LOVE IN A SUNBURNT LAND

ANTHOLOGY

LEANNE LOVEGROVE   SUSAN MACKIE

EMMA POWELL   RHONDA FORREST

LOUISE FORSTER

SMALL TOWN PUBLISHING

MEET THE AUTHORS

In 2020, **Susan Mackie** floated her vision to bring together a group of authors to create an anthology of rural romance stories that would encompass various unique Australian rural and small-town settings.

The vision became a work-in-progress when **Rhonda Forrest, Louise Forster, Leanne Lovegrove** and **Emma Powell**, without hesitation, joined with Susan to form the group of writers who now bring you — Love in a Sunburnt Land. They write in a variety of styles and share a love of storytelling; their words bringing to life vibrant Australian regions filled with authentic characters.

Regular online meetings became not only a place to bounce ideas around and plan the publication of their anthology, but turned into something so much more. A strong friendship through a love of writing, publishing and support for each other developed, and one can sense there will be more to come from this group of dedicated and passionate Australian authors.

The Sunburnt Land authors hope you enjoy their stories as much as they loved working together to bring you laughter, tears and most importantly – *Love in a Sunburnt Land*.

FIVE FABULOUS STORIES

Love on the Sweeping Plains by Leanne Lovegrove

Desperation drove Tori back to her home town, but that's not why she stayed.

Vowing never to be hurt again, Tori Christensen flees home to *Cedar Creek Plains* and the loving grandmother who raised her, after the devastating end of her marriage.

Zac Coleman has lived in *Cedar Creek Plains* his whole life. His family operates the Coleman Cattle Station and Zac has a Vet practice in town. After a health scare, he's given up on love. His sisters are keen to see him married with a family and sign him up for the reality country television show, *Local Lads Looking for Love*. He begrudgingly agrees to be the star of the show to keep his sisters off his back. And it's good for the region, including Tori's grandmother's B&B.

Tori returns on the first day of filming, blundering into the show's cameraman. Zac and Tori have history, but that was years ago. Now she's a single mother and Zac is dating four women as the eligible bachelor.

Set on the sweeping outback plains of Queensland, will Tori and Zac get a second chance at love?

Love in the Ragged Mountain Ranges by Susan Mackie

She swore she'd never trust again.

Buying the old courthouse near the Barrington Tops ragged mountain ranges was a fresh start for Nicole and daughter Lucy. Renovating the run-down building into a home and B&B accommodation would help them recover from the trauma they had endured. Nik promised Lucy it would be just the two of them. Always.

But the removal truck getting stuck in the driveway on the first day threw them into neighbour Robbie's path. He sorted the problem, then returned with son Harry to help them unload. Nik instinctively liked him, but she couldn't trust her instincts. And more importantly, she vowed to keep the promise she'd made to Lucy.

Far Horizons by Emma Powell

When a second chance at life gives Molly a second chance at love.

When Molly returns to her birthplace to start a new life, she was sure her old one wouldn't catch up with her.

But after a run in with a rotting floorboard at her late mother's decrepit farmhouse, Molly finds herself face to face with her past.

She also finds herself face to face with the local police sergeant who reminds her what it feels like to be loved. He's THAT hot!

Can she trust him? After all he is a man and that hasn't worked out well so far.

And when her past and present collide, she has to fight to save herself to ensure she has a future.

Love by the Jewel Sea by Rhonda Forrest

Frankie knew one thing. She'd return to the city when the job was done.

When Frankie grasps an opportunity to advance her career, it means driving from the Gold Coast to North Queensland to sign off on a new development. Close to her destination, an accidental meeting with local farmer Simon has her arriving in a manner completely unlike anything she is used to. Tense and frustrated, her brief stay is extended, when all she wants is to do her job and head back to the city. Will the serenity of the tiny beachside community full of local characters change her perspective on what is important in life and remind her of her ethics, or will it send her running in the opposite direction?

Core of my Heart by Louise Forster

He's hungry for more than her baking, but she's on a no-man diet.

At forty-two, Madeline was forced to rethink her future.

At seventeen, a tragic event had Madeline spend many school holidays with her Aunt and Uncle at their bakery in Liana Valley. Bea and Pete taught an enthusiastic teenager how to bake and let her experiment. Much later, Madeline took their teachings further and spent years travelling the world looking for new and traditional recipes. She compiled her discoveries into bestselling cookbooks.

Buying her Aunt and Uncle's bakery was an opportunity she could not resist. The Australian high country was just what she needed to fortify her future. Settling into her new role and reconnecting with the locals was easier than she expected. Until early one morning, standing outside with her wake-up coffee, an old van slowed as it passed. The driver smiled and sent her a quirky salute. This daily ritual became a moment she looked forward to every day.

Then one morning, to her surprise, the driver stepped into the bakery ... leather-clad Ash Cooper rocked her world — but would he accept her past?

Desperation drove her back to her home town,
but that's not why she stayed.

love
on the
sweeping
plains

Leanne Lovegrove

Love in a Sunburnt Land anthology

LOVE ON THE SWEEPING PLAINS

LEANNE LOVEGROVE

To the fabulous ladies and authors I have met by participating in this anthology. Thank you for your encouragement, support and friendship. It means a lot to me.

Leanne Lovegrove

1

Tori Christensen banged on the glass sliding door. It rattled under the pressure, but no one came.

The dazzling morning sun beat down upon her back and moisture gathered in the dip between her breasts. Her reflection glared back at her and she knocked again, pausing before shading her eyes and squinting to see through the pane.

'Hello!' she shouted.

Nothing. Not a shadow, nor a murmur from inside. Glancing around, she registered the sign above the door that read *Cedar Creek Plains Vet Surgery* in faded red ink. Surely they were open.

She glanced at her wristwatch. Shit. Maybe not. It seemed later but it wasn't yet eight o'clock. They'd been driving for hours.

The two tiny animals she cupped in her other hand didn't make a sound. She shook them, hoping for a miracle. When had they stopped squeaking? Hiccupped sobs rose from the little girl beside her who gripped her skirt.

Tori thumped on the glass harder until the crunch of boots on loose gravel behind her caused her to swirl around, her heart hammering hard in her chest.

A tall, lanky man carrying a bulky camera on his shoulder raced towards her across the carpark, fumbling over his undone shoelaces. If he didn't fall over his own feet, the size of the camera would topple him at any moment.

Tori released a breath. It wasn't Todd. Of course it wasn't. Thank goodness. She was being ridiculous peering over her shoulder like a nervous ninny.

But who was this guy carrying a movie camera? And where was his pet?

As he reached her the man manoeuvred the camera off his shoulder, fiddling with a couple of buttons before positioning the equipment back in place. He loomed the lens so close to her face she veered backwards.

'Who are you?' And, just in case, she asked, 'Did Todd send you?'

Mirabelle howled louder and tugged on her skirt.

Out of the corner of her eye she caught a shadow move inside so Tori knocked again, rapping until her knuckles hurt.

The glass panel slid open. *Phew.* She jostled on her feet, ready to race inside but the figure stepped forward into the daylight and she stopped.

Zac.

It took a moment for her brain to catch up. Zachary Coleman. Her mouth opened and shut, her eyes blinking a few times too many.

He was still here. The quintessential country boy and lad next door. Her first kiss.

Embarrassment and shame washed over her as if it was yesterday. Heat crawled up her neck and she flushed.

Of course, Zac was the town vet. That was all he'd ever wanted.

And now he here was in front of her. And she needed a vet.

How strange she'd ended up here first. She'd never contemplated making a mad dash to the surgery before arriving in town. Damn pets. How was she to know they might croak it on the trip?

Neither had she thought coming home would erase all memories of the past, had she? No, but she hadn't expected them to be thrown up in her face so fast. *Welcome home, Tori.*

'Victoria?' He'd always called her by her full name. Always so polite. And she loved the way it rolled off his tongue.

Zac's brow creased in confusion.

He hadn't changed. Same blonde tousled locks that he wore too long and maybe a few more lines around his eyes and across his forehead. But he still resembled the boy she remembered. Focusing on his face, she saw his lips move. Those lips transported her back in time and she remembered the feel of them against hers and how much she'd enjoyed it.

Oh God, a thrill raced straight through her.

'Is this the first contestant? I was told they weren't arriving until this afternoon...' came a muffled voice from behind the lens.

'What?' Zac turned his attention to behind her and lifted one hand to place in front of the camera, preventing it capturing the unfolding scene. 'No,' he said.

Undeterred, the cameraman shifted position to avoid Zac's hand and kept shooting.

'What are you doing here?' Zac asked her.

A good question. It brought her back to earth.

The guinea pigs!

'Can you save them?' Tori held up the duo of what she hoped were not lifeless furry bodies.

'Oh, you have a sick animal. Of course, come on in.'

Why else would she rock up to the vet surgery at this hour?

Zac ushered them inside towards a consulting room. Mirabelle was sniffling but trailed behind, followed by the camera guy.

Zac slammed the clinic door shut and blocked him out. 'Man, that's not the deal...' the cameraman yelled.

He took the two creatures from Tori. They were tiny in his large hands and he placed them on the examination table with care. Mirabelle moved in closer beside him and peered up with those large round almond eyes of hers. Wet trails made their way down her dirty cheeks and she stifled a further sob before rising on her tiptoes. She was so small she couldn't see over the table. Zac paused, watched her and then dragged over a chair and lifted her up.

'Are these your pets?'

The little girl in her fairy outfit nodded. 'Are they sick?'

'I don't know. Let's have a look.'

The door opened a tiny crack and the camera lens snuck in; the man's legs visible underneath.

'Get out!' Zac yelled and Tori jumped.

'Who is that guy?' she asked.

Bent over, he glanced up through his long floppy fringe. The gaze that seared into her asked a thousand questions. Tori balanced from foot to foot, uncomfortable with his scrutiny.

'It's a long story,' he answered and went back to work.

'I think,' and this time he addressed Mirabelle, 'these guys went a little too long without water. So, I'm going to give them a big drink.'

'Oh, thank goodness. They're going to be okay, aren't they, Zac?'

Mirabelle inched closer and leaned her elbows on the table to watch his every move. Tori did too and propped herself against the hard bench.

Once the guinea pigs were hooked up to some fluid, he said, 'I think they'll be okay. They'll need to stay here for a few hours for observation. Are you in town long?' This question was for her. He rose up tall and waited.

'Um, yes, maybe. I'm staying at Nanna's, of course. I'm so grateful. Thank you, Zac. We'd all be very unhappy if these little critters hadn't made the journey with us.' She stroked the curly, dark hair of her daughter as she spoke, avoiding Zac's eye. 'When should I come back and collect them?'

Tori tried to focus on the detail of what Zac was saying. Instead, she became intensely aware of every detail around them. Where Zac put his hands. His Adam's apple as it bobbed when he spoke. How he scratched the itch on his back. The clean medical smell of the surgery. It's too bright whiteness. The sterile instruments lined up on the side table in the room and the timbre of his voice. And suddenly the room was suffocating her. This town had that effect. She hadn't been back for five minutes and already it was getting to her. Already she was morphing back into the young woman she once was. The young innocent girl that had once lived in this town.

And fled.

Zac chatted to Mirabelle allowing Tori to get lost in her daydream. Every now and then he furtively glanced up as if checking she was still there. Fair enough, she deserved that. In the middle of a sentence, Mirabelle turned to her. 'Mummy, can we take Puddles?'

'Mummy?' the words slid off his tongue. She jerked her head up and held her chin too high. Defensive perhaps?

Yes. Circumstances had changed and so had she.

'Yep. This little rascal is Mirabelle, my daughter,' and she clasped the girl's hand.

Time for them to go. She needed to let her erratic heart calm the hell down and pull herself together. She tugged her daughter towards the door. 'We can't thank you enough…'

Zac strode ahead and reached for the door handle. For a crazy moment she thought he was preventing their exit. Did he want her to stay? Ridiculous. He turned the knob and moved aside to let them go first.

The doorframe wasn't large and Tori's hips brushed against his hand. A rush of warmth spread to her erogenous zones. She glanced up, fearing he could tell. Zac continued to watch her. Did he hold his breath?

Before the door had fully opened, the guy jumped up from the plastic waiting-room chair, camera in position, the red light on top flashing.

Her eyes on him, Zac shrugged. 'It's a reality TV show.'

2

Tori parked her car off to the side of the long drive to her nan's B & B. She let the dust settle and focused ahead, on the house. Tears pricked her eyes and a funny excited flutter went crazy in her tummy.

She hadn't been home for years. So many, she'd lost count. Long before Mirabelle, four years old, had been born anyway.

The place appeared the same; worn, but welcoming. Her nan's house was rusty red and it contrasted against a vibrant blue sky and sat on a pillow of verdant grass. Occasionally there was a spot of white as a duck or a lamb or a goat wandered past.

On the outskirts of *Cedar Creek Plains*, the farmhouse stood solitary, an upright double-storey timber building lumped in the middle of broad, golden sweeping plains. The plains that had named the town surrounded the area on all sides.

The smell of bacon wafted out through the open kitchen windows, the aromas mixing in with smoke billowing from the chimney. Her stomach turned. She sure was back on the farm and undeniably in the country. Trying to distract her senses from the frying pork, she listened to the chickens clucking and laying their morning eggs. The familiar sounds of a new day.

'Out,' Mirabelle sang from the back seat.

She was *home*. Her nan's home anyway. Where she was raised.

Tori reached in and extracted Mirabelle from her car seat and bunched her up in her arms for a quick cuddle. She checked her daughter's face. She seemed to be coping okay, but who knew. It hadn't been very long and her father was unlikely to be a distant memory yet.

'Let's go and find Nan.' Mirabelle nodded, giggling as a noisy duck crossed their path, its loud quacks resounding across the yard.

Entering through the back door, the cooking smell became overwhelming and Tori gagged.

Her nan was bent over the old-style aga cooker.

'Nan!' she called out when Rosalie didn't hear them enter.

Her nan turned and a broad smile opened up her face. Dropping the spatula onto the bench, she rushed towards them.

'Tori. Mirabelle. What a lovely surprise!' She squeezed Tori into a tight hug, the type only a loving grandmother can offer, before bending low to Mirabelle and kissing her sweet cheeks.

The skillet hissed and exploded.

'Oh, bugger. You'll never believe it. Helena, the girl who helps me out around here, usually cooks and tidies up, hasn't turned up this morning. I've got a few guests in and more arriving today to a full house.' Rosalie Stanhope fluttered her arms like a bird and turned back to the stove.

'I can help,' Tori offered and retrieved an apron off the back of the door and searched the pantry for ingredients. 'You finish off the bacon though, and I'll prepare something else. Remind me what you usually serve for breakfast?'

Nan giggled. 'Are you still on that silly diet?'

'Nan, it's not a diet. I'm vegan. I don't belong to a cult. A lot of people don't eat meat or dairy these days.'

With her back turned, Nan said, 'Maybe in the city, but not the country. We haven't advanced that far yet. A wee bit set in our ways. I'm sure your poor pet would love a rasher of bacon, nice and crispy on a slice of buttered white bread. You used to love it as a child.'

'I loved a lot of things as a kid. Didn't mean they were good for me.'

Already she was whisking and mixing. Calm washed over her and happiness at being in the kitchen; anyone's kitchen, although her nan's was pretty special.

'Well, the bacon is done anyhow. How about I take little Mirry out to feed the animals and collect the fresh eggs and you can finish up in here?'

Mirabelle squealed with delight and placed her tiny hand in Nan's. She'd loved doing the same when she was small. *Back then, before.* She smiled watching them leave, then opened all the windows to rid the kitchen of the odour of over-cooked pork.

'NAN, IS IT OKAY IF WE STAY FOR A WHILE?'

The breakfast rush was over, relaxing, they sat together on the spacious front deck, enjoying a cuppa. Green tea for Tori.

'Will Todd join you?'

'No.'

Nan waited, maintaining the silence. She was good at that.

'You'll never believe what happened.' Tori looked away to hold in the tears that threatened. 'I busted him having sex with the new Pilates instructor in the change rooms at work. I can't get the image out of my mind. All bronzed skin and platinum blonde hair and pert breasts! How could he do that to me, Nan? To Mirry?'

'Ouch. The bastard. Can't say I'm surprised though. He was a nice bloke but a bit light on. Maybe too nice, hey, to all of the girls. What will you do now?'

'Dunno. I'm not sure yet. But I intend to get myself sorted with some good old-fashioned country living for the time being. And maybe lots of Nanna cuddles.'

Nan turned serious and placed her palm over hers. 'Oh, Tori. It's wonderful to have you back. I miss you and you're always welcome here. It'll be nice to bring some life back into the old place with some young blood.'

'Yeah, and don't worry about finding someone else to help out. I'll do it. That's how I'll earn my keep. Obviously I'm skint and have no job, but you won't turf me out for not contributing will you?'

It was supposed to be a joke. She thought her nan got it.

'I'll eat your organic vegetable food if it means you're cooking,' Nan offered a cheeky smile and continued, 'that sounds perfect, love, thank you.'

Tori searched the yard for Mirry who wasn't used to all the space. The country was nothing like the congested and built-up city. So much room to breathe.

Mirabelle swung on the old rubber tyre hanging from the oak in the front yard. Her long hair flew behind her with each swing and she giggled with glee.

'That could be you out there. She is so like you as a child.'

'We had a bit of an incident on the way out. Mirabelle has two pet guinea pigs. I put them in a box with her in the backseat. Who knew they couldn't survive a few hours without food and drink? Most animals can, can't they? Anyway, as we entered town they were lifeless and not moving. I stopped at the vet surgery. Zac is the town vet.' She stated it as a question.

'Yes.'

'You never told me.'

'You haven't been concerned with the news around here since you left. I tried a few times to keep you informed but you weren't interested.'

'That's not true. I was probably distracted with other issues.' But Tori knew that wasn't the case. After leaving, she didn't want to associate herself with the old hick town she'd grown up in. She'd fled to a new, better life. Or so she thought.

Nan didn't respond. A goat approached Mirabelle and she crouched and tried to pat its fur but pulled her hand away each time it moved closer. They all had some adjusting to do.

'Well, okay. Whatever. I'm knocking on the door not realising it wasn't open yet and the strangest thing happened. A cameraman appeared from the carpark and flashed his camera in my face. Zac seemed annoyed but said it had to do with some reality TV show.'

'Oh yes!' Nan slapped her knee. 'That's what's happening today. They're my guests. It's a scoop. The four young girls are staying here for the duration of the show.' She chuckled. 'Imagine,' and she swept her arms wide, '*Cedar Creek Plains Farm Stay and B & B* is the next bachelorette pad. It might make me famous. Be good for future bookings at least. Well, if we can pull it off.' She sat up and placed her tea on the low set outdoor table. 'What a time for Helena to go missing.'

'What on earth are you talking about? Why is the farm going to be a bachelorette pad for a vet doco?'

Nan sat back then. 'It's not a vet doco. It's like one of those reality dating shows. But a country one.' She clasped her hands together trying to remember the name and muttering under her breath.

A light sheen of perspiration broke out across Tori's brow. The sun was high in the sky now, bearing down upon them from its orange orb. The heat of the country was like no other. Another wash of nostalgia came over her of long hot summer days, running around barefoot playing games until diving into the river to cool off.

'*Local Lads Looking for Love*! That's it. It's a regional show, not a fancy one like *Bachelor* or *Farmer Wants a Wife*. This one is local lads.'

'You're telling me Zachary Coleman is a contestant on a local dating show and his prospective girlfriends are staying here. For how long?' Tori detected the high intonation in her voice.

'A month!'

Tori took a large gulp of her tea that burned her throat on the way down.

'The cabins are ready but need a last check. I have some lovely flowers fresh from the garden to be placed in vases. Nothing like a homely touch.' Her nan stood and got moving. There was no stopping the old girl. You'd easily forget she was well into her seventies.

3

———

'So, looking for love, huh, doc? Today might be your lucky day!' Bert the servo attendant sang out as Zac filled the ute. It was the third gibe this morning already. He held his hand up acknowledging the joke. The old fellow guffawed.

To top it off that bloody annoying cameraman tailed him and moved with surprising agility between Bert and the bowser. Did people really want to watch him pumping fuel?

After cornering the guy this morning, Zac had settled down. The poor man was doing his job. And his job was apparently to follow his every move. Get footage of a day in the usual life of Zac Coleman, *Cedar Creek Plains* vet and local, and contestant on the inaugural *Local Lads Looking for Love* show.

He had two thoughts about this – first, he wanted to kill his interfering younger sisters and secondly, it was likely to be a boring and short show if they wanted exciting footage of his life.

Zac fought the urge to jump in the car and race away to lose the cameraman. But that wasn't fair to the poor bloke, and at the end of the day, he'd agreed to this crazy scheme.

Best he forget about it and get on with his day.

He turned his mind back to his home visit. Unfortunately, it was to the Coleman cattle Station. His mum had rung, not his dad, and asked him to do his regular check-ups. He hadn't stayed home last night instead sleeping at the vet clinic. What a blessing! The head vet, Rob Cooper, otherwise known as Chief, was away and he'd bunked in his quarters. And he'd stay there until the boss returned from his fancy cruise.

Zac wasn't sure he could deal with his father today. It had been a strange morning already.

Victoria.

He'd waited years for her to return and she never had. Now she was here. The same day he was about to embark on a ridiculous love show. A show he was reluctant to be involved in. Oh, the irony.

With one hand on the steering wheel, Zac fiddled with the ring on his pinkie finger and pictured the older, more mature Victoria. She'd aged; he had too. Was it possible she'd become more beautiful? And she was a mother. He'd heard the odd comment here or there over the years. But to be honest, he'd avoided the gossip. It had never served him well.

Zac wound down the window and let the cool air of the morning rush in. He travelled past the bakery, the pub, the bank and drove over the river that separated the town. In *Cedar Creek Plains* you either lived north or south of the river. His family property was north. The vet clinic south; Victoria's home south. It went without saying he preferred the southside of town.

The long, majestic driveway of Coleman Cattle Station approached and the fat, round bottle trees lining the drive came into view. More like the entrance to a royal palace. The station had always been out of place and overdone.

A few Angus cows sheltered under the trees and Zac pulled up sharp, retrieved his phone from the glovebox and hopped out. With the sun filtering through the branches of the trees and the positioning of the cows, it was a perfect shot. He snapped, discarding a few dodgy images and sat in the driver's seat whilst he uploaded the pic.

#serenity #idylic #farmlife #cows

His brief stop caught the cameraman off guard and by the time Zac posted the shot, the man was still fumbling around with his camera from the boot. Zac chuckled and drove off, leaving him by the side of the road.

He parked the ute in the circular drive and before he'd even had the chance to exit, Holly and Lara bolted out the door.

'Why are you working today? You should be at home getting ready, showering and dressing for the big night!' Holly squealed into his ear and tugged on his arm.

Conscious of the footage being captured on camera, Zac acted all cool and stand offish. How much to give away?

He kissed Holly on the cheek but didn't reply. Did likewise to Lara. 'Can't wait to hear how it goes,' she yelled as she departed for the primary school where she worked as a teacher. She blew him a cheeky kiss.

'Should I come over later and help you choose your clothes?' Holly asked.

'No.'

'Aw, come on, it will be fun.'

'No way. I think you've done enough little sister.'

His father walked around from the sheds and the banter stopped. Holly took off and he extracted his gear from the car.

This time he waited for the camera. This footage he could deal with – him doing what he did best.

Tori knew she shouldn't, but it was like the show was playing out in front of her.

One of the girls, no, *woman*, looked towards the farmhouse and Tori dropped the curtain to avoid detection. It was stifling in the kitchen as she prepped for the welcome dinner and she pulled her long hair back into a makeshift pony, holding it away from her neck. The relief was immediate but she was pretending to be distracted and glanced out the window again. She did live here after all, but to be found snooping, no that wasn't cool. And why was she peeking anyway? Curiosity was the answer.

The group of four women exited the shiny black Prado and circled around themselves, taking in their home for the next month. Tori tried to imagine what they saw. She guessed it depended on where they came from. For a country girl there'd be no surprises but what about a city girl. A culture shock?

She admired the four eligible women and wondered what type Zac preferred. She didn't know. When she'd left town all those years ago, he'd been dating her best friend, Susie. Susie had been the quintessential country gal, all long legs and leather-brown skin and hair bleached from the outdoors. Country life was in her blood from centuries ago.

Whereas she'd always been the odd one out. Dark hair, dark eyes, exotic French influence from the father she never knew while her mother was fair like her nan. And the glasses she couldn't see without making her a geek. Not the fun-loving kid who ran carefree through the fields. Tori was the one to fall over, scrape her knee and end up worse for wear. She'd given most things a good go, though. Maybe she was half tomboy.

At the time, Zac and Susie had seemed like a perfect match. Similar interests – both loved sport, commitment to their families with country living in their veins, a bright bold future ahead of them. What happened to Susie? To Tori's shame she hadn't kept in touch. It was all too hard when you were taking different paths. She was forging a life in the big city. A different life. Not to mention the guilt at what she'd done.

There had been one passionate, well, very passionate kiss between her and Zac on their graduation night. It had caught her by surprise but man, what a kiss. She still remembered every detail after all these years. Once their lips had touched, it was as if they'd let go a long-held passion for each other. Passion she certainly hadn't been aware of until he'd awakened her desire.

The kiss may have started fast and furious and a bit fumbly, like a roll in the hay, but it had ended tender, deep and oh so intimate. Tori swore she'd never been kissed like that since.

She held her left fingers up to her lips reliving the sensation and dropped them just as quickly.

Any recollection of that night and she hated herself. Cheating on your best friend and enjoying it – it doesn't get much worse. She blamed herself but how had Zac allowed it to happen when he'd been dating Susie? And now she knew what it was like to be cheated on. She was no better than her unfaithful husband. Back then, her penance had been to flee, escape the scene of the crime.

But that was a long time ago.

Today, she was married, had a child and was recently separated from her lying, cheating, filthy husband. The husband she'd loved; the husband who had introduced her to a new life; the man she credited with helping her find herself. But had she? Or had it all been convenient at the time?

How did these women compare?

One looked comfortable in her surrounds wearing jodhpurs and R.M William boots and an Akubra hat. Had to be a true-blue country chick. Based on appearances she might be a winner. The thought make Tori's chest go tight.

A blonde-haired girl giggled in a cute and feminine manner and the sound drifted in. Would Zac find her titter attractive? The woman was overdressed in a short skirt, small heels and too many bangles that jingled up her arm. Tori was sure she was a very nice girl.

Another wore her longish red hair in a loose bun with runners and her active gear appearing ready for a yoga workout.

The fourth lady was different to the rest and stood out. Goosepimples spread across Tori's arms. Would Zac appreciate her uniqueness? The woman had dark features but it was the way she held herself that caught Tori's attention. Tall, straight, elegant. Yes, beautiful.

Her nan entered the kitchen.

'Love, will you come and help me show the ladies to their cabins and explain the basics?'

'Sure. Are there cameras out there?'

'No. They've arrived alone with the host. She's a local TV journalist. Nice lady. I think the idea is to commence filming tonight at the welcome dinner. It's a big deal. You feeling okay about preparations?'

Oh yes, she was sure the ladies would love her vegan Bombay burritos and vegetable biryani.

4

———————

Her mobile buzzed again. Tori pulled it out of her apron pocket and checked the screen. Todd, for the hundredth time. He'd been ringing all afternoon and she'd ignored him. She understood avoidance wasn't an option, and she'd accept his call when it suited her.

Now didn't suit.

And, what would she possibly say to him? Act all civil as if their relationship was hunky dory? Or God forbid – forgive him? Maybe she needed to wait and see what he said first. See if he apologised, begged her forgiveness and asked her to return? The whole thing gave her a headache and she needed to concentrate.

Tori whipped off the apron and flung the phone on the bench.

Not for a moment had she considered she'd be on TV. Pretty stupid when you remembered the television show's welcome dinner was at the farm. And this wasn't a fancy five-star restaurant with wait-staff. Her and Nan were the cooks and waiters and on clean-up duty. But as Nan reminded her numerous times that afternoon, they were being paid.

Murmurs of conversation drifted in from outside. The women had arrived at the homestead and were having a drink on the deck. The sun was slowly kissing the horizon and providing them with a golden glow. Tori had to admit it was a special scene. In every direction were sweeping plains of gold and green grass that billowed gently in the breeze. Bottlebrush trees grew sporadically breaking up the flat prairies. Their branches forming perfectly rounded foliage that was lush and heavy and coloured deeper than the grass it sat upon. The trees were framed by a sky of muted pink. Further in the distance the main street of town was evident, like an oasis in a desert.

Nan had jazz background music playing and everything was ready.

Ducking into the downstairs bathroom she reapplied her light pink lipstick. *Stupid Tori, you are not a contestant.* She rolled her eyes at herself. Nonetheless she patted down the wayward strands of hair until they sat flat and pinched her cheeks until colour returned. Unlike the ladies outside dressed for a cocktail party, she wore dress jeans and a white blouse. One of her favourite outfits and very comfortable, but perhaps not what she'd choose for TV.

Excited conversation became louder and the host commenced her rehearsed speech. Zac must have arrived. Exiting the bathroom she collided with Nan. 'We're on darling, all ready to go?'

Offering Nan a broad smile, she nodded. 'I'll grab a stubby from the fridge and meet you on the verandah.' Beer used to be Zac's favourite drink. Was it still?

Zac slid out of the Prado that had delivered the contestants hours before.

Her breath hitched. Had his shoulders always been so broad? Had he always filled his jeans so well? No doubt about it, Zac was one fine strapping man. His clothes appeared crisp and new. Resplendent in blue, his chambray shirt matched his dark jeans perfectly. Polished leather boots completed the outfit. Only his hair gave the slightest hint of character with his sandy blonde hair long and tousled on top, like he'd recently had a shower.

Gulp.

He stood next to the car and looked towards the deck where all eyes were trained on him. His eyes skittered back to the ground and with one hand he slammed the door shut. His other hand lay bunched to his chest, grasped there in an awkward position. The bulk of his chest rose and fell before he took a couple of tentative steps toward the house.

Zac Coleman was nervous. But wasn't this exactly what he wanted – to find love? His future wife might be standing before him. What had happened in the last few years that had caused Zac to resort to a reality dating show?

Tori assumed he'd have married long ago, maybe even to Susie and had a bunch of kids. At thirty-five, the same age as her, there'd been plenty of time for him to meet the right girl and settle down.

Perhaps all would be revealed during the taping of the show? She was the hired help anyway and it made no difference to her.

Tori was transfixed though, not unlike the contestants, as he swaggered towards them.

Expecting Zac to approach each of the women and greet them, he instead walked in the opposite direction once he reached the verandah and headed for her. What?

'Victoria.'

His voice ran like honey down her throat.

'Hmm,' she said, conscious the camera was rolling and Zac was not talking to the gorgeous women on the deck but to her instead.

He looked down at the bundle in his arms and said, 'You forgot to come and collect them, so I'm home delivering.'

Zac held Puddles and Rainbow.

Tori blinked. 'Oh, sorry,' she babbled. 'I forgot all about them with the preparations for tonight and helping Nan. Thank you, Zac. Mirabelle will be thrilled they're back and well.' She sounded formal and stiff. *Get a grip, Tori!*

Zac held them out but wasn't quick enough. One of them peed and a little trickle of urine dribbled down his shirt leaving a strong and acidic smell.

'Oh, Zac, so sorry. Now you'll stink.'

He smiled and she saw his shoulders loosen. 'Well, at least I know your guinea pigs are feeling better,' he said and handed them over.

Turning, he approached each woman. Like the good country gentleman he was, he shook their hands politely. But these women didn't appreciate his good manners and pulled him in close for a kiss instead. Zac's cheeks flushed and Tori stifled a giggle as they all avoided his urine-soaked shirt.

After the introductions, the ladies surrounded him like a school of piranha, talking rapidly, their words spilling over one another. Her nan stood to the side, grinning before gesturing for Tori to offer the drink to Zac.

She handed the pets to Nan and stepped forward, but the girls didn't let her penetrate the circle. 'Zac, would you like a drink?' Her voice rose over the top of the blathering.

All heads turned towards her and she held out the can of beer with the condensation pooling down its sides.

Zac moved through the small group and stood before her. 'Thank you.' His voice came out croaky and he cleared his throat.

Tori swallowed, her throat suddenly dry as she pushed her pesky glasses up on her nose. Zac stared hard at her and she also felt the weight of four pairs of other eyes. He paused too long. Was he going to take the drink? About to ask if he'd prefer something else, he reached for it.

'Thank you, Victoria,' he turned towards Nan too, 'and Rosalie, for hosting us. I'm glad you're here.' Then he took a large swig of the beer. Her mouth went drier as his Adam's apple bobbed.

Once again she imagined those lips on hers and her mind wandered until one of the ladies asked him a question. It snapped Tori out of her, what? Nostalgia? Lust? How ridiculous. She was fleeing a cheating husband and didn't have time for any man. And particularly not another two-timer, nor, one dating four women at once.

'I'll get the nibbles for you to enjoy with your drinks whilst watching the sun set.' Geez, now she sounded like a tour guide.

Nan gazed at her with a puzzled expression, her head titled in question. Tori moved away and Nan swiftly followed.

'You okay, dear?'

'Sure, why?'

Nan gave her a silly grin but she ignored her and busied herself preparing the platter of delights. 'These look delicious,' Nan said, but her voice was sing-songy and too high.

'I'm not sure what you're getting at, this is almost ready,' Tori sighed.

'Tell me what we have?'

'There is hummus, spring rolls, aubergine and chickpea pieces and carrot and caraway crackers to compliment.'

Tori had taste-tested everything and it was good, even if she said so herself. She'd perfected many of these recipes from catering events and the guests had loved them, so she hoped tonight wouldn't be any different.

'I'm thinking I might be able to continue my catering business whilst I'm in town. I used to do so much in Brissy. The timing is terrible because I was building a fantastic client base and now I've left.'

Nan stopped fussing over the plate. 'Tori you're a brilliant cook. Even as a child you were happiest in the kitchen baking up treats or preparing meals. I think it's fabulous to have a goal and Brisbane would have been a great market for your vegan business. This platter looks divine but let's take one step at a time and see how tonight goes.'

Nan leaned over and kissed her cheek. Tori smelled lavender talcum powder and inhaled deeply. It was her Nan's scent and transported her back to her childhood.

Laughter drifted indoors and she handed Nan the plate. 'You take this and I'll continue prepping dinner.'

5

———————

Tori moved around the oblong oak table refilling the champagne flutes. It was impossible not to listen to the chatter. The host, a confident, dark-haired woman in her thirties, sat at the head of the table and acted as interviewer. She tossed out questions randomly which broke the silence and prevented awkwardness.

'So, Zac why did you sign up for the show?'

Tori paused, desperate to hear the answer. The bottle of bubbly was only half-empty, but she retrieved another from the sideboard, deliberated over popping the cork and slowed her steps. Anything to delay.

'Well,' he stammered, 'actually, I didn't sign up for the show.'

The ladies all spoke at once before the host settled them down and asked Zac to elaborate.

'My younger sisters, Holly and Lara applied and didn't tell me. The first I knew about the show was when I received a call to let me know I'd been accepted and the details for filming would be sent through to me.' He paused letting the statement sink in.

The cold bottle of Dom Perignon slipped in Tori's hand and drops of liquid spilled onto the lap of the lady seated in front of her. Clare, the country girl, dabbed at the wet spot on her dress but never took her eyes off Zac.

'But clearly,' the host continued, 'you want to find love?'

Zac glanced at each of the ladies who in turn either crossed their arms, took another sip of their drink or replaced the napkin on their lap.

'I'd love to meet a nice girl.'

Lame, Zac, lame.

There was silence, except for the sound of the cameraman sweeping the room to capture expressions before they vanished.

'And what would you say you're searching for in a partner?'

Man, the host was persistent, but it was her job after all.

Instinctively Tori glanced up, eager for his reply and their eyes connected. Her heart did a little pitter-patter in her chest. His mouth opened to speak but then Nan bustled into the room too fast and the door swung against the frame, slamming loudly and stealing away the moment. Zac jumped up to take the two plates she carried, placing them on the table. Tori distributed the fresh and still warm sourdough bread.

Saved by the bell?

The room remained quiet, the chatter commencing again after the meal was served.

'Are you vegetarian, Zac?'

He shook his head.

'Interesting. As a cattle farmer I imagined you'd love your red meat but there's no meat in this meal tonight?' asked the exotic Asian woman. Even her voice was fine, like silk.

Tori was on her way towards the kitchen with her back to Zac and the table. 'Well, firstly, I'm not a cattle farmer, but I do love steak but I eat it all the time. So I arranged something different tonight.'

That was a lie. Tori smiled and left the room.

~

Dessert had been served and thankfully she and Nan had a moment to sit on the bar stools in the kitchen, enjoying a cuppa before the clean-up.

Her body sagged with relief at the first hot sip. It was short-lived. A shrill squeal rang out, followed by a second and a third. She jumped up quicker than Nan and raced into the dining room.

'Something ran over my foot!'

'Mine too.'

'Is it a rat?'

Tori dropped to her hands and knees and scoured the floor.

'Puddles! Rainbow! Come here you pesky creatures,' she thought she whispered.

'Puddles!' Tiffany, the blonde wearing the short skirt upon arrival, jumped up and stood on her chair. 'What is it? A rodent?'

'Technically they are a breed of rodent...' Zac didn't finish the sentence before two more of the women jumped up on their chairs. Only the country chick, obviously not afraid of critters, remained seated.

Zac crouched down too. Puddles darted across the rug. 'He's under the table,' Tori yelled.

Tori crawled under one end and Zac came from the other. She shuffled backwards, checking under each chair, lifting the rim of the plaid rug. Nothing. Half-way and she bumped into Zac. Both swivelled to face the other. In the semi-darkness Tori could make out his wicked grin, his teeth all white and gleaming. A twinkle spread to his eyes and they crinkled at the edges in mischief. She sat back on her haunches and placed her hand over her mouth to stifle her giggle. Zac put one finger to his mouth urging her to be quiet.

'Are you two okay down there?' The host asked but Tori couldn't respond lest the giggles break free.

'Yep, almost got him. Stand still up there until we do.' With his grin becoming even wider, Zac lifted up a hand to reveal the runaway guinea pig securely fastened in his grip.

Tori dropped her hands and placed her palms flat on the floor. Her laughter fizzled away like the bubbles in the glasses of champagne sitting on the table. Zac sat so close, the heat radiated off his body. It mixed in with the scent of dried pee and the musty smell of hair from the bundle he held. The two of them were alone and Zac was making no effort to move. He kept staring at her as if seeing her for the first time. 'It's nice to see you again,' he said, all innocent-like, as if they weren't hiding from a roomful of women vying for his attention.

Puddles squeaked.

'I can hear it. Where is it?' one of the women shrieked.

The long tablecloth was lifted in one corner letting in the light. 'Yoo hoo under there. What's happening?' Nan sang out.

With their eyes glued to each other they both backtracked out from opposite ends of the table. Not paying attention, Tori clocked her head on the thick leg as she climbed out.

'Got him!' Zac yelled from the other end of the room. A cacophony of noise erupted and chairs scraped as bodies came back to the ground.

'Oh, it's so cute,' they exclaimed in sexy voices.

Tori rose to her feet and rubbed the bump on her head. The four women surrounded Zac petting the guinea pig.

She hoped it shit all over them.

6

Tori stood at the washing line at the rear of the farmhouse and hung the white sheets and towels her nan had forgotten about earlier. She sent Nan to bed and insisted she'd hang the linen they needed for tomorrow's clean sheets.

An ocean of darkness surrounded her, with only the lights from the homestead to guide her. Plus, the stars. She'd forgotten about the vastness of a starry sky, its sparkling array of beauty. You never saw skies like it in the city. And a sight she must show Mirabelle.

There was something about the isolation of the country; it made you feel small and unimportant but also part of something incredibly special. Tori soaked up the contentment it provided her.

Hushed voices came from her right followed by the sound of heels on the pebbled path. She peered in that direction and saw the silhouette of a man and a woman. Even wearing her glasses she couldn't see them clearly. This path led to the cabins where the contestants were staying. Who would it be?

After the guinea pig debacle she'd departed the evening pretty quickly, not wanting to cause any more trouble. How much of the footage would make the show? She knew these productions edited and manipulated the material for prime TV viewing and hopefully it wouldn't look too bad for the B&B.

But she'd really disappeared to hide from Zac. What was that display under the table? They weren't eighteen anymore playing childhood games. But it had been kind of funny. Thinking about his mischievous grin, her tummy flipped.

The sounds moved closer and Tori hung the last sheet, collected the wash basket and moved into the darkness surrounding the house.

Long, wavy platinum blonde hair shone in the light as the couple passed by the clothesline, less than a metre from where she stood. Giggles echoed on the breeze and Tori saw Tiffany wobble on her too-high stilettos. Ridiculous footwear for the country, but she'd admit the narrow silver straps hugged her ankles nicely.

Of all the girls, Tori imagined she was the least compatible with Zac. But she didn't know the boy she went to school with anymore. Perhaps he'd changed?

Zac reached to steady Tiffany and she sought out his hand linking their fingers together and swung them to and fro. A few more steps and Tiffany yanked on Zac's arm and pulled him to a stop placing their bodies half in shadow. Ever polite, Zac paused, waiting. Tiffany stood on tiptoes and leaned in towards him.

Zac was slow to cotton on but as she neared his face, he leaned in with a swift jerky movement to plant a kiss on her cheek. 'Well, it's late and I must get you back to your cabin.' He turned and kept walking, stopping a little ahead to wait for her to catch up.

Tori gripped her sides to hold in the laughter.

Thank goodness she hadn't witnessed a passionate kiss between the pair. Talk about awkward. It gave her a bizarre sense of satisfaction that Tiffany's ploy had failed. Once Zac kissed any of these women they would be gone, hook, line and sinker. Well, that is, if he was still as good a kisser as she remembered.

And somehow, Tori imagined he would be.

~

'GOOD MORNING, TORI, I'M ANNA FOX, HOST AND JOURNALIST FOR THE show. Last night's dinner was delicious, thank you. I'm a vegetarian too and I appreciated the food, even if it was a bit too fancy for some.' She winked at Tori. 'The producers and I are wondering if you could be the caterer. You know, obviously for all the meals here at the farm-house, of course, but also on location. I'm not sure if you understand how the show works, but Zac will be taking each of the ladies on a date and we'd like you to provide the meals for them and the crew as well.'

Tori wiped her forearm across her brow. She was right in the midst of making savoury pancakes for breakfast and Anna spoke so fast she couldn't keep up.

'Yes, of course, I'd love to help out.'

'There's a catch. You'll need to remember your audience. After all, we feature on regional television and country folk are our main viewers. They don't want to see fancy mocked-up MasterChef food. They want locally sourced and traditional country meals.' She paused. When Tori didn't respond, she continued. 'Meat. You'll have to serve meat.' She held her fingers up to indicate inverted commas.

Oh, that was a catch. Tori hadn't cooked meat or prepared meals with dairy for, well, a long time. It went against all of her beliefs. And how could she serve that sort of food and hope to develop her vegan business? It'd be a contradiction. No, unfortunately, she couldn't help. Anna's mobile rang as she was about to refuse. Answering but holding the phone away from her ear, Anna said, 'Awesome. I'm so glad you've agreed. I'll let you know the schedule pronto!' And she left the kitchen leaving Tori with her mouth hanging open.

SHE WAS STILL WASHING THE BREAKFAST DISHES, HER HANDS IN THE SUDSY water at the sink when the cameraman strode in flapping a piece of paper.

'Here's today's schedule. Last night Zac chose Lucy as his first date and they're going fishing today in that famous river of yours.'

Tori stared at him.

'Um, you know the mass of water that separates the town and is filled with fish?' he said.

'Um, Zac chose a date last night? Was it like a rose ceremony where he had to pick one and left the others hanging?'

The man smiled and Tori noticed for the first time he didn't have his camera sitting on his shoulder. 'No, different show. We can't rip them off. He chose at the end of the evening. You'd probably knocked off by then.'

Oh, yeah, sure.

'Which one is Lucy?' she asked.

'The redhead.'

Okay he'd chosen sensible shoes and active wear.

'I understand you're going to be catering and today we need a picnic for the couple to enjoy after their fishing experience.'

Yes, she could do that. Her mind immediately conjured up delicacies. Oh, no, damn, she needed *normal food.*

'Do I need to run the menu by anyone beforehand?' she asked him.

'Nah, Anna trusts you. Just make sure there's enough for me,' he laughed, 'I'm the only crew. Anna won't be on set today as there's no hosting duties. She'll voice-over later.'

They talked a bit longer, finishing with the small details and timings. Tori shook the excess water off her hands and held one out. 'By the way, I'm Tori. We haven't met properly and if we're going to work together we should at least know each other's names.'

He reciprocated and shook her hand firmly. 'Mike,' he said and walked away. 'See you in a couple of hours.'

Two hours. Shit. There was heaps of work to do. Tori prayed her nan's pantry and freezer were fully stocked. And she'd have to ask Nan to look after Mirabelle.

But Tori didn't think about the picnic. Her thoughts were on Zac.

7

Zac glanced under his lashes at Lucy. He didn't feel anything other than uncomfortable.

Lucy was pretty with dramatic red hair, dimples in her cheeks and seemed to be a nice girl. He waited for fireworks to explode in his chest when she smiled at him. Nup. Nothing. Those were the dreams of movies, anyway.

But he wanted to feel a twinge of excitement ripple through him. It happened *every single time* he saw Victoria. His heart beat too fast and his mouth went dry. He wouldn't call it fireworks exactly, but it was a visceral reaction that had him gravitating towards her at any opportunity.

And man, today she wore a simple summer dress. It was thirty degrees out and she wore shoestring straps revealing bare shoulders and showing off long lithe legs. Her dark hair hung down her back and reached the hem. To him, she resembled the girl he remembered at eighteen.

So, right now, poor Lucy didn't have too much of a chance because it took all his effort to stop staring at Victoria. But Tori was married.

She had a daughter.

Family was important.

She didn't live in *Cedar Creek Plains*.

So, basically, he was an idiot. Zac turned his body away so he couldn't see her in his peripheral vision as she set up their picnic lunch.

Time to focus on fishing and Lucy.

This river was the major feature of the town. Tall, majestic Cedars resembling Christmas trees ran for miles along each side of the banks, hence the town's name.

It was the strangest thing, those vast and open plains that crept up upon the river. During drought the grasslands were dry and brown and filled with dust. But now, after the rains, they were plentiful and lush and sometimes green, sometimes the colour of spun gold. In the middle was an oasis. A lengthy, snaking river provided the lifeblood of the community. Made it less dry and more appealing.

'Do you fish much?' he asked. Fishing was one of the most popular pastimes in the community after team sport.

'No, I've never fished. Used to watch my dad and brother do it when I was younger.'

'Okay, here's to new experiences.' Zac clinked their champagne flutes but his was empty. As if Victoria had been watching them with an eagle eye, she appeared and filled the glasses.

He was embarrassed treating her like a maid. 'Thank you…' he started to say more but looked up, noting Victoria's red and puffy eyes. He dropped his fishing rod and stood. 'What's wrong?'

She hiccupped in response, placed her hand to her mouth and walked back to the picnic spot.

He hurried after her not glancing at Lucy. Zac placed his hand to the small of her back. Through the thin cotton fabric he felt the knuckles of her spine.

'Zac. You're on your date. Don't worry about me. I'm fine. I had a call from my husband and well, um, he's a jerk.'

He pulled her in close and cradled her head against his chest, one hand to her moist cheek and held tight. Inhaling her honey and vanilla scent, he closed his eyes a moment too long. Time and place got lost until the clearing of a throat.

Shit. He pulled away but gawped at Victoria. Her misery was like a physical pain deep in his gut. A raw and primitive urge overtook him; to protect her, keep her safe and happy, dry her tears and murmur reassurances. Instead Victoria moved away and fussed with the picnic. Dismissed, Zac turned back to the riverbank and Lucy. His arms ached to have her back in his embrace.

What the hell was wrong with him?

He had to pull himself together. Reaching Lucy, he pushed out the words, 'So sorry. I've known Victoria since we were kids and she's upset about something back at home.'

At that moment his rod bent. 'Lucy, a fish,' he laughed and pointed. 'Reel it in.' Lucy picked up the pole and held it in the air. It jerked in her hands before bouncing towards the bank and out of her grip. Zac ran after the rod and grasped it before working furiously to save the fish he'd hooked. Lucy squealed as the splashes of water wet her clothes and even louder when the fish finally landed on the earth.

'Oh, that's disgusting. It's bleeding, Zac because the hook is caught in its mouth. Throw it back in,' she demanded.

Zac stared at the fish and didn't respond to Lucy.

It was a solid catch of legal length and he wanted to keep it.

After a pause, Zac threw the fish into the river after extracting the hook. 'Let's have lunch.' He pulled his lips into a tight smile.

'Oh, this is beautiful. How perfect. Thank you, Zac.' Lucy leaned over and kissed him, like he'd set up the checked picnic blanket with low set table and a vase of wildflowers and a candle that refused to stay lit. Platters of finger sandwiches and quiches lined the table, along with jugs of sparkling cold water.

Victoria stood near the SUV packing something away. Lucy talked. He tried to concentrate, he really did, but her voice droned on. Then out of the corner of his eye he saw Victoria fall to the ground where she lay motionless. Zac dropped his glass, the liquid spilling all over the place as he jumped up and raced over. The camera loomed in his face.

'She's fainted. Get some water.'

Without releasing the camera, Mike rushed to Lucy who remained on the rug mopping up the mess. She silently poured a glass of mineral water and Mike rushed back, the liquid slopping over the lip.

Zac shook Victoria but she didn't respond. He slapped her cheeks until she roused and moved her up into a sitting position. She pushed his hands away.

'Get back to your date,' she said through gritted teeth.

'Let me get you something to drink and eat and ensure you're okay.'

Zac rushed over to the picnic and collected a handful of goodies in a napkin Lucy prepared for him. He offered her a smile of apology. 'Be back in a tic.' Lucy shrugged.

'Zac I can't eat any of this food. I prepared the chicken and water-cress, and egg and lettuce sandwiches for you and Lucy.'

'Oh, okay. What about some custard tart or a sugar rush with a square of chocolate?'

Again, she shook her head.

'You don't eat your own food?'

Victoria stood and he placed his hand under her elbow, supporting her. Slowly she took tentative steps away towards the shade and a camping chair.

'I'm queasy. I'm going to sit for a moment and have a drink. I'm probably dehydrated. It's warm today although the sun is losing some of its heat. Anyway, you need to take Lucy for a lovely walk along the riverbank and devote yourself to whatever it is she wants to talk about. Whether it's the latest fashion, movies or osteo technique.'

'Osteo technique?'

'She's an osteopath, Zac. Geez. Pay attention. Get it?'

Her gaze seared into him. She was right of course; he was being disrespectful. His sisters would be ashamed of him. He was ashamed of himself but there was no way he wouldn't have helped when she'd collapsed. But now he had to do the right thing. The only way to do that was to be far away from Victoria and near Lucy.

Zac nodded. Why then did his heart feel so heavy in his chest?

8

———————

ori had to admit she loved watching *The Bachelor*; had watched each season. There was something about observing two people fall in love. The romantic in her enjoyed the intimacy of it, but not so much the gossip and dramatics. The producers were clever at delivering good television. It worked though, because people were glued to the screen.

But *Local Lads Looking for Love* was not *The Bachelor*.

Anna and the crew seemed to make up the rules as they went along. As best Tori could work out, similar scenarios were playing out in nearby regional towns. Other Aussie blokes were hosting four contestants in their hometown and escorting them on dates. Occasionally, like tonight, they would have a hook-up to share stories and check on progress and, hopefully hear a country-boy had fallen in love.

Unlike the national show where there were numerous dates and contestants all vying for the attention of the bachelor, the regional show allowed for only one date with each lady. Otherwise, they spent time eating dinners together and similar to a camp atmosphere, they might play games or host a Q&A. All with Zac as the special guest of course.

Rumour (from Mike) was that Zac could send a woman home at any time.

Yesterday after her fainting episode, she'd devoured a generous slice of the custard tart she'd made for the picnic. It was part nostalgia and part desperation. It was Nan's recipe and she'd made it religiously with Tori as a child. It had been Pop's favourite too.

Tori remembered many occasions sitting on the kitchen barstool as her nan worked her magic. Her grandmother had nurtured her love of cooking and being back home with her was making Tori happier than she'd expected. Despite her unfaithful husband and her heart being shattered into a million pieces, each time Nan cuddled her or helped in the kitchen, she felt healed.

But Tori hadn't eaten a tart or any sort of pastry for more than ten years. It had been a trip down memory lane making the treat: rolling out the sugar-laden base, beating the eggs and stirring the boiling custard. Like the old days it had turned out beautifully; a classic country dish.

If she'd returned to the past baking it, taking the first slice was metamorphic. There'd been an explosion of taste she'd long forgotten and it had delivered other childhood memories. Many of them contained a young Zac.

Anyway, the ridiculously delicious treat had landed her back to earth with a thump with the past and present colliding. It didn't take away her nausea, however, the sick feeling settled in the base of her stomach today.

Tonight she'd cooked two of her favourite dishes: orecchiette with cream and carrot miso sauce and vegan alfredo. The guinea pigs were locked up and she, Nan and Mirabelle ate in the kitchen, leaving the game show to play out in the living room.

Like Tori did as a child, Mirabelle shadowed her nan.

'Did you feed the chickens today?'

'Yes,' she said, 'and the little piggy. Oink, oink,' she imitated.

The three generations laughed together.

'What's next for the show?' her nan asked.

'Tomorrow night is some sort of Q&A thingo where questions are thrown at Zac. There's a cardboard box in the living room where the contestants can anonymously ask him questions, presumably contentious ones if they are too shy to ask him directly!'

'That sounds fun. We'll have to tune in,' her nan said delighted and clapped her hands.

'The next big date is an overnight camping adventure on Zac's property. A bit awkward because I'll be there with Zac, his date and Mike. I'll be in the background of course, but it was totally weird the other day serving up lunch while they're trying to get to know each other.'

'It might not have been so strange if you hadn't fainted and distracted Zac.' Nan laughed.

'Don't joke, Nan, it was terrible. Lucy sat on the picnic rug alone while Zac was busy slapping me on the face.' Nan broke out in raucous chuckles, prompting Mirabelle to join in.

'Well it sounds pretty tame tonight,' Tori commented. Not a sound emanated from the dining room. 'Why don't you catch an early night and I'll clean up?'

Nan placed her wrinkly brown hand over hers. 'Gosh, it's lovely having you back, Tori.' Nan's eyes misted. 'Thank you for all of your help.' The old woman turned to Mirabelle. 'I'll tuck you up in bed while Mummy finishes and we'll read two books.'

'Ten books!' Mirry squealed.

Tori knew Mirry would sucker Nan into reading way more than she intended.

BEFORE THE QUESTIONS HAD EVEN BEGUN, THE LADIES WERE DRUNK. SHE supposed it was on purpose but Tori noticed Anna remained sober.

And Zac, well he kept to himself not sitting near any of the women but nursing a stubby and chatting with Nan.

'Okay, Zac,' Anna's voice was too loud and Tori grimaced. The woman's hand was in the box and she extracted a small square of paper. 'First question – what is your idea of a romantic night out?'

'A night at the pub?'

'Ah, c'mon, Zachary Coleman,' Anna shouted. 'You can do better.'

Zac blushed and bowed his head, confronted over taking the lazy option.

'Enjoying a moonlit dinner under the stars with good food and wine, and of course wonderful company.'

'Well, Zac. That's more like it. What do you think, ladies?' They made appropriate comments.

'Zac, you're a handsome country lad. Why is it you haven't settled down before now?' Anna asked the next question and before Zac could answer she said, 'Great questions, ladies!'

Tori held her breath. This was her question. She'd snuck it into the box when no one was watching. She'd been dying to ask since she'd first run into Zac. Why was he single?

Zac heaved a big sigh like he was tired of the interrogation already. More likely, he preferred staying out of the spotlight. She'd always known him to be a private person.

There's nowhere to hide, Zac.

'Um, there isn't any exciting answer to this one. I simply haven't met the right girl.' He sat back defiant, not prepared for challenge on this answer.

Rubbish. Tori didn't buy it. He was being coy and secretive. There had to be more to it and she determined to find out the real answer.

'Righteo,' Anna trilled and grinned down the camera lens. 'Toilet seat up or down?' The ladies erupted in laughter.

'Down of course. I have four sisters.'

The ladies clapped.

'Next one – a bit more serious. Tell us about your relationship with your mother and your family.'

Zac took a gulp of beer. 'My mum is a strong, no nonsense practical woman who is a saint for putting up with the shenanigans of my sisters and my grumpy father.'

Tori remembered his mother as a model country wife. Running the household while her husband managed the cattle property. She'd always been welcomed with home-baked afternoon teas and a smile.

Plus, his sisters were always such great fun. To her, his loud and rambunctious family had been a great diversion from her non-existent one. She knew Zac felt differently.

'Do all of your sisters still live locally?' Anna interjected.

'Yes in the country. They don't all live in *Cedar Creek Plains*, but close by.'

Anna nodded. Zac was being a bit of a killjoy and the mood turned sombre.

'Let's keep going then shall we. We're loving getting to know you better, Zac.'

Tori sat glued to her seat at the rear of the living room, resting her feet up after another long day. The house could burn down around her and she'd stay to devour each word Zac revealed about himself even in his modest terms.

Anna raced through more jovial questions. Favourite colour – green. Animal – all of them. Food – steak.

None of them revealed much about the true Zac, but kept the contestants entertained and no doubt the audiences at home too.

Zac finished his second beer. 'Okay. It's been fun getting to know our resident Lad but here's our last question for the evening and it's a goodie. Zac, have you ever been in love?'

There was no hesitation. Zac's eyes roamed the room until they found her. The gap between them lessened while all of the air sucked out of the room. Tori shifted her feet off the seat in front and sat up with a straight back, one hand holding the tea. Suddenly, the mug she held with its cartoon design held her attention. Only fleetingly though. She couldn't avoid the pull of his stare. When she glanced back, his magnetic eyes zeroed in on her. It was impossible to look away. There was no twinkle tonight or creased lines shadowing his eyes from a smile that stretched too far. The moment dragged and Tori sucked in a breath.

One of the women turned in her seat. Another took a sip of her drink. Tori heard Anna breathing into the microphone. But it was like no one else was in the room, only her and Zac. She wasn't supposed to be in the spotlight. Little beads of sweat rolled down her chest.

Finally he broke the contact. 'Yes,' he said, 'a long time ago.'

The theme song to the show erupted and the scene, like one in a movie, ended. Mike moved in too close with the camera, but Zac shoved him away and rose to leave the room.

'Who wants another drink?' Clare asked.

9

Tori wasn't required at the camping site while Zac and Sophie set up their tents. In fact, she'd rather be skinning a goat than be hanging around like a voyeur. But there were only two cars and she travelled with Mike who had to capture every minute of the action.

Zac chose the grand sweeping plains of his sizeable family property for the overnight adventure. He'd also chosen Sophie, the exotic and alluring woman. If he chose a partner based on elegance and beauty, Sophie was that girl.

Tori grabbed the front of her shirt and puffed it out a few times to catch a breeze. It was great to spend most days in these clothes again. She mightn't look as fancy as Sophie but it was comfortable and practical. Except for those bloody flies. Them she would never like.

A cow bellowed in the near distance. A small herd of deep red cattle were bunched under a copse of shady trees. Some rubbed their necks together, others lazed on the ground. Their musty manure scent drifted towards her.

Her mind drifted to her husband and what he might be doing now. Had the Pilates instructor moved into their home? Once again she wondered where it all went wrong. She'd been a good wife she'd thought. Did men require more? Or did they bore easily?

Tori stole a glance at Zac. He seemed so different – caring, genuine, every girl's best friend. But then he'd kissed her while dating Susie. So, yeah, they might all be the same.

Thinking about her cheating husband no longer made her sick. Instead a ball of fury swirled in her chest. How dare he do that to her. How dare he ruin their marriage; their family life; not be an available father for Mirabelle? One thing she refused to do was blame herself. She wasn't the one having sex with someone else. That was him. All him. She was not responsible for his behaviour. And because he couldn't keep it in his pants. No, maybe she did feel a bit sick after all.

There had been a mixture of emotions returning to *Cedar Creek Plains* but also resolve. She could make it on her own; start a successful business and provide for Mirabelle. She didn't need Todd or any man to care for her. Tori Christensen could damn well look after herself.

Tori stood tall and stretched out her back. The horizon went as far as she could see, well past the cows and the boundary fences. In the distance, some kilometres away sat the Coleman family homestead. She could make out the main house and the surrounding stables and sheds. In front, the long flat plains supported tiny tufts of grass, their new growth swaying in a breeze so gentle it hardly kissed her skin. She wiped her forearm across her brow, the scorching sun was biting her bare skin.

Tori set up her make-shift kitchen under the nearest tree. Dinner prep was done and she needed to pitch her own tent before dark.

Heading over to the car she saw two tents circling a fire pit with matching camping chairs. Would the couple be using one tent tonight?

Zac stood to the side of the car and pitched another tent.

Her tent.

'Hey, what are you doing?'

'Oh, hey. Just setting this up for you. I'm sure Mike isn't going to do it.'

'Nor does he have to, or you. I'll do it.' She walked closer and took the canvas top out of his hands. He let her take it without a word and she draped it over the tent's canopy. Zac hammered in the corner pegs before saluting and heading back to Sophie.

When he was about half-way across, a flock of birds took off in fright and filled the cloudless sky. Zac whipped out his phone and angled it above him. He examined the shots and stood still for a moment staring at his phone.

'I'll finish this and bring over the esky and cool drinks,' she shouted to his departing back. He waved in acknowledgement.

Tori lugged over the heavy esky while Mike filmed.

'Mike, are you married?'

'Nuh.'

'Hmm,' Tori commented.

'Hey, what's that supposed to mean?'

'Nothing.'

When she arrived at the cosy site, Zac was on his mobile, listening and nodding.

Tori extracted a bottle of chilled champagne and two glasses. She indicated to Sophie who nodded.

Zac ended his call. His right hand crept up the back of his neck and rubbed his hair line. 'I'm so sorry, Sophie,' he said but glanced in Tori's direction. 'There's a vet emergency. A horse has gone into labour and is having difficulty. The farmer's worried the foal might be stuck. I have to go. I'll make it up to you, I promise and be as fast as I can.'

'Zac,' Tori said, 'what about the Chief. Is he still away?'

Zac nodded confirmation as he rushed to the car.

Tori turned to Sophie. 'The man he works with is away on holiday and Zac is the only vet in town and for miles. He wouldn't go if he didn't have to. Here have a drink.'

Sophie didn't respond but accepted the drink and downed it in one swallow. Not so elegant after all. Tori refilled it and was about to pour her own and pull up a chair when Sophie rose and marched towards her tent.

Zac wouldn't be long, she was sure. Knowing him, the guilt at leaving would spur him on to act as quickly as possible; he'd feel dreadful.

Tori busied herself with dinner. This time Mike had remained and not followed to film the action. 'Enough footage of vetting,' he muttered as he cracked open a can of beer.

The sun sank lower to meet the horizon. It was one of the best times of day in the country. Time for supper. She served Mike a bowl of simple beef stew. She'd gone out of her comfort zone to create a life-like camping experience. A lot of good it had done. Sophie hadn't come out of her tent, so Tori made knock-knock noises and served her the meal inside. 'Mike and I are sitting by the fire if you'd like to join us.' Sophie replied with a tight smile but didn't follow.

Zac returned over two hours later. The light was out in Sophie's tent and he didn't rouse her. Tori remained by the fire, enjoying the peace and quiet of country life.

'Sit down. You must be starving. I'll get your dinner.'

Mike had collapsed in the driver's seat of the car where his body hung over the steering wheel, snoring. He hadn't even bothered to set up his tent.

Tori handed over the steaming plate. 'I must say your track record with these dates isn't great.' She laughed, sat down and got them both a drink. Zac rolled the can of beer over his forehead and down his cheeks, puffing them out as he enjoyed the cool metal on his face.

'Don't laugh. These poor girls. Here they are waiting for these romantic interludes with jackass old me and it's all turned to shit.' He took a big swig of beer.

'Not your fault.'

'I know. But circumstance, right?' He spooned a couple of mouthfuls of stew in quick succession. 'Oh, this is incredible. Thank you.'

'You don't like my usual vegan, vegetarian, dairy free fare?'

Zac held up a palm in defeat. 'I didn't say that. In fact the meals we've had at your nan's have been outstanding. But I've been raised on traditional tucker. What is it with that food anyway? You never used to be vegetarian.'

'I'm vegan. Don't eat meat or any meat-based products, including eggs and cheeses etcetera.'

'Man, you're missing out. I love a slather of cheese spread over a cracker…'

Tori relaxed and slumped into the chair, leaning back. The stars twinkled at her like diamonds in the sky. 'It was a gradual thing. There is so much on offer in the city – five different varieties of coffee, and milk. Every plausible food you can think of – Thai, Indian, Lebanese and shops devoted solely to chocolates or French pastries; anything you can think of. I worked a few odd jobs here and there and tasted each of those foods. It was heaven. I joined a gym not too long after and met Todd.'

'Your husband?'

She nodded. 'He owned and ran the gym. I was exercising a lot and losing weight and feeling great. He needed help in the gym shop and it served healthy food. You know I enjoy cooking and baking. I always have.'

He agreed in between chewing.

'I experimented and made my own healthy treats. It was so easy and so much better than that sugar-laden rubbish we shove into our bodies. I developed a small range and then branched into salads and super-foods. It's all the rage in the city. But I guess, before I could blink, I was married and my entire life had altered from the one I used to know.'

'But why did you leave in the first place?'

10

─────────

Her lips pressed together in a slight grimace and her gaze turned away, looking out into the dark distance. Tori uncrossed her legs and remained silent.

Had he offended her? It was a valid question. Running away without a good-bye after all the time they'd spent together growing up. And after that kiss.

He had almost given up on her response when she spoke.

'Zac, you kissed me at graduation while you were dating my best friend. I kissed you back! You cheated on Susie and I let you. I couldn't live with myself. Plus, you were convinced country living was for you. You never wanted more. I did.'

His last mouthful of beer spat from his mouth. 'Shit, sorry. That's gross. You're wrong.' He repeated, 'You're wrong. You never gave me a chance to explain. Yes, I kissed you. It was one of the best kisses I've ever experienced. And before we'd even pulled apart you ran away. Like a child.' He swallowed. He needed another sip of beer to moisten his mouth.

Tori leaned forward resting her elbows on her knees, but he kept talking. There was no way he'd let her interrupt this time.

'And didn't just run from me. You left town. I thought I'd let you

cool off for a while and we'd talk the next day. That I could tell you…'
He shook his head and checked out the dark horizon, taking solace in
the silence and the vast openness engulfing them.

'Yes, I'd been dating Susie, but I broke up with her that night. I only
had eyes for you and it wasn't fair. I kissed you after I'd told her.'

'You broke up with Susie and then kissed me?' Her voice was a
whisper. A pause. 'Shit. I'm sorry. I didn't know. I'd betrayed her and I
couldn't face her or you. We'd done the wrong thing.'

'Everything might have been different if you'd let me explain.'

Tori sat back and he was sure heat radiated off her and not from the
raging fire. 'You think?'

Sarcasm dripped off her words. Yes, he wanted to scream. Instead,
he waited for her to digest the information.

'You were destined to take over the cattle farm and live a happy
country life. I wanted more. Still do, I guess, but maybe the definition
has changed. So regardless, even if you'd tried to convince me to stay, I
would have left eventually.'

He drank the words in. 'But now you're back.'

She cackled like there was poison in her mouth. 'I had no choice.
My husband cheated on me and I fled. I have no money and nowhere
else to go to get my shit together. I have responsibilities; a daughter.
Thank goodness for Nan. I needed to take Mirabelle somewhere safe.'

'Was he violent?'

'No. Just a lying cheating prick.' She turned her full gaze on him.
'All these years I thought you were a cheater too. In retrospect I
should've realised. You were such a nice bloke, everyone's best friend.
It didn't make sense you'd do that. It upset me again when I first
arrived. Brought all those memories back. I didn't stay in touch with
Susie after I left because I felt so guilty. What a waste.'

Victoria shook her head; her wavy long hair fell, hiding her face.
'What *have* you done since then?'

Her voice was less friendly, exasperated maybe.

'Dad is still pressuring me to take over the cattle farm. The precious
lineage. He tolerated my vet studies, said it was a valuable asset to the
station. Saving money on animal husbandry. What a coup. He tolerated it less when I returned and worked with the Chief. Even then he

hoped it was a passing fad. It wasn't. My dream is to buy the vet clinic off the Chief when he retires. That is what I want.'

'Wow. So you do have ambition. I'm impressed.'

The comments hurt. He'd always had ambition, but Victoria wasn't here, didn't know. He wasn't the hick country boy she remembered. 'The war wages on between us. No real urgency I guess while Dad is fit to run the station. I was laid up, off track for a while…'

He paused, collected himself before he could continue. Took a sip of his beer but the can was empty. Tori got up and pulled another from the esky.

'You don't have to serve me.'

'Well, I do actually. I'm paid to cater for your show and it's part of the job description.' Zac didn't agree and gave her a glare that said so with a shake of his head. He opened the can and drank before continuing.

'I was diagnosed with cancer a few years back. Had treatment, chemo. I'm in remission now and all clear but it was a bit stressful at the time.'

'Zac! I'm so sorry. I never knew.'

He shrugged. It was old news but he had to admit it still affected him. The experience had changed his view on life. Made him realise what he wanted and what he could achieve. In a cruel twist of fate, choices were taken from him too.

And yet, despite his close call with the game of life, what had he actually accomplished? Perhaps the best was still to come. He wouldn't admit it to her. Tori would think he was still a naïve country boy.

A loud snort emanated from the SUV where the door remained ajar. They both laughed.

'It seems as if we have both lived a lifetime. Grown up, hey?'

Zac agreed.

'But why the show, Zac. It's not your style. Surely there are a queue of girls lining up to date one of the most eligible men in town. You don't need to resort to reality TV.'

'My sisters signed me up!' he said in defence.

'I know but you're doing it. I'm sure you could've gotten out of it.'

'You know my sisters, right? They would have had my guts for garters and other parts of my anatomy too.' He let his words hang, hoping they might be enough. Not for Tori. 'Yeah, but seriously. It's for them. To shut them up for a while about me getting married and what not. Maybe it's time?'

'You've had girlfriends since?'

'Yeah, but honestly nothing serious. Few dates.' He shrugged but that didn't sum up how he felt about it at all.

'Zac Coleman. Are you telling me since Susie, you've not had a relationship?'

He didn't answer. Stared at her until she broke their hold. Then he gazed at the stars and the moon. It provided a silvery glow on everything in its path.

Tori rose and collected the dirty plates and glasses. Zac drained his beer and followed her to the kitchen. A wild dog barked nearby and Tori jumped. They stood so close she bumped into him and he took the opportunity to hold her arm, reassure her. She turned her head towards him and he didn't drop his grip. The barking receded into the distance and the only sound was the drone of Mike's snoring.

Zac felt her take a deep breath and her chest rise and fall. Tori's body moved sideways until their torsos met and her hips brushed his. Her hot breath smelt of champagne and berries as it blew against his cheek. They both leaned their heads in, hesitating briefly until their lips connected. It was like coming home. Tori's lips were soft and warm and delicate. Zac shut his eyes as their mouths danced together, moving apart and back with kisses as tender and light as the summer breeze. His confidence grew by her hungry response and he pressed harder, his mouth devouring hers and forcing it open with his thrusting tongue. One hand entangled the hair at the nape of her neck and the other rested to her hip, his thumb grazing the waistband of her jeans. The feel of her bare flesh under his finger sent currents of desire to his core. With that one finger, he drew her body closer, her breasts resting against his chest. His knee nudged in between her legs. He was being transported. Finally, back to the lips he'd never stopped thinking about. The girl he'd once loved.

Tori placed a hand to his chest and pushed him back hard. His dream slipped away as she shoved him with her weight.

She stared at him, her pink and swollen lips parted. He lowered his head for more, but Tori took a step backwards creating space between them. Their bodies no longer touched and he ached for her already.

'You are a cheater. No different to my husband. You're dating four women on a reality show, Zac,' she hissed his name through gritted teeth. 'You have four potential women one of whom you'll pick to possibly marry one day. You cannot be kissing me. It isn't fair to them, or to me. It isn't right!'

'Shit,' he said and hung his head, raking his fingers through his hair. He kept it long for moments like these, he guessed. There'd been a few of them.

'These women ...'

'Stop. Don't offer excuses. You're committed to the show and to them until you send them home. Don't justify your actions. I thought you were different. But that proves how stupid I am. How bad I am at trusting people. The wrong people. Or maybe it's men in general. You're all a bunch of lying cheats.'

'Tori, c'mon.' He reached for her, desperate to stop her fleeing, to feel her skin once more. To hold her. It didn't work and she backed away as if he repulsed her. He flinched as she flung the remaining dirty dishes into the plastic bucket filled with water and stormed off.

11

———————

'Mummy!' Mirabelle skipped towards her, the rose-pink dress she wore swinging as she moved, her unsuitable white patent shoes squeaking on the floorboards.

'I missed you so much!' Tori squeezed her too tight, relishing the squish of her baby folds. She released her daughter and said, 'This morning I have to do some cooking for tonight's dinner but when I'm finished would you like to go horse riding?'

Mirry's eyes opened wide. It was the one thing Mirry had been begging to do since they'd arrived. Tori had put her off too many times.

'Lovely, dear. Your old gear will be in the stables. It'll need a good clean I imagine,' Nan commented from the corner where she sat sipping her morning coffee.

Mirry hugged her fiercely and squealed yes, many times over. Horse riding had been one of Tori's favourite activities as a child. She'd had her own horse whom she'd adored and endless summer days to roam paddocks. The idea of riding out on isolated tracks and brushing the tips of the branches as you passed by, sent a wave of excitement rolling through her. They'd both waited too long. And after last night she desperately wanted to reconnect with passions she'd once enjoyed. And maybe with her old self?

This morning she'd risen early and set up breakfast before waking Mike and telling him she was taking the car back. She was good at running away, knew it was immature, but it was also liberating. Making her own choices. She didn't want to face Zac, not yet anyway. Tori needed distance to collect her thoughts. And Zac needed to spend time with Sophie before they headed back to the homestead. That was only fair.

A gamut of emotion pulsed through her. She wasn't angry even though she'd made him think that. Frightened and confused more accurate.

He'd broken up with Susie and then kissed her. She'd tossed and turned all night remembering those words. One thing Tori couldn't work out is what it meant. Had he liked her back then? Wanted more but she'd run away?

She'd enjoyed the kiss. Too much. And that scared her. A lot. It was like she remembered. Damn, Zac Coleman was a good kisser.

She'd accused him of being a cheater, but he wasn't. He hadn't been all those years ago either and he wasn't now. Zac was the one man she felt comfortable with. He was like a warm blanket being draped around your shoulders on a cold winter's night. Remembering those lips on hers sent shivers racing up her spine.

'Why don't you change out of those party shoes and go and feed the animals with Nan? Then you might like to sit here at the kitchen bench and do some drawing while I cook. I can't bear to be away from you a second longer.' Mirry rolled her eyes but tugged off her shoes, replacing them with wellington boots. It hadn't taken her long to adjust to the routine of the country.

Mirry's small hand clasped Nan's, their fingers entwined as they wandered out to the yard together. Tori's heart swelled. The unconditional love for a child was something else. Despite the disastrous situation of her marriage, she loved being a mother.

Focus, Tori. First, she needed to whip up a feast for tonight, suitable for a buffet, she decided because the urge to make herself scarce weighed heavily on her mind.

Tori didn't think twice about making good old-fashioned chicken pie given her tolerance to meat had grown considerably.

Talking with Zac about the past had reignited something within and she yearned for the comfort of tradition. Horse riding, and more cooking. Zac had reminded her of what she once was. She was still that person, wasn't she?

But she'd repressed many memories. How could she? They were her childhood highlights. Cooking with Nan for starters. In the early days when she'd missed her mother so much it felt like her heart was split in two, they'd spend hours in the kitchen with Nan taking her with pain-staking care through each step of a recipe.

The house had always been filled with inviting aromas and they'd shared the thrill of anticipation as their favourite creations were lifted out of the oven.

Had she gotten so way-laid with fancy super-foods like kale and spinach and quinoa and fast-spinning blenders that she'd forgotten real food was nutritious. You couldn't get much healthier than direct from a vegetable patch and organic chicken from your neighbour down the road. Pastry made from scratch had no preservatives or nasty chemicals.

Warmth spread through her body. More longing for the past but also, what? Contentment? Realisation at rediscovering her roots? No, it was hope she felt and the emotion stole her breath away, catching her by surprise.

The facts were harsh and she couldn't hide them: her marriage was over; she was broke; had a floundering vegan catering business and was currently sponging off her nan. And yet, being in the kitchen, like the small child she'd once been, and feeling the same sense of accomplishment, allowed her to feel certain everything would be okay.

It had to be. Tori pushed aside thoughts of Zac. The man was dating four women. There was hardly any cause for Tori to get her knickers in a knot. She had to get her own life back on track. *Even if* he liked her all those years ago, and there was a hint of attraction between them now...

Hours later Tori led Mirry on a narrow track heading towards the river. She inhaled the scent of her first love, her horse Giddy Up. His musty earthy smell was so familiar to her. A smell she'd always loved, but today, her stomach churned as she controlled a cramp of nausea. Tori reached for the water bottle on the side of her pack and Giddy Up nuzzled her, demanding a pat. She swallowed the cool water and rubbed his nose. He'd always been an obedient and tame horse, but now with his advanced age he was perfect for Mirry.

This life was enough. Her future could be the farm, like Nan. After Pop had died her nan had lived a full and happy life alone. Yes, she'd had customers to care for and the hobby farm to keep her busy, but Tori could be the same. She'd help out more and make a serious effort to get the business off the ground and make a success of it. She'd provide for Mirry without the help of Todd, and her daughter could grow up a country kid like she had.

Thinking about men … Despite her self-talk, she couldn't get Zac off her mind. Her belly tightened into knots remembering the words they'd exchanged. But then she recalled the kiss and her insides turned to liquid dissolving those same knots. Tori remembered the sensation; his thumb on her bare back, the feel of his body against her.

Shaking her head, she chased those thoughts away. It was the nostalgia of being home. That's all. Zac was *Cedar Creek Plains*. The two went together.

Zac was the perfect friend, had always been there for her. They could continue being great friends.

12

―――――

Saturday night in Cedar Creek Plains and there was only one place to be: the pub.

The lifeblood of any small town was the local. And that is exactly why Zac had chosen this as his date with Clare.

Plus, Saturday night was trivia and was always a hoot.

Clare was the perfect candidate. Zac resisted the urge to headbutt himself. Talking about candidates made it sound like he was interviewing her to be his vet assistant. That was sort of the problem though, his heart didn't flutter and his skin didn't erupt in goosebumps around Clare, or any of the women. Well, except one and she wasn't in the running.

Clare was a jillaroo. A country girl born and bred and he admired her calm demeanour and no holds barred attitude. She'd mixed in well with the other girls and could talk about anything ranging from make-up and hair which interested some of them, to horses and agriculture and the future of farming. On paper, she was his perfect woman.

She sat across from him and nursed her beer with a genuine smile. Music blared from the rock band in the corner making talking difficult. He leaned in close to chat and their shoulders touched.

Zac focused on her dark hair pulled severely back into a bun, her distinct high cheek bones and the dark mole upon her upper lip. He checked out her eyelashes too, anything to avoid glancing across the room to where Tori sat with friends.

Mike filmed as always and the locals relished the chance to be on TV.

Mayor Graham tested the mic, asking people to group into teams of six as trivia would commence in ten minutes. Two people rushed to join their table and when elderly resident, Francine, wandered past, Zac nabbed her too. She was infamous for her general knowledge on movies, pop stars and TV from reading trashy magazines. The old woman giggled and pulled herself gingerly onto the spare stool.

The Mayor wandered the room checking on numbers and asking team names. 'Are you being shy?' he yelled into his mic. 'Here is our resident bachelor Zac with his lovely date, Clare. They need another team member folks. C'mon, who is going to volunteer? Might guarantee you a spot on the telly!' The crowd roared but no one moved.

'Here's the perfect addition to any team,' the Mayor continued. 'Welcome home, Tori. Lovely to have you back. Let's hope it's for good.' The Mayor bailed her up as she stood in line at the bar. Zac's senses went on high alert.

'Come and join the *Local Lads Looking for Love* team. They've got Francine and are sure to be in with a chance!' The crowd cheered again and raised their glasses in a toast.

Tori shook her head, her loose hair swishing around her shoulders.

Zac couldn't help but drink in the sight of her. Those long, lean legs were in faded blue jeans with slight heels giving her some height. She wore a transparent loose white blouse so he could see the swell of her breasts. He flicked his tongue across his lips and took a sip of beer. God damn.

He'd tried his best to clear the air and talk to Tori since the campout. She hadn't brushed him off exactly; she'd been evasive and polite. Acted as if everything was normal. But nothing could be normal, could it, after that kiss? It was all he could think about since. For him, the flame he'd harboured all those years ago flared brightly and continued to simmer. Unfortunate, given the circumstances he found himself in. Of all the timing for him to be coerced into a reality dating TV show.

But it was all for the best.

The Mayor droned on and Zac turned back to Clare. 'Tell me about your family.' Clare was an only child who was estranged from her parents and lived alone on an outback station. Short and simple, she said. Nothing like his large and noisy family whom he argued with regularly, but loved dearly.

Clare reached out her hand and placed it on top of his. Out of the corner of his eye, he saw Tori being bustled into position at their table. His eyes were trained on the hand that had obvious sun damage but painted pink nails. With Tori approaching on one side and Clare being intimate in the rowdy pub, his heart accelerated.

It was all shades of awkward.

Clare leaned in. 'I have to tell you up front that I do not want children.' She lowered her head closer to his and his long fringe brushed her forehead. It was intimate, wrong. 'For a relationship to work, there has to be honesty. It's important you know because I won't change my mind. I understand if my view changes the situation for you, but you need to know.' Clare withdrew her hand and placed it in her lap.

Tori sat down next to him and her leg brushed his thigh. The song playing ramped up to its crescendo and thumped too loud in his ears.

The music stopped as abruptly as it started and Mayor Graham was back on the mic announcing the trivia categories.

Clare was perfect on paper and in other respects too. It didn't bring him any joy though as he sat squashed between her and Tori in the noisy pub. All of a sudden he wanted to be anywhere but there.

THE TOILET CUBICLE DOOR OPENED AS TORI SHOOK THE WATER FROM HER hands.

'Clare, I'm so sorry. I never meant to crash your date with Zac. I keep popping up but it's never my intention.'

Clare stared at her reflection in the mirror and washed her hands.

'Are you sorry?' She turned and ripped off some paper towel and threw it in the bin before facing her. 'What is it between you and Zac?'

'What do you mean?'

'Are you dating?'

'No! Zac is on the show and is dating all four of you. Not me.'

'Are you sure you're not a secret contestant that is going to surprise us in week four and run away with the prize?'

'No!'

'So, what is it then? Unrequited love? I understand you grew up together. Is there passion that hasn't been sated?' She smirked. 'Because personally I'd rather know than waste my time.'

'No, completely innocent I assure you. We were friends and ran around in the same group together.'

Clare leaned one hip against the basin as another woman entered the bathroom. She crossed her arms against her chest. 'Not buying it, Tori. The chemistry between the two of you when you're in the same room is palpable. Are you telling me you can't feel it?'

Tori went mute momentarily but found her strength and stood taller. This woman was ballsy and straight to the point but Tori wasn't intimidated. This was a reality TV show and each of these women wanted to win. It was a game after all. Who wouldn't want to win Zac's heart?

'Nah. Nothing going on. Good mates is all.'

'If you say so.' But Clare stared too hard for too long and shrugged as she dawdled towards the door, shoulders back, hips swaying. A waft of her perfume clung to the air and tickled Tori's nose. The taste lay on her tongue and lined her throat. She gagged. Bile burned before Tori clasped her hand over her mouth and rushed back to the nearest toilet. She only had time to lift the lid before vomiting.

Despite multiple rinses she couldn't rid her mouth of the sour taste of sick. What was going on? She'd drunk two beers and while the pub food wasn't great, you couldn't go wrong with a vegetable stir-fry. Urgh. She wanted to leave.

Pushing open the fling-back door she sought out Mike. Hopefully he'd give her a lift home. As usual, he had his lens focused on the contestants, filming their every word.

She approached and stood behind him waiting, not wanting to interrupt an intimate moment and good viewing. But Zac noticed her lingering and poked his head around Clare and past Mike.

'Tori?' he questioned. 'Are you okay? You're pale.'

'Yeah, I do feel a bit off. Can Mike drive me back to the farm?'

Zac stood and the stool scraped. 'I'll take you. Clare, would you like to stay or call it a night?'

Clare didn't respond to Zac but turned full circle and faced Tori, smirking and raising an eyebrow in question while her eyes twinkled.

'Don't be silly. You cannot call your date short because of me. I'm sure Mike will take me,' Tori stammered.

'I can't leave. I do the filming, Tori.' His words dripped in sarcasm.

Given there wasn't a cab rank of taxis waiting outside to take her home, she had to accept the offer.

Clare stood. 'It's fine. Let's get Tori home if she's not feeling well.'

Zac patted Clare's arm and smiled in her direction while Clare glared at Tori with what looked like smug satisfaction.

What a disaster.

13

The wind picked up and mini tornadoes of dust swirled across the landscape. The branches of the bottle brush trees surrounding Coleman Cattle Station swayed in rhythm and stray leaves rustled along the ground. The breeze cooled the sweat on Zac's skin but he ripped off his hat and wiped the sweat from his brow.

Three station cattle dogs lay on their bellies under the nearest tree, their heads alert, tongues lolling, not prepared to miss any of the action. They rolled around in the dirt to generate some cool. Zac snapped them on his phone and posted to his feed.

#cattledogs #workingdogs #mustering #coolspot

It sure was stinking hot. Too hot to be mustering cattle, but here they all were.

A hard slap landed on his back and that could only mean one thing. Turning, his anticipation built. 'G'day, Chief, you're back!' The men hugged.

'Good to see you, son. You've got a fantastic turn out today.' Mike shoved the camera in their face capturing the greeting.

Chief placed his hand to the lens. 'What's this then?' The man's smile disappeared.

'You've been away too long. I've gotten myself roped into a reality dating show. No guess whose idea it was?' Zac smirked but continued. 'Unfortunately for the time being you'll have to get used to Mike here being a right pain in the behind as he shoves that camera in our faces all the time. You get used to it.'

Chief shook his head but pulled his hand back. 'Mike, I'm Chief.' The two men fumbled to shake hands. 'Zac might have been convinced to find love on TV but give us a break and catch some real action later when the mustering starts.'

Zac nodded at Mike who he assumed had captured the footage he wanted anyway. Mike lowered the camera and wandered away.

'How's the clinic? Have you been busy?'

Zac gave his boss the rundown on births, deaths and emergencies, adding in a few funny stories for good measure. Mid-sentence he paused as his father joined them, talking over him.

'You're a sight Chief. It's great to have you back. Now my son can return to his proper focus here on the station and forget any silliness of working full-time as a vet.'

Zac's mood dipped.

The trio stood under the shade of the tree. Other men participating in the muster gathered in the circular drive, adjacent to the front sheds. Tori busied herself a few metres away, filling an esky with water and snacks for the trip. Tiffany wasn't anywhere.

'Jerome,' Chief nodded at Zac's father. 'You know I'm set for retirement at the end of the year. The valley needs Zac. Without him there's a chance the vet clinic will close and emergencies will have to be handled by the next town. It's too far away and not good for *Cedar Creek Plains*. And, Zac is keen.'

'Zac is keen to do everything possible to avoid his responsibilities here. I'm winding down for retirement too but that doesn't feature in Zac's plans. This is a profitable stud. The best around. I've slaved for years to make it what it is, you can see what I've achieved.' His father waved his hands wide taking in the magnificent homestead.

Chief knew the drill. 'Perhaps it's time to consider a different succession plan Jerome. Accept the boy isn't interested.'

'Perhaps it's time he remembered his responsibility and to do what is required. He'll break his mother's heart if he continues to carry on this way.'

A break-out cat call and whistles came from the group of men to their left. Most were smoking or getting in their last drink before the dusty job ahead.

Zac's shoulders slumped with relief. He unclenched his jaw and rolled out the fists he held at his side and turned. First, he glanced towards Tori and their eyes connected. She stood at the steps to the house, the now filled esky in front of her. Her expression was grim and he guessed she'd overheard the conversation with his father.

Like an oasis in a dry desert, Zac was transfixed by her. Today she wore her trade-mark blue jeans and a cool, light green cotton blouse. Her hair was pulled back in a low ponytail so it draped around her neck. Nothing about what she wore was special but his thirst for her was unquenchable.

He was seriously in trouble.

The noise grew more raucous close by, but Zac's attention was captured by a colourful floating butterfly soaring on the breeze. He wanted to capture it mid-flight but it floated away too fast.

Tiffany had arrived.

She was as colourful as the butterfly. Zac had suspected Tiffany was no wallflower and today proved it. She lapped up the attention from the male group, held one hand to her hip and stood in that funny way girls do, with one leg bent out and her hip angled to the side.

Normal blue-rinse jeans were accompanied by a black top but the reflection off the large gold buckle belt she wore had him squinting before he could register the bubble-gum pink knee-high boots. The colour paled in comparison to the bouffant blonde blow wave she wore. Very American.

With the crowd watching on, she sauntered over to him, placed one hand behind his head and pulled him in for a smooch on the lips. The kiss drew jeers from the men and cheers for more.

His father muttered behind him to Chief. 'And that's the other thing the boy got himself involved in. A stupid dating show. I don't know how it happened but his priorities are all screwed.'

The roars drowned out his father's voice. Zac's chest tightened and his face grew hot. Averting his gaze, he observed the red dirt on the ground and how it covered his boots but had not yet coloured Tiffany's. Glancing back up, a salacious grin greeted him and a dozen gazes burned into him, heavy and expectant. Sweat gathered on his brow, he twisted the pinkie ring with his thumb and turned his gaze to Tori who held up a bottle of water, gesturing for him to approach.

Zac nodded and grasped Tiffany's hand and headed toward the homestead. Mike filmed and Zac understood it would make terrible television. This was the moment he was supposed to dip his date and kiss her passionately to the cries of the local blokes and the women watching at home. He knew how he was supposed to act; but the only thing on his mind was escape and Tori offered it.

'Thank you,' he whispered as he clutched the icy cold bottle of water. Tiffany resisted but he dragged her along until they were inside the house and the door shut. Inside he dropped her hand and rolled the water bottle over his hot face.

14

'Anyone checked out Zac's feed today? He posted the dogs. They're so cute,' cooed Lara.

Zac's four sisters gathered around the one phone to check out the image.

'Have you seen Zac's Instagram account, Tori? It's adorable. It's all animal photos in a whole range of different shots. You won't see any family or social pics. A bit weird but super-fun.'

Tori moved closer and agreed it was a great photo and made a mental note to check it out later.

'It's so fabulous to have you back. Are you staying?' asked Eliza, Zac's eldest sister.

Tori sat at the grand outdoor table that covered the entire width of the verandah wrapping around the Coleman homestead. Today it was decked out with an excessive amount of food for lunch when she wasn't even hungry.

'You know what? I think I might.' The women cheered.

'Another eligible woman to add to the few available. If we'd known, we might not have volunteered baby brother for the show.' Lara, the youngest sister, peeked at Tori with an expression she couldn't interpret.

'I heard you signed him up. Bet he was pleased?'

'He knew when he was defeated and he'd never live it down if he didn't proceed. No was not an option. He's a smart guy; understood when to give in,' said Hollie, the second youngest and one of the duo of sisters that had written Zac's application for the show.

'I know I've been gone a long time, but why did you need to? All the girls drooled over him at school. He was voted most boyfriend-worthy and he was dating Susie,' Tori said.

'Oh, so long ago,' Eliza crooned. 'Susie, I remember her. Wild curly hair like Nicole Kidman and very sweet.'

Jessica nursed a sleeping baby of about six-months and rocked the bundle as she spoke. 'His confidence was knocked by the cancer scare a few years back and he hasn't dated much since. He needs a bit of a boost and we thought being chased by four women at once might do the trick. But we also secretly hope he might find love. He deserves to be happy.'

Each sister nodded.

'Who do you think is the front runner?' Tori asked, the question causing a bunch of little firecrackers to release in her tummy.

'Well, not Tiffany given his reaction this morning. And she was dressed like a grown-up lollypop in that outfit. Zac is so not going to go for that,' offered Hollie.

'Sophie is gorgeous,' said Tori and waited for their reactions.

'And she's a teacher which is fabulous,' said Lara, her sisters booing in response.

'Only because you're a teacher. Doesn't mean she's perfect for Zac. I think he'll be too intimidated by her perfection and elegance,' said Jessica. 'I think it's either the osteopath, Lucy, because she's so sensible or the country girl, Clare.'

'Clare gives off a funny vibe, don't you think?' commented Eliza.

There were a few murmurs of agreement.

'No matter who he chooses, let's hope he gives up that ridiculous notion of not wanting children. I mean, it's crazy. He comes from a large family, has adorable nieces and nephews whom he loves but says he doesn't want children.' Jessica held up her own bub and kissed its forehead as if justifying her argument.

'He doesn't want children?' Tori squeaked the words.

'Tori, he claims he doesn't, but none of us believe him,' exclaimed Eliza.

Hollie held her head in her hands, 'Imagine if he's told any of the women that view.'

'He can't have. They'd have run, wouldn't they? Most women want children. Tori, you do. How old is your daughter?' asked Eliza.

'Mirry is four.' She had difficulty forming the words. All of a sudden, Tori's body overheated. She gulped down a glass of water and fanned out her shirt. The sisters kept nattering on oblivious.

Zac didn't want children.

The guy had kissed her! How dare he? She had a daughter, he'd saved her bloody guinea pigs from near death after all, had tendered to them with so much love.

Tori recalled the few occasions Mirry and Zac had been together. He'd doted on her or had she imagined it? The sister's voices receded as she tried to remember. No, he *had* doted on her. They'd played together and Zac had giggled and even made faces. Mirry had found it hilarious. Something Todd had never done, come down to her level and played with her like she was important and special.

The man who tended with such care to injured animals; gave them his one hundred percent, didn't want children.

Then he couldn't possibly want her.

The realisation hit her hard.

Had she really thought Zac wanted her?

The pesky nausea that had been bothering her for days surfaced again. Maybe it was the prawns but she couldn't keep making excuses.

The sour and acidic taste entered her mouth. Tori breathed deeply in and out to make the sensation go away and to calm her racing heart. Her entire body shook with the effort. But she couldn't do it; couldn't hold it together and she raced for the railing and vomited over the edge.

Each sister rushed towards her; one patting her back, the other holding her hair, another offering a cup of water.

She'd grown up with these girls so they were like sisters. The homestead had been her playground for horse riding, bonfires and annual festivals. And now they cared for her. Who wouldn't want this for themselves? A loving family to surround yourself with; to care for you, nurture you and love you. It didn't make any sense. As an only child it was often all she'd dreamed about having when she grew up. And to be a better mother than the one she'd had.

Tori's eyes watered as her entire lunch ended up in the front garden.

15

———————

Two pink lines.

No! No! No! Tori screamed a silent scream, covered her gaping mouth and glanced around in case someone saw, in case someone witnessed her fear. She'd been blindsided. It could be wrong. It was common for false positives, right? She'd do another test.

She did the test again.

Same result.

Tori lay curled up into a ball on her side, a bed on the enclosed back verandah offering a welcome retreat. Her finger swiped over the screen of her phone.

How cute could one man be? Despite her predicament, which she was blissfully ignoring for a few minutes, she scrolled through Zac's Instagram. An entire feed of animal photos with most of them capturing large doses of cuteness.

Tears pricked her eyes at the images. The account was so adorable that she couldn't understand how Zac wouldn't want to fill a similar feed with photographs of gorgeous little babies. The idea of him not wanting to was so far out of the ballpark of anything she might imagine about Zac. Zac who was perfect in almost every way.

Instead, she focused on the baby kittens curled beside their mother not long after being born, and the sheep under a burning horizon sun and the many dogs of all breeds and poses. Puddles and Rainbow! She paused her quick finger scroll. When did he capture those two rascals? Tori spread her fingers wide and zoomed into the background. Nan's house. Must have been when he returned them or perhaps when they escaped. A line of animal emojis featured as his comment.

His sisters were right. Not a single photo of anything else, no previous flames or drunken Saturday night shots at the pub. All animals in their glorious rural outback.

Her stomach cramped again and she curled up tighter.

Tori placed one hand on her belly. A little life grew in there. She didn't feel nauseous anymore but wretched in every definition of the word. And oh, so tired. Right at this moment she wanted to lay on this bed for a week and not move; let the world continue around her.

She wished. Reality had hit her smack in the face and she had to rise to the challenge.

And she would, but, oh, how could she have been so stupid? Dumb enough to get pregnant again to her loser of a husband who preferred sex with other women.

But even worse how could she not have realised? She knew the signs for goodness sake; had been pregnant before. In fairness she'd been distracted recently. Yes, with leaving that same unfaithful husband, caring for her daughter and relocating themselves to the country where she hoped to develop a thriving business. Not to mention Zac.

After vomiting, the sisters had ushered her inside to clean up and rest. In the bathroom at the rear of the house, she'd washed her face and tidied her hair, and searched for some light make-up to hide the circles under her eyes and make her lips shine again.

She didn't mean to snoop. But as soon as she saw the pregnancy kit hidden amongst the bottles and tubes, she'd realised. She'd fallen back onto her bottom on the cold tiled floor and pieced together the obvious signs over the last couple of weeks.

It wasn't like her to steal someone else's stuff, but she'd been unable to resist. Tori had to know for sure. Right then.

Yep, she was pregnant.

Tori flicked off the phone and pushed her face into the pillow and cried. She'd never felt so alone.

∿

TORI ROUSED TO RAISED VOICES OUTSIDE THE WINDOW. STRETCHING OUT her legs it took a few moments before realisation kicked in and the world crashed back down around her.

Instinctively she patted her stomach again before raising up onto an elbow and peering out the window. The sun was less ferocious and a shadow had commenced to creep across the back yard. The manicured lawn and garden beds blossomed with reds, pinks and yellow. Tori had to admit, the vista was pretty idyllic. There was something about dry sprawling plains creeping up to meet vibrant green grass with the explosions of colour.

To her left Tiffany came into view. She was nothing like the woman who had left mustering this morning, not a sign of the gusto and confidence she'd displayed as she'd kissed Zac.

This woman dragged her no longer pristine boots against the ground as she walked with a slight limp. The magnificent bouffant curls were flat and hung lifeless around her shoulders, an Akubra hat hanging from her hand. The left leg of her jeans was smattered with brown patches that also crawled up her shirt sleeve. When she turned in Tori's direction, both cheeks were caked in sticky wet mud with little bits flaking away as she walked.

But it was her scowl that had Tori stifling a giggle.

Pinching her own cheeks to add colour to what she was sure must have been a pale complexion, Tori wandered out and through the homestead.

Jessica held an awake baby now and stood watching the show on the deck as it unfurled in front of her. Both Hollie and Lara were fussing over Tiffany who swatted their hands away.

For once Tori wished Mike was here to capture the footage. This is exactly what the viewers wanted, didn't they?

'What's happened?' Tori asked.

'Apparently, she was attacked by a stud - her words - and had to run for her life but no one came to her assistance,' Jessica's eyebrows were raised, her eyes twinkling.

'So she's come back early and alone?' Tori searched for Zac.

'Yup.'

'How on earth did she find her way?'

'She was mounted on Rufus. That old girl would find her way back to the homestead through a blizzard. So lucky for Tiffany she would have led her right home,' Jessica offered.

Hollie and Lara attempted to placate an enraged Tiffany with kind words, wet towels and a cold drink. Tiffany rejected the offers and stormed off to the sheds.

'It won't be too long until the group is back,' Jessica said, 'We're hanging out in the kitchen. Come and join us.'

Tori nodded and followed.

'Are you feeling better?'

16

Zac pulled open the heavy oak doors to the barn and all he could think about was quenching his thirst with an ice-cold beer.

The lads surrounding him jostled for a spot to cool down their horses or park their motorbikes as quickly as possible to allow the celebrations to begin.

His eyes adjusted to the dimness of indoors and he spotted two figures in one of the bays; Zac pulled up sharp. A couple of musterers bumped into his back before going quiet and then all six of them exploded into raucous guffaws and wolf whistles, their profanities loud and unruly.

Tiffany gasped. She twisted around towards the commotion, her bright blue eyes wide like her gaping mouth.

In front of her stood a young rouse-about employed by Zac's father. His lips were in a smooched position, one hand clasped to Tiffany's waist, the other clearly inside her top, enjoying the curves of her voluptuous bust.

Tiffany's mouth closed and with alacrity she extracted his hand and slapped the young guy hard across the cheek.

Mike arrived on the scene. Skidding on his feet in the dirt and fumbling to get his camera rolling. Zac had seen him over by the entry stairs, looking exhausted when he'd briefly put his camera down for a rest.

Tiffany didn't acknowledge the gathering crowd. Instead she turned and stormed off through the rear door of the barn. Mike swung the camera in Zac's face to catch his reaction before swinging back away and chasing after Tiffany.

A few men approached the jackaroo and slapped him on the back, congratulating him on the conquest. Zac approached and stood in front of him and the group hushed, aware the young man, whose name no one knew, had been making out with one of Zac's contestants.

The man flinched as Zac reached up and whacked him on the back too. 'Looks like you saved me a whole lot of trouble. Thanks mate.'

The men cheered.

It didn't take long for word to travel. By the time Zac had cleaned up and changed clothes, Anna Fox was at the station. Mike stood by her side while the crowd sat on hay bales shadowed by flickering fairy lights hanging from the trees.

Zac's heart sat heavy in his chest as he took in the scene.

His four sisters stood to the side and Eliza moved forward in step with him. She grasped his arm in solidarity but dropped it as he moved away towards Anna. Tori stood further back, closer to the verandah and his whole body came alive with longing.

He had almost reached Anna when from his right a figure barrelled towards him in a flurry of colour and floating on a cloud of strong perfume. A flat palm was to his cheek before he could blink.

'Bastard. You should have rescued me from that cow. It could have killed me!' Tiffany's face was scrunched in fury before she circled and stormed off.

'Well, there you have it folks,' Anna crooned into the camera, 'love doesn't always run smoothly. Tiffany has decided farmer Zac and rural life isn't for her and is the first girl to leave the show. Three remain, which one will Zac choose?'

Mike filmed a panorama of the celebrations in front of him and then followed Tiffany's departing back.

'Zac, we want you to give us a round-up of how you feel about Tiffany leaving. Okay?' Anna prompted when he didn't respond.

'Okay,' he said and reached for the beer he'd been dreaming of.

Anna approached Tori and with their heads bent, Anna whispered something to her. Tori nodded and glanced in his direction but her expression was blank.

Victoria.

The wind rustled her loose dark hair and her skin dazzled in the afternoon haze. All of the commotion around him receded, forgotten.

She was the one that brightened his spirits. Her presence that made his heart skip a beat and was always the only one he wanted to talk to. It was Tori who mattered. Always had been. He'd known it but had gone along with this ridiculous façade. A cracking pain shot across his chest, physical confirmation of the disaster he'd created. What the hell was he going to do? At the moment he couldn't be with her.

But that was all he wanted.

Victoria stared right through him. Her mouth was downturned and her eyes hooded. Sad. Lost. Like an invisible pull of gravity he moved towards her. If she was in pain, he wanted to help. Needed to help.

But the next time he looked up, Tori was gone.

'Mummy!' Mirry cried and rushed towards her car as it pulled to a park outside of Nan's place. 'Daddy's here!'

Tori's head jerked up so fast it cracked. Sure enough, short blonde curls on a lean frame sauntered out of the shadows and into the glare of the afternoon sun. 'What the fuck?' she muttered as she unclipped her seat belt and opened the door, her movements in slow motion to allow her to regulate her breaths and calm the hell down.

The little girl jumped up and down on the spot. Tori leaned down to her height and squeezed her in close for a cuddle. Something hard jabbed at her belly and pinched. Tori pulled back and Mirry squealed again and held up three new Barbie dolls. Two wore active wear and the third some ridiculous pale lemon ball gown. For some reason the active wear bristled. Old life and sore memories perhaps?

So, Todd was going to be one of those dads, prepared to pull out all the tricks in the war for Mirry's affection.

He approached and stood before her. 'Hi.'

'You could have told me you were coming to visit.'

'Would you have let me?'

She scoffed. 'Of course. You can visit Mirry anytime. You are her father, after all.'

'I wanted to see you, too.'

Tori stared incredulous. 'What for? To tell me all about your new love pad? Shacked up together now, have you?'

Todd moved in closer and clasped her elbow. There was slight yet familiar body odour, tangy and acidic; like he'd been working out. He leaned too close. She'd forgotten how strong his grip was.

'I'm sorry. It didn't mean anything. I love you.'

Tori ripped her arm away. His touch repulsed her.

'It meant something when you were going for it up against the wall. You weren't even hiding. So desperate to get into each other's pants were you?' Tori lashed out at him.

'Daddy, c'mon. I'll show you 'round. There are so many animals. Do you want to say hi to Puddles and Rainbow? They almost died!' Mirry tugged her father's hand but his eyes remained fixed on Tori, pleading. Their connection broke as Mirry pulled him away to see the farm.

'Urgh!' She slammed the car door shut too hard and stormed inside.

Nan found her kneading the dough for the fresh bread she planned to serve with dinner. Her stomach churned, a mixture of nausea and anger.

'Go easy or the bread will never rise.' Nan patted her on the arm.

'Who does he think he is, Nan? Coming here, turning up whenever he chooses.'

'He hasn't seen Mirabelle for over two weeks. She's delighted to see him.'

'He can see Mirry and she deserves to spend time with her father. It's not that. He can't turn up whenever he likes.'

Nan smiled, her wise green eyes crinkling.

'God, I can't even put into words what I'd like to do to him. That image of him, him, *fucking that woman*,' Tori whispered the phrase, 'is back bouncing around in my head. I'm not like my mother, weak and forgiving, a dreamer.'

Nan interrupted her again. 'Your mother was not weak. In fact, she was the opposite: strong and headfast and determined. You have all those qualities too and they are not bad traits.'

'I don't want those qualities if it means you leave behind your responsibilities to chase bigger and better opportunities. Opportunities you couldn't have with a little girl in tow. I understand more now I'm a mother. I could never, ever, leave Mirry, not ever.' Tori paused her overzealous mixing and blew her fringe out of her eyes.

She kept on. 'I can't believe you still defend her after all these years. She's cut both of us out of her life and yet you speak fondly of her.'

'If Mirry abandoned you, regardless of the circumstances, you'd still love her too. Doesn't mean you love her behaviour or the way she's treated you, but she's my daughter. And the best thing she ever did was leave you with me. I adored having you around when you were growing up. Kept me young again.'

Tori wiped her flour-covered hands on her apron while tears rolled down her cheeks and they held each other tight.

'I did the same too, anyway. I shouldn't criticise. I left you, too.'

'Ah, that was more spreading your wings, I think. Discovering who you were. And look at you now, a mother, business owner and fabulous cook!'

'Hardly, but said like a true loving grandmother. Sorry, Nan. But I know one thing I am not and that is a pushover. Some people are prepared to give philandering husbands another go, I'm not. If he didn't want to remain married to me and wanted to be with whatever her name is, he could have gone about it the right way. He didn't. I could never trust him again. And thanks to him, I may never trust a man again.'

'Okay, so you treat this as a father visiting his daughter. He can stay for dinner. For longer if he makes arrangements to stay.' Tori went to butt in but Nan held up her palm. 'I didn't say here. We're fully booked anyway. Give him some time to work it out.'

Wiping her moist cheeks, she nodded. 'You're right. And I have a dinner to prepare.' She kissed her nan's cheek and went back to her happy place.

17

———————

Tori was deliberately being a bitch. But damnit, she couldn't help it.

Sure enough Todd was hanging around and joining them for dinner. Well, eating with Mirry, as Tori wouldn't be sitting down nice and cosy with *her husband*. She had to work anyway and prepare the dinner for the show tonight. Plus, she had to get away from Todd's puppy dogs eyes that followed her every move.

Because of their special guest, she took extra care with the meal. Todd had converted her to veganism but she wasn't strict compared to him. He was hard-core about the food he ate. So, she'd cooked a good old-fashioned roast beef with all the trimmings, including gravy with animal fats and vegetables soaked in dripping. The bread was vegan but she'd keep that to herself. Dessert was cheesecake because Todd loved his gelatine…

Tori gripped her belly as a wave of nausea washed over her. That would teach her for being evil. But still, she couldn't wait to see the look on his face as dinner was served. Would he make a fuss or enjoy dinner with his daughter? This wasn't an *a la carte* restaurant; there was no sending your dinner back.

Todd positioned himself at the high benches in the kitchen in readiness to eat with her and Nan. Nice try. Tori directed him to a special table for two in the alcove where the other B&B guests would dine while the television show was filmed in the main room.

'This is romantic,' Todd said as his eyes sparkled in her direction.

Tori clasped Mirry's hand and guided her to the table. 'Yes,' Tori smirked, 'a special daddy and daughter dinner.' Todd didn't even mimic a smile. But Mirry felt special.

The main room hummed with activity as the remaining three contestants and Zac dined with Anna, Mike trawling the room as usual.

'Where's Tiffany?' asked Clare.

Anna stood at the head of the table and advised Tiffany had left the show that afternoon. Mike's camera scanned their faces for reactions. Anna's words took a few moments to sink in and the reactions varied – relief at less competition, to sorrow (such a terrible way to go) and pure nasty happiness. It took less than a refill of their drinks for the women to forget about poor Tiffany. Their focus intensified on Zac; he was prey in their sights.

'Zac,' Lucy sidled up to him and clutched his arm. Her preferred casual workout gear and flat shoes – heels are so bad for your back – were nowhere in sight. Tonight she wore a little black number that showed off her shapely legs and accentuated her red hair. 'Let's go outside for a chat while we wait for dinner.'

Zac gazed back at her like a deer stunned in headlights. 'I'll bring you both out a drink,' Tori jumped in, feeling uncomfortable on his behalf. Nice one Lucy. A Bachelorette type move. Would it pay off?

Tori delivered the drinks, but clearly she didn't work as fast as Lucy. They stood in the far corner of the verandah with Zac's back to the balustrade appearing as if he was trapped.

Tori lingered out of sight behind the open French doors while her fingers frosted around the cold drinks.

She couldn't see what Lucy was doing but she imagined the woman's hands pawing at Zac's chest, her fingers twirling through the smattering of hair escaping the top of his shirt.

'Zac, I've enjoyed your company. I know it's not just me. You know we have a fantastic future together. It can work for us. My business is transportable and perfect for the country.' Did she purr? Lucy stepped closer to him, any closer and she'd be straddling him. 'I'm falling for you,' her voice was low and husky.

Tori growled low in her throat. Her gaze lowered to the golden Aperol Spritz she held. It would go nicely down the front of Lucy's dazzling black dress. Okay, she wouldn't. Imagine that being caught on film? The viewers would love the twist. A crew member goes off script the headline might say.

No, she wouldn't toss the drink at Lucy, but she damn well couldn't stand still either. Her feet moved and she clomped out the door. Zac flinched and tried to move away but Lucy was attached to his face.

Grow some balls Zac, she wanted to scream. Hurt someone's feelings for a change. Instead, she said in a high-pitched voice, 'Here are your lovely cool drinks. It's warm out here tonight.' She stood behind them as Lucy stepped back from Zac but didn't turn. Zac accepted the drinks and handed one to her.

'Dinner won't be long,' she said in her sing-song voice.

'Thank you, Victoria.'

'Yes, thank you Tori. You're always around at the most convenient times,' Lucy said as she swirled around and offered a saccharine smile. Her body jerked on the turn and she tugged at one leg in an unladylike fashion. The orange liquid spilt over the lip of the glass and dripped down her leg. 'Argh,' Lucy said. Her stiletto was caught in the gap of the old timber floorboards.

Leaning over and showing off too much butt, she yanked at the shoe that wouldn't budge. Removing her foot from the stranded shoe, she stood lopsided.

'These were new and expensive. Now one is stuck in your deck,' Lucy said to Tori.

'I'm awfully sorry. I'll find something to wrench it out with.'

Lucy skulled the remnants of her drink and handed the empty glass to Tori before smiling through tight lips and hobbling away unevenly.

Tori scampered away, too, to avoid Zac. She didn't want to look at him and know what he was thinking. Didn't want to communicate about what had happened and how she'd acted in successfully sabotaging their intimate moment. She should feel ecstatic, but her belly churned.

As she moved away she observed the full and bright white moon illuminating the sky, twinkling stars surrounding it. Ah well, the romantic setting hadn't worked.

18

Tori stepped into the bright lights of the dining room. Mike and Sophie moved swiftly apart and Sophie wiped one finger along the corner of her lips. Mike rose from the seat at the table, his belt buckle loose.

What was that? Mike and well, anyone, but Sophie? The most elegant lady in the group groping the cameraman, who in Tori's view was a lazy misogynist. Geez, what was Sophie doing?

With wide eyes and unable to hide her surprise, Tori turned back to Zac as he followed behind her. Lucky, his head was lowered so he hadn't seen anything.

Even Clare was glassy-eyed and sat slouched in her chair with one arm slung over the back. The number of empty glasses on the table in front of her, the answer.

The night sure was taking an interesting turn.

Zac sat and Tori scooted off to serve dinner. Some food in rumbling tummies might ensure everyone behaved themselves. Even her?

Nan had served the other guests whilst she was interrupting Zac and Lucy so Tori delivered the main meals to the *Local Lads Looking for Love* crew and contestants. The group concentrated on their meals but tension filled the air.

She stepped into the alcove. 'Well done with your dinner, sweetheart. Did you like it?' she asked Mirry taking in Todd's uneaten plate. He'd nibbled at a few of the vegetables. The slab of meat remained untouched, its bulk congealed in gravy soup. The bread was gone.

'Yummy, thank you Mummy,' Mirry said as she yawned.

'Time for bed, kiddo. Kiss Daddy good night and head upstairs. Nan will come and see you soon.' The little girl rose on skinny legs and hugged her father.

The moment Mirry left the room, Todd clutched her arm, the grip too tight. 'We need to talk.'

'Stop grabbing me like you never intend to let me go.' Tori pulled her arm back and her glasses slid down her nose. She pushed them back up with too much force. 'You have no right to touch me.'

Surprisingly, Todd let go. Her tone was harsh, she guessed, and she'd rarely spoken to him like that before.

Tori left him and entered the main dining room.

'I love you,' Todd yelled and the room fell silent.

Tori paused mid-step and hoped by some miracle the ground would open up and swallow her. Instead, Todd chased her. He stood so close behind she heard his intake of breath before he kept speaking.

'I'm sorry for what I've done.'

Tori did not want to turn; did not want to acknowledge him. But all eyes in the room burned into her.

She glanced around in slow motion. Todd was on one knee and holding up a blue jewellery box.

'Let's start again.'

Mike moved to her left, focusing the camera on her and Todd. Tori shook her head towards the camera but Mike either didn't see or choose to ignore her plea. He would do pretty much anything to capture good footage, so it was probably the latter.

'I love you, Victoria Christensen. I made a mistake. Please forgive me?'

'What did he do?' Clare sang out.

'Slept with the Pilates instructor at their gym,' Mike responded.

What the? That man had eyes and ears everywhere. Important to remember.

'Bastard,' both Clare and Sophie echoed.

At that moment Tori liked them very much.

Todd shoved the box into her hands and Tori pushed it back, but Todd kept ramming it into her palm.

Embarrassment pulsed through her and Tori glanced at Zac. He'd know what to do, how she should react. Her childhood friend had always been a calming influence. His eyes were wide and they were streaked with sympathy. No, she'd wanted to draw strength from him. But his concern almost undid her and the tight control she was holding onto. Suddenly she was tired. Tired of fighting, working so hard to always be the good girl, to be the best wife and parent, always being responsible.

Zac gathered himself and rose and stood next to her; he didn't speak or touch her, knowing his presence was what she needed. That she could look after herself, that even though she might need it, she didn't want to be saved. It was an act of solidarity that she loved and it spurred her on.

Loud, ugly sobs rose out of Todd that caused his face to turn a blotchy red and scrunch up in an unattractive way.

Of course it wasn't the right time or place. Oh, well, he started it.

'The answer is no. You ruined our marriage and our family by sleeping with someone else. You made a mistake and I no longer trust you nor love you.' Tori placed the blue box on the ground in front of him. He picked it up and threw it at her. Zac reached across her to catch it but he missed and it fell onto the rug. Sophie jumped out of her chair.

'That is no way to treat jewellery. It deserves respect.'

Tori's head went heavy on her shoulders and she swayed. A kaleidoscope of colour flickered behind her eyelids. She reached for the dining chair for support and Zac placed his hand to her back.

'I'm pregnant!' Her voice was too loud and out of control. *You stupid idiotic fuck,* she wanted to scream. 'While you were busy screwing someone else, I was carrying your child and looking after Mirry.' She held back her tears, did not want to be weak.

'Who's the dad?' Mike asked, his head popping out to the left of camera. 'I mean you are separated and all.'

'Are you for real?' she replied with venom.

'Yeah, who's the father? How do I know it's me?' Todd joined in.

Tori's fury dissolved like a deflating balloon. All of the oxygen left the room as she tried to think of a riposte.

'You're a terrible husband. I hope you're a better father to our children.'

She'd moved beyond anger to not caring anymore. It was an unusual sensation. It created a sense of power and control she relished. Todd was a waste of her time. She left the room and clicked the kitchen door shut behind her. The dining room erupted in a cacophony of noise as people spoke over each other. Mike would be loving this, Anna too, or perhaps not, because the drama didn't relate to the show.

Tori stood leaning back against the door listening as if she was someone else.

19

———

Zac downed the last of his beer. What a crap night. Good television viewing? He wasn't sure. Did people want to watch all that drama?

Luckily the segment with Lucy wasn't captured. It was embarrassing. For both of them. Thank goodness Victoria had arrived in time.

A baby goat wandered past the front stairs where he sat. Its white fur illuminated in the verandah light. It paused and stared at him with glowing eyes. One go and he had the perfect picture. It was a beauty. The tiny goat was outlined by the bright moon high in the sky but was contrasted with the deep green of the grass it stood upon, its captivating gaze staring down the lens. It gave him a lift. He loved capturing creatures in their natural environment.

#goatlove #kids #farmlife

The door creaked open.

He knew it was her without looking.

'I'm sorry about that rat of a husband of yours,' he said as Tori sat next to him on the top step.

'I'm sorry that scene ruined the evening and probably the show.'

Zac shrugged. 'It was all a bit of a disaster. But is it congratulations about the baby?'

Victoria shrugged now. 'Yes, and no. The circumstances suck. A poor baby being welcomed into a fractured family with a less than perfect father. But it is what it is, I guess. I'll love it regardless and do my best to be a good mother.'

'So, it's one lucky baby indeed.'

Victoria lightly shoved her shoulder against his in thanks. 'Only the cocktail party left. Do you know what you're going to do?'

'No.' He answered. 'I honestly don't.'

'I still don't get it. You say you didn't want to be on the show but here you are. It's all been, well, mundane from what I've seen. The dates haven't been great, is that fair to say? I don't understand why you bothered. These girls have feelings and real lives. They may have entered the show hoping to find love.'

'I did too, after the initial shock and anger. I agreed because I thought maybe, I might meet a nice girl.'

'A nice girl?' Victoria challenged him. 'Zac, you are the most eligible bachelor in town. All of the girls lust after you and the women on the show would match up with you in a heartbeat. It doesn't make any sense.'

'I've fought them off over the years.' Victoria laughed and held her stomach. He loved the sound. 'Sorry, I don't mean there's been hundreds of women beating down my door. I mean there's been a few, but, I don't know. It was never right.'

'But don't you want a relationship? Have a family? Settle down? Be loved?'

He turned sideways to face her. 'I want all of those things.' His words were forceful. 'But I can't.'

'Of course you can. You have a loving family, a job, dreams, a life. Lots of women would fall for you. Plus, you're the nicest bloke I know.'

He paused. Maybe it was time to be honest with Victoria. 'You know how I told you I had cancer?'

She nodded, watching, waiting for him to continue.

'The treatment left me sterile. I'm unable to have children.' He let the revelation sink in. 'It's unfair to ask a woman to accept that. I know the value of family, I grew up with lots of siblings. I don't want to be responsible for robbing someone of their dreams. So, I'm not a great package, regardless of the rest. I made a decision a long time ago that I'd be fine by myself. I love my nieces and nephews and my animals. I can have a full and happy life.'

'But it isn't that simple, is it?' Victoria reached over and held his hand in hers. It was warm and soft. 'I'm so sorry you had to go through that experience. But you know what? The power of love is incredible. If someone loves you for who you are, they are enormously forgiving. Particularly of flaws, not that I'm saying it's a flaw. More of an obstacle. And plus, this is the twenty-first century. There are so many options.'

'Clare told me she doesn't want children and it wasn't negotiable. Said it was important I knew.'

'Did you tell her?'

'No. I've never told anyone.'

'What? You haven't told your family you can't have children and that is the reason you've remained single all these years?'

Zac nodded.

'Man, that's crazy. Zac, they love you. And would regardless. Perhaps it might have kept your sisters off your back about getting married.'

'I've been living in the shadow of my family forever. They're so suffocating and noisy and demanding. They think they have a right to know everything. I guess it's one reason I've kept it back. My way of keeping some control.'

'Your dad is one tough cookie.'

'You think? Dad interferes in my work and my sisters interfere in my personal life. All bases are covered.'

'They love you though. It sounds like a dream to someone who has no family. That's why I'll welcome this baby because I never had a family and I want one.'

Zac slapped his knee and the sound reverberated through the dark and still night. 'Exactly my point.'

'Maybe it's time nice-guy Zac stood up for himself? It doesn't mean people won't like you. People will admire you for chasing your dreams, for sticking up for yourself. It's time.'

'When did life become so complicated?'

'When we grew up, I guess.'

Victoria placed her arms around his middle and held him close. His breath caught. This was the reaction he searched for with each of the contestants. With her it felt good, and right and he always wanted her close.

'What will you do now?' he asked her as he inhaled the vanilla and raspberry scent of her hair.

'Work out how to be alone.'

'So, no forgiving Todd?'

'No, I'm certain. But otherwise, I'm thinking of staying. I've missed out on so much time with Nan. She never sees her daughter, my mum, and she's here all alone. I know she's fine. But I want to spend time with her and I love this lifestyle for Mirry. She adores the animals and learning to care for them; horse riding and running around barefoot each afternoon.'

Zac tried not to move. It was hard when butterflies were going crazy in his belly and he wanted to dance with joy. Plain and simple, he liked having her around. He put his arms around her shoulders and together they cuddled.

'I think you can achieve anything you want.'

'Why is it that I don't trust men and yet feel comfortable with you Zachary Coleman?'

A faint click in the front yard had them both on alert. Zac felt empty the moment Victoria removed her arms. He wanted them back on him, their bodies touching and skin close.

'What was that?' They both scanned the yard.

'Is that a glow in my car?' Zac sat up taller to gain a better vantage.

'Sure is, maybe the light from a phone screen,' she offered. A person lifted their phone closer to their face and they could see.

'Sophie. She's sitting in your car.'

Zac's body sagged. 'The night is not yet over…'

Victoria got a fit of the giggles. 'Does she think you won't notice her holed up in your car? Hoping you'll drive home and she'll jump out and surprise you? Hope she'll strike it lucky?'

Zac stared at her and held his lips together in a tight line. 'Clearly she doesn't know me well. I'm not that sort of guy. Sometimes I wish I was. I could have a bit of fun and forget about it all tomorrow.'

'But then you wouldn't be Zac anymore. You'd be like every other guy.'

She kissed him on the cheek. It was innocent, but her eyes remained shut and her moist lips lingered; he inched his body closer. Did she savour it as much as he did? All too soon it was over.

20

The next morning after a restless night tossing and turning and thinking about Zac, Tori poured Nan a coffee.

He did want a family.

In the early hours when she couldn't sleep, she'd made decisions, but not about Zac. About her.

Tori handed Nan the mug. 'I love you, Nan,' she said and Nan glanced up from the morning paper.

'I love you, too, honey.'

'I want to stay here with Mirry and the baby. Can I help run the farm and B&B and take some of the load off you a little. I'll be responsible for all of the meals, of course. And I'll continue to try and get my catering business up and running as well. But, well, can we stay?'

Nan's eyes misted over. 'I'd love that so much, Tori. I don't need your help, girl, but I'd like it and your company and to spend precious time with your children.'

Tori hugged her from behind then served up scrambled eggs and generously buttered toast.

'You've made a decision about the type of catering too, then?' Her Nan asked pointing to the dairy injected eggs.

Tori smiled. 'Well, yeah. A less restrictive menu might be more successful. Particularly here in *Cedar Creek Plains* and local areas. Plus, all of a sudden it feels like that life was all about Todd. I remember now about the origins of food and how healthy and delicious home-made can be. You can't go wrong with home-grown and fresh ingredients, right? It's better than nouveau vegan food that excludes a number of food groups. And plus, it's been so much fun making those scrumptious desserts from my childhood.'

'It must be the French in you.' Nan smiled.

'Maybe. But they're so damn yummy too!'

There was a faint knock to the back door and it pushed open to reveal Todd.

Tori placed the spatula she held on the bench and took a breath. 'Morning,' she said.

Taken aback Todd paused and his eyebrows rose in question. 'Morning,' he replied hesitantly. He stood like he waited for the spatula to be thrown at his head. And of course, he deserved that. But after chatting with Zac something had clicked and Tori knew she had to sort out her relationship with her children's father plus her future, and that's exactly what she intended to do; starting now.

'Come in,' she continued. 'Nan, is it okay if Todd and I go for a walk? I think it's time we chatted about the future and the arrangements for him to see Mirry and the bub when it arrives.' Tori patted her belly.

'What? You're staying here?' he spluttered.

'Yes, it's time for a chat,' Nan agreed. 'I'll hold the fort. Off you go,' and she shooed them out of the kitchen.

Tori hugged her grandmother again and squeezed tight.

Nan whispered in her ear. 'Now you need to find a hard-working, reliable and loyal country boy. A man who will love you ferociously.'

'Even if I find him, Nan, how will I ever trust him?'

'Chief, I owe you. I can't ever repay what you've done for me. Thank you, for everything.'

Zac's fingers danced across the paperwork.

Chief slapped him on the back. 'My time away made me realise I'd like to travel more and work less. I've loved this job and this town and the animals, but it's time to stop now. I have an itch to get into the caravan with Joan and travel around Australia, see what else is outside of these plains.'

He continued, 'I'm so happy to know the clinic is in good hands and so is the future of this region with you responsible for the animals. That's the reason I've brought forward my retirement. I trust you. You'll do a great job. The time is right.'

Zac choked up. His dream was coming true. He was forging his own future and breaking free from control. He finished his signature with a flourish and hugged the man who'd taught him all he knew and acted more as a father figure than his own.

'Do you want me to come and see your father with you?'

'Nah. You don't want to be part of any fiasco. You'll hear his reaction from here anyway.' Zac grinned, but his insides churned at the showdown about to occur. It wouldn't be pretty.

'Good luck, son. I'll pass this to my lawyer and we'll do a formal handover this week.'

They shook hands and Zac hopped straight into his ute and headed to his folk's place. Best to get the confrontation over with. Checking the time on the dashboard he hoped he'd catch his parents at smoko.

The dust from the road billowed behind him as he drove too fast. Adrenalin spurring him on.

'How lovely, dear,' his mother said as he arrived on the verandah. 'Have a seat and I'll get you a cup.'

His dad grunted and prattled on about the weather. 'Dry out there. Need some rain soon, the ground is cracking. We can't afford another drought…'

Zac let him chatter. His mother returned with a fine china cup and lavished a scone with jam and cream. As he bit into it, Victoria sprang to mind. His mother was a great cook, but these scones were not as light as Victoria's. He shook images of her from his mind.

Stay focused Zac.

With a lull in conversation, he gathered his courage. 'Mum and Dad, I have some news.'

His mother's head popped up. He knew what she wanted. News of finding love; the cocktail party was days away.

'I've signed a contract to purchase the vet clinic from old Chief. He's been talking about retirement for years and is finally doing it. It's mine.'

His mother coughed and snuck a furtive glance at his father.

'Don't be ridiculous boy. We've been over and over this. I'm tired of it when there is so much to discuss about the future of the station.' His father rattled his cup in his saucer.

'It's time to listen, Dad. I will not be running the cattle station. You'll have to find an alternative plan. I'm the new owner of the vet clinic and it's what I want to do. I've been telling you this for a long time.'

His father held his head low and talked through gritted teeth. 'I have one son and four daughters. It's proper process for you to take over the property. And it's tradition. If you do not do this, you are no son of mine.' Jerome stood and left the table.

'He'll come 'round,' his mother said, placing her hand on his.

'He won't, Mum, but thanks for saying so.' Zac noticed she didn't congratulate him on one of the biggest decisions he'd ever made.

Edith rose, patted him on the shoulder like he was a teenager and went after his father.

Usually, he'd race after his father too, reassure him they'd work it out; the future of the family and the station was all that mattered. But it wasn't true. He wasn't going to chase after him and say those words today. Damn it, his father should be chasing after him. But hell would freeze over before that happened.

He was done with these endless arguments. The burden he'd carried on his shoulders for years, loosened, and his body became lighter. This was what he wanted and his family would have to accept it. And even if they didn't, he could do it without their support. He loved his bulldog of a father and his timid mother regardless. At least his sisters would be ecstatic.

Thinking of his sisters gave him a new idea. Why hadn't he considered it before? It was so obvious. Jessica's husband Earl was keen to be involved in the future of beef. The property could stay in the family and the tradition could continue. Ownership might be a little different to what his dad expected but The Coleman Cattle Station could still be in the family.

What a bonzer idea. Zac raced away to talk to his sister.

21

———————

Almost the entire population of the town – at over four thousand people - had turned out for the live *Local Lads Looking for Love* grand finale and cocktail party.

Well, perhaps not the entire town, but the front yard of the *Cedar Creek Plains Farm Stay and B&B* was crammed with people.

The regional television station had found a budget. Fairy lights adorned a white-picket fence leading to a rolling red carpet. It was a bit lumpy here and there from tuffs of underlying grass. Snow-white balloons were tied to each available post and provided a carnival atmosphere. It looked festive, Tori decided. She also had to agree the event may have copied the idea from the popular mainstream series, but hey, she didn't think anyone would raise an objection about that tonight.

The weather was on their side, with clear, midnight blue skies and a silver crescent moon. The humidity was kept at bay with a gentle breeze and the mood was jubilant with soft background music playing from a live band located over near the sheds mixing in with the pleasant sound of laughter and chat.

Tori inhaled a deep lungful of air. She'd slaved all day on finger foods. Technically she was hired to feed Zac, the contestants and crew.

But how could they invite the town and not give them an hors d'oeuvre too? It was inhospitable and un-country like. So she'd made extra, a lot extra.

She set up a drink station on the deck. There wasn't any fancy bar tonight, but she'd roped in a local lad - another one looking for love perhaps - to man the drinking hole.

A hand grabbed her around the leg and Mirry clung tight, her little chest heaving. She was dressed for the occasion in a pink tule dress like one of the fairies who might inhabit the wood; or perhaps she was a princess, who knew? Her daughter fitted in perfectly and could be whatever she wanted to be tonight. Just as quickly as she arrived, Mirry raced away playing chasey with some of the local kids.

There was a stir to her right and she glanced in that direction. Zac arrived to slaps on the back and cheers from the crowd. He wore a dark black suit hugging his shoulders and chest. He matched it with a white collared shirt, the contrast striking. He wore his standard R.M Williams boots and his too-long wavy hair was mussed on top, as always. She curled her fingers in and out, releasing the itch to run them through his head of hair.

The sight of him sent her body into overdrive but she quashed down those feelings. Tonight was his night.

A goose raced across his path, chased quickly by a gaggle of ducks. The menagerie of animals roamed free, never restrained on Nan's farm. Why should tonight be any different? Zac pulled out his phone and captured the retreating animals who scurried amongst the chairs set up on the lawn.

Who would he choose? She couldn't decide. But if he truly thought he was destined to live a life without children, and he couldn't rob anyone of that right, Clare was the obvious choice. But really? She couldn't imagine it. Clare was so officious and thorough. Tori imagined she needed everything in her life to be perfectly ordered, arranged and scheduled. Not suitable to farm life where things often went wrong.

Clare along with the other girls wouldn't be far away. Tori moved back inside to collect the first platters of hot food. Trays of crackers and dips and cheeses were already scattered around the grounds.

Zac entered the warm kitchen as she removed mini quiches from the oven, her hands in mitts.

He lit up the room. A smile flitted across her face while her skin burned hot and warmth flushed throughout her body. Once again, she ignored the sensations. 'Hey, what are you doing here? You should be out mingling and enjoying your special night.'

'Victoria, I wanted …'

Nan entered, blowing her hair out of her face and puffing out her cream blouse. 'Full crowd out there,' she said and kissed Zac on the cheek. 'Good luck tonight Zac. I hope you find all that you're looking for.' Nan's eyes connected with Tori and her stomach dipped.

Mirry raced through the door, squealing as she exited straight out the back. Mike followed in between the two other children, chasing her with equal excitement.

'Anna is here and needs to see you before we start live streaming.'

Mike had scrubbed up for the occasion but missed the mark with a tux and bright red cummerbund and bow tie.

'Are you the one getting married tonight?' Tori said to him with a smirk.

'Married?' he said. 'Do you know something?' and he turned to face Zac. 'Is this serious mate, you going to propose?'

Zac held up his flat palm. Tori intervened.

'I'm joking. You're dressed like you're the groom at a wedding.'

Mike didn't smile. 'I look alright don't I? Reckon I might have a chance with the rejects?' he asked, his face deadpan.

'No,' Tori and Zac said simultaneously.

Zac's name was being called beyond the door. Tori leaned across, took off one mitt and held his forearm. It was firm under her grip. 'Good luck,' she said. Other words died on her tongue. It felt a little like saying goodbye.

He opened his mouth, closed it again and seemed to be about to say something when the door flew open and in strode Anna Fox.

'Whoa, Anna,' Mike was the first to speak but his eyes were lost on her chest. The low-cut ball gown left nothing to the imagination. It was black, diamantes and gemstones featuring on the fabric, the full skirt billowing around her. Did she get the memo this was regional television?

Tori had purchased a new dress too. It was short, showing off her shapely legs, the long billowing sleeves and frill surrounding the high neck, complimenting her slender figure. Nothing like Anna's but it was light and cool and comfy and she felt feminine in the deep magenta cotton.

Zac still stared at her, his eyes pleading. 'What…' she said but Anna clasped his arm and he walked out of the kitchen backwards and was gone.

22

'And here we are everyone. We've reached the finale of Zac's search for love!' Anna's voice was loud through the microphone. The crowd cheered.

Zac bounced his knee up and down. He placed his palm on it to stop the shake, then used those same fingers to tug at his too-tight collar. The bright lights made him squint. He'd never wanted to get out of somewhere so much before. He couldn't remember the last time he was so nervous he wanted to vomit.

The three contestants sat on high stools on an elevated timber stage with their legs crossed. He sat to the left and had a clear view of both the crowd and the ladies. Zac didn't want to look at either.

Anna droned on, recapping each of their respective dates and funny anecdotes. Some he'd never heard and he was sure she was making them up for entertainment. Then the questions began. He focused on each one, taking his time to reply.

'What's been your highlight?'

'Are you pleased you came on the show?'

'Is it a difficult choice?'

Anna ran to a commercial break and footage of Zac and the women played on a large screen backdrop. Mixed in were live streams to simultaneous finales around the country region. None of those blokes looked as nervous as him.

And then before he was ready, they were cutting to him. The crowd went silent. He stood and wiped his hands down his pants.

'Clare,' he said and everyone went berserk catcalling and wolf-whistling. 'Shush,' he commanded them with his hands urging them to quieten down. 'Clare,' he began again. 'It was lovely getting to know you. I love your brutal honesty. A man will always know where he stands with you because you'll tell him! You have a no-nonsense approach to life, taking what your heart desires and grasping it, not wasting time on the minor issues. These are all wonderful qualities. We have a lot in common particularly our love of the country and farm life. You must be a fantastic jillaroo and would be a wonderful addition to any team. I think we also have shared goals and common perspectives on life. Turns out your trivia knowledge is not so great.' A light chuckle rose from a small bunch.

He'd vaguely been looking in the general direction of the stage as he spoke, but now he focused on Clare. He shouldn't have. She sat stony-faced and hard to read. Fitted perfectly with the attitude of, her way or no way, that Zac had detected. This woman would break his balls he was certain.

Clare turned her head away and stared at the throng. He followed her direction. Clare stared at Tori standing at the far rear of the group. Zac swung his gaze back. Thinking of her right now would undo him.

'Lucy,' he said next and smiled. 'We enjoyed a romantic date down by the river and a fish. We didn't catch much though. You're a fun girl to have around and always have a smile on your face and are happy to laugh at yourself. You don't take life too seriously and giggle a lot, it's infectious. I could do with a few pointers. But underneath your pretty face you are tough. And strong. Someone to be admired.'

'Pick her then!' someone heckled from the yard.

Zac paused to settle his nerves. He cracked a smile at her before moving on.

'Sophie. You are the rose and elegance and charm all men seek.' Oohs and aahs drifted up from the audience. Anna chimed in, too.

'He's a catch, ladies, with words like those!'

'Who would have thought a city chick like you could handle the dirt and the dust, and the outdoors as well as you did whilst wearing your designer clothes and immaculate hair styles. But you have. It was a lovely surprise. You are a full package of beauty and adventure all mixed into one. Underneath your exterior is mystery and intrigue that is fascinating but difficult to crack. The man that you let in will be special indeed.' Zac paused. 'But all of you have embraced country life and weren't afraid to pitch in and experience it for all it was worth. You've made this a pleasant experience. Thank you.'

'I …'

'Hold it right there, Zac. Before the big announcement, we're crossing to a commercial break!' Anna worked up the crowd and they cheered and clapped as the ad commenced.

Mike stood with the camera in his face. Tonight he was overshadowed by stationary cameras in strategic locations to capture the stage. Mike wouldn't be cast aside though and was in the way at each opportunity.

'Can I have a drink of water, mate?' he asked Mike who handed one over. Zac drained the glass.

Like a premiership football game when they'd focus with their eye on the prize, Zac zoned everything out. The noise receded and fell away. His heart rate slowed and his muscles relaxed. He was ready.

'The lady I've chosen tonight is someone special. She's hasn't had an easy life but has managed it with grace and humility and achieved great things even though she may not realise it. She's always loved country life, but perhaps forgot how much until recently when that love was rekindled. She is family-oriented, warm, and funny and kind, especially to others and often the first to lend a hand to a person in need. She is fit and works hard and has an opinion on most issues. But by golly, if you scorn her, she'll hit you hard with her caustic tongue.'

People murmured in response, turned to their neighbour, shrugged their shoulders and whispered. The contestants frowned, realising some qualities belonged to them, but not others.

'More than any of that though, she's captured my heart. To be honest she captured my imagination a long time ago and I've never forgotten. I wish I'd taken my opportunity then. But now I'm asking her for a second chance at love. Perhaps she ruined me for others. It was her I pined for in the knowledge of what true love and attraction was. She's had her heart broken and stamped upon, shredded apart and has lost trust. Most men might be difficult to trust, but not me. In me, I will be her greatest advocate. I will help her achieve her dreams. I will stand alongside her, holding her hand and encouraging her. I will protect her heart and nurture it and build her trust until there is no doubt she can rely upon me. I sincerely swear I will never let her down. She has become everything to me, I come alive in her presence, and she makes me a better person. I count the minutes until I see her again.'

'I'm not perfect but I hope she'll accept me as I am. The country vet with a big heart and lots of love to offer. This woman is a great mum and fabulous cook and I hope she'll risk everything again for love. I choose Victoria Christensen.'

Silence descended on the people present. A horse neighed at the fence.

Sweat broke out on Zac's brow. He searched the crowd. Where was she? Isn't this where she finds him and embraces him until he can't breathe and expresses her undying love? She no longer stood at the back. She wasn't inside was she? There's no way he could repeat that soliloquy.

Anna and Mike were muttering. Anna wanted to cross to another show with a real winner, but Mike refused. The viewers would love it or hate it, he said, but either way it was fantastic viewing and he was determined to capture every second.

Clare stood in her satin black pants suit, hands on hips and feet standing width apart.

Sophie brushed her long dark hair off her shoulder and brushed imaginary fluff from her billowing egg-shell blue sleeves.

Lucy, resplendent in a vibrant emerald frock to match her red hair, hung her mouth open and searched the gathered crowd.

Everyone held their breath until the crowd parted and Tori walked towards the stage.

23

———————

Holy shit, Zac Coleman was talking about her.

All of a sudden everything made sense. He made sense. It was like the whole world opened up.

Tears didn't pool in her eyes; bucketloads of water ran down her cheeks as she blubbered. Happy sobbing of course. Tori ripped off her glasses and rubbed at her eyes. She didn't want to lose sight of him. The sea of people standing in front parted leaving a wide path leading her to Zac. Hands shoved her in the back forcing her forward. She both wanted to run to him and simultaneously wait.

The moment he spoke, she'd known. His deep honey voice had caused her stomach to flutter. As his words sank in, her heart hammered in her chest, her eyes pooled with water and she hadn't stopped crying since.

Zac moved one tentative step closer to her and she couldn't control herself any longer. She ran the last few metres to him. Her wedged heels sank into the grass but they reached each other and she collapsed into his open arms. He held her tight. Tori squeezed her eyes shut, blocking out everything else.

Eventually, he let go. Tori wanted to stay safe and secure in those capable and strong arms forever. Zac cupped her head in his hands, peered deep into her eyes and claimed her lips. The kiss was light and gentle. Their third only ever kiss. She sensed him holding back, perhaps conscious of the ogling crowd.

It didn't stop her body reacting though. Heat emanated off him and she melted; they became became one hot wrangling mess together. His stance relaxed as her hands raked down his back and she felt the full force of him, pulling him closer. Her erect nipples brushed against his chest but his lips remained tender. Their mouths met in perfect precision, lip upon lip, wet and warm and inviting. Spirals of ecstasy shivered through her veins and her mouth parted in response. Raising her mouth from his, she gazed at him; he stared back with utter happiness. He pulled back and took shallow breaths. The deep pools of his expressive eyes spoke to her and sent flutters straight to her groin. Her body ached for more of his touch. Thank goodness he showered her with more kisses, to her eyelids and along her jaw and chin until he reached her mouth where he pressed against her with sudden force once more. Every nerve ending tingled.

Something tugged at her chest. A large hand was pinning something to the neckline of her dress and she turned. Bloody Mike. Still being such a pain. Tori moved out of his way but he wouldn't have it.

'It's a mic. You're the winner, the audience wants to hear from you.' He stood back for a minute. 'Who would have thought, hey?' He elbowed Zac in the arm before gaining a better camera position.

The crowd came back into focus as they huddled closer to them, closing the gap. Her cheeks warmed at the scrutiny and she was sure they must be pink. For once, Tori didn't care. The mass responded with hollers and cheers, their excitement palpable and it lifted her. Zac scored a few slaps to the back.

But then Zac was back in her focus.

'No one has ever said such beautiful words about me before,' her voice wobbling yet magnified by the close microphone. Those closest hushed.

'Zac, you are truly the kindest of men. Everyone's best friend. Reliable and friendly and one of the best. I'm so comfortable with you, have always been comfortable with you. I can talk to you and you listen. You are different from other men. You have confidence in me I'm sure I don't deserve and you make me a better person, too,' she hiccupped. Zac tugged a loose strand of her dark hair and placed it behind her right ear.

'You are not a cheater and I'm sorry I ever said that. I know you'd never do that to a woman. You are tender and sincere and true. I don't think you're real.' The crowd laughed. 'Perhaps you are too good to be true,' Tori clasped one of his hands.

'I'm not an easy package. I have a daughter, *an ex-husband*,' she emphasised those words, 'and I'm…with… having another baby. It's a lot for anyone to take on. A ready-made family.'

Zac didn't hesitate to speak up and say what he meant. 'That is exactly what I want and you know why. I might not be able to give us our own children, but your family is my family. We can all be together and I will love your children as I love you.'

Happiness threatened to bubble out of her. Could this all be happening? But for once, the first time ever, she knew without a doubt she could rely on him, trust him.

'It's crazy Zachary Coleman, but I love you too. You've taught me to trust again. I'm prepared to take a second chance and we won't blow it. I believe in you, I trust you, I want you to be by my side forever. I won't let you go, you understand. This is for the long-haul, forever.'

The gathering went from silent to rowdy and back again, captivated as she was with the man in front of her.

'Say something,' she urged him softly.

'You've made me the happiest man alive. I know the future is bright if we can face it together. There's so much to look forward too. And I can't wait.' Into her ear he whispered what he'd like to do to her later. Pulling back, he smiled the broadest she'd ever seen. Then he whooped her up off her feet and she shrieked.

In the beckground the band commenced playing as Anna Fox tried to call order to the show and Mike fought for footage. There were more shrieks to the right.

'Something just ran over my foot…'

THE END

She swore she'd never trust again

love
in the
ragged
Mountain
ranges

Susan Mackie

Love in a Sunburnt Land anthology

LOVE IN THE RAGGED MOUNTAIN RANGES

SUSAN MACKIE

For Gordon, my very own horse whisperer.
Love you Dad.

Susan Mackie

1

Nik turned onto Copeland Road, the surface was old and pitted bitumen, and barely wide enough for one car. She flashed a bright smile at Lucy. 'Just a few minutes now, Luce. I can't wait to see it again.'

Concentrating on the rough and winding road, overhung with huge gumtree branches, Nik leaned forward. The day was already warm but turning onto the smaller road the temperature seemed to drop, just a little. The high peaks of the Barrington Tops loomed closer.

The road narrowed further, and she slowed the car to a crawl, while drawing in her breath. 'Funny, but it didn't seem this rough back in September.' She felt, rather than saw, Lucy glance at her. She was leaning forward too, and Nik risked a quick sideways look. Her daughter's usually pensive expression had lightened. She seemed almost eager to get there. A wave of relief washed over her. She was doing the right thing. For Lucy. And for herself. This was a fresh start. Nodding, she told herself moving here was the right decision.

They passed a couple of narrow driveways, their entries obscured by large cedar trees, each with its own leaning letterbox.

'It should be the next one to the left. The old Copeland Courthouse, built in the eighteen eighties at the height of the gold rush.' Nik grinned across at Lucy, who smiled tentatively back. 'And it's ours now. Our home.'

'Stop, Mum. You've gone past.' Lucy turned in her seat, peering out her side window. Nik stopped and reversed slowly. 'Yes, there's the sign. It says Courthouse. Oh, the entrance is pretty isn't it?'

Nodding agreement, Nik paused. The sign Lucy had spotted was on an angle, the lettering worn, the paint faded. But the entrance was gorgeous, if a little overgrown. Large posts stood on each side of the driveway, a rusty iron gate swung back against the inside fence, the dirt and gravel driveway leading up to the high set building just visible through thick native foliage.

'It will need some work. Not just the house, but the whole block. Fences need repairing and this driveway will have to be graded and gravelled. But we're not in a hurry. We'll work out what needs doing the most and we'll start there.' Driving further in, the building came into view. They sat in the car for a moment, peering up at the house in front of them.

The old courthouse had been turned into a family home in the early nineteen hundreds and lived in by various families for over a century, some renovating and extending as they went. Nik knew the ground level had been a jail and quarters for courthouse staff in the early days. The upper level was split in two, with the courthouse itself at the front, and the magistrate's accommodation at the back. Several outbuildings squatted in the undergrowth, including the original stables that had been turned into cottage accommodation at some point. It was all a bit rundown. Heaps of potential though.

'Gold was discovered around here in the eighteen seventies, or maybe eighties. The real estate agent told me there were twelve pubs and about four thousand people in this valley then. That's why the courthouse is so big.' Nik had told Lucy this when she first found the property but said it again to remind herself that the history of the place, the valley and the buildings, was significant.

Lucy nodded, then opened her door and scrambled out. Nik did the same. Walking to the front of the car she slung an arm around her daughter's shoulders, giving her a quick squeeze. 'You'll help me plan this out, won't you Luce?' She kissed the top of Lucy's head as she spoke.

Tears came to Nik's eyes as Lucy leaned into her. Her voice a murmur. 'It's just us now, Mum. You and me. We can do this together. We don't need anyone else.'

'You're right. It's ours. We'll plan it together. But Luce, we will need help. We'll have to get tradespeople like an electrician, and maybe a carpenter or builder. And someone to grade the driveway. But they won't live here. It will just be us. Well, maybe some guests eventually when we have the bed and breakfast part ready.'

Lucy stretched and turned in a circle, long legs belying her tender years. 'I know. But it's ours. I like that it's ours.'

Walking toward the house, Nik glanced around. It was greener than last time, the drought had broken. Everything was overgrown, but that was easily fixed. There was a large yard in front, and she knew there was a fenced paddock behind and another to the side. Big enough for a pony, or maybe two. Lucy was horse-mad and hopefully she could find a quiet horse for her to begin.

THE DAY WORE ON AS THEY UNPACKED THE CAR, CRAMMED WITH KITCHEN items and clothes. The removal truck should have arrived around lunch time, but it was almost three and there was no sign of it.

After a good look through both levels of the house, they decided they would live upstairs themselves. The ground floor was already set up for separate living, with a small kitchen and bathroom, two bedrooms and a lounge and living area, perfect for guests. Doors that led out from the rear opened to a small courtyard, the paving neat, the original hand-made bricks laid in intricate patterns. It would be excellent accommodation once she upgraded the kitchenette and bathroom. Fresh paint inside and out and the right furniture and it would be ready. They would focus on that first.

Upstairs needed more work. There had been so many renovations, alterations, wallpaper, and paint over the years, that it needed to be brought back to the original timber boards before contemplating anything further. It also needed a new kitchen and bathroom and maybe an ensuite. But it was liveable, and downstairs should be renovated first.

About to head out to the cottage that in years past was the stables, they heard the removal truck struggling along the driveway in low gear. The high back of the truck was dragging through the tree branches and Lucy cried out when a large branch snapped off and bounced off the side of the truck, hitting the ground before rolling under the back wheels and stopping the vehicle altogether.

'Wait here Luce.' Nik strode forward to meet the driver as he climbed down from the cab. His face was florid, and he wiped the back of his neck with a large cloth as he stomped towards her. His passenger, a younger, fit-looking man had walked to the back of the truck and was trying to lift or pull the branch out, but it was firmly stuck, the truck wheels sitting squarely on it.

'You didn't mention the trees over the driveway when we quoted this job. I'm going to need either a tow out, or someone with a chainsaw to cut that branch up and get it out from under the truck. Either way, we are not going to get your furniture unloaded before dark and you will have to pay accommodation for me and Jimbo.' Hands on hips, he glared at Nik.

'I'm sorry Dave, I didn't recall the entrance being this overgrown when I was here last.' Nik smiled, hoping if she stayed polite and friendly, he might calm down. She glanced behind her to see if Lucy was nearby, but she had vanished. She hated confrontation; Nik knew she would stay out of the firing line.

'Look Nicola, I realise it's not your fault, but we need to get some help here quickly or we'll lose light altogether. And the truck is blocking anyone getting in or out now.' Somewhat mollified, Dave turned back to look at Jimbo still pulling at the tree branch. He shouted, 'It's no good Jimbo, we need a chainsaw. It's too big!'

'Can you try backing over it, do you think Dave?' Nik felt sweat beginning to trickle down between her shoulder blades. She wiped her arm across her eyes, her shoulder length dark bob curling at the ends in the heat and humidity.

Sighing, Dave nodded at Jimbo. 'I'll have another go at backing over or rocking back and forth to see if I can get the wheels off it. Stand back though in case it snaps or flicks out at you.' Dave climbed back into the cabin of his truck, while Jimbo moved to one side.

The truck revved as it was thrown into reverse, the wheels spinning on the solid timber. He then put it in gear and tried moving forward. Again, the wheels spun. Several attempts to move forward and back made no progress.

'Damn.' Nik pulled her phone from the back pocket of her jeans, turning her back on the truck, hoping to google some help. She had no idea if there would be a tow truck in the area and if there was any hope of finding someone with a chainsaw on Boxing Day. The service was only one bar, and she struggled to get any search results. Perhaps she could call the real estate agent, Ben Evans, or his offsider Harriet Russell. She tried Ben's number, but it rang out.

'Hey there. Perhaps I can help.' The deep voice was right behind her. Spinning around the phone flew from her hand, landing at the feet of a man she could only describe as a cowboy. Hat pulled low, collared shirt with sleeves rolled up to large biceps, broad chest, faded jeans and work boots. She glanced at his face, partly shaded by his hat, squinting a little to read his expression.

'Excuse me.' He removed his hat with his left hand, holding his right hand out. 'I'm Robbie Stewart. Live just up the road, saw the truck, ah, wedged in the driveway. Thought I might be able to help.' Reaching down, he scooped her phone from the ground and handed it over with a lopsided grin. Her fingers touched his as she took it from him, bringing a flush of warmth to her face.

Smiling tentatively, Nik shook his hand. The warmth receded from her face but settled somewhere lower. Ignoring it, she mentally shook her head, then looked him in the eye. His grin broadened, deepening the laugh lines around his eyes.

'Nicola Reid. Nice to meet you. Thank you. Yes, we need some help. Branch came off and is wedged under the back tyres. Dave, the removalist, hasn't been able to budge the truck either forward or back. Do you know of a tow truck in the area?' She sucked in some air as Robbie strode toward the truck and waited as Dave climbed out.

They spoke for a moment, then Robbie squeezed past the side of the truck, heading toward the road. Nik walked over to Dave.

'Is he calling a tow truck?'

'No love. He's got a chain saw in the back of his ute, parked at the entrance back there. He's going to cut up what he can get too, then we might be able to shift the truck a bit.'

'Oh. Good. Well, that's very nice of him.' Nik turned around to check on Lucy. She was up on the veranda of the top floor of the house. She gave her a wave. Lucy smiled and waved back. Good. Best she was out of the way.

Robbie reappeared with a chainsaw and began cutting the timber up, with Jimbo moving the heavy pieces and stacking them to one side. Trying to relax, Nik told herself at least she'd have some firewood when the weather cooled. She stepped forward to offer help, but Dave touched her on the arm. He was leaning against the front tyre, lighting a cigarette. 'Let the young blokes do it. They look fit enough.'

Nik moved forward when Robbie crawled under the truck, chainsaw in hand. 'Is he going to use that thing under there? Laying down?' She was incredulous. Jimbo just grinned and crawled under behind Robbie, pulling the large pieces out as they were cut up.

Twenty minutes from start to finish and Robbie was standing back, the chainsaw at his feet. 'Try to edge forward now Dave but turn the wheel a bit as you go. I think if we can get one side over, the other will be easy. We'll have some traction on the driveway.' He picked up the chainsaw and moved back a few paces, touching her lightly on the arm to indicate she step back too.

Dave revved the engine and edged forward, spinning the wheels again. He threw it in reverse and edged backwards, then back into gear, the truck surging forward, on a slight angle. A loud crack signalled that the end of the branch had broken under the tyres; the vehicle moved forward again, rolling effortlessly over the last piece.

'Yay!' Nik fist-pumped the air as Dave grinned from the cab of the truck, a cigarette dangling from his mouth. Jimbo leapt forward to pull the last two pieces to the side. The truck came in and turned side on to the house, barely stopping before Jimbo had the rear doors open and the ramp pulled down.

'You need to tell us where you want everything, love. I don't fancy finishing in the dark.'

Looking up, Nik knew there would only be an hour or two of daylight left, so she resigned herself to just getting everything unloaded as quickly as possible. She looked around to thank Robbie, but he and his chainsaw had vanished, his vehicle no longer at the end of the drive, so he must have left. She should have thanked him properly or at least offered him a cold drink.

Dashing into the house, she found Lucy at the top of the stairs. 'Do you want to help, Luce? Are you able to show Dave and Jimbo where everything should go?'

Lucy chewed on a fingernail and shook her head. Taking a breath, Nik walked up the stairs and hugged her tightly. 'It's okay, Luce. I'll get them to bring the beds up and when I find the boxes with our bed linen, perhaps you can make them for me?' Lucy withdrew her finger from her mouth. 'Okay Mum. I can do that.'

'Good girl,' she said, hugging her briefly before running back downstairs to provide a few directions to the men. Although Dave was quite rotund, he was strong and she was pleased to see he was lifting as much as Jimbo, even if he didn't move as quickly. Nik dashed out of the house, intending to jump into the back of the truck to find the bedlinen boxes, when she walked straight into the back of Robbie. He was walking backwards with her dining table, a large solid timber piece she knew was heavy. At the other end of the table was a younger version of Robbie. Tall, good looking, dressed in faded jeans, tee shirt, work boots, and a big grin. They lowered the table to the ground for a moment.

'Nicola. This is my boy Harry. Harry, Mrs Reid.'

Wiping his hand on his jeans, Harry stepped forward. 'Nice to meetcha Mrs Reid.' He was young, late teens maybe. Nik shook his hand firmly. 'Please, call me Nik. Nice to meet you too.' Turning to Robbie she added, 'I looked for you to say thank you. I didn't expect you to come back and help with this.' She waved toward the truck. 'Happy you did though, we had no chance of getting it all off before dark without you. I'm not sure how I can thank you for your help today. Umm, I can pay you, and Harry, of course.'

Robbie looked at her for a moment. He spoke slowly, quietly. 'We're neighbours. It's what we do out here. I'm sure there'll be occasions when we help each other out. Don't give it another thought. Now, tell me where this goes.' As he finished, his smile broadened, and his eyes crinkled a bit. She wasn't sure how old he was, mid-forties maybe with a grown son, but she instinctively liked him.

'You may regret choosing to bring this monster in. It goes upstairs.' She grinned back at him.

Picking up the table, he nodded at Harry. 'You right at your end son?'

'Good as gold Dad.'

Turning to Nik, he said 'Lead the way Nicola. Or can I call you Nik too?'

Running up the stairs in front of them, she called down. 'Nik. Please. All my friends call me Nik.'

SHE WIPED HER BROW AS THE TRUCK DROVE AWAY. IN THE END, DAVE hadn't charged anything extra, as Robbie and Harry had provided free labour.

'I can't thank you enough. I mean it. For cutting up the tree, then unloading the truck.' Although exhausted herself, she knew she should offer something for their trouble. 'I don't have any cold beer, but there are a couple of bottles of coke in the esky, if you'd like a drink. And I can make some ham and cheese toasted sandwiches ...'

Putting his hat on, Robbie patted her shoulder gently. 'We're fine thanks Nik. We've got steaks to throw on the barbie at home. And cold beer. You must be exhausted. You've worked as hard as any of us today. Make those toasted sandwiches and wash them down with a coke.' She nodded gratefully. 'And you might want to fix something for the little ghost who has been busy upstairs all afternoon. It seems she has made the beds for you and set up your bookshelves.'

She looked at him, surprised. Lucy had been almost invisible, disappearing when she heard anyone coming upstairs. 'My daughter

Lucy. She's very shy.' A movement at the top of the stairs told her Lucy was hovering just out of sight, listening.

Slightly louder, Robbie added, 'Lucy is a good little worker then. You'll be as pleased as punch when you see how much she's achieved.' A muffled giggle from upstairs warmed her heart. Quietly, she looked at both men, Harry standing as tall as his father. 'Thank you for today. For everything.'

'No worries Nik. We'll see you soon.'

'Bye Nik.' This from Harry.

Dragging her tired feet up the stairs, Nik found Lucy's arms around her waist, her lovely face looking up at her. Holding her tightly, Nik brushed the long brown hair from her forehead before leaning down to place a kiss on the tip of her nose. 'Was it okay for you today Luce? You didn't mind so many people here?'

'No. I was a bit scared at first. I don't think the men from the truck saw me at all, but the cowboys did. They pretended they didn't. After a while I wasn't frightened of them at all.'

Ruffling her daughter's hair, Nik took a deep breath. 'You know what? I don't think any of them were scary. Or bad. And I think you were very brave to help as much as you did.' Taking her hand, they walked to the kitchen. 'Would you like a toasted sandwich? And a drink? I see you have the beds made and found our towels and bathroom things. How about something to eat and drink, then a quick shower and straight to bed for us. What do you say?'

'Yes please Mum. It's been a big day. But I think I'm going to like it here.'

'I hope so, Luce. I've got a feeling this is the right place for us.'

2

Waking in a pool of sweat, pre-dawn light creeping through the bedroom window, Nik sat up quickly, her heart racing. Faint sounds came from inside the house. Unsure if it was just the normal creaking of the old building or if someone was moving around, she glanced at the other side of her bed. Lucy had slept with her last night, not keen to spend the first night in her own room. The bed was empty.

Probably Lucy then. She sat on the edge of the bed for a moment, hand on her heart, willing it to slow down. Taking two deep breaths, she called out. 'Luce. Is that you?'

Silence for a moment. 'Yup. It's me. Stay there, Mum, I'll be right in.'

Moments later Lucy appeared at the bedroom door, carrying a mug of steaming tea. Grinning, she walked carefully to the bedside table, placing the mug down. 'Thought I'd surprise you. Good morning, Mum.'

'Thank you, sweetheart, good morning to you too. What a lovely thought. Have you been awake long?'

'About an hour. I slept really well, but when you started to get restless, I got up and left you to sleep. You worked really hard yesterday.'

Sliding back on the bed, Nik rested her shoulders against the wall and took a sip of her tea. She'd kill for a coffee. Barista made. But this was nice. And Lucy having the confidence to move around the house while she slept. That was extra nice. A really good sign. She rolled her head from side to side, releasing the tension in her neck.

'Yup. I'm sore in all sorts of places. Especially my legs. Carrying stuff up and down the stairs will have done that. A quick breakfast and then we can unpack the rest of our stuff up here, get this area feeling like home.' Reaching out to Lucy, now sitting on the edge of the bed, she opened her arms. Lucy fell into them, half laying across Nik's lap, her head burrowed into her shoulder.

'What do you think so far?'

Sitting up, looking into her mother's eyes, Lucy reached out and tucked Nik's hair behind her left ear, gently sweeping it back from her forehead. She traced the jagged scar, beginning to fade, that ran from Nik's forehead, almost in her hairline, to her ear.

'Does it bother you Mum? The scar?'

While not surprised by the change of subject, Nik hesitated for a moment. 'No, the scar doesn't bother me. I don't care about this scar, or any of the others. I'm simply happy we're together. And safe.'

'I'm always safe with you Mum.' A tear trickled down Lucy's face. 'I'm sorry he hurt you. I'm sorry I couldn't stop him. I tried.'

Pulling her daughter into her arms, Nik gulped, trying not to cry. 'It's not your fault. None of it was your fault.'

'It wasn't your fault either, Mum.' They held each other tightly, memories flooding Nik's mind as she drew a sharp breath. They had to stop reliving it. They had to start living beyond it. Months of counselling and Lucy could at least speak of it, but Nik worried it would always be her first thought on waking each day. They both needed to move past that. She kissed Lucy's forehead, and gently moved her to the side, reaching for her mug of tea.

'Well?'

'Well what, Mum?'

'What do you think? Of the place? Have you had a bit of a look around?'

Lucy smiled, stood, and walked to the window overlooking the paddock beside the house, the ragged mountain ranges of the State Forest and National Park rising steeply beyond. The distant peaks were tinged with blue, a trick of Australian eucalypts. The heavily forested hills flowed down from the mountain peaks to rich green farmland below. Patches of black and bare spots were a roadmap to the destructive fires that had burned through thousands of hectares the previous summer.

'Yes, I like it. It's peaceful, but sort of wild at the same time. There was a kookaburra just outside the kitchen window earlier. It made me laugh. And I love that we're going to plan the renovations together, and even do some of the work ourselves. It will be like episodes of The Block.'

Warmed by the enthusiasm in Lucy's voice, Nik stood and stretched, swallowing the last of her tea. 'I'm going to throw some shorts and a tee shirt on, like you. It's going to be hot again today. Can you get some toast started? Or would you prefer eggs?'

'Toast is good. I turned the fridge on earlier and moved everything from the esky into it.'

'Good thinking. You start the toast; I'll be there in a moment.' Nik padded to the bathroom down the hall as Lucy returned to the kitchen.

Brushing her teeth, then washing her face, Nik looked at herself in the old, discoloured mirror. Taking a deep breath, she pulled her thick shoulder-length hair into a ponytail. It made her look younger than her thirty-eight years, but the scar in her hairline was visible. Other scars, one across her ribs and another on her shoulder were rarely seen. Throwing on a sleeveless tee and yoga shorts, she glanced at the back of her legs. A faded welt was visible where her shorts ended. Shrugging, Nik glanced in the mirror again. Wide-set eyes stared back at her with a few small lines creasing their corners when she smiled. Her lips were plump and naturally red, her nose was straight and her brows dark and arched. She touched her cheeks, thankful her skin was lightly tanned, with a few freckles across the bridge of her nose.

A faint smell of mould permeated the room. She wrinkled her nose. Maybe they could re-do this bathroom when they did the downstairs one. It would certainly be more comfortable.

The kitchen was large, with timber cabinets and benchtops most likely put in during the eighties and the old electric stove had seen better days. There was no dishwasher, but a large cement sink crouched beneath a large window, which Lucy had opened, letting in fresh air and a light breeze.

Lucy was standing at the toaster humming quietly to herself, two plates already piled with thick toast. Nik paused in the doorway. Her sweet daughter at eleven was long-limbed and coltish, her arms and legs lanky and thin. Wearing denim shorts and a pale green tee shirt, her thick, long dark hair was pulled up into a high ponytail, complete with multicoloured scrunchie. That was a good sign too. For months she had preferred to keep her hair down, hiding behind it when anyone spoke to her.

Lucy turned, waving a piece of toast in her hand, a small smear of vegemite on the side of her mouth. 'Started without you,' she giggled and raised an eyebrow, her face a girlish twin to Nik's.

'Good. I'll have butter and vegemite too, thank you.' Turning around in a circle Nik gestured to the room. 'It's a good size, don't you think? Perhaps we don't need to do much here. We could paint the timber cupboards and laminate the benchtop, put in a new stove, preferably gas. There's plenty of bench space and I really love the old sink, it might be the original.'

'I love that idea!' Lucy's eyes were shining.

'We could get it done soon, too, if we don't have to replace the cupboards. We could do most of this ourselves.' Nik waved her arm at the cupboards as she turned around.

'Okay, we'll look at paint colours for the cupboards online, I'll get my iPad.' Nik walked back to the bedroom, grabbed her iPad from her tote bag and sat it on the kitchen bench. They scrolled through several ideas on Pinterest, eating their breakfast standing at the bench. A few ideas seemed good, but they needed to get to a hardware store for paint samples.

Breakfast finished; they placed their plates into the large sink. 'I know the drought has broken but let's not fill the sink until we have lunch dishes too. It will save water.'

Lucy laughed. 'We might need a dishwasher Mum. You hate

washing up in the sink. Using the drought as an excuse is kinda funny.'

Nik poked her tongue out. 'We're on tank water out here, I need to check the tanks are full. The solicitor handling the sale made enquiries with Council. If we start offering short term accommodation we may be required to put in more tanks.'

Continuing to laugh, Lucy said, 'Yeah, I totally get that. But Mum, you really do hate washing up.'

Laughing together, Nik gave in. 'You're right. We need to make room for a dishwasher.'

SORTING THROUGH THE KEYS THE REAL ESTATE AGENT HAD PROVIDED, THEY strolled around the side of the house to the cottage. Originally stables, the lower walls were built from hand-made bricks, then timber boards above that. The paint was peeling on the outside at the front, but a veranda had been added on each side, with doors opening onto it. They were the original stable doors, with a top and bottom half. Nik and Lucy looked at each other, hand over mouths, exclaiming in unison. 'I love these doors, they're perfect!' Nik added, 'they need sanding and repainting, or we could even take them back to the original timber because I suspect they are Australian cedar under all those layers of paint.'

Lucy nodded and took her mother's hand, leading her around to the front of the building. The front door was a wide, modern double door. Nik unlocked it and they walked in, looking back at the entrance. 'Hmmm. Cheaply made and doesn't fit with the look of the building. Those doors have to go.'

'Hey Mum, do you think the entrance originally had a big sliding stable door, or perhaps heavy timber double doors? Because I think that would look awesome.'

Nik glanced at her daughter's excited face, then walked back to the entrance, studying the opening a bit closer. 'It may have had no doors, just been an opening big enough to get a horse and wagon through. But there's no reason we can't get a door made that fits the style. Like a big sliding stable door.' Turning she winked at Lucy. 'You have great ideas.'

The inside was an open living area with a kitchenette at the far end and bedrooms on one side. Dated carpet covered the floor, plus the building needed painting inside and out and the kitchenette was just a small sink, aged cooktop, and a freestanding cupboard. 'We can pull this out ourselves and replace it with a neat little prefab kitchenette in a heritage style.' Nik took Lucy's hand, walking toward the bedrooms.

Two enormous bedrooms with a bathroom between them opened up to the veranda, taking up the whole length of the building on one side. They were completely bare of cupboards or furnishings. Lucy frowned. 'Would we put in wardrobes Mum? The rooms seem really empty.'

'People don't always unpack, but I think we could do a chest of drawers and maybe some hanging space. Folks don't need a lot for short term stays.' She walked into the bathroom, which had a door leading into it from each bedroom. It was a dark, narrow space, with just a basin, shower, and toilet. No frills. It all needed to be replaced. Nik stepped into the next bedroom, then back through the bathroom.

'The bedrooms are huge, and the bathroom basic and narrow. What if we took another metre from the side of each bedroom to add to the bathroom? That would give us about three point five metres by four metres. We could set it up really nicely with a large double shower, put the toilet in its own little room at one end and put a big claw foot tub on the veranda end, maybe add in a window there for extra light and ventilation.'

'I love it! It will be luxurious on the inside, but rustic on the outside. I can't wait to get started. Will we get this ready first, or the bit underneath the house?' Lucy was almost dancing on the spot with enthusiasm.

'I planned to do the house bit first but seeing this now, makes me believe we could get this cottage started straight away. We can finish by Easter and have guests staying, although probably just on week-ends, and that will help us kick on with the house. It would be nice to get our own kitchen and bathroom done sooner, rather than later. I need to make a budget and we can schedule the work in stages. I have enough left from the sale of our old house to do the cottage, at least.'

They walked back toward the main house. The driveway stretched before them, deep potholes in the ground, long grass to the sides and many of the trees still reaching out across the road haphazardly. 'We need to get these trees cut back, just a little, and the driveway graded, and some gravel added. The recent rains have made it really rough and people coming from the city won't be keen to drive their cars in here, like this.'

'Do you think the cowboys could cut the trees back? Cowboy Dad has a chainsaw.' Lucy looked up at her mother.

'Maybe. I didn't get his number yesterday, but his name is Robbie Stewart. I can google, see if I can find him. He may be able to quote.' Nik pulled her phone from her back pocket. 'He might recommend local builders and tradespeople too. I was going to get recommendations from Ben Evans, the real estate agent, but I doubt he'll open again until Tuesday.'

Nik couldn't find anything under Robbie Stewart, or Robert Stewart. She tried R. Stewart. Up popped a listing *R & J Stewart, Builders. No job too big or too small. Carpentry, fencing, tree lopping.* He had a mobile number. Nik looked at her watch. It was nine o'clock, but Sunday morning. Her finger hovered over the call button.

'I could just ask if he is interested in the tree lopping, giving a quote. It doesn't have to be today.' Lucy nodded, her face bright and excited. Nik pushed the button.

It rang a few times, then went to voicemail. A recorded woman's voice came on: *You've called R and J Stewart, builders. Please leave a message and we will return your call as soon as possible.*

'Um, hello, um Robbie. And Harry. It's Nicola Reid, your new neighbour. Can you give me a call back on this number when you have a moment please?'

3

They hadn't heard the vehicle, but a car door slamming, and a man's voice brought a look of terror to Lucy's face. Nik glanced at her, saying calmly, 'Just stay up here, Luce, I'll go down and check who it is.'

Lucy nodded but stayed where she was, sitting on her bed. They had been sorting out her clothes and books and putting them away. There hadn't been much cupboard space in her bedroom, so together they had half dragged, half pushed a chest of drawers from Nik's room. They had cleaned a bit too and Nik was hot and sweaty and pulled at a piece of cobweb that had found its way into her hair as she ran down the stairs, two at a time.

Opening the front door, she saw a large Landcruiser ute, with a black and white border collie tied in the back, its tongue lolling in the heat. 'Hi Nik!' Robbie Stewart walked from the side of the house, a tin doggie bowl full of water in his hand. He placed it down in the shade of the veranda, then spoke as he untied the dog. 'Hope you don't mind, but Scout has been in the back of the ute on the way back from town, and she could do with a drink.'

'Hi Robbie. No, I don't mind at all.' She stood back as he let the dog jump down, the lead rope in his hand. Scout walked over to the bowl and began to lap thirstily. He dropped the lead on the ground, gave the dog a pat, and said 'Stay.' Scout immediately sat on her haunches, her tail swishing the veranda boards, her mouth half-open in a happy doggie smile.

'I got your message this morning, Nik, but had to finish a small job off in town. Thought I'd drop by on my way home. Is there something I can help you with?' He glanced at her shorts, and Nik suddenly felt exposed, tried to give her shorts a surreptitious tug. There was something about the way he looked at her.

'We've been unpacking. It's a hot day.'

He smiled, folded his arms, and leant back against the veranda post. 'I can see that.'

'I didn't get your number yesterday, but I googled you. I'm needing quotes for a few things and initially thought you might be able to recommend builders and tradespeople, but I see you're a builder yourself. I'm not sure what your workload is like, but are you interested in doing some work here?'

'We've got a few jobs on the go, and one big one up at Rawdon Vale, but Harry is staying up there this week to finish that off. Tell me what you need, I can work out some costs and timing for you.'

Relieved to be talking business, Nik said, 'I'll just nip in and get my iPad. We made a list of priorities this morning.'

Running back up the stairs, she saw Lucy hovering. 'It's Robbie, from yesterday. He's going to give me some quotes.'

'Cowboy Dad?'

'Yes. The son is called Harry, but he's somewhere else this week.'

'Okay.'

Back outside, Nik pulled her list up on the iPad.

'The driveway is my most immediate concern. Are you able to lop some of the trees back a bit? I could use the wood for firewood in the winter.'

'Sure. They don't need much. You won't often have such large vehicles coming in like yesterday. Some of the branches are overhanging too much. I would just cut those back. They make quite a nice avenue in the entrance. Better to cut them back every year or two, than to go hard and lose the aesthetic appeal of the driveway.'

'Yes. Good. Right. I'll need a price for that. And do you know anyone who could grade and gravel the driveway? The rain has made big pot-holes and some folk in city cars might find it tricky to navigate.' Noting his raised eyebrows, she added, 'I'm going to offer short term accommodation.'

Taking his hat off, he ran his hand though his thick chestnut hair, walking back to the worst of the holes in the driveway. 'Grading and adding crushed metal, then rolling it to compact it a bit would be best. But if we get heavy rain it will wash out again.' He strode further up the driveway, then walked into the long grass beneath the trees on each side. 'I recommend we dig a small drainage channel close to the trees, direct the water flow away from the road and back into the paddocks on either side. That will help the driveway last longer.'

Nik had followed him, not sure what he was thinking as he walked under the trees, even peering over the fence into the paddocks beside the driveway. She couldn't help but notice his long legs, clad in the same faded jeans as yesterday. Broad shoulders, tall, lean through the middle. Not a heavy drinker then.

'The paddock on this side of the fence is mine, so that's okay, but the other side is my neighbours, and I would need permission to redirect rain run-off in there.'

Robbie beckoned her forward, walking to the fence of the neighbouring property. The trees were on her side of the fence. Robbie had one elbow up on a fence post. 'There is an old bathtub in there, it's a water trough for cattle in this paddock. The trough is slightly downhill, we could capture the run-off in a small tank in the ground here, then gravity feed the water run-off to the trough, using a poly pipe. It's a little more to set up but will mean you won't need to keep grading and gravelling the driveway after heavy rain.'

'It sounds sensible Robbie, but I still need to talk to the neighbour. Do you know who owns this piece?'

Robbie turned to her, grinning, then jammed his hat back on his head. 'I do, Nik. My place starts here at this paddock, then runs along the road apiece, some of it running up into those hills there.'

She looked where he pointed. Surprised, but pleased, too. 'I understood all the forest area was owned by the State?'

'Not all, a lot of it on this side of the hill is privately owned. Over the hill it gets steep. That's all State Forest. And further up the road toward The Tops, it's National Park.'

They began to walk back toward the house. Nik caught a flash of colour on the second-floor veranda. Lucy was sitting in the shade, watching.

'Did you know the previous owners? Why did you never work out a deal to fix the drainage on the driveway with them?' Nik knew she sounded suspicious, but she wanted to make sure she was trusting the right person. She'd been wrong before.

'Yeah, you'd think. The last owner was elderly. When her husband was alive, he had his own grader blade on the front of a small tractor and used to keep the driveway neat himself. It was never a problem. But he died several years ago, she stopped having guests stay and it just got away from her. She had a stroke about a year ago. You bought it from her estate. Her kids live in the city, never come out here. They just wanted it sold.'

'Oh.' That made sense. All the buildings had an uncared for, unlived in feel. The agent said it had operated as a bed and breakfast until recently, but maybe that was more than a year or two ago.

Back at the main house, Nik reached down and gave Scout a pat. She rolled over on her back, her tummy rounded, the nipples visible. 'Is she …?'

'Pregnant. Yes. She'll whelp in about three weeks. She isn't doing any real work on the farm but loves coming with me in the ute. She's a fabulous working dog, has a lovely nature too.' He knelt, taking the dog's head in his hands, giving her a slow, luxurious pat. Nik's tummy flipped over. He was so gentle. Such big, gentle hands. She stepped away. Seeing such gentleness in a man, after the violence she had experienced, sent her heart racing.

'Can I offer you a drink, Robbie. Coke? Water?'

'No thanks, Nik. I'll work out a price for the driveway grading, crushed gravel, and the tree lopping. I have a grader tractor myself, so I can do it all, no need for another contractor. I'm not going to charge for the drainage and poly pipe, as I will get the benefit of the extra water in this paddock for stock. It'll allow me to run a few more heifers here.' He pulled out his phone and tapped a few figures into his calculator. Looking up, he named a price. Much less than Nik had expected.

'Really? Oh, that's good. Thank you.' Nik watched Robbie untie the dog, tip the remaining water out of the bowl, then open the tray of the ute for her to jump up. 'When do you think you could start on it?'

'I'll come back after lunch to get the trees sorted today, grade tomorrow morning, bring a load of gravel in the afternoon, then roll it on Tuesday. If we get a few showers later in the week, I'll roll it again then. We aren't expecting heavy rains just yet, but when Harry returns next week, we can dig the drain and set up the water diversion.' He stepped forward, holding his hand out. Nik shook it.

'Do you want this in writing, Nik? I can send it through tonight.'

'That would be good. I need tax invoices, you know …'

'Sure. I'm not great with the bookwork, but I can do that.'

Robbie nodded, then walked swiftly around the side of his ute, jumped in, and pulled away. Leaning out he waved, looking up at the second floor.

Confused, Nik took a step back and looked up. Lucy was standing at the rail, in full view. Her hand still raised, waving as the vehicle made its way along the driveway to the road.

4

____

Lucy ran down the stairs as Nik stepped inside, the house several degrees cooler than outside.

'Did you see the dog, Mum? She's beautiful. All shiny and black and white and her tail kept wagging the whole time!'

Nik smiled and held her arms out. Lucy's face was radiant as she ran into them, quickly hugging her mother, then stepping back. 'What's her name? Did he tell you her name? I'm sure it's a her because I saw her nipple thingies.'

Laughing, she was delighted to see Lucy happy and chatty. Like she used to be. Before him. Before Nik's big mistake. 'Her name is Scout. You know, like the girl in *To Kill A Mockingbird*.'

'Scout.' Lucy said the name out loud, as if trying it on for size. 'Scout. I like that.'

'And she's going to have puppies in about three weeks, Robbie said.'

'Puppies? Really? How lovely.' Lucy was almost dancing on the spot. 'Is he going to do some work for us? Cowboy Dad?'

'Robbie. Mr Stewart to you; perhaps.' She laughed. Lucy's nickname suited the man. 'Yes, he is. He's going to come back after lunch and cut back the trees that are sticking out too far,' she pointed to the

138

driveway, 'and then he will grade the driveway and add some crushed metal over the next couple of days. When his son, Harry, is back from another job later in the week they are going to dig a drain on that side,' Nik pointed to a dip in the grass, 'and send the rain-water into the paddock for his stock. He owns that piece and right up there to the mountains, so he's our neighbour. We're pretty lucky, he's going to do that drain bit for free, because he gets the water for his cattle.'

'That's good. Do you think he will bring Scout again?'

'I'm not sure Lucy, her puppies are due soon, so he said she isn't doing any farm work, just riding around to jobs with him in the ute.'

'Well, if he comes back in his ute, he might bring her. Do you think I could come down and pat her? You know, when he's working on the trees?' Lucy looked happy, and hopeful. It warmed Nik's heart. 'I was on the veranda. I let him see me. He saw me yesterday too, but he didn't say anything. Then I saw him put his hands on Scout. He has gentle hands. Someone who is gentle with a dog couldn't hurt a person, could they?'

'I don't think he would hurt anyone either, Lucy. And it's great you let him see you. Remember Doctor Slater said some people will just have a way about them that makes you feel safe. I think Robbie might be one of those people. If he brings Scout back, I'm sure you can pat her while he's working.'

They made lunch upstairs and ate their sandwiches while unpacking Lucy's room. It was looking good and would be even better when they painted and re-did the carpet. Or maybe pull the carpet up and polished the old floorboards. She'd have to see what condition they were in.

Nik hadn't asked Robbie to have a look at the cottage. She wanted to be sure his work was good first. She wondered what his wife was like, the woman on the voicemail message. She must be the J. in R and J Stewart.

Robbie came back after lunch, the back of his ute full of equipment, including a chainsaw. This time Scout was riding beside him on the passenger seat.

She walked out to greet him. 'I see you've brought Scout back. Lucy was quite taken with her earlier. You can leave her on the veranda again if you like.'

'Sure.' He smiled, his grey-blue eyes crinkling at the edges. His face was tanned, his teeth straight and white when he smiled. 'Scout's great with kids. I'll leave her bowl here, and perhaps Lucy can give her some water.'

Reaching into the back of the ute he lifted out his chainsaw, a small can of fuel and a pair of earmuffs. 'This may be noisy for a while. I'd recommend you do something inside while I get this bit done.'

Nodding, Nik watched him walk to the far end of the driveway with his gear. He was going to start there and work his way closer.

Lucy popped around the door, kneeling as she patted Scout, exclaiming at her softness. Scout gave her hand a couple of happy licks then laid her head in Lucy's lap, her tail pumping the veranda floor.

'Don't get too settled. Robbie asked if you could give Scout some water.' Nik handed the metal bowl to Lucy, who leaned close to the dog, explaining she would be back in a moment. She jumped up and ran to the tap at the side of the house under the water tank, filling the bowl and returning moments later, carrying it carefully.

'Would you like to make a jug of lemonade and some pikelets for afternoon tea?'

'We don't have any lemons.'

Taking Lucy by the shoulder, Nik turned her toward the water tank. 'See that tree just behind the tank? What does it look like to you?'

'Lemons! It's huge. Wow. I'll just get a basket from the kitchen.' Lucy shot off, returning with a wicker basket. 'I'll pick a dozen. Can I take Scout with me?'

Nik looked at Scout, who had sat up, looking eagerly at Lucy. 'Alright but take her on the lead and keep her close and in the shade. She's expecting puppies, remember.'

Nik checked her phone for the time, watching as Scout trotted happily at Lucy's side. She could probably do two hours of work while Lucy made afternoon tea and played with the dog. A room on the ground floor would be perfect for an office. It had an old solid timber countertop and may have been the reception desk for the police station at one time. She brought her laptop and work bag down and set it up, using a kitchen bar stool as a chair for the high counter. She had organised Wi-Fi connection before they arrived, so it didn't take long to get everything connected. This way she could offer free wi-fi to guests, too, when they eventually came.

In the meantime, she would continue to run her book-keeping practice from home. She had only retained a few long-term clients who could manage working with her remotely. It would be enough to keep them going and would help pay for any renovations that were beyond the money she had put aside. Perhaps she'd even be able to pick up a couple of local clients. Robbie mentioned he didn't enjoy the paperwork side of his business, but maybe his wife did that for him. He said Scout would be alone at home, so it's possible his wife was away. Could be worth asking though.

Lucy returned and went upstairs to make afternoon tea, leaving Scout laying on the veranda. The noise of the chainsaw slowly grew louder, as Robbie worked his way closer to the house. After almost two hours it stopped altogether and Nik looked up, expecting to see him coming in for a cool drink. But he had gloves on and was working his way back up the driveway, stacking the sawn wood into piles as he went. Nik pulled on the gardening gloves Lucy had set aside after picking the lemons and strode down the driveway. She nodded at him, then began picking up some of the pieces, watching how he stacked them and following suit.

'This is heavy work for a woman and you're paying me to do it. You don't have to help.' It was quietly but firmly said.

'And I'm sure the cost of the drain is going to outweigh the financial benefit to you. So, I'll pick up a few logs and stack them.' Also said quietly, but firmly. He chuckled and kept working. She liked the sound.

At the end of the driveway, they stood for a moment, looking back towards the house. It was more visible now from the entrance, but Robbie had left enough foliage to create a welcoming avenue of green. Pulling her gloves off, Nik nudged Robbie with her shoulder. 'Nice work, Cowboy Dad.'

'Cowboy Dad?' he laughed loudly, a rich, hearty sound.

Nik chuckled. 'It's what Lucy calls you. Cowboy Dad. And Harry is

Cowboy Son. She knows your names, but it's how she sees you.' Turning to him, she frowned slightly. 'I hope you're not offended. And she's made some lemonade from our own lemons and pikelets for afternoon tea. She's a great little baker.'

'Not at all. To a girl from the city, I must look like a cowboy. Pity I didn't ride a horse over to complete the look.' They began walking toward the house. 'A cold lemonade and pikelets sound perfect. I hope she lets me thank her.'

'Horse. You have a horse? Do you keep it nearby?' Nik looked across his paddocks, which seemed empty of stock.

'Horses. Plural. We have several. Harry rides in the camp draft and what we call 'sporting' at the local rodeos. Australian stock horses mostly. Quiet, good natured. Smart animals.'

'Oh. That's lovely.' Nik was deep in thought as they arrived at the house. Stepping inside she saw that Lucy had set a small table up in her office area, its surface neatly covered with a gingham cloth, a jug of lemonade, two glasses and a platter of pikelets with jam and cream positioned nicely in the middle.

Robbie hesitated in the doorway. 'I'll just nip around to the tap and wash my hands. Back in a moment.'

Nik went into the downstairs laundry to wash her hands and realised she was pleased to be sharing afternoon tea with him. Working alongside him had been good. Neighbourly. They arrived back together. Their first glass of lemonade went straight down, but they sipped on the second one. Robbie ate a pikelet, 'Delicious.' Nik knew Lucy would be listening at the top of the stairs.

Leaning back after his third pikelet, Robbie patted his flat stomach. 'Couldn't fit another thing in. Thank you, Nik. You must know a good bakery around here because I'm fairly sure the local one is closed today, and they are the best pikelets I've had in a long while.'

He was rewarded by a little giggle from the top of the stairs. Nik said, 'Wait until you taste her scones.'

Lucy called out from the top of the stairs. 'Lemon Meringue Pie!' Nik's surprise was evident, and Robbie looked pleased with himself. While he didn't know their story, he had surmised Lucy was shy with strangers.

Standing, Robbie nodded to the computer set up at the counter. 'Working?'

'Yes. I'm a bookkeeper. I had a practice in the city but sold it to make this move. I'm just keeping a handful of clients I've had for a long time, who don't mind working with me remotely.'

Robbie nodded. 'Good for you.'

She stood on the veranda while he reloaded his ute, putting Scout back in the passenger seat. He looked up and waved. 'Thank you for afternoon tea, Miss Lucy.'

Her girlish voice called down, 'My pleasure, Cowboy Dad.'

His eyes met Nik's as he looked across the bonnet of his ute at her. He smiled and nodded, and she grinned back, waving as he drove away.

Lucy flew down the stairs, giggling. 'He called me 'Miss Lucy' like a real cowboy would.'

'Yes, he did. And he is a real cowboy because he told me today, he, and Cowboy Son, have horses.'

'Ohhh! Horses! Maybe I can see them some time.'

'Sure. I'll check on that.'

5

———————

The next few days flew by and Nik and Lucy focussed on setting things up inside the house while Robbie graded the driveway, delivered crushed gravel, then rolled it several times. Light overnight rain had created the perfect environment to get the job finished.

While she'd offered lunch each day, Robbie brought his own, including a small esky of cold drinks. He took his lunch break in the shade of the front veranda, where Scout lay as he worked. Nik often sat with him, but Lucy chose to stay inside, although she baked something for afternoon tea each day. Nik knew she heard his comments of appreciation for her efforts and was thrilled to see her lovely face glow with happiness at his words.

At times, while he was working at the far end of the driveway, Lucy would creep out to the veranda to sit with Scout, ensuring she had water in her bowl. The expectant dog's tail wagged madly when she appeared, and after a while she began to wriggle forward to lay her head in Lucy's lap.

By Friday morning Robbie had completed the driveway, coming to the front door later to advise Nik he would be taking his roller home, but could he leave the tractor around the back of the house, as he would use it with a different implement on the back to dig the drain down the side of the drive.

He leant against a veranda post, casually stroking Scout's head. Looking at her, his keen eyes taking in her appearance, he added, 'Harry will be home today, so we'll come back this afternoon with more equipment, and if it's okay with you we can get the drain finished over the weekend.'

Nik had pulled her hair back into a headband and knew her scar was visible. Somehow, she didn't mind him noticing and didn't feel she needed to provide an explanation. 'That's great. I'm thrilled with the driveway; it should hold up now even for the fussiest city driver.' She smiled broadly. 'Do you have an account for this work? I'm happy to pay it straight away.'

'Darn! I knew you'd ask me that. I'm not great with the bookwork. Harry will do the account for me later. We upgraded to Xero Accounting a few years ago, but I've never got the hang of it. Prefer to be doing the work than billing it.' He chuckled.

'You'd be surprised how many of my clients, especially tradespeople, feel the same.' Nik nodded as she spoke, but in the back of her mind wondered why his wife wouldn't be helping with the bookwork.

'Alright then, Nik. I'll head off. Will be back later today with Harry to drop the equipment off. We usually go into the pub on Friday night for a quiet ale and wood-fired pizza. Have you been into town at all?'

'I've nipped in a couple of times, picked up some sample paint pots from the hardware store. Most of the shops have been closed, but I did get a really good coffee from the place on the corner.'

'Oh, that's Debbie's place. Great business. Really good baked goods too, although you won't need that, you have your own baker on site.' He smiled warmly at her as he picked up Scout's almost-empty water bowl, tipping the last of the water onto the lavender growing to one side.

The warmth of his voice, the understanding implied, brought sudden tears to her eyes. She knew Lucy was hovering just inside, so she took a step forward. Reaching out, she touched his arm, speaking softly. 'Thank you. For all you've done this week.'

If he noticed the emotion in her voice, he didn't comment. He gave her a quick smile, slapping his hat on his head. 'All part of the service ma'am. See you later then.' Turning, he strode to his vehicle, his dog trotting beside him.

❧

Sitting down to a lunch of fried rice made from leftovers; a favourite of Lucy's, Nik asked her how she was feeling about all they had achieved in their first week.

'I really love it here Mum. It's quiet and peaceful and I love it when Cowboy Dad brings Scout with him. She's so beautiful.' Lucy smiled shyly at her mum. 'Do you think we could get a dog one day? One like Scout?'

The thought had already crossed Nik's mind and she wondered if all Scout's puppies were spoken for. She didn't want to suggest it to Lucy in case they were. 'I think a dog is a lovely idea. You would need to look after it and train it if we got a puppy, or we could try the local pound and adopt a grown dog. Let's get some of this work done first, and then look into it.'

Lucy nodded happily as she took her plate to the sink. She had taken to plaiting her hair each morning and Nik could see she had gained confidence. While Lucy hadn't spoken directly to Robbie all week, she had waved at him from afar a few times and called out a greeting from the safety of the top balcony. Better than previous months when she wouldn't show herself to anyone at all. Nik had been home-schooling her for the last six months and was prepared to continue for a further year, at least. But now she wondered if Lucy would be okay to go to school. The nearest one, in Barrington Village, was small. They still had almost four weeks before first term began; perhaps she would be ready.

As they washed up together, they chatted about the cottage. 'I think we're ready to get some quotes for the cottage, Luce. We've got our part of the house clean and settled, and my office downstairs. I like the little sitting room you've created down there too. Robbie is a builder, how about we ask him to quote on the work? He would know plumbers and electricians too.'

'He's really nice Mum. I think it would be great if he could do the work on the cottage.' She drew in a breath. 'I'm going to talk to him soon. About his horses. Maybe not today, but soon.'

Nik put down the plate she was washing and hugged her daughter hard. 'That's brilliant, Luce. He's a kind man and I think he'd love to talk to you about his horses. When you're ready.'

THEY WERE IN THE COTTAGE WHEN ROBBIE RETURNED LATE IN THE afternoon, his ute full of black water pipe and other equipment. Harry drove in behind him in an older, battered ute. Nik walked from the cottage, wiping her hands on her cut-off jeans before raising one in a wave.

'Hi Nik.' Harry boomed out, already standing in the back of his vehicle, passing equipment down to his father.

'Do you need a hand?'

'Nah, almost got this lot unloaded. Did Dad tell you we're going to the pub for a cold one and some pizza? Welcome to join us if you like.'

'Oh, thanks Harry. Sounds delicious, but my daughter is a bit shy, so we don't go out to eat.'

Robbie walked around the back of the ute, giving his son a friendly pat on the shoulder as he jumped down from the tray back. He was dressed in dark jeans, dress boots and collared shirt, sleeves rolled to the elbows. What is it about him that set her hormones racing? She glanced at Harry again, also dressed in clean jeans and tee shirt. Drawing in a quick breath, Nik smiled to herself. The boys were in their going out gear. They scrubbed up okay.

'Can I ask you a favour, ladies?' Robbie glanced at Lucy, who was now standing in the shade of a large plum tree beside the house. Scout had jumped out of Robbie's car and was sitting at Lucy's feet.

Nik glanced at Lucy, pleased to see she was close enough to hear the conversation, and delighted to see her nodding and smiling shyly. 'Sure. How can we help?'

'We usually leave Scout tied in the back of the ute while we have a bite to eat at the pub. But she loves it here so much with Lucy, I wondered if we could leave her here for a bit and I'll pick her up around seven.'

'Yes please.' It was almost a whisper, but Nik heard it. Robbie looked directly at Lucy. 'Thank you, Lucy, I really appreciate that. By way of thanks, can I bring some pizza back for you? The pub does great takeaway.'

She glanced at her daughter. They both loved pizza, especially wood-fired, but lately they made their own at home. Lucy nodded eagerly. Nik laughed. 'That would be great. Thank you. We eat any pizza, but no anchovies or chilli.'

'Done. See you around seven.'

6

Nik cleaned up the downstairs sitting area while Lucy played on the lawn beneath the plum tree with Scout. The dog's water bowl, some doggy treats, and an old tennis ball had been left with her, and Lucy sat on the grass, throwing the ball a short distance. Scout ran to it eagerly, then trotted back, tail wagging and a doggy smile plastered on her face. After half an hour or so Nik noticed Lucy laying on the grass reading a book, Scout stretched out beside her in the shade. A lovely scene.

After doing some bookwork for a client, and answering a couple of emails, Nik went upstairs to have a shower. She washed her hair, leaving it to dry naturally into a wavy shoulder-length bob. She slipped on a sleeveless cotton dress, brightly coloured, that stopped short of her knees. Her legs were slim and tanned and she felt feminine for the first time since the move.

She set the table downstairs for dinner. They didn't need much, a couple of plates, a jug of homemade lemonade and two glasses. She had planned to make a salad but knew Lucy would love just eating pizza from the box.

Scout pricked her ears as Robbie drove in, her tail thumping on the veranda. Lucy had been sitting beside her, but she stood and moved inside the house as Robbie got out, two pizza boxes in his hand.

'Hi Nik. Hope you're hungry, I've brought Margarita pizza and one with the lot, except anchovies and chilli.' He walked to the veranda and handed the boxes over, before bending down to pat Scout.

'Harry not with you?'

'Nah, he's catching up with mates. If he has a few beers he'll stay in town, come back here after breakfast to start on the drain job. Nineteen. I'm pretty lucky, he enjoys a few beers but doesn't overdo it, and he never drives if he's had a few.'

'What about you, Robbie. Do you enjoy a few beers? Or wine?' Nik asked, smiling, her eyebrows raised.

'I admit I used to hit it hard in my younger days, especially when I was on the camp draft circuit. But marriage and kids set me straight. Now I enjoy a couple of cold ones, may even crack the top off another one once I'm home, but that's it for me.' He glanced at her. 'What about you? Do you have a beer or glass of wine at the end of the day?'

'I used to. Wine mostly. Sometimes a beer. But lately, well, I need to be in the present, as the gurus say. Sometimes I yearn for a glass of wine. Especially after a busy, hot day. But it passes quickly.'

The aroma from the boxes was making her mouth water and Lucy hovered just inside the open door, waiting until Nik passed the pizzas to her. She looked at Robbie, saying almost apologetically, 'I'd ask you to join us …'

'Not at all. I've had my fill but thank you. Another time perhaps?' He whistled to Scout, who followed him to the car, jumping into the front when he opened the passenger door. He called, 'Thank you for looking after Scout, Miss Lucy. See you tomorrow.'

Lucy came to the door, not quite meeting his eye, her voice quiet. 'I love looking after Scout.' He waved to her and shot a grin at Nik, who beamed back at him. While he didn't know of their recent past, and the trauma they had suffered, she knew he sensed it. She felt herself warming to him and reminded herself he was married; she had noted the ring on his finger. She needed to establish a community here; friends, neighbours, people she could grow to trust. He hadn't mentioned his wife, but perhaps she was away. Nik hoped she was as welcoming as Robbie; it would be great to have adult female company here too.

⌒

THE BOYS WERE BACK ON THE JOB NEXT MORNING BY EIGHT O'CLOCK. IF Harry had a big night, he certainly didn't seem any the worse for wear. In fact, she could hear him chatting to Robbie as they worked, and occasionally breaking into a song, something country, in a sweet, strong voice that carried. More than once she heard father and son joking and teasing one another. Nice people. Nice family. She would ask about his wife when they stopped for lunch. To raise a young man like Harry, she would be lovely, she was sure.

The drain seemed to have progressed well over the morning, and by noon the day was hot. Harry had taken his shirt off, his tanned torso rippling with muscle and the vigour of youth. They were tall, well-built men, Robbie broader at the shoulders, his biceps bulging as he worked with shovel and pickaxe while Harry operated the backhoe on the tractor.

Nik had a bucket filled with ice, several cans of coke, squash, and water chilling. Robbie looked back at the house, saw her standing there, one arm raised to shade her eyes. He looked at his watch, then called out to Harry, who stopped the tractor.

They walked toward the house, chatting. Harry grinning broadly. 'Put your shirt on son.' Nik heard Robbie's quiet words as they veered off to the side of the house to wash up at the tap from the water tank.

Faces washed, hair damp, they reappeared and sat on the veranda steps. 'Cold drink?' Nik gestured set the bucket near them.

Harry took a coke; Robbie grabbed a water. 'Thanks Nik,' they said in unison. Robbie pulled their own esky closer; he had left it in the shade of the veranda when they arrived. He passed a wrapped pack of sandwiches to Harry and an apple, pulling another out for himself. 'Sandwich, Nik?' he opened his pack, holding it out to her.

'Oh, thank you. No, we've got some salad ready for our lunch. Happy to share too, though.'

'All good. Sandwiches fill us up. The carbs are good for an afternoon working.'

Nik stepped inside, she had two bowls of salad on the downstairs table. Lucy was there. She silently handed a bowl, with fork, to Nik and nodded. Nik smiled and stepped back onto the veranda. 'We might join you if that's okay?'

'Sure.' Harry slid down to a lower step, Nik taking the spot Harry vacated, next to Robbie. Lucy dragged a chair from inside just to the doorway, eating her salad quietly. Scout got up from her place beside Robbie, sauntered over to Lucy and lay down at her feet.

Laughing, Harry looked directly at Lucy, then back to his father. 'Watch out Dad, Scout may have switched loyalties. It seems she's taken to Lucy.'

'That was obvious from the first day, son. Young Lucy has a way with animals, that's for sure.'

Nik turned around, curious to see if the men's comments would send Lucy back inside, but her cheeks were flushed, her head down. When she glanced up, she caught her mother's eye. Nik mouthed 'love you' to Lucy, who wrinkled her nose before going back to her salad.

To change the subject and take further pressure away from her daughter, Nik turned to Robbie. 'Your business, R and J Stewart. Is the J your wife Robbie? Is she away at the moment?'

Both men stopped eating. The silence stretched and Nik could see tension in Robbie's face. Jaw clenched; he drew in a deep breath. She glanced at Harry, who was looking at his father with … interest? Concern? Damn, she knew she had put her foot in it, but didn't know how to undo her words. About to speak again, apologise, change the subject, anything.

Robbie stood up, his voice low. 'Jessica, my wife, passed away three years ago. Planning to change the business name to R and H Stewart, now Harry's finished school and decided to work the business with me. Need to do that sooner, rather than later.' He picked up his esky, walking toward his ute. 'We'll get back to work now Harry, if you're done there.'

Placing the esky in the back of his ute, he stalked up the driveway toward the tractor. Scout whimpered and walked to Harry, who stood.

He patted her head. 'It's okay, Scout. Stay here with Lucy.' He added with a sad smile, 'Mum had an aneurism. It was sudden. No warning at all. Dad … well, Dad struggles with it still. It's Mum on the voice-mail message on the home phone, he won't change it.' He reached out, touching Nik's shoulder. 'There's no way you could have known. He'll burn some energy off working and will be fine in a while.'

As Harry walked away, she stood and moved quickly into the house, brushing past Lucy in her haste. Reaching her study, she sat and cried. The tears fell silently, she reached for a tissue and blew her nose. Small arms wrapped around her shoulders. 'It's okay, Mummy.' She hadn't called her Mummy since … before.

Nik wiped her eyes. 'I'm sorry Luce. I don't know what came over me. Why it affected me so much. Their story. Losing his wife, Harry his Mum. We didn't even know her.'

Lucy smiled wanly, before climbing into her mother's lap, putting her small hands on each side of her face, looking into her eyes. 'It's the love, Mum. The cowboys really loved her.' Sobbing again, Nik buried her head in Lucy's shoulders. She felt Lucy's tears too, her small sobs shaking her body.

Wetness on her arm made Nik jump. Scout was there, licking her arm, nuzzling Lucy's leg. They looked at each other, tears still falling, and began to smile, then laugh. Lucy slid off Nik's lap and threw her arms around the dog's neck while Nik slid to the floor with her, patting Scout with one hand, stroking Lucy's hair with the other. The noise of the tractor outside continued and she wasn't sure how long they sat there. Lucy looked up at her.

'You okay now, Mum?'

'Yes. I am. I really am. Perhaps a good cry is what I needed.' She kissed the top of Lucy's head. 'How about you, sweetheart, are you okay?'

Lucy turned into her mother's body, hugging her tightly. 'Getting better every day.'

'I love you, Luce.'

'Love you too, Mummy.'

7

———————

Nik was working at her desk when she heard the tractor stop. Looking at her watch, she saw it was almost five. A long day for the men in such hot weather. She stepped on to the veranda. Lucy and Scout were laying under the plum tree, Lucy reading aloud from a favourite book, the dog's head in her lap.

Robbie was doing something at the back of the tractor. Nik worried he was still upset, but she saw him look up at Harry, in the driver seat, and say something with a broad smile. Harry bantered back. Good. She wouldn't mention his wife again. They could get back to normal.

Harry started the tractor and waved to her as he turned it around and began driving away. Robbie strode toward her. 'You'll be pleased to know the noisy part is finished. Harry is taking the tractor home; I'll follow in his ute. Is it okay if mine stays here overnight?' He flashed her a relaxed smile and she smiled back. Good. The tension was gone.

'No problem at all, it's not in the way.'

'We'll be back tomorrow to finish running the poly pipe to the new tank, then to the water trough in the paddock. Should be hooked up and going by the end of the day.'

'You've done a great job. Really quick too.' They sat together on the veranda steps, Robbie accepting the bottle of cold water she handed him. 'I have plans for the cottage out back. Some renovations to update it for short term accommodation. Some of it needs a builder, but I also need a plumber and electrician. Are you interested in having a look tomorrow, listen to my ideas, and provide a quote? It would be great if you would project manage the other trades. I understand if you have other work on though now that the holidays are over.'

Turning to look at her, he spoke quietly. 'Harry's still working on the job up at Rawdon Vale. I'll have to go up there for a day mid-week to check on it, order more materials. We're building some new horse yards. The two boys from the farm up there are helping, they're a bit younger than Harry, but are working well and it's saving them some money.' He took a drink of water, his eyes on her as he did.

'I'd be keen to have a look at the cottage. I have a builder's licence, so there's no worries there. If you're not making changes to the footprint, extending, then you don't need to apply for Council approval.'

'No, not extending. All the changes are under roof. But I want to see if it's possible to move some internal walls, create a bigger bathroom space. Bathrooms and views seem to 'sell' holiday accommodation. I've certainly got the views, and proximity to National Park for walks and hiking.' Nik couldn't keep her excitement for the project from her voice.

Robbie was smiling and grinning. It seemed to Nik her enthusiasm was contagious. 'I work with all the local trades, I'll have a walk through with you tomorrow, then get back to you with some quotes. You mentioned paint samples the other day, are they for the cottage, or the house?'

'Both!' Nik giggled. 'Lucy and I got a bit carried away with our ideas. There are little splotches of paint all over the place. It will be hard to choose. But the cottage first, to get some paying customers, while we do up the downstairs part of the house. If possible, we'll make some changes to the kitchen upstairs, we need a bigger commercial style oven, plus upgrades in the bathroom. I was thinking of putting in an ensuite too, but really, with extra bathrooms down here it's probably not needed.'

'Okay. Cottage first then.' He stood, looking down at her, still smiling. 'Well, I'll be off, back again tomorrow.'

'Thanks again. You and Harry are quite the team. Can't believe how much you got done today.' Nodding happily, he got into Harry's ute, settling the dog beside him before driving away.

If he looked in his rear-view mirror as he drove slowly out, he would see Lucy step on to the veranda, to wrap her arms around her mother's waist.

~

TOSSING AND TURNING THAT NIGHT, THE SHEETS TWISTED AROUND HER legs, her hair damp, Nik finally got up and sat in a chair by her bedroom window. The window faced the ragged mountain ranges, the moon providing enough light to see the steep hills climbing skyward. Robbie's home was out that way. She could see lights twinkling in the distance. Drawing her knees up, she rested her chin on them, staring pensively out the window.

Hot and sweaty, the vivid dream had awakened her from a deep sleep. Not the recurring nightmare she had been struggling with for six months. This dream had been slow, gentle. She had been laying under the plum tree in the soft grass, Robbie's dog, Scout, sprawled nearby. A man had appeared, she couldn't see his face at first, but knew it was Robbie. He lay beside her, on one elbow, tracing the scar on her face with tender hands. He kissed the scar, as she smiled through soft tears. His lips moved across her face, to her mouth. Kissing gently, he nibbled her bottom lip. She shook her head, smiling and crying all at once. He kissed her eyes, kissed her tears away. Then moved slowly down to her mouth. Shaking her head, she kept her lips closed but he persisted, gently, looking into her eyes. Tingling, she closed her eyes and opened her lips. As he took her mouth with his, heat rose from her body. Her arms came up around his neck, tugging him closer. He kept kissing her, running one hand down her side, tentatively touching her breast, before moving lower. Her thighs were bare, she was wearing the bright cotton frock. He moved his hand upwards, along her thigh to her hip, then across to the centre of the heat that pulsed within her. And she woke.

This was no good. She couldn't have romantic thoughts about her neighbour. About anyone for that matter. She had to think of Lucy. She would always come first. She would never make that mistake again. No matter how genuine, or caring the man seemed to be. She couldn't, wouldn't, take the risk.

By morning she had set the dream, and the feelings it engendered, aside. Robbie would be a friend. A good friend. He was still in love with his dead wife. He hadn't shown any interest, hadn't made any suggestions, or even looked at her in a way that might indicate interest. It was just her fevered, hormonal body that had betrayed her in the dream. She would remain friendly, build a community around her as she planned. Friends, neighbours, townsfolk. She would build a life here for her and Lucy. A life that would keep them safe. Keep Lucy safe. Help her heal. They would never forget, but they could heal and move past it.

8

———

Nik had finally returned to sleep in the early hours of the morning, only to wake with Lucy shaking her shoulder and the sun shining brightly through the window. 'Mum, Mum! Cowboy Dad's back. He has a horse Mum. Hurry, you need to see this!'

Jumping up, Nik pulled on denim shorts, bra, and tee shirt. Lucy hovered while she brushed her teeth, then ran downstairs together. Scout was sitting on the veranda, her tail thumping against the floor-boards when she saw them. Lucy grabbed Nik's hand, pulling her down the steps, heading toward the fence of Robbie's paddock.

Sure enough, there he was with a chestnut horse, still saddled, out by the water trough. Lucy waved and called out, 'Cowboy Dad!'

He grinned, then walked over to the fence, leading the horse behind him. 'This is Honey, I'm going to leave her and another horse in this paddock now that I have the water trough working. Thought I'd ride her over.'

Lucy stepped forward. Nik was amazed. 'Oh, she's beautiful. Can I pat her?'

'Of course. Let me help you over the fence.' He held the wires apart as Lucy slipped through, her shyness dissolving in her excitement.

'Honey is a mare and is carrying a foal, she isn't due for another six months so I'm still riding her. She's quiet, but you must always speak to her as you walk towards her, so she knows you're there. Never come up behind her quietly, as she might get a fright and kick, or take off. Come close to me, you can pat her neck, like this.' Robbie demonstrated. Lucy, eyes shining, imitated all he did, listening carefully as he explained some basic horse lore.

Nik was speechless as she watched Lucy act without shyness around Robbie. Her daughter's confidence grew as he walked her around the horse. Climbing through the fence, Nik approached the mare, petting her gently on the side of her face, before scratching under her chin and smiling as Honey nuzzled her.

'Would you like to sit on her Lucy, while I lead you around?' Robbie smiled gently and Lucy nodded and grinned. 'Yes please.' Not a whisper this time.

Holding Honey's bridle, Robbie explained how to mount using the stirrup. Lucy wasn't quite tall enough to get her foot in the stirrup, so Robbie told her to put her left foot in his linked hands, then to swing her right leg over and settle into the saddle. Once mounted she laughed happily. 'Mum, look at me. I'm riding Honey!'

Nodding, Nik grinned back, while Robbie took the reins and walked the horse, with Lucy holding the front of the saddle, across to the water trough, around it, then back to Nik. Just then, Harry's ute idled up the driveway.

'Harry's here. I'll unsaddle Honey now. We need to finish the last bit of the drainage and check it's all working. Then I'm going to have a look at what you and your Mum want to do with the cottage.' He spoke directly to Lucy. She nodded.

'Do you know how to dismount? Left foot in the stirrup, then swing your right leg over. You might have to make a little jump at the end.' Holding Honey's head, he looked up at her. 'Want to give it a try yourself?'

Lucy nodded. 'Yes, thank you.' She managed to get off without incident, receiving a quick grin from Robbie. 'Well done, you're a natural.' Turning to Nik he raised an eyebrow. 'Would you mind if I left her tack here, Nik. On the side veranda perhaps? Harry's brought a box of kit with him, her brushes and spare halter.'

Lucy was nodding wildly at Nik, her eyes shining. 'Of course. But perhaps better to put it in the laundry, there's plenty of room. I'd hate possums to chew the leather if we left it out.'

'Thank you, that's perfect.' He unsaddled the horse, explaining everything to Lucy as he went.

Harry appeared at the fence beside Nik. 'She's a lovely mare. Nice and quiet. Dad has two more he'll move into this paddock to keep her company. I've brought a bale of hay too, although the feed in here is quite good.' He called out to Lucy, holding a brush in his hand. 'I have Honey's brush here, Lucy, if you'd like to use it. Always good to brush her after the saddle comes off.'

Eyes wide, Lucy looked at Harry. He was holding the brush out over the fence. She hesitated, looked down at her feet, then at Nik. She recognised the sudden look of fear in Lucy's eyes and was about to intervene, not wanting to spoil the moment for her daughter, who had taken such big steps already, in just a few days.

Lucy looked up, directly at Harry. She gave him a tentative smile, then walked over to the fence and took the brush from his hand, turning quickly and walking back to the horse. She reached up to stroke the brush down Honey's shoulder, then looked back. 'Thank you.' It was said quietly, but Nik and Harry heard it.

'Right then, Nik. Show me where I can put the bale of hay and I'll get it unloaded while Dad brings the saddle and bridle back to the house.' Harry held the fence wires for Nik to step through, giving her a friendly pat on the shoulder as they walked back to his ute.

Glancing over her shoulder, Nik saw Lucy walking back with Robbie. He had the saddle over one arm, while she held the bridle. He was speaking to her as they walked and she was looking up at him, nodding every now and again. Taking a deep breath, Nik directed Harry to leave the hay bale outside the laundry door. Robbie stepped up on the veranda, then through to the laundry as she held the door open. There was an old wooden chest against one wall. 'Right there would be good, and there's a hook on the wall you can hang the bridle on, if you like.'

'Right-oh, that's perfect. I hope it won't be in your way.'

Lucy handed the bridle to Robbie, who hung it on the hook. 'Well done, Miss Lucy. You're going to be a fine horsewoman.' She giggled, leaning into Nik's side.

'I think you're right Robbie.' Nik ruffled her daughter's hair.

HARRY LEFT AFTER LUNCH. THEY HAD ALL SAT ON THE VERANDA, sharing sandwiches and the scones Lucy had baked during the morning. Robbie stood, picked up his hat and turned to them. He had a small notepad in his top pocket and a pen, which he pulled out. 'Let's go and inspect the cottage, see what you want to do over there.'

Nik stood and looked at Lucy. Do you want to come too, Luce?'

'No thanks, Mum. I'll take the glasses and plates in, then I'll play under the tree with Scout for a bit.'

Walking across to the cottage, they didn't speak. As she opened the front door, Nik turned to see Lucy taking their lunch things into the house.

'I want to thank you, Robbie, for all you've done this week. With Lucy. Bringing Scout and now Honey. This is the happiest she has been, in a long time.' Nik wanted to tell him more, felt she should explain, but her eyes filled with tears. The morning had been beautiful. Watching Lucy so animated, and fearless.

He closed the door behind them and turned to her. He reached out and took her in his arms, holding her against his chest while she sobbed. 'I don't know what you've been through, Nik. You and Lucy. But I can see it was traumatic. For you both. Lucy reminds me of a young horse; skittish, shy, and fearful. She needs to learn to trust again, to feel safe. Being around animals, dogs and horses, will help.' Nodding into his chest, Nik's sobs subsided.

Nik took a step back, slightly embarrassed. Robbie gave off an air of quiet understanding.

'You're right. I was letting her hide away. I haven't wanted to force Lucy to face her fears, instead I was hoping the fresh start would eventually do that for her. We need friends here, like you and Harry. Thank you.'

Robbie smiled and looked down at her. 'We are friends. And neighbours. We're going to be living side by side for a long time. We're off to a good start.'

'Now, about this cottage.' He pointed to the front doors. 'I hope you're going to tell me those cheap and ugly doors have to go!'

She threw her head back and laughed. 'Yes. First thing to go. Absolutely. Lucy wondered if we could do a big sliding stable door instead, something in solid timber.'

Glancing at her, Robbie grinned and walked back to the doors, pulling out a tape measure as he went. 'Yep. That would work.' He looked around the big living area, a frown on his face. 'You know, I recall a big set of double doors here before. Solid rosewood. They'd been painted over a few times and I'm not sure why they replaced them. Probably for a nineteen-eighties style upgrade.' He snorted. 'But I wonder if they are still here, stored in one of the outbuildings. We should check first.'

'Really? Rosewood? Wow, it would be fabulous to find them. I'll have a good look around. We haven't even looked in the garage, but it seems full of old bits and pieces. Perhaps there are some treasures in there we can re-use.'

As they walked through the building, Robbie took notes and measured as he went. They spent ages in the bathroom, while he measured the two bedrooms and sketched a new, bigger bathroom into his notepad. He understood the look she wanted to achieve and even suggested some money-saving tips to get it done.

After one last walk around the main room, they headed back to the front doors. Robbie stopped, touching her arm. She turned and looked at him as he pulled a neatly folded paper out of his back pocket. Handing it to her, he said, 'Our bill for the driveway. Harry did it for me last night. But he whinged the whole time, telling me our accounts are a mess.'

Nik looked at him, slightly surprised, and opened the bill. It was exactly what he had quoted. She nodded, refolded it and put it in her back pocket. 'I'll pay this today, Robbie, thank you. I still think it's cheap, you did all the drainage for free.'

'There's something else, Nik.' Again, she looked at him. He seemed nervous, and she nibbled at her bottom lip, suddenly feeling unsure of him. 'Would you be interested in doing a deal with me?'

'A deal?' she raised her eyebrows. She had not expected him to say that.

'Would you be interested in taking over our accounts, the book-keeping for the business?'

'Yes, of course. I'd love to.' Knowing there was more, she waited.

'I'd give Lucy riding lessons in return. Not just riding lessons, but horsemanship lessons. However, many hours a week you need to be at my books, I will give lessons in return.'

'Wow! I didn't see that coming, but it's a perfect arrangement. In fact, I think Lucy and I will get the better end of this deal.' Grinning, she held out her hand. Robbie smiled back, taking her hand, and shaking it firmly. Her shoulders relaxed. He was genuine. Friend. Neighbour. Nothing more. Never anything more. But this was enough. Her steps were light as they headed back to the house.

9

———

And so it began. Robbie took his ute home that afternoon, but returned the next morning riding a large black gelding, leading a small grey mare, fully saddled, Scout trotting beside them. Lucy had seen him riding down the paddock from her bedroom and was out at the fence before he reached it.

'Good morning Cowboy Dad.' She waved and called out, before leaning down to pat Scout who promptly planted her backside on Lucy's foot.

He raised a hand in greeting. Stopping just a few metres from the fence, he said, 'This is Blackjack. He's the one I ride myself, so I'll ride him home this afternoon. The grey is Diana. She's sweet-natured, like Honey, but a little smaller. She might suit you better for a start.'

'Oh, really? She's very pretty.' Lucy was about to climb through the fence.

'Just a minute young lady.' He looked at her shorts and tee shirt. 'Jeans and boots please. And let Mum know you're out here.'

'Okay!' Lucy sang out over her shoulder as she bolted inside to get changed, meeting Nik on the stairs. 'He's brought another horse. A smaller one. For me to ride. Her name's Diana.' Breathless, she disappeared into her room. Nik bounded down the stairs two at a time, herself dressed in shorts, tee shirt and canvas runners.

'Good morning!' She called out. He'd tied the big black horse up at the trough and was walking back to the fence, where the grey mare was quietly grazing.

'Morning Nik.' He smiled in welcome. 'Thought Diana here might suit Lucy better. I want to see if she can reach the stirrup to mount by herself.' He looked at Nik's shorts, grinning. 'I sent her in to get changed. Jeans and boots for horse riding.'

Nik looked down at her long, tanned legs, suddenly self-conscious. 'That's great. But just so you know, I'm not riding, so my attire is perfectly suitable.'

'I thought about that too. Wondered if you might like a riding lesson yourself. Honey would suit you. Then you can ride with Lucy once you both know the basics.' He was chuckling, looking really pleased with himself.

'Well. I don't know. I hadn't really thought about it.' Confused, she blushed and glanced over her shoulder. Lucy was dressed properly, and tearing across the grass toward them, Scout at her side.

He opened the fence for Lucy to climb through. 'Good girl.' He glanced at her laced-up hiking boots.

Nik watched as he introduced Lucy to Diana, in much the same way he had with Honey the day before. After a few minutes, he held the stirrup for Lucy to try. She got her toe in easily and bounded into the saddle with all the vigour of youth and enthusiasm. He handed Lucy the reins, showing her how to hold them. He led the little mare around holding the bridle, speaking quietly to Lucy, who listened intently. Nik sat on the grass with Scout, absorbing the lesson herself.

After half an hour, they came back to the fence. He helped Lucy unsaddle, remove the bridle, and let the horse go. She cantered back to the other horses, standing together at the trough, tossing her head as she went.

'Go and put the kettle on, Luce. We'll have a cuppa with Robbie.' Lucy skipped back to the house, the dog beside her. They watched as she patted Scout at the door, telling her to wait on the veranda. The dog did as she was told. Nik laughed, delighted.

'Thanks Nik. A cuppa will be lovely.' At the veranda, he turned and said, 'Lucy needs a riding hat, we don't have one the right size for her. Good if you got one too. And riding boots. The lace ups are okay for now but riding boots will be needed once she's riding on her own.'

Looking at the boots Robbie wore, Nik realised the difference. Yes, she would get hats and boots for them both. 'What you said before. About me learning to ride too. I'd like that, it's a great idea.' She smiled up at him. 'I don't think doing your accounts will really cover all of this.'

Laughing, he said, 'Wait until you see my accounts. They're a mess. I'm behind in everything …'

Robbie mounted Blackjack. 'I won't be back today; I'm picking up supplies and quotes for the trades we need for the cottage.' Nik waved as he nudged the big horse into a slow canter, watching until horse and rider became small in the distance, grateful for this quietly spoken man, her neighbour and perhaps her friend.

Nik decided to drive into town, there was a saddlery that would sell riding hats and boots. She needed groceries too and wanted to drop in at Evans Real Estate to say hello. She asked Lucy if she wanted to come into town, try on boots and hats, pick up groceries and maybe grab a cold drink from the café. She was expecting a no, but Lucy nodded. 'I can do that, Mum. I'll come with you.'

While Lucy didn't speak to the people in the saddle shop, she happily tried on boots and hats. Walking to the café, they stopped at Evans Real Estate. Nik smiled to see her property in the window with a large red SOLD sign across it.

Lucy hovered behind Nik when Ben Evans stepped forward as they walked through the door. 'Nicola.' He held his hand out to take hers. Looking down at Lucy, he added, 'And you must be Lucy!' She nodded, not looking at him, but he didn't seem to mind.

'How are you settling in out there?' He offered them chairs in front of his desk, taking a seat himself.

'Please, call me Nik. Good actually. It's even better than we hoped.

We've had some work done on the driveway by our neighbour, Robbie Stewart and his son, and he's quoting on some reno's for the cottage now.'

Ben nodded. 'Good man, Robbie. Hard workers, him, and his boy. He's fair too.'

'Yep. Lucky to have him next door. He's going to manage the trades too, which is a big help. But Lucy and I will do some of the smaller jobs, like sanding and painting.'

'And picking paint colours.' This from Lucy, who smiled shyly at Ben.

'Just as well. Most of us blokes are a bit colour blind, Lucy, much better that you and your Mum pick the colours.'

Nik leaned forward. 'I want to ask if you know much about the place. It's history? Robbie thinks there were solid rosewood doors on the front of the cottage at some point, but someone replaced them with cheap modern ones, and I'd love to get the original doors back, if they can be found. Do you think they were sold, or taken away? We haven't looked in the garage or sheds, it's possible they are still on the property.'

'Robbie's right. I remember those doors. There was a time they weren't appreciated, and they'd been painted over. More than once I should think.' He tapped a pencil on the desk, thinking. 'There's never been a clearing sale out there. Unless they were sold privately, you might find them in storage. If they've been kept in a dry place, they would be fine to sand back and refurbish.' He looked across at Nik. 'In fact, see what's still in those sheds. There may be good quality items you can sell, if you wish, or re-purpose. I'd have buyers if you find solid timber pieces you want to sell.'

Standing, Nik said 'Thank you Ben. I'll have a look at what's there. Perhaps you'd care to come out and see what we've got once we've unearthed everything?'

'Just let me know when you're ready. I'll come out and will bring Harriet Russell with me, she has an eye for good pieces.'

'Yes, Harriet. You know she found the place for me in the beginning. We wouldn't have come to this area if not for her.'

'Yes, I know. We're lucky to have her here. She's away for a few days, back in the big smoke, but I'll let her know you came in.' Ben walked them to the door, Lucy smiling at him as they left, her hand in Nik's.

As they strolled up the street, Nik gave her a wink. 'Nice work, Luce. You did well.'

'He is very tall, but nice. I think everyone in this town is nice, Mum. Not like city people.' Releasing her hand, Lucy gave a little skip. Nik nodded, but inwardly wondered how her daughter would cope if they met someone with an unpleasant manner, or scary personage.

10

The next few days passed quickly. Robbie arrived early each morning in his ute. Lucy would meet him at the laundry, already dressed in her riding gear to help him carry the tack out, bring Honey and Diana to the fence and brush them before they put the saddles on. Nik arrived in time for a lesson each day. Robbie walked them around in the paddock, at first adjusting stirrups and the way they held the reins. In just a few days they could ride to the trough and back on their own. Nik admitted she enjoyed it, not just to see Lucy so happy, and gaining confidence each day, but being in sync with Honey, feeling the power of the horse beneath her as she went from a walk to a trot with ease, responding to Nik's hands and knees like the pro that she was.

On the third morning, Robbie told Lucy she could bring the horses over and start brushing them. He had a building job to do. Nik stood on the doorstep, taking in the sight of him lifting a long post out of the back of his ute. She hurried over, taking one end of the post in her hands. 'Morning.' He grinned at her as she helped him carry it to the fence, before walking back to get a second, then a third one.

'Whew.' Nik wiped her forehead with the back of her hand. 'Heavy. What are we doing with these?'

'Well. I thought I'd set up a hitching rail inside the paddock. Safer to tie the horses up to and a bit away from the wire fence. With your permission, I'd like to set a timber gate in here too. Provide access into your place from mine.'

'Okay. Sounds good. Can I help?'

'Not really. I'm going to bring the tractor and post hole digger over, will set the two poles in first, then the pole between them. I'll do it this afternoon, just wanted to drop these off first.' He looked at Lucy, standing in the paddock, brushing Diana down. She had taken a piece of hay in with her, so the horses were content to chew as she brushed them. 'Smart girl.' He nodded to Nik.

'Born cowgirl, I think. Loves it here.' She turned to him, her smile wide. 'Thank you. The horses, and Scout, have done a lot for her. For both of us, actually.' Chuckling, she added, 'I've wrangled your accounts into order already. I've emailed the reports to you. I really think I owe you something. This deal is entirely in my favour.'

He touched her arm. 'It makes me happy to do it. I haven't enjoyed myself so much since… Well, since Jessica was alive, to tell the truth.'

It was the first time he had mentioned his wife since that first day, and Nik looked at him closely. His jaw was a little tense, but his smile reached his eyes. 'Thank you.' She leaned forward and kissed his cheek. It was barely a touch, a mere whisper, but the contact sent blood rushing to her face. And her nether regions. His eyes widened, as did his smile.

They both looked at Lucy, now busy brushing Honey. If she had seen the exchange, she didn't let on. 'Let them go when you're done there, Luce.' Robbie called out. She raised a hand to him. 'Okay!'

Looking at Nik, Robbie said, 'Harry will be over later. He's finished the other job. We're going to pull the existing kitchenette and bathroom out of the cottage. Removing the old tiles may take a bit of time. We want to set the frame for the expanded bathroom up tomorrow morning, as the plumber is due in the afternoon. I couldn't get Sandy Cooper, the local bloke, he's off until late January, having a break with his family over on the coast. I'm using Brandon Baxter, from Stroud, although he does a bit of work locally. His price is right, and I made enquiries about his work, but I really don't know him at all.' Robbie sounded apologetic.

'It's okay. I'm sure he'll be fine. Just pleased you're managing the trades. You know, keeping them honest. And I expected delays, so early in the New Year.' She smiled reassuringly.

Robbie continued. 'I thought I'd give you a hand to pull out some of the stuff in the old garage. We can lay it all out on the grass, check it out. Anything timber, or quality, we can put on the side veranda of the cottage for now, so you can sort through what might be worth keeping.'

'Oh, yes, sounds good. We opened the doors to the old garage the morning before last, intending to make a start. There were scrabbling noises in there. Not sure what it was. Possum, rats, snake?' Nik shuddered. 'I'd feel so much better if you helped us make a start, make sure there's nothing, ugh, *poisonous* in there.' She took a step back.

'May be a possum, but more likely mice. Once we start moving stuff, we'll flush them out.' He didn't mention snakes, but Nik knew it was a very real possibility.

'We might leave our jeans and boots on for this, I think.' She smiled grimly at him. He laughed, touching her shoulder. 'You'll be fine.'

'Quick breakfast first? Lucy has oranges to squeeze, and I'll scramble some eggs on to a bit of toast for us.' Nik inclined her head, smiling.

'Lovely. You're lovely.' He looked across at Lucy, leaving the horses to their hay, Scout trotting beside her. 'I'd love to have breakfast with you. With both of you.'

THE GARAGE DOORS CAME OPEN EASIER THAN THEY HAD FOR NIK. THE DAY was already warm, but Nik kept her boots on, with gardening gloves at the ready, and made sure Lucy did the same. There were pieces of timber, old bed frames, ancient farm equipment, piled almost to the ceiling.

'I reckon this calls for gloves, Luce.' Nik pulled on her own. 'Yuk.' Lucy followed suit. Robbie chuckled.

'I'll climb up, pass some of these pieces down from on top. Let me know if anything is too heavy, and I'll jump down.' Robbie climbed up onto the pile and rummaged about. He passed down a few long pieces of timber, which Nik managed to take, and with Lucy's help stacked them into a pile on the grass outside. Next came a bedhead, then the rest of the bed frame.

'That timber is Australian cedar. We might be able to do something with that,' Robbie called down. Next, he passed down section after section of wrought iron lacework, paint-chipped but in good condition. She held a piece up in front of her, each section was about a metre wide. 'Is this from a veranda do you think?'

'The upstairs veranda on the house had wrought iron lacework at one stage, but a long time ago. You could put it back there, but I think it could work nicely around the veranda of the cottage.'

Lucy looked at the piece Nik was holding. 'Could we do that, Mum?'

'We could paint it white; it would set off the colour we've chosen for the outside walls nicely.' Nik turned the piece as she studied it. 'If there's enough, but if there's not we could just use it on the front part, that people see.' Nik was pleased. She could sand it back and she and Lucy could paint it, so it wouldn't cost anything, really, and it would look great on the cottage.

Robbie started laughing. 'Wait 'til you see what's in here, girls.' He handed down piece after piece of wrought iron. 'There's enough for the whole veranda of the cottage. This would have been around the top and bottom of the house, originally.'

'I'm tempted to put it back around the house, but the upstairs balcony has cleaner lines now. So maybe keep it at the cottage. Either way, we'll use it. What a find.'

Robbie had moved further into the garage, now passing out old tractor seats and rusty farm equipment. Nik couldn't see any use for it, except perhaps as garden ornaments. But she didn't want the place to look kitschy. By mid-morning they had a pile of junk, and another pile of good pieces they could re-purpose. Lucy had gone to the house, bringing back bottles of cold water and a plate of carrot cake. She stayed out the front of the house, playing under the plum tree with Scout, who seemed to be moving more sluggishly.

Robbie stood beside Nik for a moment. 'I think she's due in about a week, maybe two. Could be sooner. She'll lay down in the shade there and rest. Lucy's worked hard with us this morning.' He turned to Nik. 'How old is she? Lucy, I mean. She's quite tall, like you, but I'm guessing about twelve.'

'Eleven, not twelve for another six months. Yes, Lucy is going to be tall, I think.' She looked up at Robbie, standing well over six foot. 'Tall for a woman, that is. I'm five-nine. She might make my height.'

He smiled at her. 'Most kids that age won't stay and help as long as she did. Harry used to disappear after about half an hour unless it was tractor work.' As he spoke, Harry's ute came slowly up the driveway. 'Speak of the devil.' He chuckled, but Nik clearly saw the pride on his face as his strapping son stepped out of his car. He paused at the plum tree, speaking briefly with Lucy, patting Scout, then sauntered across to them.

'Hey Dad. Hi Nik.' He looked at the pile of wrought iron pieces. 'Awesome! Looks like you've found buried treasure in here. Want a hand? Or should we start with the bathroom demolition?' He looked from Nik to his father.

'Another half-hour here, with the three of us, would be perfect.' Nik was enthusiastic and excited to see if there was anything else of value hidden in the old building.

Harry immediately jumped up on the pile, now much lower, and began handing things out to them. 'Oh wow! Hey Nik,' he called, 'there's a lovely old chest of drawers in here, and an old kitchen dresser. Dusty, but doesn't look damaged.'

Robbie waded back in, carrying the two pieces out with Harry. Nik pounced on them. 'The drawers are beautiful.' She opened a couple, running her hands over the timber. 'Is this walnut, do you think?' Robbie had a close look, pulled a whole drawer out and scratched the inside gently.

'Better than walnut. This is rosewood. Sand it back and oil it, the lustre and grain will be stunning. I think it could be more than a hundred years old. Look at the way it's made, all tongue and groove. Beautiful craftsmanship.'

'Oh. What a find. I can't believe it. It would be perfect in the cottage, but I'd love it in my room in the house.' Nik walked from the drawers to the kitchen dresser. 'And this. Stunning. Needs a bit of work too, but how lovely. Also, for the house, I think.' Lucy had wandered over and was busily opening the drawers in the dresser. One small one was stuck. 'Mum, this one is stuck.'

'Don't force it. It may be swollen.' Harry stepped over. 'Let me try.' He pulled at the drawer, tugging gently, then looked underneath. 'There are some papers in the drawer, and one is stuck in the back.' He slid the drawer out about an inch, then slipped two fingers in, pushing the papers down a bit, then inched the drawer out further. After several attempts it was open, and Lucy fell on the contents.

'Be careful, the papers will be old.' Nik looked over her shoulder. Freeing a couple of pieces, tied up with string through a hole in the corner, Lucy turned around, eyes shining. 'They're recipes. Really old recipes.' She gently pulled the bundle out, then reached in, bringing more bundles out, then a couple of envelopes. Turning to them, she commanded, 'Don't touch these, I'm going to get some plastic sleeves from Mum's office to put them in, they're very fragile.'

'Yes ma'am.' Harry grinned at her as she shot off. Looking at Nik, he said, 'we're nearly done, I'm going to see what else is at the back. There's something leaning against the back wall that looks a bit like old doors.'

She nodded eagerly as the two men rummaged around behind an old tractor body, eventually emerging, carrying a large door between them. They strode back in and returned with another, leaning them against the chest of drawers, before grinning in unison at Nik.

'Are these what I think they are?' She rubbed the dust off a section of the door. 'They're so thick. And heavy.'

Harry, dust in his hair, slapped Robbie on the back. 'Yup, they are. Not just the original doors of the cottage. They're the original court-house doors. Solid rosewood, they'll be beautiful after they've been sanded and polished.'

Nik laughed, but threw a questioning look at the two men. 'How do you know they're the original courthouse doors?'

Robbie laughed and turned over the door nearest to him. Rubbing with his elbow, he cleaned an old brass plaque in the centre. Nik leant closer. *Barrington Courthouse, 1891.*

She hugged them, first Harry, then Robbie, before calling out to Lucy who was walking back from the house with plastic folders in her hand. 'Luce! See what we've got!'

Running the last few metres Lucy had a look. 'Wow!' She hugged Nik. 'Do you think we should put them on the house, though?'

'No, I don't. They would have been on the top part, with external stairs going up to the courthouse. The stairs have long since gone. No, I think they're perfect for the cottage. It's just what we hoped to find. I can't imagine why anyone would have replaced them in the first place!'

Robbie raised his eyebrows. 'Remember all those solid timber kitchens our grandparents had in the sixties? Replaced by bright orange and green Formica in the seventies? And solid timber tables replaced by laminate ones? Fashion trends. Not always good.'

He looked around, at the pieces on the ground, and leaning against furniture. 'There are a couple of old tractors still in there. I suggest we stack the pieces back in that you don't want. There is a second-hand store in town. They'll come out with a truck and take what you don't need, you might even get a bit of cash for some of it.'

Nodding, Nik glanced around. 'Good. Thanks. I'll call them today. But all the wrought iron, the furniture, and those doors. I need to store them safely for now, away from the cottage while the work is going on.'

'How about downstairs in the house. The back bedrooms. If you're not going to work on those until the cottage is finished, that may be the place. We can make some room around the chest of drawers, the kitchen dresser and the doors, so we can get to them for sanding and polishing.' Robbie nodded at Harry, who was already lifting pieces of wrought iron. 'We'll get the good stuff safely away first, son. The rest can lay out here today, it's likely they'll come and look at it tomorrow.'

Nik and Lucy began to work with them, carrying the lighter timber pieces back to the house. They laid everything on the ground, letting the men stack it inside in a sensible manner. Lucy chatted as she went, occasionally asking Robbie, or Harry a question about a particular piece. What it was used for, how old it was. She was no longer shy or reticent with them.

Nik hadn't felt so happy in a long time. Every now and again she met Robbie's eyes, to find him looking at her, amusement clear on his face. Once, when she passed him a piece of timber, his hand touched hers. She blushed and looked at him quickly. Robbie stood still for a moment, the muscle in his jaw twitching slightly. Taken aback Nik looked away and kept working.

11

Faint beams of sunlight tumbled through the window, waking Nik just after dawn. Stretching, she yawned and threw back the sheet. The night had been warm. Clad only in singlet and knickers, she padded through to Lucy's room. The bed was empty, the covers pulled up haphazardly. Smiling, Nik went back to the window in her room that overlooked Robbie's paddock. Lucy was down there, feeding hay to the mares.

Capturing her hair in a high ponytail, Nik threw on her jeans from yesterday, with a bra and clean tank top. She added canvas runners. Nik didn't think they'd have time for a riding lesson today, as they hadn't finished the demolition in the cottage yesterday and the plumber was due mid-morning.

Hurrying downstairs, she noted her legs and shoulders were stiff and sore from yesterday's exertions. Lucy walked through the door, smiling happily. 'Morning, Mum. I've fed the horses. Robbie and Harry are already in the cottage and he said he'd give me a lesson this afternoon, after the plumber has been.'

'Good girl. Can you pop some toast in while I dash over and see if the men need anything?' Nik was out the door as she spoke, but she saw Lucy nod while taking her boots off.

The front doors had been taken off the cottage and all the windows and doors were open. Dust swirled around in the main room, the men wearing masks over their nose and mouth, oblivious she had arrived as they ripped up tiles in the kitchen section, the old cupboards and stove already gone.

Stepping closer, she covered her mouth and nose with her hand. Robbie looked up, saw her, and reached out to tap Harry on the shoulder, who looked up and stopped his work too.

'Morning, Nik. Don't stay in here while we're doing this, at least not without a mask.' Robbie straightened as he spoke, pulling his mask down, flashing a quick smile in her direction.

'Morning Nik.' Harry echoed, putting his tools down and stretching his arms over his head.

'You started early. Thanks so much.' She stepped closer. 'Have you had breakfast? I can bring some toasted sandwiches out, or you can come back to the house.'

'We had something at home before we left.' Robbie gestured towards the floor, more than half of the tiles already removed. 'The bathroom's done and we removed the walls to the bedrooms yesterday, just leaving the main studs and beams in place until we're ready to put the new walls in.' He wiped his eyes with the back of his arm, leaving a smear of dirt across his forehead. 'I reckon we'll be done here in another hour. If it's okay with you and Lucy, we'll come over and have a cuppa with you then. After that Harry will take some of this rubbish to the tip. The plumber, Baxter, should be here by then.'

'Great. Come over when you're ready. Is there anything we can do here to help?' Nik looked around, it was mostly done, and the last bit required plenty of strength.

'Thanks, but we've got this covered. I've left a plan of your proposed new bathroom on the front seat of the ute. Can you get it out and have a look? I want to make sure you're happy with it before we get Baxter to locate the pipes.' Nik nodded as he added 'It's not a problem to move things around if you want to reconfigure it.'

'Okay, I'll grab it, we'll have a look while you're finishing this bit.' Nik turned to leave, then turned back. 'Is Scout with you today? I didn't see her as I came over?'

Robbie stood, looked at Harry for a moment, who raised his eyebrows in surprise. 'She came with us. She's close to having the pups, she might just be laying somewhere cool. Can you please check on her, but come back if you can't find her? I don't want her getting under the house or somewhere it'll be hard to get her out of, if she's ready to whelp.'

Nodding, Nik hurried back to the house, checking in the shed first, then under the plum tree. Lucy was on the veranda. 'Have you seen Scout?' She shook her head but started to pull her boots back on. 'Can you lay down and look under the house, Luce?' Worried, Nik bit her lip, wondering where else the dog may be resting. The noise and dust in the cottage would keep her away from there, but she usually lay on the veranda or under the plum tree during the day.

Standing up, Lucy shook her head. 'She's not under there, Mum. Have you checked she's not in the shed we worked on yesterday? Nik nodded. 'We'll find her. Robbie said she might be looking for somewhere quiet and cool to have her pups.'

Standing still Lucy looked at Nik, her mouth a round 'O' shape. 'Her pups? You think she'll have them here? At our house?' She was delighted.

'Maybe. He thinks they're due any day now.'

'The laundry!' Lucy shot around the side of the house, Nik right behind her. The laundry door was closed, and Scout was nowhere about.

'I'll go over to Robbie. They'll have to help us look.' Nik left Lucy on the veranda, jogging back to the cottage. She returned a few minutes later, Robbie and Harry on her heels. Lucy wasn't where she had left her, but perhaps she'd gone upstairs.

'Scout may have headed for home, perhaps back through the paddock. I'll take one of the horses and look that way.' Robbie turned to Harry. 'Can you go back to the shed, she might've gone right inside, under one of the tractors.' About to head their separate ways, Lucy appeared, a happy smile on her face.

'I've found her. I called to her when Mum ran across to the cottage. She was right here the whole time.' She gestured inside the house. 'The front door has been open all morning, since I got up to feed the horses.' They followed her inside, to Nik's little office.

Looking under the desk, they found Scout, curled up on a cardigan Nik had left on the back of her chair days ago, which had fallen to the floor. Lucy had pulled the chair out, and was down on her haunches, speaking quietly to Scout.

Robbie knelt beside her. 'Hey girl, are you ready to have your babies?' He reached in, scratching Scout behind the ears. He was about to slide her out from under the desk, on the cardigan, when Harry, who was laying on the floor now, half under the desk, help up his hand. 'Stop, Dad. We can't move her now. Have a look.'

Harry shimmied out and Robbie took his place. He shuffled to one side. 'Lucy, come under here, Have a look.' Lucy didn't hesitate, dropping to the floor and crawling under the desk, right beside Robbie. Nik tried to peer in, but it was dark under there. 'Oh, there's one already! No two!' Lucy's excitement was evident, although she was trying to whisper.

Robbie backed out and stood up. 'Sorry Nik. She's started whelping. I'd rather not move her just yet. But, um, your cardigan …'

Nik touched his arm. 'It doesn't matter. It's an old one. What can we do to help her?'

Lucy backed out. 'Now there's three. She's licking them. They're tiny and their eyes are closed.' She was breathless with excitement.

'We need to bring her water bowl in here, and one of us needs to stay with her. She'll let us know if she's in trouble. She'll yelp or get agitated.' Robbie looked at Lucy. 'What do you say, Lucy, do you want to sit with her, make sure she has water and tell us if you think she's upset?'

Nodding wordlessly, Lucy shot outside, returning with the water bowl, half full, in her hands. She slowly slid it under the desk, where Scout could reach it. Wagging her tail, she lapped at the water for a moment, her eyes thanking Lucy. 'There's four now!' Lucy slid back out.

Nik dropped to her knees, reached under, and patted Scout gently. 'Okay, Luce. You stay here. I'll bring some toast down for you and an orange juice. I'll be nearby too.'

'How many will she have Mum?' Nik turned to Robbie, who shook his head slightly. 'Hard to say, this could be it, just four, but she could have seven or eight.'

'She seems okay though. Not upset or having trouble?' Nik frowned a little as she asked.

'It's her second litter. She had four last time, no problem at all. Best just to have someone nearby, she'll let us know if she needs help.' Robbie smiled reassuringly, before moving back to the veranda where Harry was already putting his boots on. 'We'll be over for that cuppa in less than an hour. She should be done by then. But come and get me if you need to.' He put his boots on, nudged Harry, who nudged him back, laughing, then strode off toward the cottage, his son by his side.

Nik went back to Lucy. 'Five now Mummy. Scout is licking them all. They are crawling around near her tummy.'

'Okay, sweetheart. I'll fix us some breakfast and we can sit down here and have it while we keep an eye on Scout and her puppies.'

Less than ten minutes later, Nik was navigating her way down the stairs, a plate of toast in one hand and a glass of juice in the other. About to set them on her desk, Lucy cried out. 'One of them isn't moving Mum! Quick, get Robbie. It's really small. Smaller than the others. It's number seven!' Lucy sounded distressed. Nik dumped the items she was carrying on the earnest surface and slid under beside Lucy. Scout was licking the tiny pup, but it wasn't moving at all. She nudged it toward Nik and Lucy. Nik reached out, speaking softly to the dog. 'We'll have a look at your baby, Scout. Don't worry.'

Nik had the puppy in her hand, sliding out from under the desk she sat up, Lucy beside her, starting to cry. 'Don't let it die, Mummy, do something.'

Nik held the puppy up, sticky stuff covering its mouth and nose. Afterbirth, she thought, this is what Scout was trying to lick off. She pulled up the hem of her tank top and gently cleaned the mucus from the tiny pup's face and mouth. It didn't move. She gently prised its mouth open, putting her finger in, cleared more of the stuff out. It still didn't move, and Scout was starting to whimper. Lucy stood. 'I'm getting Robbie!' She ran from the room, crying.

Nik wiped a tear from her eye as she placed the little pup close to

Scout. 'I'm sorry. I don't think this one is going to make it.' She watched, crying softly as Scout licked and nudged the pup. Hearing footsteps on the veranda, she turned as Robbie came in. He put a hand on her shoulder. 'This happens sometimes, with a big litter.'

He slid under the desk, talking to Scout quietly. Moments later he was back out, smiling at Nik and Lucy. 'Have a look.'

They shimmied under, the littlest pup was moving its head, searching for a nipple at Scout's belly with its siblings. Scout thumped her tail against the floor, a doggy smile on her face.

Nik came back out, leaving Lucy to watch. She stood, and Robbie put his arms around her, holding her tight for a moment. 'Lucy told me you cleared the mucus off its face, even out of its mouth. You saved it, Nik, good job.'

Smiling through her tears, she stepped back, but felt a brief sense of loss as Robbie released her from his embrace.

12

———————

The sound of a vehicle driving in sent them outside. A large grey van, *Baxter Plumbing* across the side and rear doors, drove over to the cottage.

Robbie and Nik walked across together while Harry stepped out from the cottage. Brendan Baxter was a solid man, not as tall as Robbie, but broader through the shoulders, hips, and legs. He had a strong face, large nose, prominent jaw. Handsome in an obvious sort of way, Nik thought.

He greeted the men with a handshake but brazenly looked Nik up and down before taking her outstretched hand by just her fingertips, giving a quick shake. She frowned. It was one of her pet hates when men wouldn't shake a woman's hand properly. He made her uncomfortable, his look intense, almost a leer.

Robbie stepped forward and she could tell he wasn't impressed either. 'Just in here, Brendan. Can you confirm the price you gave based on the plans I emailed through?' Directing him inside, Nik wasn't sure if she should stay, or just leave it to Robbie.

Harry followed them in then popped back out to Nik. 'Dad says you might want to see if the second-hand bloke can come out for a look at the stuff in the old shed today, or tomorrow. He doesn't think you need to hang around for the plumbing.'

Nodding, Nik said quietly, 'Thanks, Harry. I'll give them a call now. And I also told Ben Evans I'd give him a call. If Harriet Russell is back from Sydney, they might want to have a look too.'

Back at the house Nik checked on Lucy and Scout. Seven was the magic number, and all the puppies were feeding while Scout lay back. Lucy had given her more water but wasn't sure what else she should do. 'Just stay nearby I think, Lucy.' Nik hesitated. 'The plumber is here. Um, Luce, just stay away from the cottage okay? He's not like Robbie and Harry.'

Lucy looked startled but nodded. Nik went upstairs and changed from her figure-hugging tank top to an old, baggy tee shirt, which she left out over her jeans. Baxter's eyes had roved over her body, making her feel uncomfortable. She wasn't going to give him anything to look at in the future.

About an hour later, they heard footsteps on the veranda. Nik walked out, cautiously. It was Robbie. 'You alright?' He looked at Nik with concern. If he noticed her change of top, he didn't mention it.

'Sure. I hope his work is better than his manner with customers.'

'Agreed. If Sandy wasn't away until the end of the month, I'd send Baxter packing. He was rude, Nik. I'm sorry.'

'Not your fault. But I don't want him near Lucy.' Nik spoke quietly, glancing over her shoulder to make sure Lucy was out of earshot.

'Harry's going to hang around in the cottage while he's here, do a bit of work on the new walls.' Robbie didn't have to add that Harry wasn't going to let the plumber come near the house, but Nik knew that's what he meant. She was grateful. Just meeting him had her nerves on edge. He was exactly the personality type that would terrify Lucy.

'Thank you.' She gave Robbie a small smile. Lucy popped out, a wide smile stretched across her face. 'There's seven puppies. Minnie was the last one.'

'Minnie?' Robbie and Nik spoke together.

'She's smaller than the others.' Lucy sounded defensive but couldn't seem to take the smile off her face.

'Minnie she is then.' Robbie gave Lucy a quick grin as he spoke. 'I'll check on them, then we might leave Mum with them while we have a riding lesson.'

'Oh, good. I'll get my boots.' Lucy rushed upstairs. They moved into the study. 'We need to move Scout from here, but I'm not sure about taking her home today. Do you think she could stay in the downstairs laundry for a few days, until the pups are a bit stronger? And just so you know, Minnie may get pushed around by the bigger pups. Natural selection kicks in with a big litter, and I may have to hand feed her if she weakens.'

'Oh, I didn't know that. About the pups.' Nik clarified. 'And yes, I'm happy for her to be here. What can I set up in the laundry to make it comfortable for her?'

'An old blanket or a couple of towels will be good if you have them. I can shoot home and bring her normal bedding back with me later, and some food for her.' Lucy reappeared, all geared up and ready. 'I'll take Lucy for a lesson, then we'll see if Scout's ready to move when we get back.'

'I'll stay here. I've got to do a load of washing, and I'll move things around in the laundry to make a cosy spot for her.' Nik and Robbie exchanged quick smiles as they watched Lucy hurry toward the horses.

It was almost two hours later when Lucy reappeared, her face pink with excitement. 'I went for a proper ride. Not on the lead rope, but *by myself!*' She emphasised the last two words, adding, 'we rode all the way to Robbie's house. Well, not quite, but we could see it in the distance. And there was a paddock with Blackjack and other horses. He has a lot of horses!'

'Wow! You're really doing well. Where's Robbie now?' Nik looked past Lucy, in the doorway, but couldn't see him.

'He went over to the cottage to check on the work. He helped me unsaddle, then I brushed them and fed them by myself.'

'Good girl. How about you run up and take a shower, put some clean clothes on. You smell like a horse.' Nik wrinkled her nose, laughing.

~

THE AFTERNOON WORE ON. NIK HAD CALLED BEN EVANS. HE AND HARRIET were going to come out at ten the next morning to check out the pieces they'd found in the old garage, see if any of it was worth selling. She was looking forward to seeing Harriet again. She was younger than Nik but had lived in Sydney for a long time and now had a good life and thriving business out here, helping people like herself relocate to the region.

It was late in the afternoon when she saw the plumber drive out in his van. She breathed a sigh of relief. He really had unnerved her. Lucy was sitting cross-legged a few metres from where Scout lay with her puppies, reading quietly. Nik had told her to stop handling the puppies, to let them feed and rest. Scout seemed rested too.

Robbie and Harry appeared on the veranda.

'How'd it go?' Nik looked from one to the other.

'There's more to do, once we get the walls set and ready to put the fixtures in. But that won't be until later next week.' Robbie looked at Harry, then Nik. 'We won't use him for the work we do here, in the house, later on. Sandy Cooper will be back for that.'

Harry added, 'His work is fine, I really can't fault anything he's done today. But I've seen him in the pub a few times. He gets a bit aggressive after a beer or two. Dad's right, you don't need tradies like that hanging around.'

They took their boots off and came in to visit Scout and the puppies. Robbie explained to Harry and Lucy that they should stay for a few days, but they needed to move them to the laundry.

'I've put down an old blanket, and a towel, and made a bit of a nest in the corner behind the door for her.' Nik put her arm around Lucy. 'What's the best way to move them in there?'

'We'll get Lucy to take Minnie, and we'll each pick up two pups. I'll call Scout and she'll follow us in.'

Lucy shimmied under the counter, speaking softly to Scout. After patting her gently she picked up Minnie, cradling her against her chest.

Robbie called Scout to him, and she quietly stood, and walked out, looking behind at the pups that were all bundled together, crawling over each other and whimpering. Harry slid Nik's cardigan out, the pups huddled together on it. He handed a pup each to Nik and Robbie and scooped the rest up in the cardigan. Robbie picked up the water bowl and they walked around to the laundry on the veranda, Scout right beside Lucy all the way.

They settled Scout on the blanket and gently placed all the pups against her belly, where they immediately squirmed and nudged each other, seeking a nipple to feed from. Robbie put the water bowl down close to her head. Harry had the cardigan in his hand. 'I'll take this home and wash it Nik.'

She laughed and took it from his hand. 'We're in a laundry right now. I'll rinse it, then soak it. But if it can't be saved, I'll put it back in with Scout once it's dry.'

'Will I put the kettle on, Mum?' Lucy asked.

'How about a beer, boys? I bought some when I went into town. I think we should celebrate the new arrivals.' She raised her eyebrows in question.

'I won't say no.' Harry laughed. 'Show me where the fridge is Lucy; we'll get the drinks. Do you want one too, Nik?'

'Sure. And Lucy you can have a coke.' Harry followed Lucy out, while Nik and Robbie continued to watch the pups. Nik turned to speak to Robbie but noted a look of concern on his face. She looked back at the dogs.

'What is it?'

'The little one, Minnie. The bigger pups are pushing her away and she isn't getting a feed. If she doesn't drink soon, she might not make it until morning. Nik, I hope you don't mind, but I need to stay here overnight to hand feed her. I don't want to lose her; Lucy is already so attached.'

Surprised, she looked at the puppies again. Robbie was right. Every time Minnie latched onto a nipple one of the bigger puppies pushed her out of the way. Scout gave her a few licks but seemed resigned to the situation.

'Of course, you can stay. I'll sit up with you, we can take it in turns to feed her. How do we do it, I really have no idea.'

'Warm milk and an eyedropper. Her tummy is tiny, she needs milk every couple of hours.'

Lucy and Harry returned, handing around drinks while Robbie explained the situation. Harry nodded. 'I'll go home and get a few things for Scout, and for you Dad for the morning. After that I'll pick up pizzas from the pub, if it's okay with the girls, we can all eat here tonight.'

'Yes. Good thinking, son.' Robbie turned to Nik and then Lucy. 'Does this work for you?' They both nodded but Nik didn't miss his real concern and added 'Yes, of course.'

HARRY LEFT AT NINE, HAVING EATEN A WHOLE PIZZA WASHED DOWN WITH two beers. Lucy helped feed Minnie twice, then Nik sent her to bed, promising she would wake her if the tiny pup wasn't doing well.

'Why don't you go to bed too, Nik? I'll feed her again at midnight, then two in the morning. We should know by then if she'll make it.' Robbie smiled tiredly at Nik.

She looked at him. He had arrived at dawn and worked hard all day. He must be exhausted. 'I'll sit up with you. If you doze off, I'll feed her. I want her to live as much as you do.'

So, they sat, on the floor of the laundry, backs against the wall, occasionally chatting. Robbie told Nik about his early life camp drafting, then meeting Jessica when he was nineteen. 'Harry's age. We were married inside two years. She worked in childcare, but once Harry came along, we bought the farm, and she helped run it while I ran the building business. It was my father's and I had completed an apprenticeship before I went on the camp draft circuit. At the time I wasn't keen to take over the business, but having a wife and child changed all that. By the time I was twenty-five I was running it with Dad. He died when Harry was twelve.' Robbie looked down. 'I miss him every day. Almost as much as Jess. And Isobel.'

'Isobel?' Nik saw raw pain in Robbie's eyes.

'Our little girl. She only lived three weeks. Born early, too tiny. Her lungs never fully developed.' He looked at Nik, raw emotion etched into his face. 'She'd be twelve now. Close to Lucy's age.'

13

The catch in his voice, pain on his face, made Nik reach for him. They were sitting side by side. She took his face, leaned in, and gently kissed his cheek. He moved his head and caught the edge of her mouth with his. Closing her eyes, Nik moved her mouth against his. It was a tender kiss, full of promise, but she forced herself to break contact.

'Nik?' his voice was gravelly, his need clear.

Shaking her head, she swallowed a sob. 'I can't Robbie. You're lovely. Warm, gentle, strong. But I can't.'

He took her hand in his, but she pulled away. 'What happened to you Nik? To you and Lucy? Who hurt you? Let me understand.' But she shook her head.

'I will tell you. One day. But you need to know it was my fault. It was all my fault. I made a terrible choice. I chose someone, after my marriage ended. A long time after. We were on our own for five years. I fell for him. Trusted him. Quickly. Too quickly. By the time I realised he wasn't who I thought he was, it was too late. The damage was done.' She angrily swiped tears from her eyes with the back of her hand, ignoring Robbie's look of sympathy. 'He hurt us. Physically. Emotionally. It can never be undone. Never be forgotten. But we're learning to live with it. These last couple of weeks have been amazing. Lucy gaining confidence. You, Harry, Scout. The horses. But Robbie, I promised her I would never let a man into our lives again. Into our family. Friendship is all I can offer.'

He withdrew his hand and nodded, leaning his head back against the wall. 'I understand, Nik. I haven't been interested in anyone since I lost Jessica. And you are lovely. And there's Lucy. I imagine Isobel would have been like her, crazy about horses and dogs. Gentle. Smart.' He nudged her gently with his shoulder. 'But I can be friends. Friendship is good. Strong. Friendship will last. You're okay with me Nik. I won't push.'

Looking at him in the dim light, hearing the sincerity in his voice, the affection, she almost caved and reached for him. But she'd promised Lucy. She smiled, not sure if he could see her expression. 'We'll be great friends, Robbie. I'm so lucky we have you and Harry in our lives.'

Scout raised her head, then stood. Robbie scrambled to his feet. 'I think she needs to go outside for a minute. I'll take her if you can watch the pups.'

Nik scooted closer to the pups, who were sleeping together like a big bundle of wriggly fur.

SHE WOKE WHEN ROBBIE GENTLY TOUCHED HER ARM. THE SUN WAS coming up, and the puppies were squirming against Scout's belly. She looked at them, thumping her tail on the floor a few times. He reached over, extracting Minnie from the bundle. They had last fed her at two. He turned her over, her little tummy was as tight as a drum.

'She's had a feed by herself. I watched her shove one of the bigger ones away about an hour ago. I think she'll be okay.' They smiled tiredly at each other as he gently placed the pup against her mother.

Lucy appeared in the doorway, still in her pyjamas. 'Is Minnie okay?' she whispered.

'Come and see.' Nik held out her arms and Lucy plonked down on her lap, looking closely at Scout and the puppies.

'Oh, look Robbie, she's drinking by herself. That's good, isn't it?' Lucy looked hopefully at Robbie.

'It sure is. She's a determined little thing.' He cleared his throat. 'You know the pups won't open their eyes until they're about ten days old?'

Lucy nodded. 'I looked that up on google last night.'

Robbie continued. 'We're going to be here almost every day for the next couple of weeks. If it's alright with you and Mum, I think Scout and the pups should stay here. She'd be alone during the day at home, but here she has you to look after her.'

'Can we, Mum? Can we keep them here? I promise to look after her and clean up after the pups.' Lucy screwed up her nose, then pointed to the damp mess on the old towel.

'It's a great idea. And I'll help you. If you can show me, and Robbie, how responsible you are with them, he might let us keep Minnie when she's old enough to be weaned.' Robbie and Nik had talked about it during the night and agreed that Lucy could have Minnie.

'For real? True?' Lucy hugged her mother, then threw herself into Robbie's arms, giving him a giant hug, before scooting over to the pups and extracting Minnie for a cuddle. Robbie was surprised, and moved, by Lucy's show of affection.

Standing, he walked to the laundry door, looking out at the horses in the paddock nearby. 'Let's get the horses fed Lucy, then I'll have a quick shower and change.'

Nik joined them at the door. 'There's a fresh towel in the bathroom upstairs and I'll whip up some scrambled eggs on toast. It's been a long night.'

14

Harry arrived, and although he said he'd had breakfast at home, tucked into a serve of scrambled eggs too. Lucy dragged him to the laundry to show him how well the pups were doing. It was amazing how comfortable Lucy was with him. Like a big brother. Nik swallowed a lump in her throat, stealing a look at Robbie. He was staring at the doorway, where the kids had been a moment before. Turning, he looked at her, his eyes dark with emotion, and pain. Breaking his gaze, he took his plate to the sink.

Gathering herself, she cleared the rest of the table. 'I'll do these. You've been working every day for the last couple of weeks. Are you sure you wouldn't like to take the day off, spend some time at home? Catch up on some sleep?'

'And do what? Harry fed the stock at home this morning. We can get those new walls up today, and I'd like to be here when Ben and Harriet come to look at the pieces we found. We might call it a day after that, if you and Lucy are fine with Scout and the puppies.'

Nik washed and Robbie dried. The horses were in clear view from the kitchen window. Harry carried some hay over, Lucy beside him with a brush in each hand. It was obvious they were talking, while they brushed the two mares. Then Harry put the brushes on the top of a fence post, picked up some straw from the hay bundle and threw it at Lucy, before taking off toward the trough. She raced after him, laughing. She chased him around the trough twice, then reached in and flicked water at him. He flicked her back, then chased her to the fence. With his long legs, he could have caught her twice over, but he stayed just behind while she squealed in mock terror.

Nik looked at Robbie. He just nodded at the window. 'He's a good lad. Good-natured. But he'll fire up if someone, or something, is unjust or unfair. Got into a few scraps at school, but generally he was standing up for a mate. Can't criticise him for that.' Hanging the tea towel in front of the oven, Robbie turned to Nik. 'He took it hard when his mother died, he was only fifteen, but in a way, it's made us closer.' She glanced out the window, Lucy and Harry were no longer in sight. She nodded her understanding.

A bellow from downstairs made them laugh out loud. 'Hey Dad, are you going to come and finish this job in the cottage, or are you up there baking cakes or something?' They heard Lucy giggle. Then Harry added, more quietly, 'Honestly, the only thing Dad can cook is steak on the barbecue. Or sausages. Oh, and chops and bacon. We'd starve to death if it weren't for me; and Debbie's café in town.' Harry laughed again, Lucy giggling with him.

Grinning, Robbie called back. 'I heard that, Harry Stewart. Be prepared to work up a sweat because we're going to finish the bathroom walls this morning!'

'And I'll bake you a cake!' Lucy's girlish voice rang out.

'Excellent, Luce. I was hoping you'd say that.' Harry's voice was light and teasing.

'Behave, Harry Stewart, or you won't have any cake,' Lucy responded, using Harry's full name like Robbie had, making Nik snort with laughter. Robbie grinned, winked at Nik then ran downstairs, two at a time.

NIK CHECKED ON THE PUPPIES, FILLED SCOUT'S WATER BOWL AND GAVE HER the dog food Harry had brought from home. Leaving the laundry door ajar so she could slip out if she needed to, they went back to the kitchen upstairs. Lucy baked a carrot cake while Nik made another big batch of lemonade.

At exactly ten, Ben and Harriet arrived in a modern Range Rover with *Evans Real Estate* lettering on the doors. Harriet was small and slim, with thick honey blonde hair, dressed in capri pants and a loose cotton peasant top, canvas runners on her feet. Lucy smiled shyly as they walked out to greet them, standing back a bit until Harriet asked her what the delicious smell was. 'Have you or Mum been baking, Lucy?'

'I have. Carrot cake for morning tea.' She looked up at Harriet, adding, 'Mum made lemonade. From our own lemons. It's for you and Mr Evans. And Robbie and Harry.'

'I knew a morning visit was a good idea.' Harriet nudged Ben, who smiled warmly down at Lucy.

Nik led them to the old garage. Robbie and Harry joined them. 'Morning Ben, Harriet.' They shook hands warmly.

Robbie and Harry dragged a couple of the old tractors out for Ben to inspect, and Harriet and Nik found another old kitchen dresser, falling apart, but stacked with old china; platters, cups and saucers, mismatched pieces, some quite lovely.

By eleven-thirty they had another small pile of stuff to keep and a stack for the second-hand store. Ben made an offer on the old tractors and farm equipment, saying he had a couple of buyers for those. Nik took Ben and Harriet into the back bedrooms of the downstairs section of the house, showing them the chest of drawers; the dresser, plus the wrought iron lacework they would use on the cottage veranda, while Robbie and Harry brought the few extra pieces including the tableware, in for safekeeping.

Lucy had set up a folding table on the house veranda, with checked tablecloth, and laid out the carrot cake, plates, lemonade, and glasses.

'You've got so much done already, Nik. Much quicker than I expected. And your ideas for the cottage and house are great. I don't think you will have any trouble attracting guests here. In fact, you're such a success story for my own endeavours, bringing folk here for a permanent tree-change, I'd love to recommend your accommodation when I have buyers in the area needing somewhere to stay for a few days. Seeing how well you're doing will make my job,' Harriet turned to Ben and smiled, 'and Ben's so much easier. You're a walking advertisement.'

Nik happily agreed. Seeing the bathroom taking shape in the cottage, with all the old tiles and fixtures pulled out, had created a blank canvas and she was eager to start putting it together. 'I'll set a launch date, Harriet. Wondering if I should hold an event, you know, a morning tea or something out here for locals to see it.' She nibbled her bottom lip. 'And I need to find someone to help with a marketing strategy, a website, social media, publicity. I know a little bit about such things, but I'm no expert.' She sighed, 'I'm an accountant, we're not usually known for our creativity.'

'Oh, I don't know Nik. You might be selling yourself short. But Harriet can give you some guidance.' Ben cleared his throat. 'And there is a woman just up the road we can introduce you to. She's a graphic artist. Did the design work for our new branding.' He inclined his head toward the signage on his vehicle.

Looking over at the signs, Nik admitted the branding was eye-catching. 'Okay. All recommendations gratefully accepted, thank you.'

Robbie and Harry had returned to the cottage, close to finishing the bathroom walls while Lucy wandered off to see the puppies.

Walking Ben and Harriet to their car, Nik thanked them for coming out. Graeme from the second-hand shop was arriving the next day and would pick the tractor pieces up for Ben at the same time. Standing with Harriet for a moment before she stepped up into the car, Nik said quietly. 'Thank you, Harriet. I'm so glad I responded to your marketing message. This move is already working out better than I hoped. Especially for Lucy.'

Harriet gave Nik a warm hug. 'This place has a way of getting to you Nik. I was just passing through more than a year ago, when a mishap with my car left me stranded for a bit. Best thing that ever happened to me.'

Waving them off, Nik felt a lightness in her shoulders and an unfamiliar feeling in herself. She analysed it as she strolled back to the house. It was happiness. She was feeling happy. For the first time in almost a year.

THE WORK ON THE BATHROOM WAS LARGELY FINISHED, BUT ROBBIE, AND sometimes Harry, turned up most days, sanding back the floorboards inside and around the deck. The new bathroom fixtures were due in at the end of the week when the plumber would come back to install them. The boys had put in a basic kitchenette, the cupboards had a heritage look and Nik and Lucy decided on the final colour scheme, buying the paint from the local hardware store.

Mid-week, on the way back from town, Nik pulled into the little Barrington Public School. It was school holidays and empty, but they had a walk around and peered through the windows of the three class-rooms. 'Do you think you'd like to come here, Lucy, at the start of term? I had thought to keep home-schooling you, but Harry went to this school and said he loved it. It has about sixty students and only three teachers. Not big at all.'

Lucy didn't answer straightaway, but she walked around thought-fully, pointing out the tennis court and playing field to one side of the buildings and the library now in the original old schoolhouse. A sign proudly declared the school was established in 1864. 'Look, Mum, gosh, it's really old.' She turned around in a circle, taking in the small, neat campus. 'I think I'd like to come here. Is this really where Harry went to school?'

'It is. I think Robbie went to school here too. And his father. What do you think?'

Tucking her hand into Nik's she leant against her briefly. 'Well … I've still got a year before High School. If I start here next term, I might make some friends to go to high school with later.' This was said with a firm little nod of her head. Nik squeezed her hand lightly. 'Good idea. That's a really positive way to look at it. I'm proud of you.'

ON THURSDAY MORNING A LARGE TRUCK PULLED IN, UNLOADING ALL THE bathroom fixtures. Lucy watched from the veranda as Nik directed the burly delivery men to place everything just inside the main room of the cottage. Harry had gone to Rawden Vale for the day to finish work on a fence and Robbie said he would be at home working with his young horses, but to call him if they needed help unloading.

Everything was out of the truck inside an hour, with Nik choosing not to disturb Robbie who had been at his own place so little in the last three weeks.

Robbie had advised the plumber, Brendan Baxter, that the fixtures would be delivered and expected him to come over the next day to begin installing them.

15

The plumber's van arrived that afternoon and as Nik walked across to speak to him, she secretly wished he hadn't come until the next day, as Robbie had requested, when he would be there too. She really didn't like the way he looked at her.

Baxter was already in the cottage, unwrapping the new bath.

'Hi Nik. Thought I'd get a start on this. You've chosen some great quality pieces.' He smiled at her, but she saw his eyes rove over her body as he did.

Looking directly at him, she stepped into the room. 'Thank you, Brendan. Good bathrooms seem to attract guests. I'm pleased with what we've chosen too.' She was standing by the large claw foot bath, deep and wide, big enough for two, it would take pride of place in the new bathroom.

He stepped closer to her, stroking the edge of the bath. 'Oh yes, this is a beauty. Who wouldn't love to take a soak in this one, especially with a sexy woman?' He winked at her as he spoke. 'Perhaps we should take it for a test run, once I've got it installed.' Nik took a step back.

'That won't be happening.' Turning, she walked to the door. 'I'll leave you to your work.'

'Aw, don't be like that. You're an attractive woman, living here by yourself. You must be missing a little male company.' He walked toward her. 'I'd be happy to help you out, if you know what I mean.'

With her heart suddenly racing, Nik tried to remain calm. 'I'm paying for your plumbing services, Mr Baxter. Nothing else.'

She stepped outside and closed the door firmly, but not before she heard him snarl, 'Bitch. Who do you think you are?'

She fled across to the house, pulling out her phone to call Robbie. As she reached the veranda, she slowed down, the phone in her hand. She shouldn't call Robbie. Baxter was a tradie and sometimes they could be a bit rough. She should learn to handle men like him, not let them frighten her. She slid the phone back into her pocket but stayed by the house all afternoon.

When the plumber's van drove out, she walked across to the cottage to see what he had achieved. She had to admit his work was good. All the pieces, except the large bath, were in the right place, and he had some of the connections and taps on too. She knew it would take two men to lift the bath in, but also knew Robbie wanted to tile the floor first. Sighing, she closed the door. He'd only be here a couple more days, then they would use Robbie's regular plumber when they started the renovations in the house.

Nik had the nightmare that night, for the first time in three weeks. Her ex-husband Patrick had been standing with his new wife, holding his baby in one arm, pulling on Lucy's hand with the other. Nik was pulling on Lucy's other hand and they were tugging so hard Lucy was crying out in pain. Just as Nik was about to give up, let Patrick take her, he morphed into HIM. The other one. Michael. Her big mistake. Michael was huge, he grew larger in her dream, knocking Patrick out of the way with a sweep of his hand. Sneering, he yanked Lucy to his side. His massive hand, a fist now, came for Nik. Hitting her in the ribs, then, once again on her feet, when she rushed to get Lucy. Pain swept through her and she tried again and this time his fist connected with her head, his ring slicing her open. Blood in her eyes, she screamed for Lucy, but he pulled her away. As he grew larger, Lucy seemed to shrink, until Nik could barely see her.

Waking in a cold sweat, Nik rushed to Lucy's room. She was asleep, curled up with a book about dogs lying beside her. It was a book Robbie had loaned her, about training a working dog. Climbing into bed beside Lucy, Nik curled up and eventually fell asleep.

'Mummy?' She opened her eyes. Lucy was facing her. She reached out and pushed Nik's hair back from her face. 'Are you okay, Mum? Did you have the nightmare?'

Blinking once or twice, Nik nodded. They studied each other. Nik noticed Lucy was more 'present', less inclined to disappear inside herself. Even asking the question was a sign of her growing confidence, and maturity.

'Why, Mum? Why did you have a bad dream?' Nik shook her head, not wanting to mention the plumber, not wishing to scare Lucy, or God forbid, set her back.

'I guess it just popped into my head while I slept. I'm fine, really. I hope you didn't mind me coming in here to you.'

Lucy snuggled closer. 'I don't mind. But we are getting better, aren't we? Remember how in the beginning, we always slept together. We needed each other 'cos of the bad dreams.' She patted Nik's shoulder. 'But I haven't been having the bad dreams at all. Lately I just dream about horses and puppies.' She giggled and Nik smiled, relieved.

'Good. Let's get up, have a juice, then check on the puppies and feed the horses. Do you think we could go for a ride together, along Robbie's paddock and back?' Nik stretched.

Lucy was out of bed as Nik spoke, pulling on her jeans and hunting around in a drawer for clean socks. 'Yes! Let's do that. We can have our ride before Cowboy Dad gets here. Won't he be surprised?'

Laughing, feeling better, Nik got out of bed. 'I'm going to get dressed, then race you downstairs.'

'You're on!'

Pulling on the faded jeans she now thought of as her 'riding jeans,' Nik added a sleeveless cotton shirt and ran a brush through her hair before running downstairs, boots in hand, right behind Lucy.

Scout wagged her tail when Nik opened the laundry door, standing and letting the puppies roll away from her as she stepped outside. Lucy filled the water bowl and gave all the puppies a pat, with a generous cuddle for Minnie, while Nik changed their bedding.

It was only just after dawn and Nik felt a growing sense of confidence and peace as she nudged Honey into a trot, then canter, Lucy beside her on Diana, as they rode in the direction of Robbie's place. Nik had not been this far, and she was curious about his farm and house. Lucy had ridden this way with Robbie a couple of times and knew the way. Navigating into another paddock, she saw the farmhouse in the distance. A single level timber home with a high roofline and two chimneys.

Looking at her watch, Nik slowed her mare to a walk. 'We should head back now. Robbie is probably on his way over in his ute.'

'Okay.' Nik was careful to walk on the way back as Robbie had warned her the horses may try to break into a gallop when heading home.

Nik noticed the plumber was already at work as they hitched the horses. She unsaddled while Lucy brushed them down. Nik frowned and looked at her watch. Robbie and Harry hadn't arrived yet. They were usually here by now.

Back in the house, Nik checked her phone. Robbie had sent a text.

Will be late today, sorry. Vet coming to look at injured horse. Harry still at other job. Call me if you need anything.

Nik nibbled on her lip while she looked at the phone. She would prefer Robbie to be here to deal with the plumber, but if he had an injured horse of course that would take priority. She messaged back.

All good here. See you later. Hope horse is ok.

Upstairs, buttering toast, she told Lucy that Robbie would be late, and Harry was at the other job. Lucy nodded, then announced she was going to sit with the puppies and study the dog training book.

Laughing, Nik said, 'they haven't even opened their eyes Luce, I think they're a bit little for training yet.'

'I know, but I'm just going to read about it anyway. And Scout likes me to be there.' Nik nodded. Lucy was happy, relaxed. That's all that matters.

Nik chose not to go over to the cottage; the bloody plumber could just get on with it. She didn't want to give him another chance to leer at her. She showered quickly and changed from her riding gear into beige capri pants and a sleeveless top. Checking it didn't show any cleavage, just in case Baxter came to the house, Nik went into her downstairs office and began answering emails and responding to client requests.

Mid-morning, she saw Lucy out with the horses, brush in hand. She shook her head. They'd be the best-groomed horses in the district.

Heavy footsteps on the veranda broke her reverie. Nik stood, pushing her chair back. Stepping toward the open door, Baxter loomed in the entrance, his bulk blocking out the light.

'Do you need anything?' Nik knew her tone was cool, but she didn't want to give him any encouragement to be fresh with her. She hoped Lucy was still in with the horses and out of earshot.

He leaned against the doorjamb. 'There's no need to take that tone *Nik*.' He straightened. 'I'm sure we can be friends.' He towered over her, and she was tall. But she held her ground although her voice was dripping with tension.

'Let me get this straight, *Baxter*. You are here to complete a plumbing job. Nothing more. You are deliberately trying to intimidate me. It's unprofessional and unnecessary and certainly won't lead to *friendship*.'

'You already giving it to Robbie Stewart?' His tone became more aggressive, and he took another step toward her. She prayed Lucy was out of earshot. 'Old Robbie hasn't had any since the beautiful Jess died. Still grieving.' He touched his crotch with one hand. 'But a woman like you. A woman like you could help a man get over his grief.'

Nik stepped back, drew herself up and straightened her shoulders. 'You're a bully and a creep. And you're fired. Bill me for the work you've done.' She was almost shouting now but needed to keep momentum. 'Pack up your tools and get off my property!'

'You heard the lady.' This came from behind Baxter. It was said quietly, but with murderous intent. Robbie stood on the veranda, feet apart, body poised for a fight.

Baxter swung around. He was bigger than Robbie but seemed to deflate. 'It was just a joke mate. Chick can't take a joke.' He swaggered, stepping towards Robbie.

'Get your tools and piss off, Baxter. Don't make me say it again.' Robbie stood firm, arms crossed, chin up. For a moment Nik thought Baxter would swing at Robbie, but he stepped to one side and walked toward the cottage.

Nik put a hand up to her face, trembling. Robbie stepped inside, wrapped his arms around her, holding her for a moment. Releasing her, he stepped back as the van sped down the driveway, kicking up gravel with its tyres.

'You did well, Nik. You held your own. I'd heard rumours about Baxter but had no idea he was a bully. And a sleaze. I'm sorry to have brought him onto your place.' He looked across at the cottage, a muscle in his jaw twitching.

'It's okay. I don't think he would have attacked me. All talk, I think. But he scared me.' She looked around. 'I hope Lucy didn't hear.' But she knew the conversation had become loud. Knew in her heart Lucy would have heard some of it. It suddenly became important to find Lucy, make sure she was alright.

'Lucy.' Nik looked at Robbie. She pushed past him and ran around the veranda to the laundry, Robbie on her heels. Scout was there, with all the pups except Minnie. Outside, Nik looked around wildly, fear on her face.

'The horses! Diana is gone! Her saddle too!' Robbie yelled. 'Where do you think she'd go, Nik?'

Nik shook her head, panicked. 'Maybe your place. We rode that way together early this morning.' Moving quickly, Nik grabbed Honey's saddle.

Robbie put his hand on her arm. 'I'll go on Honey. I'll be faster. Call Harry, he should be home by now. He can watch for her from there.' He touched Nik's face, wiping her tears. 'She'll be okay. But you should stay here in case she comes back. In case she didn't go this way. Nik, you need to be here for Lucy.' Nik nodded, pulling out her phone. Robbie had the saddle on Honey, as Harry answered her call. She handed the phone wordlessly to Robbie, unable to speak.

'Lucy has taken off son. She might be heading towards our place on

Diana. Baxter had words with Nik, we think Lucy overheard and was frightened.'

'The bastard!' Nik clearly heard Harry's response. 'I'll saddle Blackjack and start toward Nik's. We'll find her.'

Robbie handed the phone to Nik, leant in, and kissed her on the mouth, gently, then said firmly. 'We'll bring her home safely. Stay here.' He leapt on Honey and nudged her with his heels. She leapt into a canter, crossing the grassy flats swiftly.

Hand over her lips, Nik ran inside, checking all the rooms just in case. She knew Lucy was on the horse but had to do something. She went back to the laundry, the door wide open, her phone in one hand, the other stroking Scout as she peered down the paddock past the water trough, searching for a sign of her daughter returning.

The phone rang. Robbie. She answered hurriedly. 'Is she there. Have you found her?' Robbie's quiet, patient voice answered. 'Lucy's right here. With me and Harry. She's fine. Put the kettle on, we'll be with you in twenty minutes.'

Crying with relief, Nik patted Scout. 'They've got her, Scout. She's okay.' Scout licked her hand, thumping her tail.

Nik ran upstairs and put the kettle on. From the upstairs window she could see the three horses with their riders, walking back together. Downstairs, Nik ran out to the hitching rail, waving madly. Lucy waved.

Within minutes they were at the fence. Lucy slid off Diana and ran to Nik. Nik knelt, wanting to hold her daughter tightly, but Lucy stood back, smiling through her tears. Something was wriggling inside her tee shirt. She reached in and drew out the puppy, Minnie. 'Minnie needs to be with her Mum too. I have to take her in to Scout now.' She leaned forward, kissing Nik on the cheek, before climbing through the fence, heading for the laundry.

'Thank you. Where was she?' Robbie and Harry looked at each other. 'Almost to our place. She knew the way and would have got there sooner, but she didn't want to shake the puppy up too much.' This was from Harry. 'I'll go check on Scout and the pups too.' He strode off.

Nik looked at Robbie. 'Was it because of Baxter? The argument?'

'It was. But Nik, she said she came to get me, and Harry, because she knows she's safe with us. She came to tell us Baxter is not a good man and that you, Nik, aren't safe with him. Her fear for you was much stronger than fear for herself.'

Amazed, Nik shook her head. She slipped her arm through his as they walked towards the house, where Lucy and Harry were standing together, waiting for them. 'Let's make a pot of tea, Mum.' Lucy put her hand in Nik's as they walked upstairs together.

LATER THAT NIGHT, NIK SAT ON THE EDGE OF LUCY'S BED. ROBBIE HAD ensured Baxter had taken all his gear. Nik knew he had phoned the man, who insinuated Nik had led him on. Robbie had stopped him, saying firmly, 'There'll be no more work with me, Baxter. I'm recommending Nik make an official complaint. You might want to consider relocating. I can't imagine anyone will use your services once this gets out.' He paused. 'Better still, why not mend your manners. Your business, and social life, will surely improve.' While Nik didn't hold great hopes for Baxter to change his ways, she felt sure he wouldn't be back to bother her.

Stroking Lucy's hair, Nik asked if she wanted to sleep in her own room or would she prefer to sleep with her.

'It's okay, Mum. We're safe now. And Robbie told me you were really strong, and that man wasn't able to scare you.' There was pride in Lucy's tone and Nik didn't want to admit that Baxter had scared her, although she now realised that she had stood up to him and he was backing down when Robbie arrived.

'Remember the promise I made you, Lucy? That I will never let a man into our home again, to live with us. That I will keep you safe, always.' Nik watched as Lucy nodded.

'But Mum. I think you're wrong. I don't need that promise.' Nik sat back, confusion on her face as Lucy spoke earnestly.

'I rode to Robbie's place for you, not me. Not because I was scared, although I was, but because I wanted to protect you.'

'What do you mean, sweetheart?'

'I know no one will ever hurt me. I know you will always protect me. I wasn't really hurt last time, Mum. You were. You were hurt protecting me. Us. I've been afraid something will happen to you. Not to me. But I haven't been able to explain it properly.' She stroked Nik's hand as she spoke. 'I rode to Robbie's because I trust him. He's a good man. Harry is too, although he's silly sometimes. Robbie will protect both of us. He loves you, Mum.' She looked down at their clasped hands, then looked up, tears in her eyes. 'I think Robbie loves both of us. Like he loves Harry. I don't mind if he's here all the time. I like it when he's here. Harry too.'

Nik hugged Lucy close. 'I like it when he's here too, Luce. Harry too. I like it a lot. But first things first. Let's all be friends first, okay? If it works out, maybe one day we can be something more.'

Lucy muttered into Nik's shoulder. 'We can be a family one day. I think we can be a family.'

16
___

It was late March. Nik, Robbie, and Harriet were sitting on the veranda, waiting for Lucy to be dropped off by the school bus. Minnie, the puppy, was curled up on Nik's lap.

'So, she likes the school, Nik?' Harriet took a mouthful of scone, sighing as she did. 'That Lucy, she knows how to bake.'

Chuckling, Nik nodded. 'She loves it. She's topping the class in English, but Mrs Merrington told me last week that every story she writes stars at least one dog and several horses.'

Robbie laughed too, then poked Nik's arm. 'You know Lucy's trying to train this pup, and you keep picking her up and taking her on your lap. You're going to be in so much trouble if she sees you.'

Nik hastily set the puppy on the ground, its sharp teeth promptly latching on and chewing on Harriet's laces. Robbie threw the tennis ball under the plum tree and Minnie scampered after it.

'Tell me about this new idea you have for the accommodation Nik. It's gorgeous by the way, I love the cottage so much.' Nik followed Harriet's gaze toward the cottage, the beautiful rosewood doors standing sentinel, the wrought iron lacework painted white, wrapping around the whole building on the veranda.

'The cottage is exactly as we planned. Short term accommodation. We'd love to have your clients stay here when they're looking at relocating to this region.' She shot a glance at Robbie, who nodded. 'But we've changed our minds about the rooms downstairs in the house. There's now two bedrooms, a big bathroom, two living areas and a full kitchen.'

Harriet smiled, but her brow was creased as she considered this. 'Self-contained accommodation. That's good.' She nodded encouragingly at Nik.

'We aren't offering this to holidaymakers. Or house hunters.' The school bus had stopped, and Lucy was now running down the driveway, Minnie tearing toward her full pelt. Nik watched as Lucy knelt, the puppy leaping into her arms, licking her face while Lucy laughed with delight.

Turning back to Harriet, Nik said firmly, 'This accommodation is for women. Women who need it. Who need a place to go because they don't feel safe, or they have nowhere else to go. Or they just want a break. Women with children. Young mothers with babies. Women, girls, who have been through trauma.'

Harriet sat back surprised. A broad smile appeared on her face. 'Really? How wonderful! I love this idea. How can I help?'

Robbie spoke. 'That's not all. Nik and Lucy will offer the accommodation. Those that come can stay as long as they need to. They can help with the gardens, the vegetables. Cooking. Servicing the cottage if they feel up to it. But we are also offering horsemanship lessons. To be with the horses, groom, feed and ride them. A sort of equine therapy. Harry and I will provide the horses.'

'And anyone staying in the cottage that wants to ride, or learn to ride, can have lessons too. Or just go for a ride with one of us if they have some experience.'

'Harriet, we hope you'll help with the marketing. Get the word out to the right places.' Nik rose to hug Lucy, finally at the house, Minnie at her heels.

'Hi Mum, Robbie.' Lucy gave him a peck on the cheek. 'Harriet.' She sat down, reaching for a scone. 'Has Mum told you our plans? It's a really good idea, don't you think?'

'I really do, Lucy. I'm thrilled to be included. I'll help as much as I can.'

Lucy stood, 'Have you seen the cottage yet, Harriet?'

Harriet rose. 'I saw it last week, but I don't think you had the final colour in the kitchen. May I take a look?'

'Sure. Come with me.' Lucy turned, smiling at Harriet. 'Minnie, stop it! Leave Harriet's laces alone.'

Nik stood beside Robbie, loving the feeling of warmth his arm around her shoulders generated. She picked up the puppy, which squirmed against her chest.

At the door of the cottage Lucy raised her eyebrows at Harriet. 'You know I'm getting a brother, don't you?'

Harriet glanced back at Nik and Robbie. It was common knowledge they were seeing each other. But no one had mentioned a baby.

Looking at Lucy, she said, 'Really? Is your Mum expecting a baby?'

Lucy snorted. 'No, silly. Harry. Harry's going to be my brother.' She opened the door and skipped inside.

THE END

far horizons
love story

Emma Powell

FAR HORIZONS LOVE STORY

EMMA POWELL

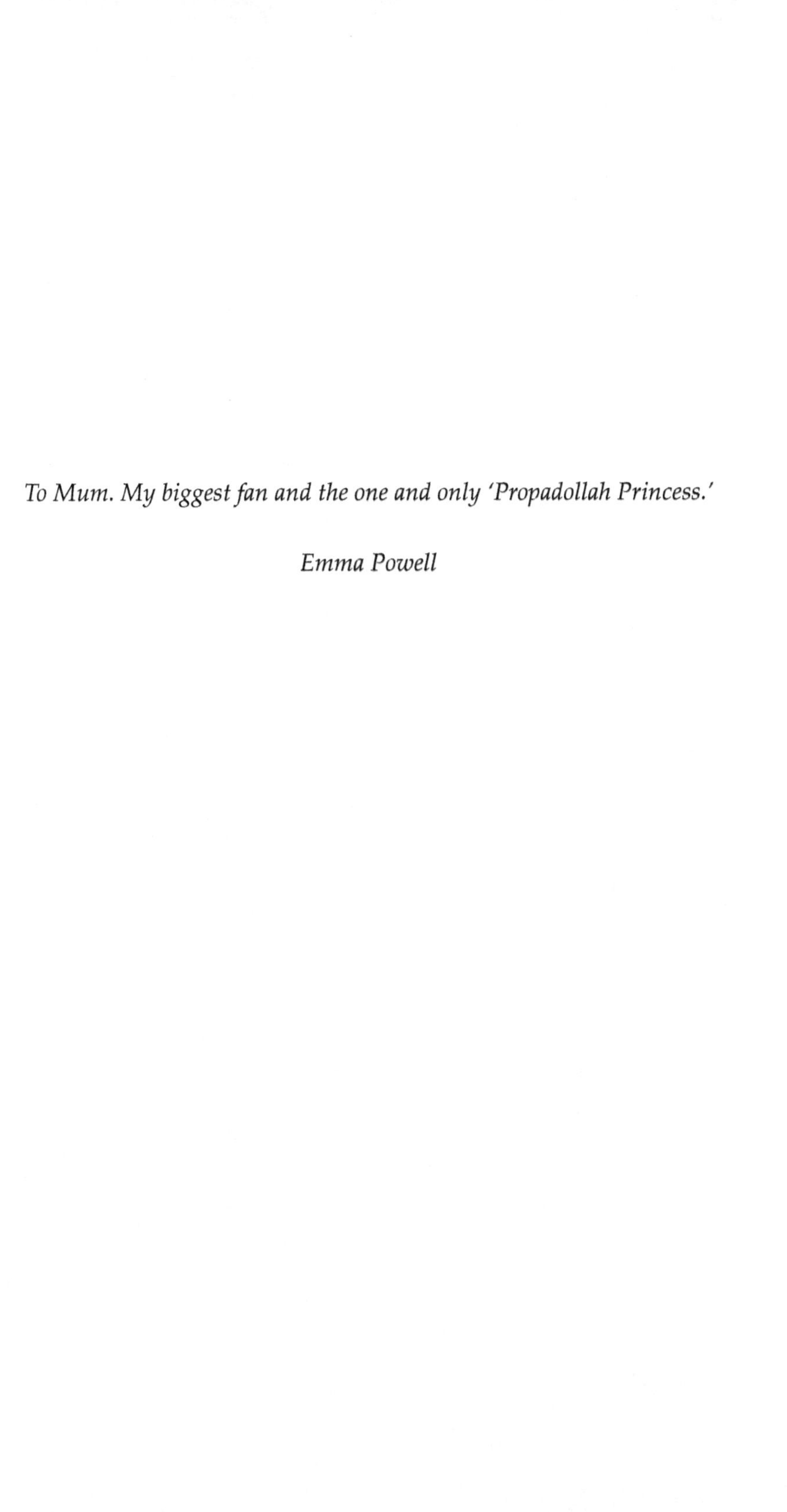

To Mum. My biggest fan and the one and only 'Propadollah Princess.'

Emma Powell

1

———————

It seemed like a good idea at the time.

To pack up her life in Melbourne and head north. To the wide brown land of the Wimmera. Land of wheat and far horizons that went on forever.

Her mother's childhood home and her own birthplace. Nhill.

For most of her thirty-six years, Molly had a running gag that she told over wine and cheese at some fancy-schmancy alleyway bar.

I was born in Nhill, zero, nada…which has no bearing on my personality whatsoever.

It usually got a good chuckle from her equally citified friends.

So, WTF did she come back for?

That was a question for her therapist for the next session she'd have to do via Zoom.

Molly sighed deeply and in so doing, ingested some sort of bug into her mouth. She spat it out and resolved never to breathe with an open mouth again.

Standing at the barbed wire fence, she held her skirt down so the hot northerly wind wouldn't blow it into the mini steel pikes. After all that skirt cost her $250 at SABA.

Wearing that skirt had seemed like a good idea at the time too.

Marrying Tony had as well. In the wise words of Julia Roberts...*Big Mistake. Big. Huge.*

Molly shook her head to drive out the memories and stared directly at the ruin in front of her.

A small sign, almost obscured by tall dry ryegrass read:

Propadollah State School est. 1915

And propped up by sheer will and the three timber walls that were left – Molly had no doubt if they could talk they'd have stories to tell – was the little one-roomed school her mother had gone to.

It reminded her of *Little House on The Prairie,* and it wasn't until her mother told her about her childhood that she realised little schools like this weren't just written about in fiction books or in TV series.

She waved a flurry of sticky little flies away from her face. Taking in the dilapidated wooden schoolhouse, she marvelled at how her mother went on to get a full scholarship at the University of Melbourne, becoming the first in her family to go on to further education.

And here she was complaining about a few sticky flies and pointy wired fences.

People had always said she looked and sounded like her mum, but that was about it. Molly knew she didn't have any of the resourcefulness or optimism that her mum had had. After she died Molly had vowed to try and be more like her. Fat chance.

Perhaps that was why, when the opportunity presented to move back to her birthplace, away from all the grief in the city, she'd jumped at it.

As if by cue, a mini whirlwind of dust and grass whizzed around her, and in that moment, she determined that Propadollah would be her sabbatical, her pilgrimage, her resurrection. As a non-religious person, she was feeling pretty bibley... Out with the old in with the new. *A new Molly.*

With one final gust, the hot wind flung her skirt into the barbed wire and as her mouth and nose filled with red dust, Molly heard the ripping of the soft linen.

Resisting the urge to scream in frustration, she repeated her mantra with an addendum.

A new Molly. A new wardrobe. A new Molly. A new wardrobe.

Plonking into the driver's seat of her totally-inappropriate-for-country-driving-Prius, she grabbed her bottle of water. Having sat in the car for only fifteen minutes in the hot sun - she would've parked under a tree if there was one - the water was luke-warm. That didn't stop Molly from screwing up her nose and taking a large swig to rid her mouth of the grit, swilling it around then spitting it onto the ground.

The hungry, dry earth sucked up the water.

She closed the door, started the car and cranked the air-con to full, sticking her red-hot face in front of the vent to cool down. Of pale complexion due to her Scottish and English genetics, she reprimanded herself for not donning her sunhat for that fifteen minutes. She'd probably wake up in the morning with another twenty-five freckles on her already freckled nose.

Face cool and steering wheel able to be touched without 3rd degree burns, Molly pulled out onto the dead straight, dirt road and headed back towards Nhill. The corrugation on the road slowed down her progress until she came to the well bitumened Western Highway. Breathing a sigh of relief on behalf of the bottom of her low sitting Prius, she turned the radio on loud and pressed down on the accelerator so she could get back to her air-conditioned rental house asap.

Senior Sergeant, Jack Meadows, sat in his patrol car, which was hidden behind the *Welcome to Nhill* sign, his speed radar at the ready.

A white ute whizzed by, just under the speed limit giving a toot as it passed, the driver flipping Jack the bird out of the window.

The locals knew where his hiding spots were.

And Jack knew that ute anywhere. Bluey the Blue Heeler - how original - riding shotgun in the ute tray, mouth open, tongue flapping in the wind. Eighty-two-year-old Carl the owner of Bluey and the vehicle, never missed an opportunity to give Jack the friendly finger.

Jack tooted his horn in reply, resisting the urge to send a one-fingered expletive back. It didn't suit the uniform. But next time he was off duty and in the pub, he'd make sure Carl shouted him a beer for the digit misdemeanour.

His phone buzzed. He clicked it on and a familiar voice boomed through the car speakers.

'Mate!' he exclaimed.

'Mate!' the caller replied, his voice echoing through the cabin.

'How the hell are you? Zoe? The kids?' Jack asked, lifting his radar to another car that was, thankfully, well in the speed limit. He hadn't spoken to Doug in a long time and didn't want to interrupt the phone call with a speeding infraction.

'All good here.' Doug paused. 'Ah sorry I haven't called since...'

Jack interrupted to spare him the embarrassment.

'Mate it's fine. I get it. Life goes on and all that. And let's face it, I probably wouldn't have answered anyway. Wasn't feeling particularly sociable back then.'

'Still...bad friend. Sorry buddy.'

There was a shared moment of silence, which on a phone call might normally be uncomfortable but instead, it communicated shame, grief and forgiveness in a matter of seconds.

'So, what's up?' Jack broke the silent reflection.

'Well, I know Zoe has a go at my memory all the time, but I do remember you saying at the funeral that you wanted to leave. And a position has come up in my department so if you were still keen to get out of there, I can put you forward.'

Jack didn't remember saying he wanted to leave, but sadly everything was a blur then. Then again, a move might be a good thing.

'You're still in cyber?' Jack asked.

'Yup. They're on a recruitment drive at the moment. Cybercrime has gone through the World Wide Web roof.'

'Okay thanks. I will definitely think about it. When do you need my answer?'

'Next few days I reckon. It's moving pretty quickly cause there's a big case we're investigating and we need extra eyes on it.'

A red Prius raced past him at seven kilometres over the limit.

'Sorry gotta go mate, I've got a car to chase. I'll let you know.'

'Righto. Go get 'em!' Doug replied.

Jack flicked on his siren and lights and pulled out onto the highway as he clicked off the call. Planting his foot on the accelerator, the thought of moving to the city filled him with excitement. A feeling he hadn't had for a long time. A new beginning. And if he was being honest, there was nothing keeping him in Nhill anymore.

THE BLINKING OF LIGHTS IN HER REARVIEW MIRROR CAUGHT HER attention.

Police… Shit!

She punched the off button on the radio and the car's cabin filled with the sound of the police siren. Molly slowed down hoping that he was on his way to a robbery in town, or a fight at the pub and would pass her by — but no — the siren was wailing at her to pull over. So she did.

Her temperature was starting to rise even though she'd kept the car running so the air-con could keep going.

She hadn't been going over the limit even though she didn't know what the limit was. There were hardly any signs. It was one of those country things where everyone just 'knew' how fast to go and cityites like her had to guess.

The cop approaching in her side mirror had a certain swagger. She wondered whether they taught that in the police academy. That somehow it gave them confidence and an air of Eastwood about them. Most cops just looked like they'd done a poo in their pants. But this guy had it down. It was sexy. And with the aviators and the snug, short-sleeved shirt showing off his tight biceps, Molly squirmed in her seat, feeling a bit more hot and bothered in all the wrong ways.

He rapped lightly on her window with his knuckles and gave her a signal to wind it down.

She followed his order and spoke quickly, wanting to get in first.

'I wasn't speeding officer. But even if I was it's because there are absolutely *no* signs to tell me what the limit is. In the city they're everywhere.'

'You were doing eighty-seven in an eighty-zone ma'am…'

'There was no sign!' Molly blurted out knowing that she was arguing with an officer of the law which never ended well.

'There's a sign about five k's back,' he stated.

'Well, that's why I didn't see it. I came off the Propadollah road.'

Molly shut up shut up shut up. Just take the ticket and go.

'Ahh okay,' he said, cocking his head at her. 'You're not from around here are you?'

'No. Do I have to be?' She cocked her head right back at him.

He laughed. 'No. I'm just curious why you'd be coming from Propadollah. It's a no-through road.'

'Is this an interrogation now?'

She glanced up at him and saw him trying to stifle a smile. He cleared his throat, readjusting his mouth to a stern policeman mouth and pulled out a small pad from his shirt pocket.

'No of course not. So how about this…because you were doing less than ten k's in excess of the speed limit, I'll give you a warning today. And I'll ignore the fact that you're arguing with a police officer.'

Molly smiled up at him while at the same time keenly aware how his low, soft, in-control voice made her stomach flip flop.

'Thank you officer…' she replied, looking at his name tag, '…Meadows. Can I go now?' His presence was making her feel wobbly.

'Not just yet. You've got something hanging from underneath your car. You'll need to stop in town and get that looked at.'

If Molly wasn't red enough from the heat flowing in through her window, her embarrassment from being argumentative with a hot cop was enough to make the blood rush to her face.

'Okay thanks…again.'

'You're welcome…?'

'Molly.'

'You're welcome Molly.'

He wrote on the pad, tore out the page and handed it to her.

'That's my mate who runs the servo. He can get under there and see what's going on.'

I'd like you under me.

Molly pushed the thought away immediately.

Stop it Molly. You're a no-man zone. Remember!

'Just tell him Jack sent you,' Officer Meadows, aka Jack continued as he pulled his sunnies down his nose, peeking his eyes over the top.

If eyes could be even brighter than the sun, Jacks were the ones to do it.

Or perhaps it was the sun behind him that made her squint, but either way she felt like she needed to shield herself from the sparkling blueness of his gaze.

She felt a tingle in her nether regions that she hadn't felt in a long time and shifted in her seat.

'Okay well, yes. Good. Thank you, I will definitely go there to get him under me…under the car.'

Jack smiled and pushed his glasses back up. 'Make sure you do. I'll let him know to expect you.'

'Rightio. I'll be off then,' Molly chirped, feeling like she was fifteen again. But at thirty-six, her hormones were obviously still working their magic.

Buzzing the window up, she waved to him as she pulled away and watched him wave back in her rearview mirror.

She checked him out as he walked back to his car. Yep, that swagger was real. Real nice.

2

'Hand on heads!' bellowed a red-faced Nora, to the twenty-eight over-excited six-year-olds who paid no attention to her as she placed her hands on her own head.

Molly followed suit; her eyes wide with mock terror showing the kids how important it was to behave around Mrs. Flanagan.

This was a very different Nora who had cornered Molly at her mother's funeral six months earlier and regaled her with stories of their first teaching assignment together. The only difference in their fate was that her mother left Nhill, but Nora had stayed.

Irish by name and Irish by nature, Nora was quick-tongued and quick to ignite. Forty years as a teacher had done nothing to inject patience into her personality. And by the looks of the sweat trickling down from her greying hairline and the flush on her wrinkled face, forty years in Nhill hadn't changed her DNA sufficiently enough to deal with the heat either.

Molly could see why. She just hoped the white tee she had on would hide the wet patches under her own sweaty underarms.

Eventually, all of the kids, except one, did as they were told and stood to attention, hands on top of heads. Well, standing to attention was a bit of an overreach and Molly tried not to smile as their wiggling little bodies gave away their inability to stay still.

'Lachlan!' Nora barked. 'Hands. Head. Now.'

Molly glanced over at Lachlan, who was picking his nose as if the booger was all the way up in his brain. He glared at Nora, daring her to stop him.

It was a stare-off.

Eventually, Lachlan found what he was searching for, pulled his finger out of his nose, shoved the treasure into his mouth and planted his hands firmly on his head.

In a moment of final defiance, he took a big swallow. 'Ahhh yummy,' he sighed.

Molly caught a laugh just as it was about to reward little Lachlan for his excellent timing and it came out sounding like a cross between a cough and a raspberry. The kids giggled in response.

Nora looked across at her. 'Don't worry, you'll get used to him,' she whispered, a smile touching her lips. Pressing them together again as a sign of control, she turned back to the children.

'Thank you, girls and boys. Hands down now and sit.'

They followed her instruction, even Lachlan, who went back to digging away for the holy grail of nose treasure.

'Remember I told you you were going to have a wonderful new teacher because Mr. Holt was leaving?'

The kids nodded in agreement.

'Well, here she is. May I introduce to you Mrs...'

'Miss,' Molly stage whispered.

'Miss. McDonald. Now as we rehearsed. One, two, three.' Nora conducted the children.

'Hello Miss. McDonald,' they chorused in the usual classroom rhythm, with some missing the beat completely. Lachlan being one of them. Instead, he raised his hand.

'Yes Lachlan?' Molly asked, smiling at him. She was determined to make him like her so he'd do what he was told.

'McDonald?'

Molly nodded.

'Are you old McDonald?' he asked.

'I'm thirty-six. Some people think that's old,' Molly replied, knowing he was going somewhere with his line of questioning but not quite sure where.

'Do you have a farm Miss?' he asked, his head cocked and his brows knotted in curiosity.

'That's enough Lach...' Nora began.

Molly threw Nora a quick *I got this* look knowing that if she didn't rein him in at the beginning it would be all over for the rest of the year.

'Well, I don't. But my Mum did. Right here actually.'

The kids gazed up at her, she had their attention. Even Lachlan ceased his mining expedition.

'Where Miss?' one of the girls asked.

'Propadollah. It was called The Far Horizons Farm.'

Three hands shot up. Molly called on the boy with the tight blond curls and the missing front teeth.

'Is that the old haunted one Miss?' he asked in a whisper, his eyes wide with wonder.

'No. Ghosts aren't real,' Molly said.

'Yes they are! I've seen one.' Lachlan exclaimed.

There was a collective gasp from the kids and they started to become rowdy again, talking amongst themselves about ghosts and ghouls. Molly shook her head, six-year-olds were the most dramatic people on the planet.

Nora clapped her hands three times. 'Okay that's enough talk of haunted houses girls and boys. It's time for some real-life learning.'

She looked across at Molly and smiled. 'You alright to take over dear?'

'I've been teaching teenagers for ten years I think I can manage a few six-year-olds,' Molly forced a laugh.

Nora patted her on the arm, tears welling in her eyes, 'You look so much like her it's as if she's here all over again. Thank you. Good luck dear.'

Molly watched Nora leave the classroom and paused for a moment, listening to the chatter of the children she was to spend the next year with and feeling a little daunted. Teenagers she knew how to deal with. Twenty-eight six-year-olds not so much. The only similarity was that they could smell fear. She could do this and reminded herself of the deal she'd made. *A new Molly.*

Taking a deep breath she turned back to the kids.

'BOO!'

They squealed and giggled.

'Alright, who wants me to tell them the story of the haunted farmhouse?'

Their hands shot up with little shouts of *me, me me me.*

Molly sat down on the floor with them and they gathered closer to her as she whispered.

'Once upon a time there was a property called The Far Horizons Farm…

All eyes were locked on her, except for Lachlan.

3

———————

er first day at the Nhill Primary School had come to the end of what she thought, was a pretty good day. The ghost story was a success. The house as it turned out wasn't haunted, it was just a family of chickens who lived in the run-down farmhouse and their scratching made it sound like it was haunted.

By the end of the story, she had the children up on their feet pretending to be chickens that sounded like ghosts. It was a weird mixture of boos and clucks, that the curly blond-headed boy called, Blucks.

Nora had peered into the room during the role play and gave Molly a thumbs up and a broad smile. Later telling her that her mother had played crazy games like that with her students as well. Like mother like daughter.

Molly watched Lachlan, who always kept himself on the periphery of whatever the other kids did. Even at lunchtime he sat alone with his lunchbox and watched the other kids playing around him. At one point a red-headed girl from his class pulled him into a game of footy, and he seemed to enjoy it for a few minutes but then went back to his place in the shade and his lunchbox.

Nora walked up to her at the staff room window as she watched him.

'Poor little fella,' she said, letting out a big sigh. 'Hasn't been the same since his mum died. Of course. Who would? She was too young. Devastating.'

'What happened?' Molly felt tears prick at her eyes. She'd only just met the kid, and she could tell he was a special one.

'Cancer. Awful thing. Ovarian. It was pretty quick in the end.' Nora's voice caught in her throat as she trailed off.

'Oh no.'

Nora wiped the tears from her cheeks. 'He's my favourite actually. I don't like to say I've got favourites, but he's so smart, and he's got spunk. I haven't seen it lately, until this morning. I wanted to jump with joy when he made the joke about your name. It's the first time in a long time he's done anything like that.'

It was Molly's turn to pat Nora's arm, leaving it there for a moment. 'He'll be okay. Kids are resilient. Family?'

'Just his Dad and his Mum's parents, but they're pretty useless since she died. Took it hard. And Lachie looks so much like her they've found it hard to have him in their lives. Sad really.' Nora sniffed and gestured to the staff and the kids outside. 'This place is his family now.'

'Well count me in,' Molly declared.

Nora smiled at her through her tears and then pulled her into a hug.

'You're just like her. Generous. Smart. Compassionate.'

Molly wasn't so sure she had any of those attributes. Certainly not in spades like her mother had, but she wasn't about to contradict Nora in her vulnerable moment.

She kept her eye on Lachie during the afternoon session and he seemed okay, but with the new information, she did notice a sadness in his little brown eyes. A sadness that she wanted to reach in and make better, even though she knew she couldn't.

The final bell went and some of the children raced up to her for a hug before grabbing their bags and heading out to meet their parents for pickup.

Standing at the classroom door, Molly couldn't wipe the smile off her face from the love the kids had showered upon her. Then she heard a kerfuffle coming from the Headmaster's office.

She snuck down the hall to get a closer look. Peeking inside she saw the cop who had pulled her up standing in front of Nora, his hands on his hips. She couldn't see his face as he had his lovely broad back to her, but she could tell by the look on Nora's face that it wasn't a good conversation.

Nora nodded, her face in deep concentration and concern.

'It will never happen again Jack. I'm so sorry,' she said.

Jack dropped his head and shook it. 'Thank you Nora. Sorry but you can understand.' It wasn't a question.

Nora walked around her desk and rubbed his back. Molly really wanted to know what was going on, but she also really wanted to rub his back too. Lucky lucky Nora.

'I do understand. I'll talk with his teacher.' Nora guided Jack out of the door and Molly made a quick turn to get back to her classroom before they came out into the corridor.

Too late.

'Molly? Isn't it?' There it was. That smooth low voice.

She turned slowly. 'Oh yeah. Hey. Hi. Didn't know you were there, here, in the school area.'

His face, tense from the conversation with Nora, softened as a smile touched his lips.

Such nice lips. Kissable really.

'Did you get your car looked at?'

'I forgot actually. Haven't used the car since. Everything's walking distance.'

'True,' he laughed. 'Do you have a kid here?'

'I've got twenty-eight!'

He ran his eyes over her and nodded. 'Well you look great for a woman with twenty-eight kids.'

'Oh, don't worry I am exhausted. My first day with twenty-eight six-year-olds. Put a fork in me 'cause I'm done!' Molly laughed. After a few moments she realised it was a one-way laugh. Jack hadn't joined in.

Weird. The 'put a fork in it' joke worked every time. Did he not have a sense of humour? Or had the latest gruesome crime scene just jumped into his head.

She glanced at him, his hands were back on his hips and his face had tensed up again.

'So, you're Miss McDonald?' he said, his voice low and soft.

'The one and only,' Molly bowed, hoping to lighten the mood that had turned suddenly very gloomy.

Jack walked - swaggered - towards her and it still made her tummy flip flop even though her tummy also knew something less than pleasant was coming.

'Please don't ever tell my son ghosts don't exist. It's all we've...he's got.'

Then he reached into his pocket, pulled out his Aviators, slid them onto his face and walked out, leaving a stunned Molly in his wake.

4

———

He knew he was unreasonable.

He knew Molly was only doing her job.

He knew that he was totally incapable of helping his son come to terms with the loss of his mother.

He knew ghosts didn't exist.

But he wished they did.

Walking to his police car, he slid into the driver's seat. No need to unlock it because he hadn't locked it in the first place. No need to. Not in Nhill. There was a high level of youth crime like most country towns, but weirdly people still left their cars unlocked. Old, trusting habits died hard. He always knew when a city slicker was in town because a car break-in always involved a smashed window.

Starting the car, he turned the air-con up high and sat waiting for the simmering, sauna style heat to subside. And besides, he really didn't feel like going anywhere. His mother had begrudgingly picked Lachie up because his babysitter cancelled at the last minute. But the phone call from his mother with Lachie on the other end in tears telling him *Mummy didn't really come to see him because his new teacher said so,* was what made him race down to the school to find out what the hell had happened.

It had been a year of firsts. Christmas was first which was really only a blur with a pathetic excuse for a Christmas tree because Sarah normally did the decorating with Lachie. Then Easter. Then her birthday. Then her death day soon after.

He'd done a better job on the tree last Christmas because the second Christmas seemed a little bit easier. Although he had thrown out every single decoration she'd ever used and bought a whole new collection.

Lachie had seemed to be doing a little better since then, until his dimwitted new teacher from the city, had told him ghosts didn't exist.

Jack knew that to encourage Lachie's belief that Sarah visited him every night was short term relief that would most likely create long-term problems. But it was the only thing that both of them could hold onto and he hoped that as Lachie got older his visions and imagination would fade away.

The other first had happened the day before. When he pulled Molly over on the Highway. It had been the first time he'd had any kind of attraction to another woman. He'd been quite sure there would never be another woman. That part of him had died with his wife. Or so he thought.

His reaction to Molly had been instant and visceral, catching him by surprise. That wasn't supposed to happen. She had sparked something in him that he'd been thinking about for the rest of the night. And the next day.

Thinking about her smile and how the curve of her lips beckoned to him to touch them with his own. She'd been wearing a buttoned shirt, but the seatbelt had pulled against it, revealing the soft curve of cleavage underneath. His Aviators had allowed him to take a quick glimpse before the gentleman in him forced his eyes away. Within two minutes of meeting her, he knew he'd like to 'meet' her again. And she was feisty. He liked that.

Which made the fact that she was the person who had told Lachie that his mum didn't exist, even harder to bear.

Why did it have to be her?

And there was the possibility of a job in Melbourne. The arrival of

Molly hadn't just thrown a spanner in the works, it had thrown the whole toolbox.

He punched the steering wheel and drove off, flicking the siren on to make the trip to a distressed Lachie quicker and also to drown out thoughts of Molly from his mind.

~

MOLLY WATCHED JACK SPEED OUT OF THE CARPARK.

First day ruined.

She felt Nora walk up behind her.

'Don't mind him,' she said, patting her arm. Arm patting seemed to be a Nora speciality. Such a simple action that was infused with comfort and warmth. 'He's had a tough year. Didn't take any time off and kept looking after all of us without taking care of himself.'

Molly nodded and let out a small sigh.

Nora clapped her hands, jolting Molly out of her thoughts. 'Alright let's tidy up ready for a new day tomorrow.'

Molly hadn't even noticed that the classroom looked like a bomb had hit it. Crayons and paper everywhere. The cushions from the reading corner had ended up in every corner of the room and there was a strange smell emanating from underneath one of the tables.

She crawled underneath and discovered an uneaten sandwich of salami, a very pungent cheese and what looked and smelled like horse-radish. She screwed up her nose and holding it out in front of her as far as it would go, dropped it into the bin.

'Oh, that's Fleur's,' Nora explained. 'She always has…how shall I say it…interesting lunches. I always have a pack of nut-free muesli bars in my office that she comes and gets if she can't stomach her lunch. She hasn't quite come around to the idea of throwing it out herself. Thinks hiding it will do.'

'Embarrassed perhaps?' Molly said, wiping her hands with a handful of tissues, knowing that the only way to get rid of the smell would be hot soapy water.

'Most likely. Kids can be cruel.'

'Yes, they can. But thankfully, they don't always stay cruel,' Molly said, wondering if her ex had been one of those bullies that picked on the kid with the weird lunch. Probably. She made a mental note to have a little chat with Fleur and to find ways to inspire more acceptance from the cheese and Vegemite kids.

A picture on one of the tables caught her eye. The paper was covered in black crayon with a round yellow moon in the top corner. And in the middle, a stick figure with a triangle skirt and long hair marked with a big red cross through it. On the back, in six-year-old wobbly handwriting was the name…Lachlan.

Molly breathed in deeply and berated herself.

What had she done?

5

———

Molly turned into the *Bob's Short Stop Service Station* just off the Main Road and parked in front of the service centre.

The walls of the workshop held every tool known to man. And of course, there was the obligatory erotic calendar on the office door.

She bent down to see if there was anyone working underneath the car that had no wheels or bumper bar. Nope.

'Gidday love. Can I help ya?'

Startled, Molly stood up and turned around, surprised at what she saw. She was expecting a man in greasy overalls with black oil-stained fingers and a glint in his bloodshot eyes as he looked her up and down. But what she saw, was a man well in his seventies, in well-worn but clean navy overalls, clear bright, brown eyes and well worn, clean hands that held a cup of tea. He took a sip and was way more interested in the tea than checking her out.

She breathed a sigh of relief.

'Oh, how rude of me,' he said, 'Do you wanna cuppa love?'

Molly held her hand up. 'Oh no. It's fine. Thanks for the offer. Jack…the policeman, suggested I book my car in.' She gestured to her car. 'There's something banging around underneath apparently.'

'Nuthin' worse than something banging around underneath,' he replied giving her a wink and placing his cup on the tool bench. 'And no need to book her in. I'll check her out now.'

He held his hand out to her. 'Bob, by the way, nice to meet you.'

She shook his hand. 'Molly and likewise.'

'Give me the keys and I reckon come back in a coupla hours and she'll be good as new.'

Molly handed him the keys and as he got in the car to drive it into the workshop, he gave her another wink. 'Jack said a pretty lady with a Prius might be dropping by. He wasn't wrong.'

Molly was glad he'd closed the car door before he saw the blush rise in her cheeks. She waved goodbye to him and decided to head to the Pub for a wine and a bowl of chips to celebrate surviving her first week in the Wimmera.

THE FARMERS ARMS HOTEL SAT PRIDE OF PLACE ON THE CORNER OF THE Highway and the main drag and was everything Molly had heard about country pubs.

Wide verandahs wrapped around the ground and second floors with a stained-glass double door entrance leading into a dark front bar. Decorated from a bygone era of thirsty farmers and their sidekick farmhands, everything had started to fade. It wasn't through any direct sunlight, as there was none, but rather time and feet on the sticky beer-stained carpet and tired bottoms on the worn leather bar stools.

Most pubs in the city had had makeovers, turning them into trendy café-style eateries with snazzy decor and lots of natural light.

Molly suspected that back in the day, farmers who'd spent all their day in the harsh daylight, wanted respite with their well-earned beers, so the dark dingy front bar was a welcome relief.

It wasn't busy, so she was served straight away at the bar. Molly ordered a glass of an oaky Yarra Valley Chardonnay that she loved and a bowl of chips with tomato sauce on the side.

She took a seat at a tall table next to a window, that looked out onto the small park area that separated the street. In the middle of it was a bronze statue of a draught horse dedicated to the important role the draught horses played in the wheat lands of the region.

Her mum had told her that the horse talked. Not literally talked, but there was a speaker in the foundation that when the button was pushed it gave a *history of the horse* in the area. But one night when she was teenager, after the local football team won the regional competition, revellers celebrating the win broke it and it was never fixed. Her mum had married one of those revellers. Explained a lot.

The wine and chips arrived and she took a sip, her eyes closed, trying to drum up a vision of the days of draught horses pulling trays laden with freshly baled hay.

She felt someone standing next to her and he cleared his throat.

'Molly. Hi.'

Opening her eyes, she looked up into Jack's handsome face. He gave her soft smile, his face etched with remorse.

'Jack,' she nodded, cool as a cucumber except for the warm spiral of excitement that ran up her body.

It looked as if he wanted to reach out and touch her but thought better of it. 'I wanted to apologise for having a go at you about the ghost stuff. I know you were just doing your job.'

He smiled at her. It was so soft and sincere that she felt her heart skip and a warm hum run down her body, landing between her legs.

'Pfft,' Molly exclaimed, throwing her arms in the air almost taking out her Chardonnay. 'No worries at all. I'd forgotten all about it.'

She hadn't.

'And if you think that's bad you should have seen what the parents in the city are like. Helicopter parents have nothing on those Mosquito ones.'

'Mosquito?'

'You know, mosquito,' Molly said, 'they buzz around and you never know when they're gonna attack and when they do it stays with you for days.'

Jack laughed, making his face light up, all the worry washed away.

'Thanks for understanding Molly. Means a lot.'

The way her name sounded coming out of his mouth made her

want him to keep saying it over and over and over. She felt a blush rising. As a distraction, she picked up the bowl of chips and shoved them at him.

'Chip?'

Jack had to step back to avoid being 'chipped'. He laughed. 'Okay sure. Thanks.'

He grabbed a few of the larger chips, dipped them in the sauce and threw them into his mouth.

'Best hot chips in the Wimmera,' he muttered, his mouth full.

'They sure are,' Molly replied, shoving one into her own mouth.

'It's a special salt they use. They won't tell anyone the recipe.'

'I'm hooked. I might as well just plaster them onto my thighs now,' Molly laughed, popping another one in.

Jack beamed at her. 'I like a woman who loves her food.'

'Well then you're looking at the right woman,' Molly beamed right back at him.

'Mrs Right huh? Hold that thought.' He stepped closer, bringing his hand to her face. She raised her head to him and parted her lips ever so slightly, her belly full of butterflies and want. He stared at her lips and with his thumb, wiped a smudge of sauce from her chin then pulled back, grabbing another chip.

His radio crackled to life.

'Sir, it's Raverty. Davo's at it again. Are you near the Farmers? Over.'

Jack gulped the chip down and clicked the radio.

'Roger that Raverty. I'm at the Pub now. Leave Davo to me. Over.'

He nodded at Molly. 'Thanks for the snack. That'll keep me going until dinner.'

Embarrassed that she'd thought he was going to kiss her – why would she let him? She was a no-men-allowed-zone – she returned the nod and took a large swig of wine waving him off. 'You're welcome. Anytime.'

She watched him swagger off into the back room where voices had started to get louder.

'Davo!' he yelled. 'Mate, whatever you're doing stop it!'

Molly took another gulp of wine and returned her attention to the bronze statue, wishing she could put his touch and his swagger out of her mind.

~

TWO HOURS, TWO CHARDONNAYS, AND THE BOWL OF CHIPS LATER, MOLLY headed back to *Bob's Servo*.

He greeted her as she walked into the workshop.

'She's all done love,' he said, rubbing his hand with wet wipes.

So that's how he keeps his hands so clean.

She must've been staring at his hands because he held them up to the light for her to get a better look. 'My wife, Cheryl, said she'd divorce me if I went home with disgusting mechanic hands and now here we are. Me washing my hands with baby bum wipes.' He chuckled and then reached into his pocket, pulling out her keys.

'Smart woman your Cheryl,' Molly laughed. 'So, what was under the car?'

'Just a bit of road-kill. Happens all the time out here.'

'Road-kill? What did I kill?' Molly was appalled at the thought that she'd killed anything.

'Nah I don't think you killed it. Been dead awhile by the smell of it. Your car sits so low it just picked it up…like that.' He snapped his fingers.

'Okay. And what was it?' Molly almost didn't want to know but curiosity got the better of her and if she was going to live in the place, getting used to the country way was going to have to be a priority. And that included talking about road-kill.

Bob cocked his head and looked at her. 'You sure you wanna know love?'

She nodded.

'Ok. Put it this way there'll be one less Roger Rabbit in the paddocks tonight.'

She was glad he hadn't said Bugs Bunny, but she still felt sad that the little fella had met an untimely fate.

'Circle of life love.' Bob clapped his hands. 'Now you get out of here and enjoy the rest of your day.'

Molly pulled her purse out of her bag. 'What do I owe you?'

Bob shook his head. 'Nuthin' love. On the house.'

'Oh no I have to…'

Bob raised his hand to interrupt. 'A friend of Jack's is a friend of mine. You're good to go.'

Molly could tell he was serious and any further objection would be ignored on purpose. She smiled at him and took his hand. 'Thanks so much Bob.'

Jumping into the car, she wound the window down. 'Oh and great to meet you. It's been most…illuminating.'

She waved goodbye through the window. He waved back.

'Say hello to that Jack of ours!' he yelled after her, a wide, cheeky smile plastered across his face and his baby soft thumb held in the air.

6

———

Parent-Teacher Interviews. Molly didn't dislike them. She really disliked them.

She hadn't become a teacher to have to deal with the parents. It was for the kids.

Parents were weird. Not being one at thirty-six, she'd resigned herself to the fact that it probably wouldn't happen. But it didn't matter, because her students were her 'kids'. Her friends back in the city, who weren't teachers, thought that was weird. And maybe it was. But it meant that she invested in her progeny pupils. Was that so bad?

And only one week into her job at Nhill PS what was she going to say to the parents? She wasn't accustomed to PT Interviews so early in the year. Nora told her that they liked to get a start early so that they could see change throughout the year - a baseline as such.

Molly made sure her bits and pieces were in order and waited behind her desk for the first cab off the rank.

She heard him before she saw him.

His deep voice hummed into her very core as he greeted other parents out in the hall. She heard a few of the mums giggle after he told a joke. Molly smiled. The joke wasn't that good. And they weren't giggling at the punchline. It was more of a swoon than a giggle.

So, she wasn't the only one.

Lachie bounded into the room.

'Miss McDonald had a farm Ee-i-ee-i-oh,' he sang, clapping his hands at how clever he was.

Molly figured if you can't beat 'em join 'em.

'And on that farm I had some...?' she trilled.

'Robots!' Lachie yelled.

'With a...' Molly had no idea what robots sounded like.

'A beep beep here,' Jack added as he sauntered in. He wasn't in his police uniform and although she liked a man in uniform, Molly liked casual Jack. Cargo pants, flip-flops and tight white tee that showed off his wide strong chest and firm biceps. Nice. Incredibly good looking. He'd shaved and smelt like mint and soap. It was a heady mix.

Jack kept singing then they all joined in.

'And a beep beep there. Here a beep. There a beep. Everywhere a beep beep,' they chorused.

'Miss McDonald had a farm Ee-i-ee-i-oh,' Lachie finished with a low bow, worthy of any opera house stage.

Molly gave him a standing ovation and clapped along with Jack, who threw her a wink and mouthed *thank you.*

Eventually, Jack got Lachlan under control and they sat down opposite Molly.

'Thanks for being a good sport,' Jack said, giving Molly a wide smile that almost had her slipping off her chair. She stifled a giggle, not wanting to sound like the mums out in the hallway.

'Well, it is kind of true after all. My family did have a farm here many years ago.'

'Oh? Which one?'

'Far Horizons. Out at Pro...'

'Propadollah,' Jack finished for her. 'That's why you were out there. You're a real Mac.'

'Through and through.'

'Sooooo...not married then?' Jack glanced quickly at her wedding finger. 'Or just using your maiden name?'

Molly covered her left hand with her right. She didn't wear her ring anymore but there was still a slight dent on her finger where the ring had made it's mark. It was a horrible reminder.

'Not married. No. Okay Lachie let's talk about you.'

Jack shifted in his seat, aware that he'd just been shut down.

'Dad said he wanted to talk about you,' Lachie glanced up at Jack, confused.

Jack laughed, it was forced and a little too loud. 'Ahhh mate you're a funny little bugger.' He fluffed Lachie's hair.

'Don't Dad!' Lachie pushed his hand away. 'You did say Miss Molly…'

Out of the mouths of babes. Molly fussed around with her folder of papers to pretend that she hadn't heard the exchange.

'So, how's my little buddy doing Miss?' Jack spoke loudly to drown out Lachie's insistence.

Molly concentrated on her notes about Lachlan, pursing her lips to hold in a smile in the hope that she looked suitably scholarly and serious.

Clearing her throat she looked up from her notes, straight into Jack's eyes, that were filled with concern for his son.

All thoughts of the father and son conversations about her, disappeared as the reality of what Jack was really asking, hit her.

Lachie was picking his nose again. That boy's nose was probably the cleanest nose in town. Jack followed her gaze and gently pushed his son's hand away from his face letting out an embarrassed chuckle.

Molly ignored it. 'Lachie is a joy to have in the classroom Officer Meadows.'

'Call me Jack. Please.'

'Can I call you Jack, Daddy?' Lachie asked, bumping up and down on his seat.

'No. You call me Daddy. Now let's listen to what Miss McDonald has to say.'

Lachie hurrumphed his disapproval and slouched back in his chair.

'Call me Molly,' she said to Jack.

Molly saw Lachie's eyes widen and he opened his mouth to speak, but she got in first.

'No Lachlan you can't call me Molly. You have to call me Miss McDonald.'

'Or I could call you Mummy,' Lachie exclaimed. 'Susie said I need one of those.'

If Molly had blinked, she would've missed the mixed look of anguish and discomfort that flashed across Jack's face.

She decided to take the bull by the horns and dive right in.

Leaning across the desk she took one of Lachie's little hands in hers. It was his nose picking one, but she didn't flinch.

'Oh, my goodness I'd *love* to be your Mummy,' she said, feeling Jack squirm in his seat and choosing to ignore him. This was between her and Lachlan. 'But you've already got one.'

'No, I don't. She died,' he replied, his big brown eyes clear and true and as honest as only a six-year-old's can be.

Molly leaned closer. 'Do you wanna hear a secret?' she whispered to him.

He nodded and his eyes widened.

'My Mum died too. But she'll always be my one and only Mummy.'

Lachlan cocked his head, his forehead crinkling in thought as he digested Molly's on the spot advice.

'So is your Mummy and my Mummy together?'

'I hope so, because I think they would like each other.'

Lachie sniffed, nodded his head and then smiled at her.

'Ok,' he said, pulling his hand out of what Molly realised was by now quite a firm grip. He looked up at Jack. 'Dad, can I go play?'

Jack seemed caught off-guard and Molly was sure his eyes were clouded with tears.

'Ah, yep, sure mate. Only in the playground ok,' Jack yelled after him as he ran out the door.

'Ok!' Lachie yelled back in an excited high-pitched voice from halfway down the hallway.

Jack shifted in his chair and rubbed his face with his hands in an attempt to hide the fact that his eyes had been leaking. Out of respect for his privacy Molly shuffled with her papers again. If this kept going, she was going to run out of papers.

'Well, you can stay,' Jack said, his voice husky with emotion. 'I wish I was able to be like that with him.'

'Be like what?' Molly slid her papers to the side and leaned back in her chair. Too close. She was wildly attracted to Jack and he was vulnerable. A terrible combination and one that had gotten her into her destructive marriage.

'Honest.'

'Best way to be with kids.'

'And adults?'

'Oh goodness no. Honesty with adults *never* works. They always take it the wrong way,' Molly declared.

Jack leaned back in his chair, threw his head back and let out a long hearty laugh.

His laugh was so contagious Molly couldn't help but laugh along with him. It reached deep into her, the vibration and sound of it falling from his beautiful mouth. She noticed his shoulders were more relaxed than what they were before. Not that she'd seen him very much. And if she was completely honest with herself, she really wanted to see more of him. Not just timewise. But more of him in the biblical sense. Not being particularly religious, Molly didn't really know what that meant but she assumed it was a bit naughty. And that nudity would be involved. A blush rose in her cheeks at the thought of being naked with him. Not to mention the little wave of heat that throbbed deep in her nether regions.

Jack leaned across the table and taking her hand in his, looked into her eyes.

'Thank you, Miss McDonald…ahh…Molly. I needed that. I haven't laughed like that for a long time.'

Molly felt a little bit like she was falling into his deep blue eyes and had to give herself a metaphorical slap so that she didn't say something silly like, *Well you might of needed that laugh but I need you to kiss me right now.*

Instead, she squeezed his hand and smiled at him. 'It was my pleasure. Any time.'

Jack returned the smile and she was sure she saw a wave of desire wash across his eyes. Then he blinked, pulled his hands back and rested them on his thighs.

'Well, I'd like to say the pleasure was all mine, but perhaps that's for another time.'

If Molly hadn't checked the weather app to see that there was a week of sunshine on the way she would've thought there was a thunderstorm approaching, because the electricity between them was palpable. There was also another feeling deep in her stomach. Pleasure meant pain, but before she could say anything in return, the school bell rang to indicate that their time was up and the next parent was due.

Jack let out a long sigh. 'Time flies when you're having fun.' He stood up and walked towards the door and then turned back. 'See you at tea and biccies after?'

'Wouldn't miss it,' Molly replied, her voice a little shaky with a tonne of emotion and a little bit of lust.

He smiled and nodded at the next parent entering the room, but Jack didn't miss the opportunity to give Molly a quick wink that made her nipples tighten in response.

She hoped and prayed that Mr Bartlett who sat down opposite her wouldn't notice.

7

Molly's Prius bumped along the gnarly dusty back roads of Propadollah, towards Far Horizons Farm.

She vowed to herself that if she was going to live in Nhill permanently, and the jury was still out on that, the Prius was going to have to be traded in for a more country friendly vehicle.

A Ute or a four-wheel drive was not for her and as the Prius dipped into another pothole with an almighty crunch, Molly knew she was going to end up with an SUV. A Sport Utility Vehicle. Makes sense in the country. Not so much in the city where Molly called them Stupid Urban Vehicles because they blocked everything. Views. Roads. Carparks.

But for the moment she was stuck with her environmentally friendly hybrid that was slowly but surely sacrificing its undercarriage to the back roads of Propadollah.

She breathed a sigh of relief as the entrance to Far Horizons came into view in her headlights. Turning into the driveway she stopped for a moment, deciding whether to proceed or not. Technically it wasn't trespassing if the gate was open. And as there was no gate, just a collection of old wooden beams hanging at right angles from rusty hinges it was open for her to drive in. The sign read: *Far Ho zons*. A result of years of neglect, weather and shooting practice from local kids with their pellet guns.

The property had been sold and bought many times over the last four decades. Her mother had filled her in with who, what and when but Molly never really listened. She wished she'd paid more attention.

She did remember that no one lived in the old farmhouse anymore. In the early 80's the owners had built a snazzy new sprawling homestead, on the north east side of the property where they had access to town plumbing. Her mother had chuckled at the photo Nora sent her of the new house.

'I bet they regretted building this monstrosity,' she'd said.

'Why?' A semi-curious teenage Molly had asked, her head buried in her Dolly Mag.

'A year after they built it the drought hit. All that money spent on that snazzy house, down the drain, pun intended.'

'Uh huh,' nodded Molly, making a note of the pink lipstick brand that her 'sister by another mister' Molly Ringwald used.

'Pop always used to say, you don't live on the land, you live *in* the land, *for* the land, *with* the land. And always, always know that she will turn on you when you least expect it. And boy did she turn.'

Molly smiled at the memory and at the deep respect her mother had for mother nature. She put the car into drive and headed up the long, even bumpier, driveway towards her mother's childhood home.

In the darkness of the night, the hundred-year-old house was the stuff of horror movies and nightmares.

Hollywood producers would be crawling over each other to use it as a set if they knew it existed.

Molly was glad her mother never got to see it in this condition.

She recalled seeing old black and white photos of it with her mum and her siblings in front of the verandah steps, atop of ponies, or pushbikes or in school uniforms on their first days of school, faces beaming in anticipation of what lay ahead for them.

Back then, the house was a pretty white weatherboard with a bullnose verandah decorated with intricate iron lace, that wrapped all the way around. Wicker chairs adorned with cushions, sat on the porch and voluptuous wisteria vines wound themselves around the porch columns.

According to her mother, it had three bedrooms, one bathroom, an outhouse, a kitchen which housed an impressive six burner wood-fired Aga oven, a sunroom out the back and a formal sitting room that was barely used.

Her mother and father had the main bedroom and she shared a room with her sister while her brother, *lucky bastard* she called him, had a bedroom all to himself. For many years she would exclaim to anybody who would listen *I wish I'd been born a boy!*

Molly assumed that was, in large part, why her mother became such a staunch feminist. All because her brother had his own bedroom.

The years of neglect had not been kind to the 'old girl', as her mother used to call her. And she was definitely old. The lights from Molly's car showed no sign of any white paint anywhere. The dry dead roots of the wisteria looked like it was the only thing holding the east side of the porch up. The rest of the verandah hung in various angles and the iron roof was speckled with rust and dead leaves.

There were no intact windows at the front of the house and her headlights shone all the way through the front entrance to the back-yard where the Hills Hoist clothesline sat at a tired right angle with one kid too many having swung on it. Probably the local kids with the pellet guns.

Molly parked the car and grabbed her torch. Making her way to the entrance, she stood carefully on the verandah steps, avoiding the rotten wood and aiming for what looked like solid footing. She made her way inside the house and walked straight into a spider's web, right across her face.

Spluttering and grabbing at her face and hair she ran into the entrance hall, hopping from foot to foot. She hated spiders ever since she'd had one caught up in her curly brown hair as a kid. It became a life long fear.

Trying not to scream she calmed herself down, running her fingers through her hair a dozen times to make sure nothing lurked.

Once her heart rate had settled, she moved from room to room. All dusty, dark and empty. She wasn't sure what she thought she'd find or feel. Family perhaps. Something that would make her DNA vibrate. Connection. But it was just an old house that was desperately trying not to fall down.

The only room that had anything left in it was her mother's bedroom. An old cupboard stood against the far wall, pale and weathered from the hole in the roof that let in the sun and rain and the wind.

Molly smiled at a memory her mother had shared with her.

'I loved to read. Anything and everything I could get my hands on. And my sister couldn't sleep with any light on, so I'd get into the cupboard with the torch until all hours of the morning. It was my happy place.'

The doors were hard to open as the wood had swollen in the heat and the hinges had rusted together. Molly held the torch in her mouth and tugged gently at first, and then in a moment of frustration gave one final pull. The doors flung open.

Molly squeezed her eyes shut and held her arm across her face for protection as a flurry of dust and dry leaves fell down upon her. She felt something else as well. A cool breeze, which was strange because there was nothing cool about Nhill in February. It made her skin prickle with goose bumps and a shiver move up and down her body. As she opened her eyes, she thought she saw a shimmer of something in the corner of the room. She blinked a few times trying to focus on it, but it had gone. Or most likely, there was nothing there to begin with.

Lachie's drawing flashed into her mind for a brief second, until a warm squall of northerly wind blew through the opening in the wall, warming her back up again. She shook of the heebee jeebees and shone her torch into the cupboard.

Except for a thick layer of decades-old dust, it was empty. She was about to close the doors when a sliver of white paper in the corner, caught her eye. Checking carefully for more cobwebs, she leaned in and grabbed the paper. It was an old envelope. And it was addressed to her mother with beautiful cursive handwriting. There was no postmark or sender details on the back.

Molly felt her heart rate increase. She wanted to open it. But it felt wrong. Like she was prying into her mother's life. She'd obviously left it in the cupboard for safekeeping and to keep it away from nosy ninnies.

Turning the envelope over and over in her hands she held it up to the light in case she could see what was written without actually opening it. It wasn't really prying. But she couldn't make anything out.

And then she heard the police siren.

8

Molly stood at what was left of the front door and watched as a police car, lights flashing and siren blaring, came barrelling down the driveway.

She could see the outline of a solitary figure in the driver's seat and she knew it was Jack. Her heart skipped a beat.

He came to a stop next to her car and thankfully so did the siren.

Molly leaned against the door jam, hoping it wouldn't cause the entire house to fall down but also wanting to project a casual air. Because there was nothing casual about what her body was doing at the sight of him getting out of his car – his silhouette even did that sexily - and walking towards her, illuminated by his headlights.

As he got closer and she could start to make out his hunky face, Molly gave him a smile and a small wave. 'We've got to stop meeting like this.'

'Do we?' Jack smiled back at her, throwing in a wink for good measure.

The house might not be collapsing any time soon, but Molly was in definite danger of falling down.

'Why all the fanfare?' Molly asked.

'I got a call from the owner, she said there was a trespasser on the property. We've had some squatters here in the past and I like to give them a warning that I'm coming so they can get out of dodge before I arrive. I'm not the arresting type if I can help it.'

'So, you won't be arresting me then?'

Jack stood at the bottom of the verandah steps and scanned her from head to toe, his eyes finally landing on hers, making her breath catch in her throat. In the fading light, Molly didn't miss the deep want, and then he blinked and they returned to the cheeky twinkle she was beginning to adore.

'Well?' she asked, hoping it was equally cheeky, but it was more breathy and come hither than what she was expecting.

Jack cocked his head, 'I'm thinking…'

'I think this is what's called witness intimidation.'

'Oh, you're not the witness. You're the suspect.'

'And what exactly am I suspected of doing? This is my family's house after all.' Molly planted her hands on her hips and felt immediately defensive. This was her ancestral home. Where generations of her family had been born, lived and died.

'Not anymore I'm afraid Molly. I think I'm going to have to take you in for…questioning.' He unclipped a pair of handcuffs from his tactical belt and swung them lightly from side to side.

Molly glanced at the handcuffs and even though it was a hot night, a cold shiver ran down her body and she dropped her head, taking a few deep breaths.

It was happening again.

She heard the squeak of dry wood as Jack walked up the steps towards her.

'Stay away!' she shouted, throwing her arms out in front of her for protection. The buzzing started in her ears and she took a step back away from him, straight into a hole in the rotting floor.

She cried out in pain and fell to the ground with a thud.

～

MOLLY JUST DISAPPEARED. ONE MOMENT HE WAS PLAYING 'COPS AND robbers' with her - he thought - then she shouted at him, there was a crash, she screamed and disappeared into the darkness.

He dropped the handcuffs, stupid things, pulled out the torch from his belt and flicked it on.

In the hallway just inside the door, Molly was on the ground with one of her legs down the hole in the rotten floorboards.

He raced to her and dropped to his knees.

'Molly?'

She groaned.

He knew he wasn't supposed to move an injured person, but he wanted to touch her to make sure she was alright, so he placed his hand on her shoulder.

She flinched and then groaned in pain.

'It's okay Molly. It's just me. Jack. The cop. Remember? I'm not going to hurt you,' he said, knowing that's what she needed to hear.

'What happened?' Molly groaned, trying to move her leg, which made her wince in pain.

He could see blood on her head. 'The floorboards gave way. Your leg is hurt and you've hit your head. I'll have to call an ambulance.'

'No. No ambulance please. Can't you fix it?' Molly pleaded, her words starting to slur.

Jack knew he had to get her to the hospital sooner rather than later, before she passed out from shock or pain or whatever else was going on. Because he knew there was something else.

'Molly, I'm going to put your arm around my neck. Is that okay?'

'Uh huh,' she murmured, almost imperceptible.

He gently placed her weak arm around his neck. 'Then I'm going to pull you up. It will hurt your leg, but you'll be alright.'

He wrapped his arms around her body. 'Alright, on the count of three. One. Two. Three.'

As he pulled her up, she groaned in pain and then went limp in his arms.

'Molly!'

Nothing. She was out. With a hit to the head that was not good.

'Damn it,' he growled as he carried her to his car, laying her down gently on the back seat.

Brushing sweaty curls from her forehead, he leaned down and kissed it.

'You'll be okay Moll. Hang tight.'

As he closed the cruiser door, he noticed her clutching an envelope, spattered with blood.

He jumped into the driver's seat, punched the siren and sped away from the farmhouse just as a hot gust of wind swirled around it creating a wailing siren of its own.

9

M olly reached across to her bedside table to turn off her alarm that was beeping at her but there was no alarm clock.

'Molly, Molly.'

That was her name wasn't it? Molly. Someone was saying her name. She didn't recognise the voice. It was a man. But she couldn't remember having a man anywhere near her bed. Come to think of it, she couldn't remember anything that happened after she went out to the farm.

She tried to open her eyes, but they were so heavy and they just did not want to open. Panic bubbled in her throat and she didn't recognise the voice, but maybe he had found her. Maybe he'd tracked her down. She cursed herself for not covering her tracks. Of course, going back to somewhere she knew was dangerous. But she'd never told him where her mother came from or that Nhill was where she'd been born. Sadly, he had his ways.

Finally, she was able to force her eyes open and sitting bolt upright, she came face-to-face with a man in scrubs.

'Welcome back Molly,' The scrub man said, giving her a wide smile.

He had peppery grey hair and black-rimmed glasses, so it definitely wasn't him.

Molly let out a sigh of relief and lay back down against her pillows. 'Why? Where did I go?'

'You had a pretty nasty hit to the head and you lost consciousness. We were worried there was some bleeding on the brain, but it's all okay. Your ankle has a bad sprain though.'

Movement at the door caught her attention. It was Jack.

'Yeah. It was touch and go. Almost lost your leg, didn't she doc?'

Molly's eyes widened in shock.

Scrub Man glared at Jack, then looked back down at Molly and patted her hand.

'He's telling you a porky pie, don't listen to him.'

'Jack!' Molly exclaimed.

Jack threw his arms in the air in mock surrender. 'Alright alright, I'm sorry, my bad. Just couldn't help myself what with you lying there all vulnerable and everything. It felt like the right thing to do.'

The man in scrubs who Molly had determined was her doctor rolled his eyes. 'Hilarious. Local Constabulary the envy of stand-up comedians.'

Molly laughed. 'Don't give up your day job.'

Her doctor gave her shoulder a soft pat. 'It will be uncomfortable for a while. We've strapped it and given you some nice pain relief. You're gonna be okay.' He smiled and pointed to the drip attached to her arm.

'Hey Doc!' Molly asked as he was leaving the room.

'Yes?' He replied turning back to her.

Molly was feeling the effects of the pain relief. 'If I have to wear one of those groovy moon boots can I have mine in pink. And maybe with some black spots and some purple squiggly bits?'

Jack and the doctor exchanged looks.

'We'll see what we can do,' The doctor replied giving her another wide smile and leaving the room.

Jack sat in the chair next to her bed his eyes searching hers. 'I'm sorry,' he said, 'I make really bad jokes when I'm worried or sad or concerned. And I'm a little bit all three at the moment.'

He dropped his head in contrition.

Molly looked at him and squinted her eyes, checking out the top of his head. He really did have lovely hair. All dark and wavy with a little bit of grey in there. He was going to make someone a very very nice Silver Fox one-day. He lifted his head up and his eyes were sad. It made her giggle.

'Oh, now I'm sorry. I tend to get a little inappropriate when I've been pumped with hallucinogenic pain relief. I really do hallucinate. Like just before I thought he'd tracked me down. But it wasn't him it was just the doctor.'

'Who tracked you down?'

Molly looked across at Jack, whose face was etched with worry.

'You look worried Jack. Are you going to crack a funny?' Molly giggled.

He leaned forward in his chair and took her hand. 'Who are you talking about Molly?' he pleaded, his voice soft but urgent.

Molly had to close one eye to keep him in focus. He really was worried. 'Pfft, don't worry about it really. The drugs are making me paranoid and giggly at the same time. What a combo!'

'But I am worried,' Jack let go of her hand and stood up as if he wanted to go somewhere but didn't know where.

'Hey,' Molly whispered, gesturing for him to come closer. He bent his head to her and she looked from side to side to make sure there was no one else there. It was a private room. He didn't take his eyes off her.

'He doesn't know where I am. I promise. I changed my number. I didn't tell anyone where I was going,' she said, her whisper getting quieter and quieter.

'Molly,' Jack whispered back, 'I really am worried now. Who are you talking about?'

'I think she's talking about me mate,' a soft, menacing voice answered. But the mouth that it came out of was smiling.

It was him. Her ex-husband. The one she had run from. The room started to spin and Molly felt like she was floating above herself. The beeping from the machines got louder and faster and she thought she heard someone cry out.

But it wasn't someone else. It was her.

10

____

Anurse raced in to check her vitals.

'What happened?' She asked, scowling at Jack. 'What did you do?'

'I didn't do anything,' Jack replied, staring at Molly's ex, who gave him with a smirk.

'You okay sweetie?' Asked the nurse, checking Molly's blood pressure.

All Molly was able to do was nod her head. She wanted to yell at the top of her voice that *no she wasn't okay*. The three responses to fear are flight, fight or freeze and she had frozen. In the past she had tried to fight and that had ended up badly. Moving to Nhill was the flight which she thought had given her freedom.

The nurse seemed happy once the beeping machines had slowed down. She wiggled the finger at Jack. 'Five more minutes Jack. She needs to rest.'

As she passed Molly's ex-husband at the door, she glanced up at him, 'You too.'

He furnished the nurse with a beaming smile, making her blush. He was a handsome man.

After she left, he brought his grey, soulless eyes back to Molly, the beaming smile gone, replaced with tight lips.

He walked over to her bed and took her hand. His touch and his smell, a mixture of cigarettes and spicy aftershave sent a cold shiver along her arm and down her spine, but she was unable to move. *Come on Molly! Pull your hand away. You promised you'd never let him touch you again.*

'Oh Molly, honey, I didn't mean to scare you.

'Didn't you?' Jack asked moving closer to her on the other side of the bed. 'Because it sure as hell looked like it scared the living crap out of her.'

'And you are?' Molly didn't miss her ex squaring his shoulders, trying to look even more menacing as he glared at Jack.

'I was about to ask you the same question.'

'I suppose being a cop you're pretty used to asking questions so okay I'll fold. I'm her husband.'

'Ex.' Molly croaked, her throat dry and tight all of a sudden.

'You got a name?' Jack asked, his voice low and dangerous.

'Yeah, I do,' Her ex replied, equally ominous. He stared down at Molly and although he was smiling, Molly knew that smile meant trouble, his hard, grey-green eyes telling her the same.

'What's my name honey?' he asked her, squeezing her hand just a little bit too tight.

'T…Tony,' Molly whispered.

'Tony what?'

'Please don't,' Molly whispered, bile starting to rise in her throat. She pulled her hand away.

'Okay mate I think it's time to go,' Jack said. Out of the corner of her eye, Molly saw Jack's hand move to rest on the handle of his holstered gun.

Tony saw it too.

He flinched slightly, his smile disappearing. His fists clenched and his face hardened into an all-too-familiar expression.

But it was only for the briefest of moments as he was a master of disguise. He threw up his hands in mock surrender and backed away towards the door.

'Alright officer. Nothing to see here,' he said, his voice as smooth as silk. 'You're the boss.' He saluted Jack, blew Molly a kiss and left the room.

Jack followed him to make sure he had gone. It wasn't until he gave Molly a nod – *the coast was clear*, that she allowed the tears to flow.

Jack rushed back to her and pulled her into his arms as she sobbed into his shoulder. He shushed her and stroked her hair, rocking her gently back and forth. Molly felt safe in his arms, safer than she felt in a long time.

His touch didn't repulse her. Which was a relief.

After a few moments, she felt herself relax and her heart rate return to normal.

Though Molly wasn't crying anymore, she thought it appropriate to move away, only she didn't want to. And his arms were so tightly around her it felt like he didn't want to let her go either.

The nurse made the decision for them by striding into the room and clicking her fingers at Jack.

'What did I say Jack! Five minutes. Out,' she insisted, pointing to the door.

They pulled away from each other and Jack wiped her cheeks dry. He leaned in and gave her a kiss on the forehead and she felt a nub of disappointment that he didn't aim for her mouth.

'Rest up. I'll check on you later.'

As he got to the door he turned back. 'Just out of interest what's his last name?'

'Why do you want to know?'

'Just trust me Molly.'

She did trust him. With anything. Even though she'd only known him for a short time.

'Dutton. Anthony Dutton.' It made her feel ill just saying his name.

'I like McDonald better,' Jack said, giving her a wide smile that warmed her soul, making her realise how chilled to the bone she had been.

❧

JACK STRODE DOWN THE HALL UNTIL HE WAS FAR ENOUGH AWAY FROM Molly's room to stop and take a few very deep breaths. His teeth clenched, his heart rate up. He knew he had to get that man out of her life.

As a police officer he knew exactly what had taken place between those two. He despised all men who abused women, but in this instance, it felt personal. There was a rage in him. A white-hot anger. The only other time he had felt that kind of rage was towards the cancer that took his wife – Sarah.

The intensity of his anger surprised him. He'd only known Molly for a short time, but there was definitely a strong connection.

He leaned against the wall, dropped his head to gather his thoughts and calm himself down. He took a few deep breaths and shook his head to dispel all thoughts of what he wanted to do to Tony.

Straightening up he made a beeline for the nurse's station and found Kim, Molly's nurse.

'Kim hey,' he said giving her the widest brightest spunkiest smile he could. 'So…that other guy who was in Molly's room. Do you know how he found out she was here?'

Kim raised her eyebrow at Jack to let him know that she knew what he was up to.

Jack gave her a *pretty please* look with his hands pressed together in prayer. It usually worked.

'Are you asking as a police officer or as Jack Meadows, the man who has a soft spot for the woman in there?'

'I'm shocked you even have to ask Kim,' Jack replied in mock surprise, his feelings bruised.

Kim shook her head and chuckled. 'Officer Meadows your interrogation technique needs work.'

Jack leaned on the top of the desk and gestured for her to come closer. She leaned her head towards his.

'Now, would I have seen a speeding ticket of yours come across my desk just the other day?' he whispered.

She stared at him for a moment to suss him out, then gave his shoulder a whack and walked over to her computer. She typed for a few seconds and then read from the screen.

'Okay Sherlock, it says here that he's her emergency contact.'

'She said that?'

Kim turned the computer screen towards him and he moved over to look at it.

'No. It was on her My Health record,' she said.

'Thanks a bunch. Your driving record is officially perfect again,' Jack said giving her a wink and striding off down the hall. 'Now slow down. That's an official warning!' he yelled back over his shoulder.

No time to muck around, he was in a hurry. He had to look up this Anthony Dutton and find out everything about him.

As he exited the hospital a wave of heat hit him. It made him feel lightheaded, which it never did because he was born and bred a Wimmera boy. He was used to the heat, even in March, but as he was already burning with outrage, it added fuel to his fire.

Rounding the corner into the carpark he stopped short. Dutton was leaning on the bonnet of his police car sucking on a cigarette.

Jack slipped his sunglasses on because he didn't want Dutton to see the rage in his eyes. He wanted to come across as cool calm and collected.

Jack sauntered towards his car as if he didn't have a worry in the world and like he didn't want to throw a punch at the arrogant bastard leaning on his bonnet. Ignoring him, he walked around to the driver's side.

'Sorry officer it just looked so comfy,' Tony drawled, taking another drag of his cigarette and staying right where he was. 'Do you need me to move?'

Tony opened his door and glanced up as if he was being bothered by a blowfly. 'If you like walking, might be a good idea. Up to you mate.' He dropped into the driver's seat, slammed the door and started the car.

In that moment, he was grateful that Victorian Police cars were V8's because they revved really well.

Keeping the car in neutral, he planted his foot down on the accelerator. The car's engine let out a massive growl which made Tony jump off the bonnet, the cigarette flying out his hand and onto the ground.

Jack sped away feeling like he'd won that battle and looking in the rearview mirror, he saw Tony giving him the finger.

'Is that all you got buddy?' Jack said to the image of Molly's ex-husband as he disappeared from view. 'Cause this town ain't big enough for the both of us,' he recited in his best Eastwood delivery. *I've always wanted to say that,* he thought, rounding the corner and racing towards the police station to start his investigation.

11

———

I am such an idiot.

Maybe Tony was right. Maybe I am a loser, hopeless and unworthy.

Molly couldn't believe she'd forgotten to change her emergency contact. Everything else, except for her first name had been changed and she'd started using her mother's maiden name.

And then she had to go and sprain her stupid ankle while foraging around her dead mother's crumbling old childhood farmhouse.

What did she think she was going to find? Treasure? An old secret that you read about in books or see in movies? But there was that letter. The letter addressed to her mum! Where had she left it? Maybe Jack would know.

She missed her mum terribly. It was a hard goodbye. A long goodbye. And by the end she almost thought a sudden goodbye would've been better. Either way it sucked.

Closing her eyes she let the tears escape down her cheeks.

'Did you miss me?'

Molly blinked her eyes open, already knowing who it was. Tony had done his typical thing and crept up on her. He was standing next to the bed his hand resting lightly on her injured ankle.

Molly knew he would injure it further if he wanted to and if she didn't behave.

She was so tired of him. Tired of his abuse.

'No.' Her voice was flat, empty of emotion, not wanting to give him an inch.

He moved closer to her, his hand still on her ankle and perched on the edge of the bed. She didn't move to make room for him.

'Why did you run Moll?'

He said it with such sincerity and a hint of sadness that anybody listening in would have thought it had come from the heart. Molly knew better. Sociopaths know how to play the game.

She reached for the nurse call button, but Tony snatched it out of her hand making her flinch.

'Oh, now come on Moll. We're adults I am sure we can have an adult conversation.'

He leaned into her, pressing down firmer on her ankle. His breath smelled like cigarettes and it made Molly turn her head away in disgust.

'I will ask again why did you run?'

Molly took a deep breath. 'Why do you think?'

'How should I know? That's why I'm asking you.'

She couldn't look at him in case his steely eyes full of threat, made her change her mind. 'I don't love you Tony.'

'So? I still love you and that's all that matters.'

Molly shook her head. 'Is that what you call love? Stopping me from seeing my friends. My family. Making sure I have no money to spend on myself. And what about this?' She pointed to this small scar beside her left eye.

'That was an accident,' Tony exclaimed. 'Could have happened to anyone. That's what the doctor said.'

'Yes, the doctor who just so happens to be your best friend.'

Molly was quite surprised at how strong she felt. Perhaps the drugs were giving her a false sense of security. Or perhaps being away from him had given her the chance to find herself again. She liked the feeling.

Tony's breathing started to deepen and his body tensed. All the usual signs that he was about to burst. But Molly knew she was safe because he never did anything in public. Only ever in private.

'My wife just disappears, and I do everything to find her, then a month later I get a call from a hospital in some hick country town to say she's had an accident. I mean what do you want me to do Moll?'

'What do I want? I want you to leave now and go back to Melbourne. And I never want to see you again.' Molly said her voice strong and clear.

Tony fixed his eyes on hers and growled at her.

'Oh, you'll be seeing me all right. When you least expect it.' He leaned into her and planted a hard dry kiss on her lips before she could move away. Then he left the room leaving a taste of cigarettes on her lips and a pit of fear in her stomach.

JACK PUNCHED HIS PASSWORD INTO THE COMPUTER AT THE STATION. ONCE into the system he went straight to the individual database and typed in Anthony Dutton. There were thousands of Anthony Duttons in the country, so he changed his search and came up with 1433 Anthony Duttons in Melbourne. Of those 1433, 356 of them had reports which ranged from criminal activity to overdue parking fines.

He leaned back in his chair. This was going to take some time and he was going to need Molly's help.

He chided himself for jumping the gun and not following basic investigative procedure and getting as much information about him as possible. But in the moment, he wasn't thinking like a police officer, he was thinking like a man who was trying to protect someone he cared about.

The door to the station swung open letting in a gush of hot air from outside. Constable Raverty the newest officer on the job, walked in and dropped her cap onto her desk.

'I thought you were off duty sir?' she said to Jack wiping sweat off her brow.

'I kind of am,' he replied. 'I haven't been home since last night's shift.' He took a brief moment to silently thank his in-laws who had stepped up and taken Lachie for a few days. There was definitely a change in the air. Placing his elbows on the desk he leaned forward and rubbed his face to try and get the blood flowing and his brain going. 'Ugh. I need a coffee.'

'I can get you a coffee sir,' Raverty said.

Jack looked up at her and smiled. 'That would be great thanks. Oh, and call me Jack...please. We're not as worried about titles in the country.'

Raverty nodded. 'Yes sir...sorry...Jack. That felt weird,' she laughed.

'One coffee coming right up!' Raverty declared and hot-footed it to the kitchen area at the back of the station as only an enthusiastic newbie would.

Jack turned back to the computer screen, running his eyes over the list of Anthony Dutton offenders in the hope that one would just jump out.

He really didn't want to bother Molly about her ex. It was obviously painful, but he needed more information in the hope that he could find some dirt and either get him out of town or even better, get him into jail.

He knew men like Tony Dutton and there was always dirt – but Jack had a feeling he was going to have to dig a lot deeper to find his.

12

———————

'Are you sure you don't need anything else?' a concerned Nora asked, fussing around Molly as she lay reclined on her sofa, leg up on a tower of cushions, a blanket nearby in case she got cold - not likely in the Wimmera heat - and a tray on the coffee table next to her that held a bowl of macaroni cheese for dinner, a glass of red wine, the TV remote and her mobile phone.

'Seriously Nora, I wouldn't get this kind of service in first class on Qantas. Now go home or you'll need tending.'

'Alright. But call me if you need *anything*. Anytime. I'll leave my phone on next to my bed.'

'Thank you, but I'm sure I'll be fine,' Molly said, feeling tears starting to prick in her eyes. No wonder her mother and Nora had remained such firm friends - they were the proverbial peas in a pod. And although Molly felt incredibly nurtured and loved, it broke her heart at the same time that her mum wasn't there to look after her.

She worked against the tears because she knew if Nora spied them, she would want to stay the night. But Molly was ready for her own space. Spending overnight in the hospital with machines beeping, a man who snored a lot in the next room and the ever-present hum of the nurse's chatter, had left Molly with very little sleep and a deep desire for her own bed.

Her doctor was happy for her to head home once he had eased her off the pain meds, making sure her concussion had settled and she had no discomfort.

The only discomfort she had was the heavy feeling in her gut from the last thing Tony had said to her. *When you least expect it.*

There'd been no contact from him since he had left her hospital room, but she knew when it came to intimidation, he was a man of his word.

'Get some rest my dear,' Nora ordered as she grabbed her handbag.

There was a knock at the front door.

Molly almost jumped out of her skin and off the sofa.

Nora opened the door and Molly craned her head as far as she could from her position on the sofa but couldn't see who it was. All she heard were the deep rumbling tones of a man's voice and it made her stomach drop.

And then Nora's. 'Come in. Come in. I was just leaving.'

She heard the door shut and she braced herself for what was to come. She reached for the fork that sat in the macaroni cheese, holding it at the ready as it dripped cheesy sauce onto the upholstery.

In walked Jack.

She exhaled, unaware that she had been holding her breath, but the fork still remained on guard.

'Is that a fork in your hand or are you just pleased to see me?' he remarked, holding a laugh at bay.

Molly glanced at her weapon of choice and then back up at him. 'No. It's more of a fork you.'

Jack threw his head back and laughed. 'Touche! Although I was going to ask if you were going to have me for dinner?'

Their eyes locked and Molly felt her stomach drop again but in a good way. A nice way. A sexy way. All the way down to in-between her legs way.

'Unless you're macaroni and cheese, then that's a no,' she replied.

Jack nodded and his eyes twinkled. 'Disappointing.'

Okay so that was one hundred percent flirting. Molly wasn't ready for that. She wasn't a very good flirter anyway, but Jack seemed to know exactly how to do it.

Come to think of it that's what got her into trouble with Tony. He was an excellent flirter. Compliments, dreamy eyes, the odd light touch every now and again just to keep her wanting more. No…flirting was dangerous.

'What's disappointing is that it's gone cold.' Molly pushed herself up on the sofa and grabbed the crutches that were leaning against the side.

'No no let me do that for you,' Jack insisted.

'I can do it myself.' Molly declared, giving Jack a look that told him to back off.

He obeyed and took a step back.

Molly pushed herself up off the sofa with a grunt and a crutch under each arm. If only she had three hands because no matter how much she tried to pick up the bowl of macaroni, she only succeeded in making herself feel like a new foal trying to walk for the first time.

'Okay here's the deal,' Jack said moving forward to help her. 'You do the crutches, I'll do the macaroni and we'll call it even.'

'Fine,' Molly sighed in resignation.

'Hey, you've just got out of hospital, give yourself some time to get used to this. And in the meantime, let me help. I mean what else are police for. We're here to help the community and you're part of the community so let me help.'

'I said fine,' Molly muttered hopping into the kitchen on the crutches. Just a few feet and her armpits were already sore. It was going to be a fun couple of weeks.

She opened the microwave and Jack slipped the macaroni inside. As the microwave did its thing Molly looked up at him.

'I'm not going to be a part of this community for much longer.'

'What do you mean?' Jack asked, concern lacing his voice.

Molly cleared her throat. It felt harder to say it out loud than it did in her head.

'Well, it looks like I have another teaching offer somewhere else.

Better money. At a High School, which is my preferred age group to teach and somewhere not as damn hot,' she declared with a forced laugh.

She scanned Jack's face to try and get an idea of what he was thinking. It shouldn't have mattered what he thought, but for some reason it did. For a fleeting moment disappointment flickered in his eyes then he blinked it away and it was replaced with something softer, adoring almost. He took a step towards her and her stomach dropped again. If it dropped any further, it would fall out.

He was about to say something when the microwave dinged.

Saved by the bell.

Desperate to shift the energy she grabbed the macaroni out of the microwave, making her shriek. The bowl was way too hot, she let go and it smashed onto the floor. Hot cheesy sauce and little curved tubes of pasta splashed across the floor.

That was the macaroni cheese that broke the camel's back. Molly dropped her head, rubbed her hand against her leg to take the heat out of it and started to cry.

She felt Jack's hand on her arm. 'It's fine Moll…'

'Don't call me that!' she cried.

'Alright. I'm sorry. It's just pasta. I'll go out and grab something at the shops then I'll clean this up. It'll be okay.'

Molly snapped her head up and stared at him. 'It's not *just* pasta. And it's not going to be okay. Nothing about any of this is okay. And, and, and I'm starving,' she sobbed as he pulled her into him. It wasn't lost on her that she had already cried into his chest. He was going to think she was weak and pathetic. Just like Tony told her she was.

She sniffed away her final sobs. Wiping her tears she lifted her head to Jack who pulled her hand gently from her face.

'Let me,' he whispered and slowly kissed her wet cheeks, his arms around her back pulling her even closer. The crutches fell to the ground amongst the cheese and pasta, but Molly didn't care. She knew he'd never let her fall and she felt safe in his arms.

He kissed her cheeks, then her forehead, then the corner of her eyes, then the side of her mouth. She opened her lips ever so slightly and he pulled back to look at her.

The way he was looking at her, she thought she would combust. He tucked a loose wave of hair behind her ear and bent his head to kiss her neck. Tilting her head and closing her eyes she let out a small moan as waves of heat travelled up and down her body. This was the kind of heat she liked.

'Molly,' Jack groaned. 'Is this ok?' he asked, his lips almost on hers, his eyes dark with lust and want.

'Yes. Maybe I will have you for dinner after all,' Molly whispered with a chuckle, bringing her lips to his.

He moaned softly into her mouth, his lips gentle on hers, finding their fit. And fit they did…perfectly. Their tongues sought each other out, flirted with each other, his kiss became more insistent, his breathing deeper. Molly leaned into him, feeling his hardness on her thigh.

He cradled her face with his hand, his thumb stroking her skin making it buzz under his touch.

Without the support of both of his arms, Molly had to put more weight on her injured foot, which unbalanced her and interrupted their kiss.

Jack quickly scooped her up in his arms. 'Gee anyone would think you were falling for me,' he murmured, nuzzling into her neck, his lips finding her sweet spot just below her ear. It made her giggle.

He pulled back. 'Oh, is the idea of falling for me funny to you?' he teased.

Looking into his beautiful blue eyes, twinkling with mischief, Molly suddenly felt a wave of sadness because she was actually falling for him. But nothing could ever happen because she was leaving. She had to. And she couldn't tell him where or when.

'Nothing funny about falling. That's what got me into this mess in the first place,' she whispered, pulling his head to hers and kissing him softly on the lips as if in goodbye.

'Now where's that food you promised me? I'm starving!' she exclaimed, trying not to be swayed by his look of disappointment, which he covered quickly.

'One takeout dinner coming right up,' he said as he carried her back out to the sofa, placing her gently on it. When he moved away and his hands weren't on her body anymore, she felt empty and cold, bereft. All she wanted was for him to keep kissing her, touching her, but if Tony ever found out there'd be hell to pay, for both of them.

No, she was resolved. The sooner she left Nhill the better.

13

J ack wasn't going anywhere.

It was his job as law enforcement to protect and serve. So, it was literally his job to park out the front of Molly's house to protect her from Tony.

Wasn't it?

Once they'd polished off the super supreme pizza, Molly had given him some information on her ex. She insisted that he'd never hurt her physically but that she just needed to get out of the relationship. End of story. He didn't need to be a good interrogator to tell she was holding back.

But he didn't want to push. He got what he wanted. For the moment.

He punched a number into his phone.

'Hey mate,' Doug answered, his voice groggy.

'Oh, shit sorry buddy did I wake you?'

'It is one o'clock in the morning Jack,' Doug replied.

Jack glanced at his watch. He had no idea it was that late. The time had gone so quickly chatting with Molly. Time flies when you're having fun. 'Argh sorry, I'll call you tomorrow.'

'Nah I'm awake now. I assume you're calling to say you want the job?'

'Oh, the job,' Jack murmured. He'd completely forgotten about the job. 'Sorry no, I haven't made a decision. I need a favour.'

'So, a job in the city paying twice as much as what you get now and more opportunities for you and Lachie, isn't a favour?'

Jack chuckled. 'Point taken. I need *another* favour. I need you to do a search for me on someone. Possible cyber activity.'

'Criminal activity?'

'I'm not sure. He's definitely a bad guy and he's involved in cyber security, but I don't know if there's anything else going on. He comes up clean in my searches, but you might have more luck being higher in the food chain.'

'Ok what's his name?'

'Anthony Dutton, date of birth third of May nineteen-seventy-six. He runs Dutton Holdings and lives at 345 Severn Road, Brighton. Got that?'

There was silence on the other end of the line.

'Doug, mate, have you gone back to sleep?'

Doug cleared his throat. 'No. In fact I'm wide awake. Anthony Dutton. AKA Tony Dutton. AKA David McPhee AKA Paul Phillips. We've been looking for him.'

Twenty minutes later Jack hung up and sat back against his driver's seat.

Molly's ex was a real piece of work. Doug had filled him in on the range of cybercrime he had committed over the last five years. From identity theft to theft and sale of corporate data. It was enough to put him away for up to ten years. Not long enough as far as Jack was concerned, but hopefully it was long enough for Molly.

Doug was personally going to come to Nhill the next day, but in the meantime, Jack would keep an eye out for Tony and bring him in if he saw him.

He wanted to knock on Molly's door and tell her straight away, but apart from the fact he wasn't allowed to divulge anything to anyone at this point, her lights had gone out just after he left, so he assumed she was tucked up in bed already.

He wanted to tuck her up in bed and then crawl in next to her, pull her close and never let go. Not just to protect her but to fill the hole in his heart too.

But the last thing Doug had said stuck in his mind.

'Just be careful buddy. He really is a bad guy. Who knows what else he's capable of.'

'You're not telling me everything mate. C'mon.'

Jack heard Doug take a big breath. 'There is no proof of this, but one of his aliases is possibly linked to a double homicide last year. But like I said, there's no proof, he might just be an online arsehole.'

'Okay thanks for the heads up,' Jack said, a deep uneasiness resting in his belly telling him that Tony Dutton was absolutely capable of murder.

A chill ran down his body as he looked over at Molly's house, now shrouded in darkness.

He wasn't going anywhere.

A RAPPING ON THE CAR WINDOW WOKE HIM UP.

Dammit! He'd fallen asleep. He sat bolt upright.

It was Molly. A wave of relief ran down his body that she was okay, despite his woeful protection.

Rubbing his eyes, he wound his window down and glanced up at her, giving her a sheepish grin.

'I like your new digs', Molly quipped.

'Renovator's delight,'

'Did you stay here all night?' she asked, a look of concern spreading across her face.

'With your ex most likely still around, I wasn't going to take any chances.'

'Thank you, but I'm sure I'll be ok. I've got these,' she exclaimed waving one of the crutches around in the air, almost hitting the car. 'Death by crutch.'

'Look out you're a regular Mister Miyagi,' Jack laughed.

Molly bent down, leaned inside the car and gave him a kiss on the cheek.

'Really, thank you. It's nice to know you care.'

Before she stood back up, he cradled her face in his hands and kissed her gently on the lips.

When she pulled away after the kiss, he saw a blush fill her freckled cheeks.

'Well, I do care. You know that don't you?'

'I do.' She nodded but averted her gaze.

He noted that she didn't say she cared for him too. It hurt a little.

'Okay well if you think you're going to be a-okay I've got stuff to do at the station.' He started the car and punched the air-con on. At eight in the morning, it was already starting to heat up.

Molly tucked a handful of curls behind her ear and finally looked at him. It was clear from the adoration in her gold-flecked hazel eyes that she did care for him. But buried deep in there he could sense her fear. He was a man. And he had the potential to hurt her. In more ways than one.

WITH TWO NIGHTS IN A ROW WITHOUT SLEEP JACK GOT TO THE STATION and told Constable Raverty that he was going to have a lie down in one of the holding cells. The only place in the station where he could lie flat. And luckily, or perhaps, because it was a wonderful community, there was never much use for the holding cells. A drunk and disorderly every once in a while and that was usually Carl. They always allowed Bluey – his dog – in with him.

Jack missed his boy. He was pleasantly surprised when his in-laws insisted on having him for a few days. Maybe they were coming out of their grief. He hoped so. For their sake. It gave him pause about moving Lachie down to Melbourne. They'd miss him. But, at the end of the day he had to do what was best for himself and Lachie.

He lay flat on the cold silver aluminium bench closed his eyes and groaned. Oh lord it was good to be horizontal.

The next thing he knew his face was being doused with cold water.

He sat sharply up from the shock, spluttering and spitting.

Then he heard the laugh. It was Doug.

He leapt up and feigned a boxer stance. 'Right, that's it. Put 'em up!'

'Bring it in,' Doug opened his arms and Jack stepped into them. They hugged tightly, slapping each other on the back.

Finally, they pulled apart. Doug looked Jack up and down.

'You look good my friend. With a capital G.'

Jack repaid the favour. 'You look…like you've been sitting in an office for the last twelve months,' he said, leaning forward to give Doug's tummy a slap.

'Hey! Desk duty and responsibilities will do that to a bloke,' he exclaimed. Won't it darling,' he said to his stomach giving it a loving rub.

'Well, nothing's changed then, except for that,' Jack said gesturing to Doug's soft belly.

'Nope. Okay let's see if we can find this bastard. My ever-expanding gut is telling me he's around here somewhere,' Doug said, giving Jack a wink.

'I think your gut is right, expanding or not. Let's go find him.'

14

———————

Molly sat with her injured leg resting on a child's school chair. The kids, playing doctor, had insisted that she put it there to rest. They giggled and shouted questions at her about what happened, did it hurt, would she ever walk again, their curiosity becoming more and more dramatic.

She tried to answer as best she could, but they just made her laugh at how excited they were about a sprained ankle.

Lachie declared that he wanted a sprained ankle too, but Molly warned him that he wouldn't be able to play footy or ride his bike.

He wasn't happy about that. 'So, what are you missing out on Miss?' Lachie asked.

'Well, I can't drive because it's my driving foot. But it'll be better soon.'

'And you can't dance anymore,' Lachie declared.

'That's right Lachie. No dancing for me for a while,' Molly replied.

Two nights before she and Jack had 'danced' a little bit in her kitchen, which would've turned into horizontal dancing if she hadn't put an end to it.

After they'd finished the pizza and he'd cleaned up the mess of macaroni, he admitted to her the real reason he'd come to visit.

He wanted more information on Tony.

She'd already said too much and just wanted to leave and forget about it. But Jack was on a mission, as he called it.

'Molly, I'm going to get the bastard!'

He'd wanted to know his last known address, who he worked for, the names of all of his friends and family and anything else that she thought might be of interest.

Dragging up all of that information had sent Molly down a rabbit hole which gave her a sleepless night tossing and turning. Old memories that she'd pushed down, coming back, dark, raw and painful.

She was glad when Nora had wanted her to get back into the classroom as soon as she was ready. A distraction. Bittersweet as she knew she'd be leaving the kids soon.

A quick search of teaching jobs Australia-wide had brought up lots of options, with jobs in Darwin her preference. A lengthy 4,000 kms away from Melbourne on the northern edge of the country she couldn't get much further. She'd already changed her emergency contact to Nora — who was more than happy to assist — having jumped right into the role of being a surrogate mother to Molly and although Molly wasn't looking for a replacement mother, if she was going to have one, Nora was *the* one. Fiercely loyal and protective with the kind of healthy bosom everyone expects from a maternal figure.

The only thing stopping her from leaving straight away was her ruddy foot. She had another few weeks with the crutches before driving anywhere.

The end of the day bell rang, breaking up the gaggle.

'Okay kids! Don't forget your homework.'

Most of them looked at her like they'd already forgotten. She laughed.

'Draw a picture of your favourite animal,' she said, waving them off. 'Now get outa here you rascals!'

In a flurry of squeals and energy that only six-year-olds can maintain, they left the room. One of the girls, Rabia, whose parents owned the local florist, came running back in with a posy of flowers.

'For you Miss, from Mum and Dad and me,' she declared with a huge smile on her face.

Molly fought back the tears threatening to fall. 'Oh, my goodness Rabia, they're gorgeous. Thank you.'

Rabia wrapped her little arms around her neck and planted a kiss on Molly's cheek.

'You're the bestest Miss I've ever had,' she whispered before letting out a giggle and running out of the room.

Molly closed her eyes and breathed deeply. She'd thought leaving Tony was the hardest thing she'd ever have to do because he had such a controlling hold on her, but leaving *her kids* was going to be harder because they had a different hold on her altogether.

She felt a tap on the shoulder and opened her eyes. Lachie was holding an envelope out to her, her name written in large crayon handwriting on the front. *Moly.*

Molly smiled and opened the envelope. It was an invitation to his seventh birthday party.

'Can you come Miss? Can you?' Lachie asked, unable to keep still, his legs jiggling side to side.

'Yeah, can you Miss?' Jack echoed from the doorway.

Molly glanced up and her breath caught in her throat. He was probably the best-looking man she'd ever laid eyes on. Not in a movie star kind of way but in that laconically confident amazing biceps and shoulders kind of way. The way she liked it.

'Miss!' Lachie yelled at her. He was getting impatient. Fair enough too. His teacher was ogling his dad, which although a wonderful way to spend an afternoon, was also entirely inappropriate.

She dragged her eyes away from Jack's and focussed on the invitation.

'This Saturday. Why yes, I am definitely available Lachie. Wouldn't miss it,' she said, feeling like she actually agreed to something else entirely, which she couldn't quite put her finger on. But what could go wrong at a seven-year-old's birthday party apart from too many sugary drinks and a pin the tail on the Donkey mishap?

'Can't wait,' Jack said, his voice soft and deep, reverberating through every cell in her body.

Ahhh. That. That's what could go wrong.

Molly avoided looking at him. 'Me too,' she replied, her voice just a bit too chirpy, to cover the nagging feeling that Nhill and its residents were starting to change her mind about leaving.

15

———————

Saturday. Lachie's party.

Jack and Doug had no luck whatsoever finding Tony. He wasn't in Nhill or any surrounding towns. There was a state-wide call out to be on the lookout, with a warrant for his arrest.

He'd just disappeared. Doug had decided to head back to Melbourne but had arranged for two extra officers to be assigned under Jack's command in the event something happened. They believed he would come for Molly at some point because history always repeats, so they'd put one of the extra officers outside her house during the nights.

Jack had pleaded with Doug that he be allowed to divulge what was happening to Molly. She was leaving, but if she knew Tony was locked up, he might be able to change her mind.

He didn't want her to go.

'Daddy!' An excited Lachlan barrelled into him, almost knocking him over and, thankfully, pulling him out of his musings. That's not somewhere he wanted to go on the day of his son's birthday party. And Lachie was genuinely excited, which in and of itself was something to celebrate.

Jack picked up his son and spun him around in the air. 'Wheeeeeee! Ready for your party my big seven-year-old boy?'

Lachie let out a squeal, his face bright with joy.

As if on cue the doorbell chimed.

Lachie squirmed out of Jack's arms and ran to the door. 'I'll get it! I'll get it!' he declared, well and truly the master of the house.

As the party guests started to arrive with their hands full of gifts and trays of party fare, like fairy bread and chocolate crackles, Jack felt his heart twist in his chest. He wished Sarah was there to see her little boy grow up. Ironically, he wanted her to see how well he was coping with her leaving. He knew if he said that out loud, he'd get responses like, *Oh she knows. She's here. Looking down on him and you.* Stuff like that. So, he didn't say it out loud. Life after death wasn't a thing. Or spirits or any of that. Once you're gone, you're gone. Ashes to ashes and all that.

It didn't stop him wishing it though. She would've been really proud of her little boy.

He felt a pang of guilt as the idea of Molly being the one to see Lachie grow up floated into his mind.

Sarah had made him promise to *find someone else.* He'd laughed it off and told her not to be so stupid. She was the only one for him. His first love. The mother of his child.

She'd laughed right back at him and her eyes that had become constantly dark with pain had brightened. *She's coming. Just don't be a dick and ruin it. Promise me!*

He had no choice. He smiled at her and promised, all the while his heart breaking into Sarah sized pieces.

She smiled back at him and then with all the energy she could muster, she gave his hand a soft squeeze. Then the brightness dulled in her eyes and she fell into a heavy drug-induced sleep.

She never woke up.

Molly stood in front of her full-length mirror and poked her tongue out at the reflection.

She'd made the mantra *A new Molly. A new wardrobe.* But the bright yellow sundress with spaghetti straps that Nora had insisted looked great on her in the shop was not the new wardrobe that Molly had in mind. In the shop it had felt summery and young, but Molly wasn't summery or young. She'd rather be on a Scottish Dale in a Burgundy tartan with a fur draped over her shoulders.

At thirty-six, spaghetti straps seemed more useful in a bowl of bolognese than on her shoulders. Her breasts were still relatively perky considering she hadn't had the privilege of breastfeeding, but she knew they were a lot further south than they'd been just a few years before.

She rubbed her midriff and sighed heavily. Her waist was starting to disappear into oblivion as well. She was less of an hourglass and more of a clock that was running a few minutes slow.

Speaking of clocks, she glanced at hers and saw she was running late. She didn't want to disappoint Lachie on his big day, so throwing her hands up in defeat, she decided to go with the dress. Her mum's voice rattled around in her head. *Mutton dressed up as lamb.*

'Yes, Mum thanks. I know!' she exclaimed into the ether. 'But maybe I want to be a lamb again.'

She gave herself one last look in the mirror, cocking her head and smoothing her hands over her body. 'And actually, my boobs do look pretty good in this.'

She turned to leave the room and her ankle gave a little twinge reminding her of the crutches leaning against the wall. She glanced across at them and decided that because they didn't go with the dress, she would leave them right where they were.

She made her way out to the dining table, grabbed Lachie's gift and the plate of her mum's homemade sausage rolls that she'd made that morning and walked gingerly out the front door.

'Miss Molly!'

Jack was in the rumpus room prepping Pin the Tail on The Donkey when he heard Lachie's excited announcement.

At her name, his stomach flipped and his chest filled with a warm hum.

Donkey tail in hand, he hot footed it to the front door. What he saw filled him with joy. Lachie had Molly's hand in his and was leading her to the present table.

His heart leapt into his throat as he took in the sight of her. It was as if summer had burst into the room, with all the added benefits of almost bare shoulders, a dress that showed off her slender waist and best of all the soft cleavage that hinted at the bounty just beneath the sunflowers.

She glanced across at him, her face beaming with the attention from his son. He smiled back at her.

Lachie tugged at her hand. 'Put it here Miss. And I open them after the cake,' he gushed, helping her put the beautifully wrapped gift on the table.

'Oh, I thought you would want to open it straight away,' Molly laughed.

Lachie shook his head and stood tall and proud. 'Nope. Dad said I'm a big boy now and I can do laid graftimation.'

'Delayed gratification buddy,' Jack said, ruffling his hair. 'Now go and see how your guests are going.'

He wanted a minute alone with Molly. He wanted many minutes alone with Molly but with ten crazy kids running around the backyard with only his in-laws in control, time wasn't his friend.

Lachie raced outside, screaming like a banshee who was over-loaded on sugar.

Molly glanced down at the donkey tail in his hand.

'Is that a donkey tail in your hand or are you just…'

'Yes. And I am also really pleased to see you,' Jack interrupted, his voice low and soft. He leaned forward and gave her a kiss on the cheek, just catching the edge of her lips, making her catch her breath. He hovered there for a moment and then pulled back in time to see a blush wash across her face.

She dipped her head to hide the rosiness and held the plate of sausage rolls out to him. 'Sorry I'm late.'

He took the food, his hand brushing against hers, sending a tingle along his arm.

She was turning him into a tingling, shivering, teenage mess.

'These smell amazing.' He dipped his head to take in the aroma of the fresh pastry and moist filling. 'Let's pop these in the oven,' he said as he led the way into the kitchen.

'They taste good too,' Molly said. 'One of my Mum's favourite recipes. Wins every time.'

He slid them into the oven, also keenly aware of how good Molly smelled as well. Fresh with the scent of lime and coconut - so delicious he could eat her up.

He felt her next to him and turned to her. She gazed up at him, her eyes soft and inviting and placed her hands on his chest. 'I'm pleased to see you too Jack,' she whispered as she stood on her tippy toes and kissed him so sweetly it was if angel wings had brushed across his lips, taking his breath away.

'Jack!' his mother-in-law yelled from the backyard, amongst the giggles and squeals of kids running amok.

Molly patted his chest and nodded towards the mayhem. 'Go.'

All Jack could do was nod. He left Molly standing at the oven, his trembling legs threatening to topple his journey, while the whole time Sarah's voice rang in his head, *She's coming*. And he thought perhaps Molly wasn't the only angel in that kitchen.

16

———

By all accounts, Molly's mainly, the party had been a huge success.

Only one child had vomited from a sugar overdose thanks to an overindulgence of fairy bread. There was the incident of the pin the tail on the mother-in-law that didn't go down very well and precipitated a very grumpy early exit from said mother-in-law. In little Peter's defence Jack had spun him around two times too many and he was completely off balance when he jammed the tail into her thigh.

He still got an award for participating though.

Apart from their moment when Molly had arrived, there had been no more time for her and Jack to even communicate like adults, let alone act like grown-ups.

There was something about the combination of the infectiousness of children at play and the bright yellow sunflower dress that brought out the kid in Molly.

She broke three eggs in the egg and spoon race because of her limp. Almost drowned herself in the pursuit of bobbing for apples and she ate way too much birthday cake and drank her body weight in 'grown up' apple juice…AKA Prosecco.

It was the best day she'd had in a long, long time. By the time she'd helped clean up and said goodbye to Jack and a whispered farewell to Lachie, who had passed out on the couch from all the excitement, surrounded by torn wrapping paper and gifts, her heart was full.

She stood on the front lawn waiting for the taxi she had ordered and silently thanked whatever or whoever had sent her back to Nhill. When she had decided to leave Tony, she had come up with so many different places to go but Nhill was not on that list. And then Nora had called out of the blue with a job offer. Coincidence? Or fate?

She hadn't seen or heard from Tony in over a week, so a small kernel of hope had started growing in her. Maybe he'd decided she wasn't worth the trouble. Something or someone better had caught his eye. Maybe she wouldn't need to leave after all. She looked back at the house and through the living room windows she saw Jack pick the sleeping Lachie up from the couch, kiss his forehead and walk out of sight.

She held her hands to her heart, closed her eyes and inhaled a deep breath of contentment as she heard her taxi pull up to the kerb.

THE HOUSE WAS FINALLY BACK TO NORMAL. WRAPPING PAPER IN THE BIN, leftovers cling wrapped in the fridge and a happy little birthday boy tucked up in bed. Jack plonked down onto the couch exhausted, a bottle of beer in one hand and one of Molly's sausage rolls in the other. He hadn't had time to eat properly and he was dying to try her creations. He assumed they'd be as yummy as she was.

He was about to take a bite when his phone rang. He reluctantly dropped the sausage roll back onto the plate and picked up the phone, taking a swig of beer at the same time.

'Yello Jack here,' he said as he swallowed the refreshing amber liquid.

'Detective Sergeant Meadows?' the voice on the other end of the line asked.

Jack sat up straight. 'Yes, this is Meadows.'

'It's Sergeant Jones here sir. I'm assigned to watch Miss McDonald...'

'I know who you are Sergeant,' Jack barked, a bad feeling starting to creep into his gut. 'Carry on.'

'I'm checking whether Miss McDonald has left your house yet?'

'She left two hours ago Jones. Why?' Jack set his bottle on the table, his taste for beer well and truly gone.

'Well, she hasn't returned home as far as I can tell sir.'

'Have you knocked on her door?' Jack barked at him.

'Ahh yes sir. Of course, sir. There's no answer. I called both her mobile and her landline and both are going through to voicemail.'

'Shit,' Jack muttered.

'Sorry sir?' Jones asked.

'Nothing Jones. Wait there. I'm on my way.'

Jack ended the call and forced his panic down. He was no use to Molly if he lost his shit. He was Detective Sergeant Meadows, head cop who was hoping to find the victim…subject at the shops or the pub or somewhere else unremarkable. He wasn't Jack the widower who was falling in love with Molly and was scared to death that something bad had happened to her and that Tony was involved.

He made a call to his babysitter who said she'd be there in ten minutes and he changed into his police uniform, making sure the handcuffs were on his belt and his gun was loaded. He checked twice. He wasn't taking any chances.

17

———————

Molly had seen films about people being abducted and it usually involved guns and Liam Neeson.

Hers was less dramatic. It hadn't been a taxi – she just assumed it was. The taxi she booked must've been pissed that she wasn't there because it had been Tony pulling up alongside her outside Jack's house. He'd threatened bodily harm to Lachlan if she didn't get in the car with a promise that all he wanted to do was talk. Talking couldn't hurt and besides, it would get him away from Lachie and Jack.

She got in.

Next thing she knew they were on the highway out of town and he'd not said one word.

She'd said a few.

Let me out!

Where are we going?

Why are you doing this?

All met with a grunt, a scowl and an increase in speed. He was normally a very talkative person. He could talk his way out of, or into, anything. This wasn't like him. She at least knew how to handle his loud rage, but the intense silence was making her skin crawl with fear.

She leaned against the passenger door to be as far away from him as possible, her bare arms sticking to the hot leather upholstered panelling that adorned his $80,000 Mercedes.

A heat mirage shimmered on the road in front, threatening to engulf them, which Molly wished it would. It was making her feel nauseous, so she turned her head away. Outside the window, dry, brown paddocks blended into one with only the vision of a silo on the horizon giving her any perspective of where she was. She focussed on the silo as a landmark and as they whizzed past it at 140 kms an hour, she stared at it and then closed her eyes to burn it into her brain. It was one of the painted silos. The one with the boy and the girl - one on each cylinder. She knew she would never forget the faces of those painted silo kids for the rest of her life. If she had anymore life left. Her stomach turned over at the thought. She didn't even know how long they'd been driving for. It felt like hours but also seconds. Everything was wrong.

Nobody would know she was missing until she didn't turn up to work on Monday. Except didn't Jack say there was a cop keeping watch. But that was only if something happened at her place. Tony must've known there would be someone at her house and he'd been following her. How brazen and arrogant he was to snatch her away right out the front of a policeman's house.

She felt the car slow down and turn. She wanted to look, but her eyes were so heavy. All she wanted to do was go to sleep and wake up when the nightmare was over.

The road he'd turned onto was bumpy, off the main road.

She opened her eyes just as they passed the Propadollah School House.

Her stomach wrenched, bile filled her throat and in that moment, she knew where he was taking her.

Dusk was settling in. Jack had assembled Sergeant Jones and Constables Raverty and Hanson at Molly's house once they'd checked all of the town's usual hangouts. The pub, the two cafes and the library. He had already checked inside and Jones had been right. She wasn't there. Her car was still in the driveway and he'd found the crutches leaning up against her bedroom wall and various clothes strewn on the bed. There was excess wrapping paper and ribbons on the dining room table that she hadn't tidied up yet. The kitchen smelt like the sausage rolls she'd made that morning. His heart wrenched when he walked into the bathroom, her scent filling his senses.

Taking a deep breath, he strode out to his team.

'Okay. She hasn't been home. She's nowhere in town and her car is still here. Engine cold. At this point I think we should assume that there's been foul play. No one has heard from her since she left the party. Raverty and Hanson head back to my place and go door to door to see if anyone heard or saw anything. And Jones you stay here in case she comes back and it's all been a misunderstanding.'

Jones went to speak. Jack cut him off with a raised hand. 'You've all got your orders. Let's go.'

Jones breathed out heavily.

'You got a problem with that officer?' Jack barked at him, not in the mood for ego.

'No sir! I would just like to be a part of the search that's all. I feel like I could be helpful.'

Jack nodded, keeping his cool. 'I understand Jones. But I need someone here. Just in case. If I need you, I'll call.'

Jones stood to attention and saluted. 'Sir!'

Jack shook his head. 'No need for that. At ease. I'll be in touch,' he said as he jumped into his car, hoping that Jones would be the one to contact him with the good news that Molly had arrived home safe and sound. But in his gut he knew that wasn't going to happen.

Pulling away from the kerb he wasn't even sure where he was going, but when he started heading out of town, he didn't question it. It wasn't rational and it didn't involve police work at all, but there was something pulling him that way.

As he drove West out of town the sun sat on the horizon creating a bright orange glow across the sky that reflected onto the parched summer earth, making it look like a brush fire had broken out and was about to swallow everything in its path.

18

Molly hung onto the safety handle as Tony jerked the car left, turning into Far Horizons Farm.

The setting sun created a red tinge across the sky that, in a normal situation, would be a great photo opportunity for a *no filter hashtag* on Instagram. But in a hostage situation it was foreboding. An eerie portent of things to come. The cinematographer on Liam Neeson's hostage film would die for a sky like that. Molly thought it was weird that she was thinking about a Hollywood star while she was being taken against her will to her family's old home. She heard about how the mind protected itself from trauma by disassociating from what was actually happening. So, Liam Neeson it was.

Liam would've worked out where she was by now. But in real life, no one would know where she was and she had no way of contacting anyone because Tony had thrown her bag out of the window the first time her phone had rung.

The familiar ringtone had blasted into the silence of the car's cabin. Tony grabbed the phone before Molly could answer and cry for help. Knowing what he would see on the screen, Molly braced for a slap. It was Jack calling, she'd given him the nickname Jack Yummy with a love heart emoji in her phone address book.

Surprisingly, there were no repercussions except for him grabbing her bag and tossing it and the phone out the window as they sped out of town. She assumed the consequences were yet to come.

Tony stopped the car in front of the house, leaving the engine running. He turned to her.

'When you least expect it,' he whispered, sending a shiver along Molly's spine.

'What are you going to do to me?' she asked, as her hand slid along the door looking for the handle. There was no way she was going to stay in that car with him any longer.

Her fate was in her hands, not his.

Tony laughed. The menace unmistakable. 'You were always naive Mol. I'm not sure what you expect me to do when you just walk out with no warning. It's kind of rude. I don't like rude people.'

While he was speaking, Molly had found the silver handle of freedom and curled her fingers around it, waiting for the right moment.

When he glanced across to the house, she sprang into action. Pushing the seatbelt button with one hand and pulling the door handle with the other, the door swung open. She flung herself out of the car and started running towards the driveway.

Tony was too slow to stop her but threw the car into reverse and blocked her path. She stood in front of the car staring into the headlights, her heart almost beating out of her chest, her breath rapid and shallow. But her mind was sharp. She knew she should be feeling the ache in her ankle, but there was no pain. Her body was in survival mode, adrenaline coursing through her veins.

Tony revved the engine, a warning that he was coming for her.

Not today buddy. A new Molly, remember.

Her escape route cut off, she turned and ran back towards the house. She heard the car wheels spin in the gravel as it took off after her.

She'd got a head start and bounded up the rickety verandah steps, grimacing in pain, and into the house, avoiding the hole she'd made with her ankle only days before, heading to the only hiding place she could think of.

~

JACK PULLED HIS CRUISER ONTO THE SIDE OF THE HIGHWAY AND JUMPED out, leaving the vehicle running.

He jogged back along the road to where the debris lay on the bitumen and in the tall grass on the side of the highway.

He stopped short when he saw the handbag, his heart jumping into his throat. A whoosh of blood rushed into his head and for a moment, he thought he would vomit.

Pull yourself together Jack! She needs you.

Closing his eyes and taking a deep breath, he shook his head to expel the terrible thoughts racing through his mind.

When he opened his eyes again, he was Senior Sergeant, Jack Meadows on the hunt for a criminal with all the evidence he needed to put him away for a long time, scattered on the road in front of him.

Jack collected all of the items he could find, including her smashed phone and put them back into the handbag.

He held the bag to his chest and stared along the highway and as the last rays of the sun dipped behind the horizon, he knew where Tony was taking her.

He sprinted back to his cruiser and picked up his radio.

'This is Meadows. We have a code six zero at Far Horizons Farm in Propadollah. All units to assist immediately. Over.'

'Roger that sir. Over,' Raverty's voice crackled down the line.

'Sorry sir, what's a code six zero? Over,' Jones asked, his voice tentative.

'Trouble Jones. There's trouble at Far Horizons. Get there now. Over and out.'

He threw the radio onto the passenger seat and gunned the cruiser into gear, the tyres squealing on the warm asphalt as he flicked on the siren and lights, illuminating the dark highway.

19

———

Molly huddled inside the cupboard, pressed up against the back corner, hugging her knees to her chest and berating herself for choosing the one and only hiding place in the entire house.

It would be obvious to anyone, especially a predator like Tony, where she would be.

She leaned her head against the old wood, closed her eyes and tried to imagine it as her mother had experienced it. A place of solitude and peace. After a few moments, she felt a wave of calm wash over her and she could almost feel the clothes that had hung in there, brush against her skin.

What had her mother been reading in her little hiding place? Austen? Bronte? Tolstoy? Probably all three. At the same time. She smiled at the image of her mother with her torch, inhaling any book she could get her hands on. Then she felt a small tear escape and roll down her cheek. She raised a thought into the heavens...*Yes ok Mum. You were right about Tony. I should've listened to you.*

The creak of a floorboard close by, wrenched her from her reflection, the calmness replaced with a sudden cold sweat and a stomach heavy with dread.

With shaking hands, she searched for anything she could use as a weapon. Even the hanging rail had been removed, probably by those squatters Jack had mentioned. They would've taken the cupboard too if it wasn't so cumbersome, she was sure of that.

She tried to push herself further back into the corner and her foot slipped on something. Pulling it closer with her foot, she picked it up and knew what it was straight away. An old wire hanger. She could smell the rust on it that would give someone a pretty bad case of tetanus.

The footsteps were close.

'Marco…Polo?' Tony yelled, his use of the childhood hide-and-seek game making her shiver with the memory that hours ago she'd played that very game at Lachie's birthday party.

She was almost unable to unwind the hook of the hanger because her hands were trembling so much, but finally it came apart and she had a nice sharp rusty end ready to wield.

'A cupboard? Really Moll. The *only* hiding spot on the entire property. This is why I love you,' he said, followed by a laugh that slithered under the cupboard door and into her cells.

She could imagine his face. Mouth laughing, eyes soulless.

A squeak of a floorboard just outside her hiding place, she held the wire weapon in front of her, waiting for the door to be flung open. Instead, she felt the cupboard shudder as he tried to open the door. He grunted and pulled harder. It was stuck.

'Shit,' he muttered.

He tried to pull it open again. Nothing, except she could feel the cupboard sway off its back legs slightly.

He punched the door. 'C'mon you fucker!' he snarled as if he could bully it into doing his bidding, like he'd done with Molly for years.

The wood creaked & groaned under his attack, but the door stayed shut tight.

Molly could hear him pacing around the room and muttering to himself. She could only imagine his frustration and rage at not getting his way.

'Okay Moll here I come.'

In a split-second, Molly made the decision that she wasn't going to be afraid and cower in the corner of a cupboard anymore. Enough was enough.

She leant against the back panelling and, with all her might, kicked at the door — her weapon at the ready.

The door flung open right into Tony's head. It made a loud crack that echoed through the night air and he fell backwards onto the dusty floor.

Molly lunged forward, falling out of the cupboard next to him. She felt a sharp pain in her shoulder and reaching up, she felt the wire hanger literally hanging out of it. She'd stabbed herself. One tetanus shot coming right up.

Tony groaned.

Despite the hanger dangling from her shoulder, she leapt up and away from him.

'Now look what you've done to me Moll. You bitch,' he slurred, his voice raspy and weak.

She knew what she wanted to say.

She took a deep breath.

'Go to hell Tony.'

And with that she ran out of the room towards the front door. She heard movement behind her. It was Tony.

Oh for goodness sake!

He was like a cockroach. He just wouldn't die.

And he was close behind and as she flew down the verandah steps, she heard him cry out, followed by a horrible sounding crunch.

Turning back, she saw him, stuck halfway down a hole in the hallway floorboards, the one she'd prepared earlier with her own ankle, with only his torso and head visible.

She walked back to him slowly. One of the broken floorboards had pierced his stomach. He was well and truly impaled. Alive. But impaled.

He looked at her with pleading in his eyes.

'Help me Moll. Please,' he whimpered.

She wanted to help him. Needed to help him, to show herself that she was the bigger person. But even as incapacitated as he was, he still instilled fear into her heart. In her mind he was an evil superhuman and the floorboard in his stomach was like an annoying splinter.

He reached a trembling hand out to her for help and she stared at it. Closing her eyes and taking a deep breath she stepped forward, her hand reaching for his.

Then she heard the siren.

JACK PULLED HIS CRUISER TO A STOP NEXT TO TONY'S MERC THAT WAS still running, its lights on and the driver door wide open.

Once out of the car, he pulled his gun out of its holster and shone his torch into the Mercedes. Nothing. He reached in and switched the motor off.

It was deathly quiet. Too quiet.

He crept towards the house, holding the gun and torch out in front of him, his senses on alert for any sudden movement.

There wasn't much call for guns in sleepy Nhill. The occasional handcuff for an unruly young bloke at the pub on a Saturday night. But that was about it. Jack was a pacifist by nature which ironically is why he got into the police force - to pacify. So, having to handle a gun wasn't in his wheelhouse, but he had taken to it like a duck to water. He'd come top of his class at the shooting range and his weekly self-practice with old cans on a fence post was still at one hundred percent. Walking towards the farmhouse, he was glad of his sidearm and knew, if it was needed, his aim would be straight.

As he shone the torch into the front door, he saw her. Holding onto something.

'Molly!'

'Jack help!'

He leapt up the steps and took in the scene before him. Molly trying to pull an unconscious Tony out of the hole in the floor. *Fuck!* She had a coat hanger dangling from her shoulder. Shit had gone down.

'You okay?'

She nodded and grunted as she gave another attempt to pull him out.

Jack rested his hand on her back, gently, so as not to alarm her.

'Molly I got this.'

She moved away and staggered outside, sitting on the top step, her head in her hands.

Jack holstered his gun and hooked his arms under Tony's shoulders, from behind and in one move pulled him out and lay him on the ground. For someone with such an inflated personality he was quite a small man. His pulse was weak and his breathing rapid, the wooden shard still buried in his stomach.

'Is he….?' Molly whispered from the step.

'Alive? Yes. I'll call an ambulance. Wait there.'

He raced out to his cruiser and radioed for an ambulance, but he knew it would be quicker for Molly if he took her himself. Besides, he wasn't going to let anyone else look after her. That was his job now.

'An ambulance is on its way. He'll be ok. But I need to get you to hospital.'

He helped her stand and she took one last look behind at her motionless aggressor, before collapsing in his arms.

She was going into shock.

Another police siren cut through the air.

Jack sat Molly gently into his passenger seat as Jones and Raverty pulled to a stop next to him.

'I've called an ambo for Dutton. He's just inside the front door. Out cold. Stomach injury. I'm taking Molly to the hospital myself,' he barked at them.

'Yes sir…I mean Jack…' replied Raverty who had drawn her gun.

Jack nodded. 'Okay Raverty the scene is yours.'

He jumped into the driver's seat and turning the lights and siren on, he gunned the cruiser into the driveway leaving a plume of dust behind.

Reaching across the console, he took hold of Molly's hand, squeezing it tight.

'Everything's going to be alright now. He's going away for a long, long time.'

Molly turned to look at him, her eyes filled with tears.
'You promise?'
He kissed the palm of her hand. 'I promise.'

Molly stepped out of Jack's cruiser, a little worse for wear, but putting on a brave face.

Nora raced out the front door and swept her up into a hug.

'I was so worried about you,' she sobbed into Molly's wounded shoulder that was supported by a sling.

The pain made Molly wince.

Nora pulled back, annoyed at herself. 'Oh, I'm so sorry honey. Silly me. Come inside.'

'I did this to myself Nora. I'll never mess with a coat hanger ever again,' Molly laughed, even though her shoulder had started to throb.

Nora turned and took her hands, her face etched with concern and anger. 'No, my love. He did this to you. And he'll get what he deserves.'

'He should get twenty-five and no parole if there's any justice,' Jack exclaimed, his voice barely hiding his delight, as he carried her overnight bag inside.

Nora nodded her head at Molly to put an end to the conversation once and for all and led Molly towards the house.

Molly smiled and a wave of relief flooded her body. She looked at

Nora and Jack and knew they would always look out for her no matter what. It was a good feeling. And one she hadn't felt for a long while. She felt safe. Almost. It was going to take some time.

She'd been desperate to get home and out of the hospital, even though it was only an overnighter for a tetanus shot and a clean-up of her wound.

Jack and Nora had insisted that she not be alone, so she had agreed to stay at Jack's for a few nights just to shut them up. But secretly, she was looking forward to being in Jack's orbit.

As she walked up the verandah steps she heard a little squeal.

Lachie raced out the front door and leapt into her arms, almost flinging her backwards. With his legs wrapped around her waist, he planted a kiss on her cheek.

'Dad says you're going to live with us!' he exclaimed, his eyes bright with joy.

Molly laughed.

'Just for a few days buddy,' Jack said. Molly glanced up at him leaning against the door frame, a huge smile on his face and his eyes sparkling with as much joy as his son's.

Nora peeled Lachie off her. 'Now now be gentle young man. You need to look after Molly okay. Be a big boy.'

Lachie took a deep breath and stood tall. 'Just like Daddy.'

'Just like Daddy,' Nora replied with a firm nod.

Lachie took Molly's hand and led her inside and as she passed Jack at the door, he reached out, tucked an unruly curl behind her ear and whispered…

'Welcome Home.'

Jack switched the lamp on in the living room and then plonked down onto the couch next to Molly.

Nora had left a few hours earlier after settling Molly into the guest room and then feeding them her famous lamb roast. Lachie was tucked up in bed and sound asleep after all the excitement of having a new house guest.

Jack reached over and handed her a letter. It was the letter that she'd found in her mum's wardrobe.

'Sorry, I should've given it to you sooner. I forgot I had it. I can give you some space if you want.'

'No, it's okay. I want you to stay.'

Molly slid her finger under the flap, which opened easily as the glue was decades old, and pulled out the letter.

Dear Me,

Remember what Wolfgang said: Sometimes our fate resembles a fruit tree in winter. Who would think that those branches would turn green again and blossom, but we hope it, we know it.

I think this is important, but I don't know why. So, I'm sending it to you... me in case I forget.

Kindest of Regards

Me xx

Molly smiled, feeling blessed that she'd found the letter but also sad that she couldn't tell her mum. But somehow, she felt that her mum knew.

'You okay?' Jack whispered.

She nodded and handed him the letter. 'See for yourself.'

After he'd finished reading, he folded it back up and slipped it inside the envelope. 'Your mum sounds like a wise woman.'

'A wise kid with amazing handwriting more like it.'

Jack chuckled. 'Indeed. I wouldn't say you're turning green but you're definitely blossoming,' he said, his eyes running along her body.

Molly blushed and shook her head at him.

'Drink?' he asked, breaking the moment.

'Why not?' Molly could use an alcoholic circuit breaker after the last few days.

Jack returned with a beer for himself and a glass of chardonnay for Molly. Handing it to her, he sat back down and they clinked glasses.

'Here's to…fate,' Jack exclaimed.

'To fate,' Molly replied, taking a large gulp of the wine. She moaned her approval as the honey liquid slid easily down her throat.

They sat in comfortable silence.

The sound of the cicadas and the cockatoos screeching their regular dusk chorus could still be heard even with the doors closed and the air conditioner humming away.

Molly wondered whether Jack would be able to hear her heart beating, that felt louder to her than any cicada or screaming cockatoo.

She took another sip of wine to try and calm her overexcited nervous system. There was nothing stopping her from staying in town or being with Jack anymore. Except for herself. Her choice of men left a lot to be desired, but honestly, she didn't feel like she'd chosen Jack. There was no choice involved. It just…was.

He reached across and took the wine out of her hand, placing it on the coffee table without taking his eyes off her.

His fingers made circles in her palm, making her shudder.

'Are you cold? I'll turn the air-con off,' he said, starting to get off the couch.

Molly pulled him back down. 'No. I'm feeling lots of things, but cold isn't one of them.'

She shuffled closer to him and traced her fingers along his strong, tanned forearm, watching his muscles twitch under her touch.

Lifting her face to his, he kissed her with a softness that filled her with a warm hum. He tasted of mint and beer and his one-day stubble brushed against her skin. She liked the feeling of it and kissed him harder, her tongue teasing his lips.

His arms went around her and he pulled her closer making her flinch from her shoulder discomfort. He pulled away.

'Oh, shit sorry Molly.'

'It's fine. Maybe we rain check…this. Until I'm better?'

'Whatever you want. We've got all the time in the world.'

Molly shook her head and closed her eyes. She wasn't used to being respected and it was overwhelming.

She felt Jack stiffen next to her. 'We do have time…don't we?'

Molly gazed up at him, tears in her eyes and a smile on her lips. 'You silly thing. That wasn't a no. I'm just not used to a man being nice to me. It's been a while.'

Jack breathed out a sigh of relief, his own eyes brimming with tears.

'No Molly. You're just not used to having a man being truly in love with you.'

Molly gasped and her heart flip-flopped.

'Yes. I'm in love with you,' he said as he brought his lips to hers, confirming everything she was feeling.

'I love you too,' she whispered as their lips touched and her old world slipped away.

A new Molly.

THE END

Frankie knew one thing.
She'd return to the city when the job was done.

love
by the
jewel
sea

Rhonda Forrest

Love in a Sunburnt Land anthology

LOVE BY THE JEWEL SEA

RHONDA FORREST

For Terry - so many wonderful times by the jewel sea.

Rhonda Forrest

1

———

Frankie leaned back in her car seat, the paddocks to the side of the highway a monotonous blur of grassy flats, filled with fat cattle ignoring the noisy vehicles making their way north and south. Her hands rested on the steering wheel and she flexed her fingers out straight, checking her red fingernail polish was unchipped and glossy. In the corner of the rear-view mirror, she caught a glimpse of herself and she stared back, checking her long brown hair was still sitting correctly, the usual side stray piece conforming to where it was supposed to rest. She had spent an hour straightening her hair that morning, one side pinned back, showing off her strong cheekbones, a light brush of pink adding just the right amount of colour to her skin.

Her eyes turned back to the road and she gripped the steering wheel firmly as a succession of B double trucks passed her going in the opposite direction. The highway was narrow in parts and thankfully her new white car responded to her foot quickly, picking up speed, allowing her to pass other vehicles and avoid the tedium of sitting behind slower drivers, who dawdled, showing no hurry to reach their destination.

To travel slowly or take your time were not words included in her vocabulary. Everything was undertaken at top speed and Frankie's social and business calendar was always busy and rushed, completed with an intensity like there was no tomorrow. There wasn't a moment when she sat around and did nothing and now with a new career, time was of the essence more so than ever. She stretched her legs and wriggled in her seat, impatient to get to her destination. On the side of the road, a large sign with a picture of a silver leaping barramundi caused her to ease her foot off the accelerator and she checked the name of the town – Proserpine - Gateway to the Whitsundays. Not far to go now.

The town appeared on her left; a row of houses, motels and businesses on either side of the highway, the main street directing travellers towards its array of cafes and shops. It was a popular stopover for those looking for coffee or fuel and she peered through the windscreen past the cluster of buildings. The town's mill loomed beyond, its large chimneys spewing out white smoke, reminding her she was in sugar territory. On either side of the highway, fields of cane stretched in every direction and lumbering trucks laden with short sticks of harvested cane rumbled along adjacent dirt tracks, their wheels throwing up dust, cloaking the shiny paint on her car. She'd have to find a car wash. The email from work had described the place where she was headed as a small town, but she imagined it would have a garage with a car wash attached.

Brake lights of the traffic in front slowed and then stopped. Swearing loudly she directed her glare at a series of roadworks signals and a man holding a stop sign. More dust settled on the car as trucks coming towards her slowed, their tyres finding the edges of the bitumen. Loose gravel hit the side of her car and dirt that floated in puffy brown clouds, settled on everything in its path. A large cattle truck coming from the other direction ground to a halt beside her, its full carriages clanging and heaving as it clattered to a standstill. It blocked her side vision and she looked up with irritation at the middle-aged male driver in the cab of the truck. He stared down at her, grinning and tipping his hat before sending a cheeky wink her way. She edged her car forward a little, so she didn't have to look at him, her view instead, the side of the large trailers towed behind the truck.

Rows of cattle shuffled in crowded crates that sat on the trailers of the truck. Their bodies pushed up against one another, the timber floor on which they stood covered in dirt and shit. She screwed her face up. 'Sausages,' she said out loud, taking one last look before turning her focus back to the road ahead. Suddenly a strong spray of cow urine splattered over the side of her car, causing her to jump in her seat. 'Shit.' She turned her face away from the car window as a steady trail of steamy liquid hit the glass, ricocheting off the surface and spraying in every direction. Gritting her teeth, she edged the car forward, only to be greeted by loud splats of runny cow shit. The brown slop that catapulted from the rear end of a number of cows in the trailer, hit the windscreen, splashing across the glass and covering the bonnet like a crazy abstract painting. It dripped over the edges of her car, chunks of it clinging to the side as it joined the urine that trickled down from the top of her beautiful new Mazda.

Welcome to North Queensland, she thought, as she finally moved forward in the line of traffic. The windscreen wipers squeaked and shuddered as they spread the muck even further. Gritting her teeth she gave the finger to the stop and go man, a few of his offsiders bent over laughing, one of them even taking a photo of her shit splattered car.

Her poor little Mazda. She had only bought it a couple of months ago and since then it had been garaged every night and washed religiously each weekend. The interior was immaculate, polished and shiny and she was grateful that the windows - now dripping with brown slop - had been closed.

The purchase of the car was a reward to herself. For surviving a difficult long-term relationship breakup and for gaining a new job that promised to be a big step up in her career. She hadn't known at the time when she'd bought it that she'd be driving such long distances for work or worrying about dusty roads or trucks with cattle.

Trust Enterprises had employed her only a couple of months ago. The boss, Gary, was a customer of the business where she previously worked and had poached her to be a member of his team. It was exciting to take on a new role of a personal assistant and become part of a construction and development business, focussing on bookwork and office duties as well as consulting on some of their more important development projects. A prerequisite was that she was free to travel for short stints, could take direction as needed and that she completed a quick online certificate course, allowing her to sign off as an extra on some of their contracts.

The office work was familiar and it had taken no time to settle in. The certificate course was easy, a quick process that took less than a week to complete, giving her a qualification that Gary said allowed her to sign as an extra on contracts already approved by their head management team.

Frankie's first project had been to travel to Mackay, calling in at three of Trust's regional offices on the way and ensuring everything was running smoothly. She had a list of processes to check at each one and staff to meet with. It had been an easy run so far and seemed too good to be true in relation to what they were paying her. The commitment required was similar to her previous personal assistant jobs; the same pressing deadlines, jump when asked and give a hundred and ten percent to her allotted tasks.

Yesterday as she prepared to leave Mackay and head back home, Gary had phoned, letting her know that there was an extra job they wanted her to look at near the town of Dingo Beach. She was not far south of where they wanted her to go, they'd pay her double for the extra mileage and her accommodation was already booked. It was a longer stint than they alluded to in her initial interview, but this was a one-off and a major project that Gary told her, 'Could push you up that career ladder quicker than you'd ever imagined.'

She had been surprised at his next request. 'I know you thought you'd be heading back down here to the main office and home, but this one will take a few extra weeks. Do you think you can handle it? If not, I can give it to one of the others. There are plenty here in the office that would jump at the opportunity. We thought with your skills and drive this one would suit you. What do you think?'

Of course, she'd said yes. This was the type of work that offered a different role than her previous jobs and why the completion of the certificate course was vital, plus there was nothing pressing back home that couldn't wait. Gary filled her in on the details. Once she arrived in Dingo Beach she would meet and consult with the owners of the project. There wouldn't be much for her to do after that, but she needed to stay there until they were ready to sign off on the contracts.

This would demonstrate that Trust Enterprises were invested in the complexities of the development and had not just flitted in and out.

While she was waiting for the finalisation of the paperwork, she could complete various online bookwork for Gary. The planning for the project was completed, it was now a matter of looking like she was checking it out, but really all they were after was a signature. It would be a kick start to her career.

THANK GOODNESS GARY HAD BOOKED HER INTO A MOTEL AND TAKEN CARE of the details for the weeks ahead. Because of the late notice she hadn't had time to research the town or what it offered, but after this morning's events she was going to treat herself to a long bath and an expensive bottle of champagne. She might even get room service and eat in. Spoil herself – the company could pay, and anything extra would be claimable on her tax.

She concentrated on the road, trying to ignore the mess clinging to her car as the map on her phone directed her to turn right. Heading east she steered off the highway, thankful to be on back roads and by the look of it, heading towards the ocean.

Time had got away, so she put her foot down. There wasn't any traffic and hopefully no further holdups, but she had lost time at the roadworks and now she needed to make it up. An important zoom meeting scheduled at two o'clock with Gary would fill her in on other details she needed to know. According to the map, she'd get there in plenty of time.

The road narrowed and she slowed as three large kangaroos bounded across in front of her. Once she would have stopped and watched them, following their movements to see where they went. Years ago she had been passionate and publicly vocal about the environment and protection of endangered animals. Not that kangaroos were endangered, she thought, spotting another group of them eating the long grass at the side of the road. But when she had been at university and part of a wildlife committee, she probably would have been naïve enough to fight for their protection. At least the main project she'd been involved with back then, had been for the safeguard of a platypus breeding area. She'd joined protests, collected signatures for petitions and even been on the radio denouncing the destruction of a sensitive rainforest where the platypus lived. The protest group had won and the area was listed as part of the nearby national park, protected forever.

She sighed. She hadn't been back there to look for the platypus since she'd met Ronaldo. Her life had gone in a different direction and those types of concerns weren't high on her list of significant issues. For that matter, they weren't on there at all.

Work was the priority now, there was no time for trivial sightseeing or wasting time.

Time. Time and schedules. They always cropped up in her thoughts, swinging her moods back and forth as she continually justified to herself why she was pursuing a lifestyle that had ruined her previous relationship.

She bit her lip as she thought about how she had parted ways with her last partner, Ronaldo. That fact that work was his main priority had been her main complaint. In the end he had no time for her, or anything else but his job. Yes, she agreed with him, they were both aiming for higher positions, but she was way down his list of priorities or sometimes not on it at all. He had argued that after three years she should be used to his ways, he hadn't changed, she'd known from the start what he focussed on. He couldn't understand why now - when she also was so absorbed in her work - would she start complaining about the way he lived and where his priorities lay.

She refocussed on the road, pangs of remorse causing her stomach to tighten, punching at her conscience. Onwards and upwards she had decided. If you can't beat them, then just join them. Her mind ticked over as she took deep breaths, willing her body to sink back in the car seat, her tightening muscles relaxing. Lately, she'd learnt to calm herself when uncertainties overwhelmed her. To let plaguing qualms take hold in her mind only resulted in further anxiety and worry, plus it usually ended in a migraine that often laid her up for a couple of days.

She was a different person now, a new job, a career that was going to take her places and a bank balance that was growing bigger each week. It was the way to go. Out with the old and in with the new. If she drowned herself in work commitments like she had over the last few months, she wouldn't think about needing anyone or sharing her time with someone else.

The car's indicator ticked as she slowed down, easing the car onto the grass at the side of the road. She checked her phone, noticing she had missed the first turn-off that would have taken her straight to her destination. It didn't matter though, because the directions were showing another way to go up further. It appeared there were a few different entry points into Dingo Beach and the map showed a grid pattern of roads that crisscrossed the cane fields on either side of her. As she pulled back onto the road she tried to ignore the state of her car, the muck hanging like an obstinate decoration to the shiny white paint. The map voice eventually directed her to turn left, the instructions guiding her as the bitumen road narrowed out to a thin dirt road.

Typical country roads, this one even had grass growing in the middle of it. Frankie's phone dinged; a reminder of the online work meeting to take place in half an hour. She sped up, negotiating the mounds and puddles that her precious car plunged through, trying to ignore the bumpy surface that rattled both her and her car.

Tall cane towered either side of where she drove, a cloudless blue sky bright above. The road surface evened and she looked down to check the map on her phone, pushing her foot down harder to make up some lost time. When she looked up, she was shocked to see a large tractor emerging from between the rows of cane on her left-hand side. Its metal red body loomed down on her and she braked hard and swerved, the tractor showing no signs of slowing or giving way as it hurdled through the crossing in front of her. Clenching the steering wheel and slamming her foot hard on her brakes, she veered wildly, skidding to the right, avoiding hitting the front wheel of the tractor but losing control as the front of her car slid down a small embankment and plunged into a muddy ditch.

The nose of the car sank into a hole of murky water and she looked up through the windscreen at a bank of sugar cane, the tops of it covered in pink flowers that swayed in the breeze. Rows of sturdy stalks blocked her vision and she squinted into the darkness between them, trying to take in what had just happened and thankful she had at least avoided a collision. The tractor stopped further along the road and she glanced at it, swearing hard as she threw the car into reverse, revving the engine as she tried to back out. The back wheels spun in the mud as she flattened her foot to the floor, but the car didn't budge. She was stuck fast, her precious white car sitting in a quagmire, the bonnet covered in cow shit that was now mixed with splatters of brown muck from the ditch.

Leaning across she pushed the button to open the passenger's side window. At least the electronics were still functioning. A man, probably in his thirties and a teenage boy sat calmly on the tractor, both staring back at her through the open window. The man who was in the driver's seat, swivelled his body around in her direction, positioning one of his legs on the wheel, in his hand an apple which he casually took bites from. The teenager, who wore old jeans and a t-shirt that aptly read – *shit happens* – on the front of it, jumped down from the tractor, his strides long and slow as he came towards her. He pushed a hat down on his long blonde hair, his dusty cowboy boots remaining safely on the dry land and staying well clear of the mud.

She glared hard at him through the open window. He looked about seventeen and wore a cheeky grin as he looked back and forth over her car. Frankie spoke loudly to make sure both of them could hear her. 'Are you crazy? You nearly killed me! I don't know where you get your licences from up here, but I'm on the main road and you've come flying out of a tiny track. My car is stuck, and I'm supposed to be in Dingo Sands, Bay or Beach, whatever it's called, for a meeting.'

'Is that a Mazda?' The teenager pushed down with his boot on the rear guard of the car, causing it to bounce around, the rear wheels spinning in the air. 'Looks like you're stuck.'

Frankie picked up her phone. These two obviously weren't going to be any help. She'd phone RACQ and the police. They could come and sort it out. She searched for the numbers to dial.

The man sitting on the tractor finished his apple, casually flicking the core into the cane. 'No reception here. You're in a black hole.' He chuckled and added, 'Literally.'

'You've caused this accident and I hope you have insurance because you'll have to pay for the damage to my car.' She tried her phone again. 'I was also on your right, so you're really in the wrong.'

The man on the tractor jumped down. He wore old jeans, heavy work boots and a shirt smeared with patches of dirt. The two of them looked alike and Frankie surmised they were probably father and son. The same blonde curly hair, the same stocky build and similar faces. As they looked at her through the car window, it also dawned on her that the older man was very handsome, rugged-looking, with blue eyes that locked on hers. His attitude was nonchalant though, and he appeared slightly amused and not at all like he was sorry for what he had caused.

Annoyed even more because of their unapologetic manner, she unbuckled her seat belt and tried to open her door, but the car was wedged into the sides of the ditch and there was no way out. Her anger simmered but she reminded herself not to swear. To at least show some decorum and control as she directed her words at them. 'Are you going to help me? This is your fault.'

The two men looked at each other, the younger one finally speaking. 'You might be stuck here for a while. You could always walk into town, it's a long way though.'

Frankie mumbled and started taking off her expensive shoes. She'd only bought them last month and they had cost a fortune. There was no way she was getting into the puddle with them on. She rued the fact she had worn her flared cream linen trousers. At least if she rolled the bottoms up they might escape the mud. She tried one more time. 'Do you think you could possibly tow me out with your tractor?' She couldn't help herself. 'That is the one you just ran me off the road with because of your lack of driving skills, or perhaps lack of care.'

The older man looked hard at her and tutted. 'Manners, manners.'

Frankie held back a tirade of abuse. She so wanted to swear at them, at the red tractor and the situation she was in, but she needed them to help her. If not, she would have to walk all the way to the town and without her phone she wasn't sure of the direction. 'I'd appreciate it if you helped me get my brand-new car out,' she hesitated, 'please.'

The man spoke in a deep voice, his slow manner and relaxed attitude annoying her even more. 'How about you hop out of the car and stand clear. My son and I will have a go at pulling it out.' He gestured to the teenager who jumped into action, rustling around in a toolbox on the side of the tractor before emerging with a long length of rope. At least he seemed to move with some pace and was helpful.

Frankie took a deep breath and manoeuvred herself over to the passenger side window. She lay on her back and put her feet out first, turning on her side and then wriggling her body through the narrow space. Her face burned and she tried not to look at the two men who were watching her as she lowered her body out through the open window. The younger one laughed out loud as she finally slid out, her body half disappearing in a deeper hole that unfortunately was located where she had decided to exit the car. The older man came towards her and offered her his hands. When she grabbed them, he pulled her forward, half dragging her through the mud and up the small bank until she stood beside him on dry land.

His eyes were full of laughter, his lips curled up in a smile. 'Name's Simon and this here is Eli.'

Frankie let go of his hands, her eyes meeting his as they stared hard at each other.

She flicked bits of mud off her shirt and pulled her sodden trousers up higher, throwing her shoes that had also ended up in the water, down on the ground. 'Can you see that you are in the wrong and that you have caused me to have an accident? My car is stuck and damaged, plus I'm late for a meeting and everything has gone to shit today because of you and your fucking red tractor!'

Simon was a stocky strong build and a bit taller than Frankie. He looked down at her, his lips still curling up in the corners, almost as if he was about to laugh. It was hard to imagine that he could see anything funny about the situation.

'We'll drag your car out and ring a tow truck to come and pick it up. We can drop you into town but that is it.'

Frankie dug in her pocket, closing her eyes as she remembered where her phone was. She pulled it out and shook it, water trickling out from the water-logged case as she retrieved a soggy business card, holding it out for Simon to take. 'My name is Frankie Brothrington-White. I'm staying at a place called Dingo Bay while I attend to some work. You can contact me there to discuss payment or send me the name of your solicitor and insurance details. I also need to write your name and address down.'

Eli took the card and read it out. 'Brothrington-White, that's a long name.'

'My mother wouldn't take my father's name so I ended up with both. Curse of my life but there you have it.' She shook her head and muttered to herself. 'I don't know why I am explaining myself to you.'

Simon laughed, his annoying attitude rankling Frankie even further. He swung up into the tractor seat, a smile wide on his face. 'Dingo Beach, not Dingo Bay as you called it, is a small town and everyone knows everyone, so you'll have no trouble tracking me down. The road you should have taken is the other side of those hills there. It's the only way in.' He waved his arm towards the east, a line of heavily timbered hills forming a border behind the cane. 'My property stretches from here to those hills and Dingo Beach is on the other side of them. Actually Frankie, you're standing on it now. It might be good for you to know before you go wasting money on solicitors that you weren't actually on a road when you went into the ditch. What you're on and what you had been driving on for quite a while through these cane fields since you left the main road, is nothing more than a track that runs through my farm. It's not a public road and you and your little white car are on private property.'

2

───────

The metal guard at the top of one of the large tyres provided a secure place for Frankie to sit. She perched precariously, glancing every so often at Eli who sat on the other rim as Simon drove the tractor through the fields of cane. A metal pole that supported the frame of a shade canopy thankfully gave her something to hang onto, the jerking of the tractor jarring her body as they bounced along narrow farm tracks towards the hills that rose in the distance.

The cane towered above them, blocking any breeze as sweat dripped down her back and gathered on her brow. Eventually they came to the end of the cane, the tractor chugging across a paddock, before winding its way through the bush towards a rocky trail that wound its way up through the hills. Thick scrubby bush covering the slopes offered little relief from the heat and she hung on tightly to the metal pole as they ascended through the scrub, traversing the hills towards Dingo Beach. The sun's rays were fierce, even though it was late in the afternoon and wasn't yet summer. She could feel her face burning and when Eli offered her a spare hat, she accepted, pushing it down on her head.

From high up on the tractor she had a good view of the scenery in all directions. For a short while she forgot her predicament and started to enjoy the ride, the bouncing and jolting of the tractor reminding of her when she was a kid and her dad had towed them in a trailer behind his old truck. That was a lifetime ago. The truck had been sold, the trailer dumped and her parents had long ago parted ways, finding new partners and new lives. She visited them now and again, but they'd never understood why at the age of thirty-five she hadn't settled down, why she couldn't slow down and why she was always chasing the high life, leaving behind a string of broken relationships.

Sometimes she questioned it herself but then the next big project or job came along, a new contract, different social groups and a stream of parties, lunches and networking. The bar was continually set higher, the results and income hopefully bigger.

Eli pointed to the sky and she gazed upwards and back across the fields as a huge wedge-tailed eagle spread its wings, gliding high above the cane. It floated effortlessly on the currents, its keen eyes looking downwards as it perused the fields for prey. Hurtling downwards it descended rapidly, diving without hesitation into the thick growth and disappearing from view. She swivelled her body on the guard of the tyre, excited when it reappeared with an animal, that appeared to be a mouse or small rat in its beak. It soared higher and higher, eastward bound until it was just a speck in the sky. Perhaps it had young to feed, or a partner sitting on a clutch of eggs about to hatch.

Bats squawked above them as the sun started to fade and Frankie squinted into the distance to try and see the eagle again. Her daydreams were broken when Eli shouted at her to hang on as the tractor traversed a steep slope, bouncing over a gully and onto a surface that resembled a main road.

It was dark by the time they arrived at the hotel and Simon helped her down, directing Eli to go with her to check in. She had arrived in style, barefoot, her trousers now dry but covered in mud, a dirty shirt and sitting on the back of a large red tractor. The day had been long and she didn't argue when Eli picked up her bag, which he had rescued from her car, and carried it into the hotel. He led her through to the entrance where hopefully she could pick up the key for her room.

Simon hadn't wasted any time and was already talking to the man behind the counter, their voices carrying through to her as she walked into the area where they stood. Neither of them noticed as she came up behind them.

'She's Larry's tick and flick girl,' the man said. 'Brand spanking new to the job and wouldn't have a clue. They just need her to stick around and look like she's doing what she's paid to do and then sign off. Piece of cake really.'

Simon had his back to her and shook his head. 'Nothing to do with me. I don't want to know.'

Eli banged the swinging saloon doors hard behind him, the squeaking noise of the unoiled hinges letting Simon and the man know that others had entered the room. They stopped talking and turned around, Frankie throwing the most disdainful look she could muster, their way.

The man, whose name was Sam, leaned over the bar to shake her hand. 'I'm the owner of Dingo Beach Pub and Motel. We have the best meals and accommodation on the eastern coastline and we've been expecting you. Not quite in this manner but good to see you made it. Here's your key and I've given you the best room in the house. Wait until you see the beach in the morning.'

Frankie took the key, annoyed that she had been the topic of conversation and longing for everyone to disappear so she could sit by herself, have a stiff drink and recap on the events of the day. She mustered every bit of poise she possessed. 'I'm from the Gold Coast. We have the best beaches in the world.' She took the key and nodded at Eli and Simon before walking as elegantly and confidently as she could, in her muddy trousers and filthy shirt, towards the saloon doors. She pushed them hard, but they were stuck.

'Pull them towards you,' Simon called out.

Sam yelled out after her. 'Third door on your left and use your torch because there's a large python who warms itself on the concrete there at night.'

His words were lost on Frankie who by this stage couldn't have cared if she had come across a monstrous snake or even the biggest crocodile ever seen in the southern hemisphere. She would kick it with her bare feet, use her bag to smash it on the head and stand on its back and jump up and down until it moved out of her way or she killed it. She dared anything to get in her way right at this moment because she'd take it down, human, animal or beast. Bring it on!

THE SMALL SHOWER WITH OUTDATED TILES AT LEAST HAD PLENTY OF FAST-flowing water. It was not however the luxurious bathtub she had dreamed of and with no sign of any restaurants nearby, she settled for takeaway fish and chips from the pub. She ordered a Corona. At least there was a sliver of lime to push into the top of the bottle. A small sign of civilisation. Tucking her dinner and drink under her arm she made her way back to the unit, locking the door after herself and breathing a deep sigh of relief when the fish and chips were delicious, the corona cold, and the clothes she had put on after her shower, smooth and clean against her skin.

Her beautiful Mazda, her pride and joy had arrived later on the back of a tow truck, forlorn, shit and mud-splattered, and now parked on the concrete behind her room.

The muddy water had also damaged her phone, which was dead and currently submerged in a bag of rice she had bought from the kiosk attached to the pub. The only person she would ring would be Gary anyway. If he was worried about her, he could ring the Hotel. The office had booked it, they knew where she was staying.

Her laptop sat useless on the round Laminex table. It needed re-charging and at the moment she had no idea where the cord for it was. She'd pulled apart her bags and searched her car, but the vital piece of equipment had disappeared. Something else for her to find tomorrow.

The unit's couch was hard under her body and she moved to try and find a comfortable position, a wet washer covering her eyes and forehead. The thought that no one really cared where she was niggled at her. She had plenty of friends back home, but they only contacted her on the weekends and that was only every so often. Most of them were married with kids so they were used to her being away and they'd be busy with their own lives. Too busy to worry that she had ended up in a ditch, was without a phone and was staying in accommodation with a pub next door, the music was cranking, and the conversation and swearing so loud it seemed the crowd was in the room with her. Was it bad to be this age and not have anyone care where you were? What if she disappeared for a couple of weeks? Would anyone except her boss realise?

She crawled into bed and pulled the sheets over her body, trying to ignore the loud music and a crowd of people singing loudly along to a medley of outdated Rolling Stones' songs. The pillow was thick, unlike the special thin one she preferred, which had been left at home. She pummelled it, swearing out loud as she turned on her side, a bare Besser brick wall staring back at her. It was just a bad day. Tomorrow would be better. She'd get her car fixed, there'd be a shop to buy a new phone and she'd start on the project that was going to see her advance through the ranks at her new job. It would all work out.

3

———————

Without a phone, Frankie had no idea what the time was. She glanced through the curtains on the back window, grateful to see her car still parked behind the unit. That was her first priority today, car and then phone. Her stomach rumbled. The time on the microwave said 8.45 however that couldn't be right. She hadn't slept in that long in ten years. She lay back down on the bed and did her regular morning stretches, surprised she had slept so well and the migraine that had started to creep in last night, had disappeared. Usually, she woke several times during the night. There were always new messages and emails that came through at odd hours and a multitude of ideas to think about for work the next day. The last thing she remembered was putting her head down on the pillow. What a difference a good night's sleep made. This morning she felt fresh, invigorated, and able to put the events of yesterday into order and create a plan to fix what was broken.

It was Sunday, so for once work could wait. She was due to meet with the developers on Monday, so she'd have today to herself. While she had waited for her fish and chips last night she had called work from a phone in the motel's office, leaving a message to say she'd arrived at Dingo Beach but her phone was not working. She'd get back to them once she bought a new one. Today was a good day to settle in, find a phone shop, get her bookwork in order and check out the lay of the land.

Her morning routine kicked in and she changed into a pair of denim shorts and a bright patterned t-shirt. Her hair came together easily into a thick pony-tail and she slipped on a pair of strappy sandals, turning each foot one way and then the other to admire her brightly painted toenails. The reflection of her green eyes stared back from the short mirror attached to the back of a cupboard door and she bent down to see her entire body. Her legs were long and well-shaped, and she was happy with the way her shorts fitted neatly, her backside and stomach toned and tight from the hours she put in at the gym. She pushed her breasts out and breathed in deeply. She'd never be happy with them or her hair that took hours to straighten every week.

She checked in her pocket for her phone, forgetting for a minute it was broken. It was strange not to be on it. Continual checking of emails and messages was part of her life, but now she couldn't do either and it felt like bits of her body had been removed.

A knock on the door broke her thoughts and she opened it to find an elderly man with cleaning utensils in hand. He smiled at her through crooked teeth, his shoulder-length scruffy white hair poking out from under a ragged Akubra hat. He wore patched shorts and an old t-shirt, slipping well-worn rubber thongs off on the doormat before entering. 'Good morning Miss. Seeing you're staying for a while I'll clean at this time each day. I figured you'd be getting breakfast at the pub. The name's Bert.'

Frankie picked up her purse and looked him up and down. She could only hope he was honest and able to clean. 'Good, I noticed the back window needs washing. It's covered in dirt.'

'I'll make sure to clean it. That'll be dust from the carpark behind. We haven't had decent rain in a while.'

Frankie walked outside, the glare from the sun powerful and making her reach for her sunglasses. She frowned and turned to Bert. 'Why is your vehicle parked right up near my door? That space is for my car when I get it fixed.'

Bert stood in the doorway, hesitant when he spoke. His skin was sun-damaged, tanned and wrinkled, the sign of a man who had probably lived in the tropics for most of his life. He tied his hair back with a rubber band as they spoke and his dark eyes met hers, his thin body straightening, as he stuck his chin out, his tone defiant. 'My missus, Myrtle, stays in the car. She's got dementia and has to be nearby. She won't go anywhere or come inside, she just sits and waits until I'm finished.'

Myrtle sat in the front seat of the car, the back of her head visible, a spotty hat sitting atop brown shoulder-length hair. Frankie shrugged. That sounded fair enough and besides, it might take a few days to get her car fixed. She could always get Bert to move his somewhere else once she needed the space. She went to check her phone to see what the time was. Damn, she was lost without it.

Bert started wiping the benches. 'Myrtle loves nothing more than if you talk to her for a few minutes. It would make her day.'

'Thank you, Bert. There's also a plate on that bottom shelf that has a tiny chip out of it.' Frankie turned and walked outside, heading towards the pub, a long building that was only a few steps away from the unit. She stared through her sunglasses to the area directly in front. Sunlight streamed through the branches of huge sprawling fig trees, their weeping boughs shading a sandy parkland that ran along the length of the foreshore. Beyond was the ocean, a glimmering expanse of water just visible through the gaps in the foliage. She'd have a good look later. An hour for walking was set aside in her schedule, so she'd head that way then. Now it was breakfast time and she was ravenous. Hopefully, someone could direct her to the best eatery in town.

4

———————

The Dingo Beach Pub was a low set Besser brick building, its long bar and tall slab tables already filled with customers seated on stools, laughing and chatting with each other as they ate and drank. They were a motley looking bunch and Frankie surmised they were locals. They all seemed to have the same hairstyle as Bert and wore old clothes and rubber thongs on their feet, their tanned skin smattered in spots and marks that told of a life in the sun and by the look of the fishing photos adorning the walls, a life on the sea. There didn't seem to be a dress-code sign in amongst the varied advertisements and photos. People in North Queensland must save a fortune on shoes, the rubber thongs on everyone's feet obviously the go for life in the tropics.

She wriggled her toes, trying to rid the sand from her sandals as she walked towards the counter. Large wooden tables and chairs were scattered across the sandy floor, their bright umbrellas offering shade from the north Queensland sun. It was only September but already the mid-morning heat was harsh. Shorts and a t-shirt had been a good choice of clothes and she straightened her shirt, walking briskly as she entered the area.

As she approached the bar a man came towards her. He was better dressed than the others nearby and took off his hat as he neared her. His blue coloured shirt was neatly tucked into his jeans, shiny brown riding boots and a wide leather belt completing his outfit. Short blonde hair framed a chiselled tanned face and she squinted behind her sunglasses. He looked familiar.

'G'day. You must be Frankie. I'm Steven, owner of Glenup Downs. Gary said you'd be arriving this weekend. They thought it was a good idea if I showed you around.' He held his hand out and she couldn't help but notice his strong arms, tanned and muscled.

His grip was gentle as they shook hands, his eyes looking her up and down as she smiled back at him. 'Pleased to meet you Steven. I only picked up the project files recently, so I haven't had a good read through yet, but I did see that a block on Glenup Downs is part of the acquisition for the foreshore development. It's nice to meet you.'

'Have you had breakfast yet?' he queried.

'No, I'm just about to find out where the best café is to go to.'

Steven laughed, a deep chuckle that matched the broad smile on his face. She stared at his perfect white teeth and full lips, his blue eyes that seemed to rove all over her body.

'Have I met you before?' she asked, regretting her words as soon as they came out of her mouth.

His smile widened. 'No, but I'm pleased to meet you now.' He placed his hand on her back and guided her away from the local crowd perched on their stools, steering her to a quieter part of the eating area. 'Sit down here and we can talk over breakfast. There is no other place to eat in Dingo Beach. The pub is it. Besides, they serve better food than anywhere else on the eastern coastline so you're at the best place already.'

HER MOUTH WATERED AS SHE WAITED TO START EATING, THE LARGE MEAL of bacon, eggs and mushroom impressive, with sprigs of rocket and sliced avocado decorating the plate. She declined the offer of a beer to complement the breakfast, instead choosing a freshly squeezed orange juice. Steven ordered an icy pot of beer for himself. After all he said, it was mid-morning. She watched him closely, surmising he was probably about forty, his body and tan alluding to the fact that he did physical activities and liked being outdoors. He was also charismatic, friendly and good-looking and wasted no time getting to know her, openly flirting with her from the moment they met.

She'd heard his life story by the time she finished breakfast. He'd been married twice, his first relationship resulting in two teenage boys who lived with their mother in Cairns. The last bride, as he referred to her as, was unable to cop the heat and fast pace of life that he lived. Meetings, overnight trips to the big smoke and long hours spent with business people were the essence of his work life. He might live in a tiny place in north Queensland, but his pace of life was in keeping with the big boys in the city.

Frankie listened intently. Steven's conversation held her attention and he was charming to go with it. He talked a lot about himself though and hadn't held back on his connection to the development she was here to consult on. He assured her that although Dingo Beach at the moment appeared to be filled with mostly locals and their daily socialising routine, in an hour or so the place would be packed with tourists, a live band playing and the place rocking. All it needed was some modern foreshore changes and the seaside town would be more popular than anywhere else in the Whitsundays.

He leant back in his chair; his legs stretched out in front as he stared at her. 'The foreshore plan has already been approved. The contracts are drawn up and it's only this extra signature from an external consultant to meet the guidelines that is needed. There's nothing for you to look at really. The big fellas have already done all the work.' He leant over and gazed into her eyes. 'We all know you're a newbie to the firm, so we've made it easy for you.'

He stood up and looked at his watch. 'I've got a meeting soon, so how about I see you tomorrow at nine, back here for our group conference. What about on Tuesday I take you for a spin in my new boat. I'm keen to get out to the islands, there's some good fish around at the moment. It would be a good opportunity for you to see our beautiful Whitsundays.'

Frankie stood up also. Her stomach was full, and it had been nice to sit and listen to Steven's stories. She was wary though. He was definitely flirting with her and the last thing she wanted was a romantic interlude. 'Thanks, but I don't fish. Perhaps another time.'

'I'll pack a picnic lunch and if you're lucky there might be whales. You don't have to wet a rod, you can just relax and sunbake if you want. Bring your bikini.' He smirked and winked at her. 'A couple of friends of mine will join us.' He stood near to her and gave her another one of those wide smiles. 'I don't bite. I promise you'll be safe with me. Besides it will make Gary happy for you to be seen mixing with the clients while you're here.'

He had a point. She needed to remember that part of this process was about promotions, networking and climbing the ladder. Besides he was so damn good-looking and what else was she going to do in this tiny town. The conversation with Steven had pointed her to the fact that there wasn't any phone shop in town or even another eating place. The pub with its attached petrol bowser and small coffee shop was it. There was nothing else to Dingo Beach.

Those reasons were why, Steven reminded her, they needed the foreshore development. At the moment there was only a kid's playground and some sand and trees. A concrete pool, more colourful slides and swings, as well as rock climbing walls and fancy tables and chairs would spruce it up and take away the old-fashioned feel. It would rival the foreshores in Townsville and Airlie Beach, bringing more tourists to Dingo Beach. He placed his arm loosely around her shoulders as he said goodbye, his words intended to flatter. 'She was smart, beautiful and from the Gold Coast. She was accustomed to development and knew what was needed to draw the tourists in. Progress was the way to go.'

Frankie shaded her eyes against the sun, looking towards the ocean. She had been here less than twenty-four hours but already she liked the vibe of Dingo Beach and it was obvious why others were attracted to the area. There weren't too many places like this, virtually untouched where kids could climb trees and run around, plus a pub that sat right on the beachfront. She needed to remember she was here for work though and part of that was signing off on the deal plus being friendly with the clients. 'Thanks for breakfast Steven. I will take you up on your offer. I look forward to it.'

5

———————

T he sun's rays were warm on her skin and a slight breeze
brought with it a fresh salty scent as Frankie headed towards
the beach. Several cars drove across the sandy parkland,
launching their boats on the ramp which Steven said was the only one
in the area and only useful at high tide. Barefoot kids ran around in the
shade, a dozen or so hanging like monkeys from the large branches of
the trees. Their squeals and laughter were a relaxing background noise
and reminded her of her own family picnics and school holidays.

Climbing trees was something she had loved as a kid. The feeling
of getting away from adults and pushing yourself to see how high you
could go, or which branch was strongest to hang upside-down on.
Now her exercise was regimented and she would need to do extra
push-ups and stretches back at the unit this afternoon, to catch up on
what she had missed yesterday.

Three small dogs raced in front of her, yapping and chasing each
other as they competed to tackle the one they caught, rolling around in
the sand before beginning the game all over again. A young couple
swung in a hammock, the colourful fabric pinned between two trees,
lazy long sways as their bodies wrapped around each other, their feet
hanging over the edges. She headed towards the water. Just a quick

look and then she could continue with her walk. A requirement of her exercise regime was ten thousand steps before midday.

The sandy path wound through the last of the trees, finishing on a small rise. Frankie stopped in her tracks and took a deep breath, shielding her eyes from the glaring sun and staring out towards a sparkling ocean, its surface dotted with glittering diamonds. She spoke out loud. 'A jewel sea.' In front of her the expanse of ocean stretched until its waters met the horizon. A large island and several smaller ones were scattered across its surface and a few small boats buzzed across the top of the waves, their metal hulls glinting in the sunshine that poured across the expanse of water.

Removing her sandals she stepped down onto the sand, the golden grains caressing her feet, a familiar feeling that brought a smile to her face. A few people fished at the water's edge but mostly the beach was deserted, and she walked in an easterly direction, enjoying the touch of the cool water as she waded along the water's edge. Even though she lived on the coast it was years since she'd been to the beach, her weekends and spare time filled with more important matters.

This beach was different than those of the Gold Coast. The water that lapped onto the sand was calm, the tiny waves languid, the movement mesmerising and slowing her pace as she watched the small fish that scurried through the shallows. In front of her a clean expanse of sand stretched as far as she could see, with no people in sight. A line of leaves and sticks showed the high tide line, the tufts of dry grass and small bushes beyond that protecting the foreshore and leading up to a scattering of lowset houses beyond. To the east, mountains covered in thick bush and tall trees towered over the coastline, their dark green slopes sprawling across the flats until they reached the shore. It was paradise, an undiscovered isolated beach that not only took her breath away but made her walk slow, unhurried, without even an urge to jog.

Her eyes were drawn back to the ocean and she gasped as a large stingray flew across the water. Its wing-like fins were spread wide, a long pointed tail trailing behind as it glided in flight before slicing back down into the waves. A large splash and foaming water the only tell-tale sign of its existence. She took a deep breath again, the salty air invigorating, the cool breeze and noisy calls of the seagulls diving in and out of the water revitalising her mind. Dingo Beach was not at all what she expected.

~

Walking was a good way to check out the area and after a while she left the beach, traipsing through the grassy foreshore before walking back along the road that ran adjacent to the shoreline. Bert the cleaner had passed her in his old holden, waving and grinning at her like he'd known her forever, Myrtle staring vacantly at her as they passed. She'd nodded back, hoping that he'd cleaned the windows and got rid of the chipped plate. Her mind switched back into business mode. She needed to sort out her car and just as importantly, her phone.

~

Bert had done his job properly and the unit was sparkling clean, the dishes she had left in the sink, washed and put away, the towels replaced and a small bunch of flowers in a vase, positioned in the middle of the small table. Her laptop cord lay next to the vase, a note attached from Bert saying that he had found it on the path outside and thought it might be hers. Frankie peered out through the back windows, wiping her fingers across the glass. Not a speck of dirt to be found. She looked towards her car, surprised to see that it had been cleaned, the paintwork now spotless, not a spot of shit or mud on its now shiny white surface. She wondered if Bert had cleaned it.

Her eyes were drawn to the end of the carpark. A young girl with long black hair was digging through the yellow lidded bins, pulling out cans and bottles. She threw them into large sacks that were soon full, before hoisting them over her shoulder and dragging them back to a battered old ute parked nearby. For someone so small she appeared to be strong, going back and forth, her thin arms hoisting up the sacks and dumping them onto the tray, repeating the process until the back of the ute was full.

Goodness me, Frankie thought, why would anyone do such a dirty job for probably little money. She was all for recycling, but really, so much effort for such little return. The ute took off with its cargo of tins and bottles, the dust from its tyres puffing out behind and settling on the windows that Bert had just cleaned. There probably wasn't much else for teenagers to do in a place like this and not many places to find work. Thinking about work reminded her how much she had to do. Thank goodness the place had Wi-Fi. At least she could go over the paperwork and correspondence before the first meeting tomorrow. A list – that's what she needed. Hopefully there would be emails from work that outlined the time and details of what was required. Once the consultancy was signed off, the allotted time was up and she'd delivered what they needed, she'd be able to return home, in a clean car and one that had been repaired.

That was the first item on her list – *get car fixed*!

SHE CRINGED AS SHE STARTED UP HER LAPTOP, THE CONTINUAL DINGING OF emails flooding in causing her head to tighten. Some deep breathing exercises calmed her mind and she reminded herself, that yes, her job could be stressful, but it was all about deadlines and contracts. Time was of the essence and it was good to be kept busy because it left no time to want for anything except her job.

The first email raised her stress levels even more and she looked closer at the words as if she must be reading them incorrectly, perhaps a misunderstanding. Gary was not happy that she had been inaccessible by phone and could she please ensure the issue with her communications was fixed immediately. Secondly, the contracts needed to be signed within four weeks and absolutely no later. It was essential not to sign them early, as Gary wanted to ensure the allotted perusal time for the site was given. She was booked into the motel for the next month. They would foot the bill and if everything went through correctly, they would then reimburse her for any extras, including meals, damage to her car and travel expenses for her return to the Gold Coast.

Discussions about her new role in the company would take place on her return.

Frankie read the email again. Four weeks! Gary had originally hinted at a couple of weeks. What was she going to do for a month? After all she only had to look over the site and sign off, the groundwork was complete and it was only a matter of an extra signature on behalf of their company by the set date. Why stay for such a long time when everything was already set in stone?

THE MEETING THE FOLLOWING DAY TOOK PLACE IN A ROOM THAT JUTTED off the main area of the pub. It was often used for conventions and weddings and the large table and high back chairs had a formal appearance, in contrast to the rest of the business. Frankie had been the first one to arrive and she wandered around the room, looking at the framed pictures that lined the walls. Black and white photos from another era graced the walls, with rows of men holding fish that reached from their heads down to the ground next to coloured photos of sailing boats, their sails flung open, with sailors hanging from their sides. She studied other photos that showed the pub from years gone by. Patrons stood grinning at the camera, their arms wrapped around each other, men and women holding glasses and beers high in the air, leaning into each other as they posed for the photo. She could almost hear their laughter, their camaraderie as they perched on high stools, talking and swapping stories, just like the group who sat around the benchtops today.

Her gaze left the photos and she caught her reflection in the glass sliding doors. She ran her hand over her clothes, pressing any stray creases down flat. She always liked to wear trousers for meetings, flared and well-ironed with a tucked in collared shirt completing the business look. Her hair was pulled back in a pony-tail, a turtle shell clip holding back stray bits of hair that liked to go their own way.

For a moment she felt out of her depth with this new job. The consultancy work in the past had been on familiar grounds, with smaller contracts that were based around marketing and publicity. It had been a surprise when Gary employed her and even though there had been smaller jobs she had attended to on the way to Mackay, it seemed that this project was the company's focus all along.

It was becoming increasingly apparent that all they wanted from her was a token signature. They probably didn't want to waste anyone else's time from the office and as the newbie, she was likely to do what they wanted. Who else would drive all the way up here and stay four weeks in a tiny backwater town?

Two men and a young woman entered through the glass doors. The men were probably in their forties, both dressed in jeans and polo shirts that displayed the name of their company – SheStar Developers. The woman was much younger and wore high heel shoes and a tight pencil skirt, her even tighter shirt tucked neatly in at the waist, a plunging neckline revealing a large set of breasts that were barely covered by black, stretchy fabric. Heavy make-up covered her face, glossy red lips and darkly lined eyes matching her black hair which was tied back in a neat bun, perched pertly on the top of her head. She reached out and shook Frankie's hand. 'I'm Maree, and this is Bob and Larry.'

Frankie shook hands with the men and joined them as they sat around the table, politely answering their questions as to how she was settling in. Bob and Larry were developers who had originally lived in Sydney but had been drawn in by the easy-going lifestyle of the north and the money that could be made from developments just waiting to be created. They had worked with Steven on similar projects in the past, this one being slightly different as part of the land required was owned by him. They spread the plans out on the table, quickly going over the layout of the park, rock climbing wall, play area and pool.

'Most of that rough sandy area will go.' Larry moved the plans around so they were in front of Frankie. 'There's a new mixture made from tyres, a recycled base that will look better and go with the coloured plastic slides and play equipment. Concrete paths will be nice and safe for walking and riding bikes through the area and will lead to the pool area. Most of the trees can go and there's a decent size area there for a small oval that we'll cover with fake grass. Easy to maintain.'

Bob leant over the table, his finger tracing the area where a pool and carpark was outlined. 'The pool is a long-term aim and well away from the first stage of the development. It won't be built for years. We just want to make sure we purchase the land in advance because it's all part of the plan. There's a good size bitumen car-park that will also cover much of this ground here.'

'I would imagine that concrete paths and a bitumen carpark would generate a fair bit of heat plus the trees are what I first noticed when I arrived. They give so much shade and the kids love to climb them.'

The men looked at each other and then back to the plans. 'Don't you worry about any of that,' Larry said, 'that's been taken care of, all that environmental stuff. There'll be that much shade with the new design that people will come here because of it.'

Maree beckoned the young waitress who stood waiting patiently to take their orders. 'Coffee and whatever is on the menu for morning tea and make sure you bring sugar for us and extra hot water.'

Frankie looked up, noticing the girl taking the orders was the same girl she'd seen collecting the bottles from the back of the units yesterday.

The men leant back in their chairs as Maree started to fold the plans up.

'Are those plans mine to look at?' Frankie asked.

Bob swivelled around in his chair to face her. 'Maree has the paper-work for you to sign.' Larry passed him a large envelope. 'This all needs to be back in by the specified date otherwise the entire project will fall through. There are new rules coming into place on that date, and I'll be honest with you, this project won't get through on the new laws. That's why Trust has sent you here. Being their new certified consultant, they've worked it so you're external from them on paper. They've already signed off on the project and with your signature it will be sealed and delivered.'

The waitress placed coffees and plates in front of them, her manner prompt and efficient. Maree pushed the plates around and commented that she hoped they were hot enough. 'I'm surprised you're not at school today Rose. Have you dropped out?'

The young girl looked down at the ground, her voice barely audible. 'No, I'm still at school but I take these extra shifts when they're available. Will that be all?'

Maree didn't answer and the two men hadn't even looked up, both checking their phones in between taking sips from their cups.

Frankie took a sip from hers. 'Thank you. The coffee is perfect.' She smiled at the young girl who nodded before turning and leaving the room.

After a while Maree pushed her chair back from the table, signalling the meeting was over. Her eyes met Frankie's. 'I hear you're joining us on the boat tomorrow. Steven said to tell you to meet us down at the boat ramp at seven in the morning and bring a spray jacket. The weather's kicking up a bit, but it should still be a nice day.'

Frankie wished she could think of a way to get out of tomorrow's boat trip. It was years since she'd been out on the water and she wasn't in the socialising mood. 'What time will we be back?' she asked. 'I need to organise repairs to my car and my phone's only working some of the time, so I need to get that sorted as well.'

Bob stood up and stretched, checking his watch before holding out his hand for Frankie to shake. 'It will be an all-day trip. Steven's going to take us out to the islands. Larry and I are going, plus our wives. Food and alcohol all included.' He winked at Frankie. 'All tax deductable of course.'

'We can have another meeting early next week and go over the papers again,' Larry said. 'You really need to stick around for the four weeks though, because a recent proposal was knocked back because the consultant hadn't hung around long enough - two days – so the entire proposal was under question. That's why when the main guy from your work came originally, he spent weeks here, researching and looking into everything thoroughly.' He made a clicking sound with his mouth. 'You're a lucky girl earning a job with that company. They have their fingers in some pretty big pies around the countryside.'

Frankie stood up. 'I am lucky, and it's different to what I've consulted on before. I need to study the plans before I sign anything and have a look over the site.'

Bob chuckled and put his arm around her shoulders. 'No need for that. Just check in with your boss and they'll tell you all you need to do is sign and stamp it with that big fat stamp you brought with you. She'll be apples.'

With that, the two men picked up the paperwork and left, ushering Maree in front of them. She smiled at Frankie. 'See you tomorrow at seven.'

THE FACT THAT THE PAPERWORK HADN'T BEEN LEFT WITH HER WAS NOT A good sign and she had a niggling feeling that she was well and truly being used. The trouble was she had no one to bounce her concerns off. No one back at the Gold Coast was interested and her friends had no idea what she was talking about when it came to work projects. She hadn't been at Trust long enough to make any friends, so the worries were entirely her own.

Her memory was good though and there were quite a few landmarks on the plan she had seen that stuck in her mind. She jotted down the details and drew the map again from what she could remember. After she got this stupid day out in the boat over and done with, she'd look around and go over the area herself. It wasn't such a big site so there probably weren't any problems. It would be good to check it out properly though. She did have ethics.

6

———

That afternoon she'd sat on one of the wooden chairs at the front of the pub, enjoying a cool drink. Most of the patrons sat outside and seemed to know each other and she positioned herself at a distance from the crowd that gathered around the benches closest to the bar, their laughter and chatter a muffled background noise. The tourists were easy to spot, with kids in tow, buckets and spades and their fishing rods piled on the roof racks of their cars. Dingo Beach was isolated and a perfect getaway for fishing enthusiasts and holiday makers. If she looked through the trees, she could see a few cars parked further down the street, all utes or four-wheel drives with boat trailers empty behind them.

One of the men from the local group came towards her and she cringed, hoping he wouldn't stop and speak to her. 'Aye love. Why don't you come and join us? It's a bit lonely sitting there by yourself. They said you're here for a few weeks. We're a pretty friendly bunch.'

Frankie noticed the man's bare feet, his buckled legs and a beard that hung down to his belt. A tattered old hat sat atop his head and his face reminded her of Bert's the cleaners, thin and wrinkled, like a fisherman who had just stepped off a boat or a deserted island.

'Thank you but I'm happy by myself.' She forced a smile and turned her gaze back to the ocean.

'Suit yourself lovey. Pickles is my name so if you're after a chat we're always there next to the bar. See ya round.'

You could hardly miss them, Frankie thought. A motley crew of men and women who leant on the high bench or perched on the wooden bar stools scattered next to the tables. Beers in their hands and most puffing on cigarettes, they chatted to each other, every so often loud raucous laugher filling the area from one of their jokes or funny stories. When one got up to leave, there was more noise as loud good-byes and boisterous jibes were shared. They seemed to be a happy lot, Frankie thought, just not the usual crowd she socialised with.

Pangs of loneliness had been something she'd learnt to deal with after breaking up with Ronaldo. She was better off by herself, with no one to answer to. For a while anyway. It would have been beneficial however to have someone help get her car fixed or work out how to mend her phone, someone to mull over the events of the day or share the view with. She sighed and looked towards the ocean, a sparkling shimmer beyond the trees, a moving blur of diamonds that held her gaze as she looked through the foreshore parkland.

The girl called Rose appeared beside her, picking up her empty wine glass and wiping the table. 'Would you like another drink? Prosecco again?'

Frankie dragged her eyes away from the ocean, wondering why when she was in a place where she knew no one, there always seemed to be someone to interrupt her thoughts.

'Why not? Thank you.' She looked Rose up and down. A loose cotton dress sat nicely on the girl's trim figure, the floral fabric catching her eye. 'That's a nice dress. It looks like Sass & Bide?'

'Would you like another Prosecco?'

When Frankie didn't answer, Rose started to walk away.

'Yes, but only if you tell me where you bought that dress. I don't see any designer shops around here.'

Rose stopped and turned back. 'It is Sass & Bide. There are a lot of rich people in Airlie and the op shop there has some good buys.'

'Well, you have a good eye. It looks great on you.'

Rose appeared to relax a little and put her shoulders back as she ran her hands over the fabric of the dress. 'You probably don't buy from op shops, but this dress cost me three dollars.'

Frankie laughed. 'You do know how much it's worth don't you. A dress like that off the rack would cost quite a lot of money.'

'I'll get your drink,' Rose replied as she strode off, leaving Frankie feeling like she had insulted the girl with her comments. Soon she returned with her Prosecco and a small plate of strawberries to compliment it.

'Thank you Rose.' She noticed the look of surprise on the girl's face when she used her name. 'You appear to be a local. I need to get my car into Airlie Beach somehow. It ended up in a ditch of water on the way here and it won't start. I've been told it's the electrics. I need someone to either take me and it there, or just tow it to a reliable mechanic and I'll speak to them over the phone.'

Rose had huge brown eyes, framed by long eyelashes, her skin tanned and flawless. 'My brother does odd jobs. He could tow it in. His mate's dad owns the mechanics in Airlie.' She paused and for the first time looked Frankie in the eye when she spoke. 'Is your car that white Mazda out the back?'

'It is.'

'I'm not sure they'd have the parts. They usually have to order them from Townsville or Brisbane, for cars like that. They're good mechanics though and my brother won't charge much to tow it in for you.'

Frankie sighed. It was a relief to get something happening with her car. 'I'm going out on a boat trip tomorrow.' She took a long sip from her wine. 'What if I leave the keys under the front tyre. It won't start, so no one can steal it. I'll leave my card in the car so the mechanic can give me a ring, or if he can't reach me, maybe he can contact the pub. My phone's playing up also.'

Rose smiled, a beautiful wide smile that stretched across her face, revealing a straight row of shiny white teeth. 'Sounds like you had a few mishaps getting here.'

'Nothing has really gone as planned so far and it's tricky being without a phone. Luckily the Wi-Fi works well.'

'My brother will sort it out for you. It's an hour in and one hour back, plus some time at the mechanics. Let's say fifty dollars for his time.'

'If your brother can get it all done and takes me back in to pick it up once it's fixed, I'll pay him two hundred dollars all up.'

Roses' eyebrows raised on her forehead as she smiled. 'He'll be really happy with that. Two hundred dollars it is, and he can take it in tomorrow. I'll get him to organise it tonight.'

Frankie passed her business card to Rose. The phone might not work but just ring the pub and ask for me. I'm staying in Unit 4.'

Rose nodded and took the card, turning to walk away.

'Oh, and Rose,' Frankie called out after her. 'Don't ever worry about buying clothes from op shops. Half of my wardrobe comes from them. I find more bargains and clothes I like there than online or in the designer stores. You have a neat figure. You'd look good in anything.'

THE SECOND PROSECCO WENT DOWN AS NICELY AS THE FIRST AND FRANKIE started to relax. She slipped her shoes off and rested them on a chair positioned in front of her, the sun warming her legs while the umbrella shaded the rest of her body. It was nice to talk to another female, one who wasn't only interested in talking because of a business deal or trying to network and make contacts for business.

She finished her wine. Towards the ocean and under the shade of the trees were bench seats, situated at a distance from each other for visitors to rest and take in the view. A couple sat on one close to the beach, their bodies still, the man's arm wrapped around the lady's shoulder. They had been seated there the entire time Frankie had been at the pub and now as the sun started to slide down the sky and the shadows fell long, the man hopped up and helped the lady to her feet.

Even from a distance Frankie could tell it was her cleaner, Bert, and his wife. She watched the gentle way that he straightened his wife's dress, pushing her sandals back on her feet and holding her hand as he led her back to their car, parked just behind them. He opened the door and positioned her in the seat, giving her a peck on the cheek before shutting the door. She watched as he got in, the dust from the tyres puffing up and following the car as it drove off down the street.

$$7$$

Frankie was waiting at the boat ramp just before seven in the morning. She'd scoffed down her breakfast and quickly finished her coffee while deciding what to wear. Tailored floral shorts with a white singlet top seemed to be appropriate attire for a day out on a boat and she slipped her sandals on, wishing she had some rubber thongs instead. Everyone at the pub wore them and although she usually looked down on people who flipped around in the colourful footwear, she could understand with the sandy ground underfoot, why they made more sense than a closed in shoe or sandal. Another item to add to her list.

The others greeted her as she boarded, Steven holding her hand for too long as he helped her onto the boat. Larry and Bob's wives had decided at the last minute not to come so she was thankful that Maree had kept her word and brought along another friend, Ilana. Ilana was a Swedish backpacker who spoke English with a sexy Scandinavian accent and knew her way around a boat. She worked on the tourist boats that ran out of Airlie and was on good terms with the men, her conversation leaving no doubt that she had been around for a while and was a valuable part of their social network. She had shapely bronze tanned legs and her tiny shorts and singlet showed off an Amazonian figure that left even Frankie in awe.

Perhaps the day was going to be fun after all. Maree was more relaxed than she had been in the meeting and Frankie soon found herself laughing and chatting with the girls as the boat motored out of the shallow bay and into the deeper waters between the mainland and the many islands that scattered the Whitsunday waters.

They had not gone very far before Frankie spotted the first whale. She had taken a break from talking and sat by herself on the plush leather seats that lined the deck. The water had been calm in the bay, but now tiny waves pushed up against the bow, slapping the sides of the boat as it cruised towards the open sea. She looked down, mesmerised by the vivid aqua colour and the thousands of tiny fish that swam in schools near the surface, flitting back and forth beneath the boat. Steven came and sat beside her, leaving the driving to Ilana who slowed the boat as soon as Frankie pointed out the huge whales gliding through the water not far in front of them.

A strong arm closed around her shoulders. 'Enjoying yourself.' Steven spoke quietly, his face not far from her own. 'I hope you realise how hot you look in those shorts. You've got the best set of legs I've seen in a long time.' His hand caressed her arm and she closed her eyes, wanting to look at the whale, wanting to tell him to remove his hand and wanting the squeamish feeling in her stomach to disappear.

Today he wore casual shorts, his toned legs matching his arms that were strong and tanned. His voice was low and husky. 'When we get to the island, stay back on the boat with me for a while. Let the others walk and have lunch. I'd like some time alone with you.'

She turned towards him. What a charmer and so good looking. Perhaps at another stage in her life she would have jumped in without hesitation. She took a deep breath. 'That's lovely of you to offer but isn't that a wedding ring on your finger?'

He looked down at the shiny gold band on his left hand. 'She comes and goes. We have an open marriage. I'd love to get to know you. I often come to the Gold Coast.'

Frankie leant her elbow on the side of the boat and rested her chin in her hand as she stared out towards the whales. One of them arched across the waves, its massive body emerging above the surface before ploughing back under and disappearing for a few seconds. She laughed when it spouted water high in the air, a hard splash of its tail slapping the waves before plunging down again, submerged and hidden in the deep water.

She turned her focus towards Steven. 'I'm grateful for the day out but I don't go out with married men.'

Steven swivelled his legs towards her, his eyes looking straight at her. A rugged stubble formed on his cheeks and once again she tried to work out where she knew him from. He ran his hand up and down her leg. 'I'm not really married. Think about my offer. Just enjoy the day and we can take it from there. You've got a few weeks here. Just call me whenever.'

She smiled at him, his manner so confident and charismatic. 'I'll remember that.' Steven's hand was warm on her leg, his touch gentle and goosebumps prickled on her legs, reminding her she'd had no body contact with anyone for over two years. Ilana picked up the speed and the boat bounced up and down on the waves that increased in size the further away from land they went. She peered across the waves, gaining a glimpse of the whale's back when it occasionally surfaced in the distance.

'You're very quiet,' Steven said. 'If you look over there that's Gloucester Island. No-one lives on it and there are some beautiful remote bays that are secluded and quiet. I'll take you there while you're here.' He glanced towards her and frowned. 'Are you okay?'

Frankie tried to nod but her head spun, and it felt like the entire world was swaying. Bile rose in her throat and she leant over the side of the boat, the contents of her breakfast flying out across the ocean, down the side of the boat and due to a sudden gust of wind, back onto herself and Steven.

She clung to the side of the boat, leaning out, waiting for the next lot to rise up. Steven jumped up and grabbed a towel which he placed down next to her, telling her she was okay, she was just a bit seasick.

Maree and Bob had disappeared into the cabin of the boat, both declaring if they even smelt vomit they'd throw up themselves and Larry conveniently positioned himself on a stool next to Ilana, announcing that he'd make sure the boat stayed on course. The two of them swapped stories about those that couldn't handle the waves, their words travelling back to Frankie who had eventually stopped vomiting and now lay on her side on the padded bench. She hugged her knees, the remaining contents of her stomach, rolling and churning with every wave the boat bounced over.

'I'm so sorry,' she said, turning to Steven, who stood his distance, a spare towel and bucket in hand. 'Can you let me off somewhere? It's not going to go away.' Frankie closed her eyes, even to speak was an effort.

'You should have told me you get seasick. If we turn back now we'll lose an hour, and the others will miss out on the planned events on the island. We have a long way to go yet.'

Frankie groaned. 'I haven't been on a boat for years.'

'You're from the Gold Coast for heaven's sake. I thought you'd be used to boats and fishing.'

Her eyes closed again and she tried to stop the nausea rising, wanting so badly for the swaying feeling in her body to remain still. She sat up again and what was left in her stomach was emptied into the sea; at least this time it didn't fly back on her. She was already smelly with vomit and noticed that Steven who was keeping his distance, had changed out of his clothes and into a new set.

He stood at a distance, taking out his phone and looking out across the waters. 'My brother is out here fishing. He came out at sparrow fart so he's probably ready to go back in. How about I give him a ring and he can take you back. That way we can continue, and you can get onto dry land.'

'Whatever.' Frankie whispered. 'I don't care. Just get me off this boat.'

FRANKIE PICKED UP SOME OF THE CONVERSATIONS BETWEEN STEVEN AND his brother. 'Spewed all over me, over the boat, over my fucking expensive leather seats … Yep, just needs dropping off at Dingo. Thanks Mate.'

Ilana slowed the engine and before long the sound of a smaller boat could be heard. A silver tinnie sped towards them, the wash spurting out behind it in sprays of white plumes. Just like my vomit, she thought. Hopefully she wouldn't throw up all over this person's boat. One was enough. The girls came to help her, cajoling her with sympathetic words. Funny how they hadn't been nearby when she was being sick. Even though Steven was flirty, at least he had helped her clean herself up and held the bucket for a while when she dry retched again and again. How embarrassing. Hopefully she'd never see these people again.

AS SHE MOVED TO THE REAR OF THE BOAT, STEVEN'S BROTHER POSITIONED his tinny side on, so she could climb into it. He reached up for her arm and held her tightly as she stepped down into the hull, the waves causing both boats to sway and bang against each other. She was so intent on not losing her footing, her eyes fixed on the bottom of the boat, that she didn't look up from under her hat until she was seated. Steven and the others waved and yelled out their sympathies as she huddled in the back of the boat. The man who had come to take her back to land sat down beside her and placed a towel over her legs. She looked up and stared straight into a deep set of blue eyes, a worried look in them as Steven's brother took in the state she was in.

Her teeth chattered as her stomach rose up and down and she closed her eyes and then opened them again. 'It's Simon, isn't it? You're Steven's brother.' Her words were barely out when she leant out over the side again. How could there be anything left in her stomach? 'Hang on, 'Simon said as he pushed the throttle open, the boat finding its balance on top of the curly waves as he pushed it forward. Frankie lay down on the floor of the boat and pulled the towel over the top of herself. If she could just put her head down on something solid, she might gain some relief.

He called back to her, loud enough to hear above the boat engine. 'We'll head for the island. It's rough going across that passage at the moment. You won't like it in this boat. Gloucester Island is only ten minutes away. You can get out there and put your feet on solid ground.'

Frankie didn't move or talk again until the engine slowed and the waters calmed. She sat up and tried to push her hair back from her face, chunks of vomit entwined in its curls, the smell of it making her stomach heave again. It was a relief when gusts of cool air pushed against her face and she breathed in deeply, relishing the salty spray of the waves, fresh and clean on her skin.

In front of them a mountainous island loomed, its jagged ranges lining its length, white sandy beaches and rocky headlands a border between its lands and the sea. Seagulls squawked and flew above them, and Simon slowed as a huge manta ray left the water and sailed through the air next to them. It was larger than the boat and Frankie gasped at the sight of the flying sea animal, the tips of its wings curled up, its tail trailing behind. It sank back down before wallowing in the water around the boat, a dark shape underneath the waves that had changed colour to an aqua green as they neared the island.

Simon checked over the edge of the boat as he navigated around boulders and reefs that lay just under the surface. He looked up and stared at Frankie, laughing when she shook her head. She could only imagine what she looked like and how she smelt. She pushed her hair back from her face, the rigid straight lengths now kicking up in curls, ringlets of hair sticking to her face as she tried to straighten her clothes. Her stomach calmed as the water became shallow.

They motored into a small bay, the steep cliffs lining the sides of it a protective barrier from the waves and the wind. The spray from the ocean kicked up onto the rocks, their red and orange surfaces, glistening in the mid-morning sun. The boat edged closer to the shore, the golden sand littered with driftwood and shells that she longed to put her feet onto. A surface that wasn't moving.

Simon jumped out of the boat as its hull scraped across the sand, his tanned legs strong and steady as he waded through the knee-deep water, pulling the boat behind him. He looked much the same as his brother and it was no wonder that she had thought she'd met Steven before. Simon was not quite as tall, but the curly blonde hair and blue eyes were the same. He had a cheekier smile and a kind demeanour, and she recalled how he had sat quietly and taken her abuse after he ran her off the road. She grimaced. Well not actually a road but really his own private driveway through the cane fields.

She watched as he pushed the anchor down in the sand, an esky in his hand as he made his way up the beach. Her legs wobbled and a pain throbbed in her forehead, but it was a relief to get out of the boat and onto solid ground. 'Sit down here,' Simon beckoned. A gnarled she-oak on the edge of the sand offered shade and Frankie sank onto the beach, the sand warm beneath her.

'Just sit for a while and you'll feel better.' I'll just fix some things in the boat.' His voice was deep and reassuring and as he made his way back to the boat, Frankie closed her eyes again, trying hard to relax and stop her stomach from churning.

She sat for a long while, letting the warmth from the sun pour over her body and taking long sips from a bottle of water Simon had given her. The liquid was cool on her throat and the nausea slowly diminished as she watched Simon wind up ropes and rearrange his fishing gear. The bay they had stopped at was like something out of one of the glossy Whitsunday brochures she had seen at the pub. Clear turquoise water near the shore turned to a vivid blue as it opened into the expanse of the ocean. White crests of waves balanced on top of the blue and the entire ocean continually moved, much the same as both boats had this morning. The sand was solid beneath her body and she stretched her legs, the smell of vomit hanging in the air, bits of it stuck to the folds in her shorts.

SIMON TURNED AROUND WHEN SHE CAME UP BEHIND HIM. 'FEELING better?' he asked as he splashed water on his face before putting his hat back on his head.

'I am, thank you. Is it okay if I swim here? If I duck under the water, I can clean my clothes and get rid of the smell.'

He pulled a funny face. 'What smell? Do you smell?'

'I've never felt so sick. I'm so grateful you were able to get me. I think I would have jumped overboard otherwise.'

'It's a terrible feeling. Steven should have told you to take some tablets before you left or had some on the boat. It's pretty choppy out there today.'

Frankie's stomach had returned to normal and the tickling of the sunshine on her salty skin made her feel alive, like she was a long way from everyday life. She smiled and looked at Simon. 'The vomit came back in the wind and went all over your brother and me.' She frowned. 'He was sitting very close to me and we were just starting to have a conversation about his wedding ring.'

'That's my brother.' Simon shook his head. 'We can swim here. It's winter so there aren't any stingers around.' With that, he pulled his shirt over his head and threw it into the boat before striding out into the water. He had broad shoulders and a muscly chest, his arms reached out strongly as he dove in and swam a short way out. It was a long time since Frankie had seen even a half-naked man and she stared hard, forgetting where she was until he called out to her.

The silky water closed around her as she waded fully clothed into the deeper water, sinking gratefully below its surface. She stood for a long while, scrubbing her shirt and shorts, washing her hair as best as she could. When she finished, she swam out to where Simon was diving in and out of the small waves, the water streaming off his hair and face when he popped up again.

'God, how good does that feel?' He laughed and flashed her a smile. 'I don't remember the last time I swam. I'm usually in a boat on top of the waves.'

Frankie floated on her back. 'I haven't swum in years either. It's crazy, I live right near the beach yet never go there.' She kicked her legs and stood on the sandy bottom, her shoulders and head above the water. 'Thank goodness I don't feel sick anymore. That is the worst feeling ever. You can leave me here. I'm not getting back in a boat again.' She ducked under, the water streaming off her hair and face when she surfaced.

Simon stood nearby, his shoulders and head above the water. 'By the time we dry off and you have something to eat you should be okay. I can sneak around the edge of the island and stay out of the wind. Crossing the channel might be choppy but it will only take a few minutes. There was a good swell out where Steven took you and it would have only got worse the further you went. I was just about to head home, so it was good timing.'

THEY SAT TOGETHER ON THE SAND, SHARING SANDWICHES AND SOFT DRINKS that Simon had packed for his own lunch. 'I was going to stop here and eat anyway. Lucky there's plenty for both of us.'

Frankie sat cross-legged, the heat of the day drying her hair and clothes. Her body and hair were clean and a salty tightness clung to her skin. 'I appreciate you coming to get me and bringing me back. It seems like you've rescued me twice this week.'

Simon sat with his knees up, his arms resting on top of them as he stared out across the water. 'I usually try and stay out of the way of my brother's business trips. He and I are two very different people. I'm sure you can look after yourself but if you want a tip, he's a player. He has a girlfriend in Airlie and another in Brisbane, so don't trust him as far as you could throw him.'

'I figured that from the start.' She flapped her shirt so it dried a bit quicker. 'What about when it comes to business?'

Simon turned towards her and his eyes narrowed as he stared straight at her. 'That's for you to work out. He's been doing business with those other two for years now and they've landed in trouble before. You do know that the block the pool is supposed to go on is his?'

Frankie raised her eyebrows. 'I had worked that out. They've kept the plans from me, and I was going to look into it all this week.'

Simon stood up and looked down at her. 'They're calling you the tick and flick girl. All they need is your signature. Apparently, you're the perfect option as you have the certificates, but you are separate from the initial approvals.'

She scrunched up her face, annoyed that there had been discussions about her before she even arrived. 'That's the story I seem to be getting from everyone around here.'

Simon packed up the esky and put his shirt back on. He picked up a shell and passed it to her. 'You smell a lot better now. Here, this will remind you of one of your shit days in the Whitsundays. The day you spewed.'

Frankie took it and turned it over in her hand. 'Thank you and it's strange to say, but it actually has turned out to be one of the best days I've had in a long time. I've hardly even thought about work.'

8

____

Simon managed to keep to the calmer waters that ran around the edge of the island. The wind was blowing from the east and if he kept to the western side of the island they were sheltered from the gusts. He motored slowly, pointing out small horseshoe coves where smooth boulders formed an edge to the shore, leaning pine trees hanging precariously to the slopes above them. A few small boats dotted the ocean and Simon waved to them as they passed, their occupants focussed on their fishing rods that dangled into the waters. He slowed as they came to a larger bay, the colour of the water a dark green, the sleek surface parting ways as the boat skimmed over it.

To either side of them the folds of the mountains of Gloucester Island sloped down into the ocean, their valleys and ravines an outlet for the waters that gushed down them when the rainy season came in the summer months.

'Look to your left,' he pointed to the water between them and the shore.

Frankie stood up and shaded her eyes with her hand as she watched a large group of dolphins leap and cavort in the silky waters. They moved quickly, their long snouts disappearing under the water before re-emerging, only to plunge under again. One of them spiralled upwards, the sleek grey of its body spinning high in the air before dipping down and submerging below. The boat bobbed up and down in the same spot, the motor turned off, the air silent, as they watched the dolphins circle and feed on a school of small fish before heading towards the open sea.

'That is beautiful to watch,' Frankie said, standing on her tiptoes as she followed the dolphins' path, their antics barely visible in the distance.

'They're often in this bay,' Simon started the engine back up. 'We're nearly at the end of the island, the passage is ahead. Move down the back here with me, it'll be less bumpy. It's only a short distance across so just hang on and watch the horizon.'

Frankie moved next to him and hung onto the side of the boat, praying that she wouldn't be sick again.

THE CHANNEL WAS CHOPPY, BUT IT WAS ONLY A SHORT DISTANCE ACROSS and before she knew it, they were motoring through the calmer waters not far from Dingo Beach. The boat veered in closer and Simon pointed to an area where thick mangroves lined the foreshore. 'That's Steven's block they're talking about buying for the pool area.'

Frankie looked closely at the area and then back at where the other part of the development was going. 'Don't you think it's a bit far from where they're talking about putting the boardwalk and paths?'

Simon didn't reply, so she asked him again. 'The areas don't really link, do they?'

He shrugged his shoulders. 'It seemed like an odd choice to me, but I guess if it's approved they'll have to connect it somehow.'

SIMON DROPPED FRANKIE OFF DIRECTLY IN FRONT OF THE PUB. HE HELD HIS hand out as she jumped out of the boat, helping her onto the beach and passing her bag to her.

For once she felt unsure what to say, he'd been such a gentleman and gone out of his way to help her. 'Thank you. Maybe I'll see you again while I'm here?'

He leaned back on the boat; his arms crossed as he looked at her from under his hat. 'I'm back in town on the weekend. By the way,' he asked, 'Did you put your car in to get fixed?'

'Yes. There's a girl who works at the pub called Rose and her brother was towing it to the mechanics today for me. I need to ring them this afternoon.'

Simon pulled a face. 'I hope you see your car again.'

'Please don't say that. She seems like a nice girl.'

'She's my son Eli's, girlfriend. They're a big family who live in a rundown house up on the hill. I won't say any more, but I'm interested to know how that works out for you. Adios, Miss Frankie. I'll see you next time.'

He gave her a wave and spun the boat around, seaward bound. She wondered where he was going. He hadn't taken his boat out via the ramp like everyone else seemed to. It was the only boat ramp in the area and one of the main reasons the beach was so popular. She clutched her bag, her body tensing as her phone which she had thrown in this morning, came to life. The constant dinging of emails and messages reminded her she had work to do and a pounding sensation once again thudded in her head. She pulled the shell out of her pocket that Simon had given her and held it up to the sunlight. It had been a good day, even with the vomiting. Her body was relaxed, her skin tingling with dried salty water and she didn't want to look at her phone or any stupid emails. She sighed and made her way back up to her unit. There was work to be done.

THE REST OF THE WEEK PASSED QUICKLY, AND PHONE CALLS AND bookwork took up most of Frankie's time. The mechanic had called and the parts for her car were going to take a while to come in, maybe by the end of next week. Gary had also rung, checking she was right to complete the signing by the due date. He reminded her it was just a matter of taking her time, making sure that it looked like she'd been thorough in her research.

At first, she ignored Steven's calls but eventually gave in, hoping that if she talked to him he'd leave her alone. He apologised for taking her out in rough weather and also for offloading her the first chance he could get. It hadn't been a great day but there was plenty of other places he'd like to show her. She had declined his offer to take her into Airlie Beach for dinner and assured him that she was happy where she was, with plenty to keep her occupied.

Consistent work continued to flood into her email box and even though the pressure was less with no one looking over her shoulder, she ensured she followed a routine. Each day Bert turned up to clean, his car parked in front, his wife sitting in the front seat. Frankie left as he arrived, taking the time to walk along the beach, her regimented exercise now replaced with a brisk walk, in whatever direction she desired.

Simon appeared on Saturday morning, just as she came out through the door to go for her walk. He sat on a low brick wall, watching her as she did up the laces on her walking shoes. 'Morning Frankie. I was in town and thought I'd see how you got on with the car.'

He wore old shorts and a t-shirt, his hair as usual covered with a wide Akubra hat, those piercing blue eyes staring out at her from under the brim. She turned at the sound of a car pulling in next to where they were.

Bert drove in, parking in his usual spot next to her front door. He waved quickly at them both, but instead of going inside to clean, chased Myrtle, who had opened the car door and taken off towards their usual spot on the bench seat.

Frankie straightened up and stretched her arms in the air. 'They're waiting for the parts to come from Brisbane. The mechanic rang and they've got it all sorted.'

'That's good news. I thought you might not ever see that car again.'

'Your son, Eli, seems like a nice kid and Rose works hard around here.'

'She should be at school, not hanging around the pub. I've tried to tell him that she'll bring him no good, but he won't listen. Teenagers!'

'Do you mind if I ask you something? How old are you Simon?'

'I'm thirty-eight this year. How old are you?'

'That's irrelevant. I'm thirty-five but what I'm getting at, is you sound like an old man, like my father used to talk. Don't you remember what it's like when you're that age? I've seen them walking on the beach and sitting together having a soft drink. They make a cute couple.'

He shook his head and looked across the parkland to Bert and his wife. 'Rose's family is trouble.'

'That doesn't mean she is.'

Simon stood up, took his hat off and ran his hand through his hair. 'I came to ask if you'd like to join me for a meal tonight at the pub. That's if you're not too busy.'

She thought for a moment before answering. 'I know this might seem rude, but I've been put off by your brother.' Looking directly at him she asked, 'Are you married or have a partner?'

Simon let out a husky laugh, causing her face to burn. 'It's been so long I can't remember, but no I'm not married and there hasn't been a partner for over ten years since my ex-wife left me and took our daughter with her. She left me with Eli. I'm not used to asking someone out, but I enjoy talking to you and we seem to keep running into one another.'

FRANKIE WORE HER FAVOURITE FLORAL DRESS THAT CAME TO JUST ABOVE her knee. A thin red belt pulled it in at the waist, her figure trim, her legs toned and shapely. It was a long time since she had gone on a date with someone she wanted to look good for and she ran her fingers through her hair, pushing it around until she was happy with it. Her hair was bouncy and shiny from the hotel's rainwater and for some reason she couldn't be bothered straightening it. The humidity didn't allow it to stay straight for long anyway, and for once she didn't fret about the spiral tendrils that sprung out from the edge of her face, masses of brown curls covering her head. Her skin was smooth and tanned and she ran her finger along her eyebrows, pushing them upwards in the middle to accentuate her eyes. She hadn't bothered with make-up, and only a light covering of tinted moisturiser brought an extra healthy glow to her face. The pub had a relaxed atmosphere, so it would be best not to appear overdressed. She'd been in there enough now to know that no one really seemed to worry too much about how anyone else dressed or looked.

~

SIMON LEFT THE LOCALS AT THE BAR HE HAD BEEN TALKING TO AND strolled over to meet her as she entered. He guided her to a table, away from the rowdy table of fishermen and women who looked like they had been there all afternoon. The surrounding tables soon filled up and a small band started up in the corner of the outside area. Colourful party lights flickered where they hung from the palm trees and noisy chatter and laughter filled the area.

Simon complemented her on her dress and her hair. 'Thank you,' she replied, 'You have good taste in clothing yourself.'

He raised his eyebrows as he pulled a chair out for her to be seated. 'You sound surprised. Just because I don't live in the city doesn't mean I don't dress up every now and again.'

Her lips curled up into a smile and she relaxed into the easy banter they seemed to be able to share, as she took her seat. 'It's definitely a different way of life here. I've only been here a short while but it's as if a pressure has been taken away.' She looked out across the park, the huge trees throwing their shadows over the sand as a flock of cockatoos noisily flew into the branches of one, squawking and bickering until they settled in and found their spot for the night. 'It's almost as if,' she paused, 'it sounds strange, but when you're here, it's like you could almost forget about everything else in your life and just live for the moment.'

'North Queensland will do that to you. Especially in this place, with the water and the islands. It's also the people who make it what it is.'

Frankie nodded. 'Dingo Beach is making me slow down. Who would have thought I would be happy when my phone doesn't work or when the Wi-Fi drops in and out? I don't even have a car, or my phone fixed properly.' She took the glass of wine from the waiter, lifting it to Simon's beer, the glass clinking together as they said 'cheers' at the same time.

They laughed in unison and she relaxed even more. The interaction between them was similar to how it had been the other day on the island, and they slipped into easy conversation, listening to one another and asking questions about each other's life. Simon wanted to know about her job, where she lived and her family. To begin with she had skimmed over what she'd done in the last ten years, but he seemed to have a way of asking questions that drew out aspects she hadn't talked about in a long time. Once she started talking she found it easy to open up. The good parts and the bad. She hadn't divulged much to anyone since she'd split up with Ronaldo but the more she talked, the more she remembered.

'It doesn't sound like the last few years have been that great for you,' Simon said, 'You've done well to carry on with a positive approach. Where to now?'

She looked down and played with the stem of her glass, unused to sympathy and praise bundled into one. 'I'm not sure where I'm headed. I just keep my head down and work as hard as I can and then I don't need to think about anything else.'

'Why would you do that?' Simon was intrigued. 'Time is precious, you don't want to waste it.'

'I'm not sure.' Her voice exposed her confusion and she tried to sound definite that she was happy. 'I haven't ever thought about it much, but I do okay.'

Simon leaned back in his chair, looking at her over the top of his beer, his blue eyes searching hers. He lowered his voice. 'When we get hurt we throw ourselves into whatever takes our mind off the other. For me it was the farm and Eli, perhaps for you it's been climbing the ladder, making work your priority. That way you don't have to think about the hard things.'

'That's pretty deep.' Frankie thought hard. What did she want? What was her goal? It had all been about getting a promotion, becoming successful in her career. But at the moment she was being used by a company that had promised her the world. She'd been sandwiched in between developers and a landowner who only wanted her for a signature and once she left here she'd just go back to life in the fast lane, kowtowing to everyone to try and please them. She'd only been removed from that for a couple of weeks, but she hadn't even missed it. Not once.

'What are you aiming for?' Frankie searched Simon's face, which was often hard to read. Although he was a good talker, she could tell that he only skimmed the surface and didn't reveal much about what had hurt him in the past.

'Me? Not much at the moment. Just to keep the farm going and get Eli through this last year of school. It hasn't always been easy as a single father, but I feel like we're nearly there. If he could just go his own way and not fall for Rose's ideas all the time.'

'What are their ideas?'

'He wants to head down to Brisbane and study Science and Agriculture at the main university down there. He's got the brains and the marks and I'm all for it. The problem is I'm worried now that he's thick with Rose that he's going to want to hang around here and not go to Brisbane because of her. He's been talking about a gap year, taking a year off to do whatever and then go to university the year after. I'm not keen on that. I think he needs to get away from her and get stuck into his studies.'

'You sound like my father did. Not that you're that old but that's exactly what he wanted me to do.'

'And did you listen to him?'

'I did. I went straight into uni and managed to have a job, social life and study. It worked out well as I finished my business degree and then could do the other things that I wanted to do. There's plenty of time for everything. You don't realise that when you're that age though.'

'Maybe I should get you to talk to him.'

'What does his girlfriend want to do?'

'I have no idea. Probably the same as the rest of her mob. Just hang around here and pick up odd jobs. The father's never around, he floats back and forth to family up north. I wouldn't imagine Rose has anything planned. She's in trouble here at the moment. Sam said she stole good work boots and other shoes left out the back of the units where you're staying. Someone else said they see her sneaking around there all the time, putting things in a hessian bag.'

Frankie put her drink down and frowned at Simon. 'No-one came and asked me about it. I've been staying here all week.'

'There was no need to. They know she did it. Sam's going to sack her after the weekend. He said she's a good worker, but he can't keep a thief on.'

Frankie stood up, straightened her dress and picked up the empty glasses. 'Well, I might just have to speak to Sam, because if he'd asked me, I could have told him that a large black dog has been lingering around the back of the units after dark. I've watched it take a rubber thong from the back the other night and I'm pretty sure I saw it with a boot in its mouth the next night. I also see Rose when she's out the back and she's so busy filling up huge bags with cans and bottles and lifting them into her ute she wouldn't have time to take anyone's boots.'

Simon went to speak but closed his mouth, his eyes wide, his look perplexed.

Frankie banged her empty wine glass down on the table and stalked off to the bar, annoyed that the men had all jumped to the same conclusion and not bothered to ask her about the incident. Had they thought about the fact that she might have observed something they hadn't.

When she arrived back her face was flushed, and the effects of the wine and a good meal were making her feel carefree and confident. She plonked a beer in front of Simon and raised her glass to him. 'Sam said thank you and the drinks are on him for saving one of the best workers he's ever had.'

Simon grimaced and took a long sip from the icy beer. 'Lucky I mentioned it. It's just she comes from such a rough family and usually the apple doesn't fall far from the tree.'

'Maybe you're being judgemental. I see your Eli with her, sitting in his car together around sunset. They always wave when I walk past and they never seem to be doing anything bad. Just two kids, probably madly in love.'

'Hmmph,' Simon muttered.

Frankie turned to watch the people on the dance floor. The band was playing rock n roll music and the locals and visitors were making the most of it. She laughed at some of the dancing. 'I haven't seen moves like that since I was a teenager.'

Pickles strode over to them, reaching out to shake Simon's hand. 'Gonna dance Simon? That's something I'd like to see.'

'How are you Pete? This here is Frankie.'

'Pickles nodded. 'We've met. She knows me as Pickles.' He thumped Simon on the back. 'Make sure you come over and have a drink with us before you leave. Sylvia and Wally are here tonight so it's a special celebration. She's been five years cancer free, so Wally is shouting.'

While the two men talked, Frankie gazed around the pub which was filled with loud, happy patrons, their conversation and laughter filling the space with noise. In the back bar a game of pool was under way, the room filled with players and spectators, who gave running commentaries on every shot that was taken. It was a mixture of people of different ages and backgrounds. They all had one thing in common though, they were having a good time and appeared not to have a worry in the world.

Pickles had returned to his table and she drew her eyes away from the scene, turning back to Simon who was staring at her.

'What?' she asked, scrunching up her forehead.

'You look happy.'

She smiled warmly at him. 'I am. I actually feel happy.'

As the night wore on the band continued to play, the crowd on the dance floor changing its movement with every tune. When 'The Waifs', *Lighthouse* tune started to play she felt tears welling in her eyes. It had been hers and Ronaldo's song. They had played it in the car, in the kitchen and in the backyard when they sat and cuddled, eating cheap takeaway on the old lounge on the back verandah. That had been before their careers had taken off. When they had time for each other and were happy with the simple things in life. A favourite song, a cold beer and being together.

Simon too was pensive. 'Do you have a favourite song,' Frankie asked him.

'Not anymore.' He downed the last of his beer. 'Music brings back memories though.'

'I was just thinking the same.'

Pickles and the woman he was always with at the bar, came towards them. He pulled her along by her hand and they laughed loudly as they approached. Pickles stood next to them pulling Simon up by the hands, the woman grabbing Frankie's hand. 'Come on you two.' Pickles' voice was slurred, his legs unsteady. 'You can't dance when you're dead.'

It was too late to avoid being dragged along and Frankie found herself in the middle of a bunch of people who swayed and gyrated around the dance floor. She grinned at Simon who moved his feet a little bit, a sigh of relief when a slower song started to play.

'I can't dance but I can sway.' He put his arm around her waist and held her close, her arm coming up around his back. Holding her other hand he made some attempt at what could be called a waltz and she found herself swaying in time and moving her feet with him. Her head was level with his shoulders, and hopefully he couldn't feel her heart thumping hard in her chest as she pressed her body against his. They moved smoothly around the dance floor and when the chorus played, he swung her around and twirled her underneath his arm, making it look like they both knew what they were doing. When the music stopped, she stayed next to him, the touch of his arm on her body, warm and comforting.

He looked down at her and their eyes met, her cheeks burning as they let go of each other. He grabbed her hand and led her back to the table.

'You're blushing,' he said.

'That was nice,' was all she could get out.

Simon also seemed lost for words and pulled out a chair for her before making a beeline for the comfort of the bar and another drink.

9

———————

The evening had been fun and they continued to talk and laugh even when Simon walked her the short distance back to her unit. He'd thanked her for the night and asked if she'd come for dinner one night at his place as they parted ways. 'I'd love to show you the rest of my place. All you've seen are the cane and the ditches.'

She'd fallen into bed with mixed emotions. Something was missing in her life. Why was it so long since she'd enjoyed herself like that? Let herself go, drink, dance and not worry about what anyone thought of her. Everyone else there tonight looked like they did it on a regular basis. Something was not right in her life and she'd think harder about it in the morning when she could gather her thoughts. Too many wines were probably just making her melancholy.

THE SOUND OF HER PHONE RINGING IN THE MORNING WOKE HER FROM A deep sleep. Her mouth was dry, and a slight headache dulled her mind, but it had been worth it. A message dinged and then another one. She ignored the signals, rolling over and facing the Besser brick wall, hoping the phone would die and she wouldn't ever have to answer it again. It only seemed to bring stress and more pressure. Thank goodness she'd left it back at the unit last night, Simon hadn't seemed to have one on him and there had been no interruptions to their conversation due to messages or calls.

She let her mind wander, wondering what he was doing this morning. The conversation last night had been stimulating and interesting. She thought about his face and his eyes that showed an edge of loneliness. From what he'd said, life hadn't always been easy for him and he had a problem trusting people. He'd been burnt too many times, so it was easier to steer clear of relationships and those who weren't always who they pretended to be. His words had been delivered in a way she knew he was warning her he wasn't looking for a relationship. He was happy by himself.

She'd chided him about not trusting anyone. Rose was a perfect example. He had immediately believed that she had stolen items without looking into it further. She could have been sacked. He should have been looking out for her, after all she was Eli's girlfriend. He'd actually listened to her advice. It wasn't often he took on someone else's opinions, but he had said he would try a bit harder to see Eli's point of view. In his opinion though, Eli and he were better off the way they were. 'Look at your own string of hurt,' he'd said, the beers making his advice more practical and brasher as the night wore on.

For a few days Frankie snapped back into work mode. The never-ending emails brought with them a flurry of bookkeeping and office work, leaving little time for anything else. The intensity of business processes swept back into her days and her stress levels heightened as she swore at her phone when it dropped in and out and banged her fingers hard on the computer keyboard as she battled to meet her deadlines. A meeting about the foreshore development was set for Friday and Gary had called to say she could sign the contracts on that day. When she'd questioned the feasibility of the distance of the block to be acquired, plus the new guidelines that came in at the end of the month went completely against what they were about to approve, she received a stern lecture. She'd tried to interrupt Gary's rant several times but only got a few ideas in near the end of the one-way conversation. She spoke about the shoreline with thick mangroves lining it, a breeding area for marine life. The space designated for pathways and parks was already a beautiful open area where kids and dogs ran freely, the sand and grass a soft cushioning under their bare feet. It was a natural parkland and matched the mood of Dingo Beach. People came to the pub and area because it was the way it was. If they wanted wading pools, parks and hot bitumen carparks they could go to Airlie Beach or Townsville.

There was silence at the other end of the phone when she finished speaking, Gary eventually clearing his throat. 'This is off the record, Frankie, but I'm telling you to back off on the environmental and social crap you're spouting. You have one job to do and that is to sign the contracts by this weekend. Otherwise consider yourself unemployed.'

Frankie's chest heaved and bile rose in her throat. The conversation with Gary had taken place out the front of her unit. Bert was inside cleaning and no doubt had heard every word that was said. She didn't care. Taking a deep breath, she spoke slowly and firmly. 'Are you threatening me, Gary? Because, if you are, I'd be very careful. I'm not signing off on something that is as dodgy as sin, totally unneeded and only on the cards so that your friends' pockets can be lined. I'm not an idiot!'

She wasn't sure if Gary heard her final words because her phone had dropped out or perhaps Gary had hung up. Either way she didn't care, her phone left on the brick wall as she pushed her hat down on her head and strode off towards the beach. They could all go to hell as far as she was concerned.

A MEETING HAD BEEN SCHEDULED FOR THAT AFTERNOON AND FRANKIE MET Larry and Bob in the back room of the pub. They were both seated at the table and stood when she arrived. Their attire was more formal than when she had seen them on the boat, their business trousers, collared shirts and leather shoes, official and businesslike. They had a large glass of wine waiting for her and she noted there was an envelope sitting next to it.

Larry pulled a chair out for her. 'You don't look as green as last time we saw you and you're missing your bucket.' He grinned at her, but she kept a straight face, unamused by his comments. He muttered something about being able to take a joke and sat down on the other side of the table.

Bob wasted no time and cut straight to the point. 'We've talked to Gary and he said you have some concerns about the project. He's not happy you're feeling that way and it's too late for us to get anyone else on board who can sign off on this in time.' He leaned across the table, so his face was nearer to hers. 'It's important that you come to the party and sign the contract as originally agreed.'

Frankie pushed the untouched glass of wine into the middle of the table. 'I'll not be bullied into something I don't agree with.' They'd all taken her for a fool. Young and inexperienced and willing to partake in dodgy business to get a foothold up in her career. There was no way she was signing anything.

Bob picked the envelope up and played with it between his fingers. 'We're willing to pay a little bonus if you become part of the team.' He pushed it across the table, the figure of $5000 written clearly on the front.

Frankie pushed it back and glared at both of them, her words short and sharp. 'Find someone else.' With that she stood and without a backward glance made her way through the tables and chairs.

During the night her phone rang and beeped several times as messages came through. Thankfully the battery went flat, so she hadn't needed to get up and turn it off. The issues were not going to disappear though, and she'd opened her door the next morning to find Larry, Bob and Steven sitting around the small table just outside her unit.

They tried everything to convince her the development was for the best and confirmed they'd make sure she was paid a good bonus to be on their side. 'It's not a bribe,' Steven winked at her and made a clicking noise, a sleazy gesture that made her cringe. 'Think of it more like you're part of our team. We could employ you for further consultancy work down the track. Our payment would be much more than what Gary is giving you.' The men had tried every persuasive trick there was, to encourage her to sign. They'd cajoled, joked and flattered her, the reasons endless, the promises great and the guarantees of large payments directly to her repeated over and over again.

In the end Larry became angry and waved the contract in the air. 'Gary said you wouldn't give us any trouble. You were the only one he could find at such short notice who matched the council's requirements. You were supposed to take the word of those who have looked at this before, that everything was accounted for.'

Frankie stood up. 'Well, he was wrong.'

Bert pulled up in his car just as the three men were leaving, the men paying no attention to him, not a hello or even a sideways glance. The punctual cleaner waved to her as he unloaded his cleaning gear. 'I'll do yours next, he called out. 'I'll do this other one first.'

Frankie waved back. She was tired. Tired of people putting pressure on her and tired of being treated like she was just a stupid young girl from the city. Now it appeared she had no job; she'd wasted a month driving up and down the coast for a company who had been leading her along and to add to that she was stuck here until her car was fixed.

She mulled over the last couple of weeks, and then back to the weeks prior to when Gary had employed her. Had this been his plan for her all along? Was this the reason he had employed her and not because of her skills or attitude to work? The pressure had been on her since she arrived; sign off and don't look back. It was all about money and Larry, Bob and Steven had thought they had it all stitched up. The new development rules came into force at midnight tonight. She had effectively stuffed up their entire plan.

THE CHAIR OUTSIDE THE UNIT PROVIDED A QUIET PLACE TO SIT FOR A LONG while after the men had left. Through the trees she watched the ocean, the water shimmering as the sun glinted across its surface. Small tinnies raced across the waves, probably on their way to secret fishing spots or trying to make their way into the bay before the tide became too low. A family walked through the park, two small dogs yapping at their feet as a mob of kids ran back and forth, a couple of them climbing up into the broad limbs of the fig trees.

Hundreds of lorikeets darted across the sky, their noisy calls echoing through the trees as they landed in the leafy canopies, seeds and small branches soon flicking onto the ground as the birds fed from them. The kids squealed and hung upside down from their knees, the dogs yapping louder as they tried to jump up and play with them. Her chest ached and her eyes filled with tears.

Bert appeared from the unit next door, his cleaning bucket and broom in his hands. He nodded at her, his eyes serious and under-standing. He would have heard that conversation. She figured Bert knew exactly what was going on in her life at the moment. She smiled at him. 'Do you think Myrtle would like to walk to the bench seat and sit with me? I could talk to her while you're cleaning.'

Bert's face lit up and he took a deep breath before he answered. 'That would be beaut, love. Just explain to her what you're doing and where you're going to sit. She loves to chat.'

FRANKIE SAT WITH MYRTLE UNTIL BERT FINISHED HIS WORK. SHE HELD THE older lady's attention by prattling on about her life at the Gold Coast, her family and the beaches near where she lived. Myrtle had listened and nodded, her eyes wide, her face serious. Frankie asked her about where she had grown up, what had she liked. Myrtle's sun-weathered wrinkled face scrunched up even further as she grinned, crossing her legs and sitting up straight, her hands clenched together in her lap like she was in church or school.

Her memory was clear when she reminisced back to earlier years and her stories about growing up in the area where she and Bert still lived had Frankie stepping back in time. Using intricate detail, she described the house she had lived in as a child, the wood-fired stove, the gaps in the timber floor that snakes crawled through and the damage to the roof and windows after cyclones swept over. She'd described how the whales came through in their hundreds at a certain time of the year and how huge turtles nested high up in the dunes, coming back to the same area to lay their eggs in safety, year after year.

She'd giggled when she'd told Frankie how she'd met Bert at a dance. 'I drank too much that night and I virtually threw myself at him.' She put her face right up close to Frankie's and reached up and traced Frankie's eyebrow with her finger. 'You need to pluck that stray hair. There's one out of place. He loves me. He loves me so. And one day,' she took her hand away and placed them back in her lap, sitting upright like she was a young girl. 'One day he'll ask me to marry him.'

MYRTLE HAD LOOKED AT HER WITH BLANK EYES WHEN SHE HAD WALKED her back to the car and helped her sit back in the passenger's seat. When Bert closed the car door he turned to Frankie and touched her arm. 'That means a lot to me. She would have loved chatting to you.'

Frankie held Bert's hand in hers, squeezing it lightly. 'It meant a lot to me also. How long have you been married Bert?'

'Nigh on fifty years. We married when we were eighteen and I'm sixty-eight this year. Yep, fifty years and I wouldn't change a thing. Well maybe get Myrtle her mind back, but that's not going to happen now.' He sighed and smiled at Frankie. 'You have a good day now and don't let anyone boss you around. Remember that it's your life and the choices are yours.'

She laughed and felt a burden that had been weighing her down, lift a little from her shoulders. It didn't take much. Just sharing a few thoughts and some words of support from someone she didn't even really know had made her feel a little more positive.

She had walked for a couple of hours that afternoon, hoping that exercise would clear her mind. A hammock strung between two palm trees offered a secluded, resting place, and she laid back, her wide hat protecting her from the heat of the sun. The warmth of the day filtered through the shade of the fronds and she revelled in the balminess, her legs stretched out in front as she leant back and gazed across the ocean. Fluffy white clouds moved slowly across the sky and the surface of the waves shone a vivid blue. The surroundings were perfect, and she had the entire beach to herself. But the short respite of positivity and calm began to disappear as the nagging unease returned. An empty feeling in her stomach and an anxious tightness in her chest forced her to take deep breaths, the sea air drawing into her lungs. In her mind she searched for clarity and direction. Where was she headed?

TONIGHT SHE WAS GOING TO SIMON'S FOR DINNER. IT WAS THE LAST THING she felt like doing. What she really wanted to do was to crawl into bed and stare at the Besser brick wall, close her eyes and go to sleep. She pulled out an outfit she hadn't worn since she left home. A long flowing skirt that accentuated her slim figure and fitted neatly at her waist. The nights were getting warmer and she matched it with a white singlet top, its colour contrasting with her toned arms which were getting browner by the day. Walking along the beach had given her body time to soak in the sunshine and if she went in the cooler hours she avoided getting burnt or damaging her skin. When she was a kid the Slip Slop Slap program had been in full force and unlike her parents and grandparents who wore the brunt of years of Queensland sunshine damage, she had been protected by wearing rashies, hats and sunscreen, allowing her skin to remain mostly undamaged.

She looked in the mirror, running a brush through her hair that flowed onto her shoulders, the ends kicking up in a wave that sat nicely. She pinned one side back, pressing the uncontrollable curls in place with a clip before looking closely at her eyebrows, the unwanted eyebrow hair that Myrtle had spotted, no longer there.

Watching Bert and Myrtle had brought back memories of her own family. Of special times, before her mum and dad had gone their separate ways, when the family had gathered and there had been cousins and Uncles and Aunts who had come together on important occasions.

Her grandparents had enjoyed a long marriage and it only ended with their deaths, mere months apart from each other. She could still remember the way they held hands, even in their nineties and looked at each other in that special way. It was the same way that Bert looked at Myrtle.

The only memories she held of the ways her parents had looked at each other was in anger or yelling abusive words intended to cause pain. She had spent a lot of time in her bedroom, hands over her ears and the music up loud to block out the noise. It was just her. The older sister she could barely remember had died when Frankie was only six. A heart condition from birth had taken its toll and left Frankie as the only child. She thought about that now and the impact it must have had on her parents' relationship. Perhaps the trauma had been too much, the memories too hard to deal with, their anguish pushing them apart instead of bringing them together.

She couldn't complain about too much in her childhood though. She had been given everything she wanted and was nearly sixteen when her parents had split up. Old enough to stand on her own two feet. The last year of school she had lived with her mum and then boarded at university, enjoying being by herself and setting her own goals in life.

They hadn't been bad parents, just circumstances thrown at them had changed their course in life. They'd always been there when she needed them in the years after they parted, but now they were both happy in new relationships and she only saw them from time to time. In between work schedules that was.

She took one last look in the mirror and twirled around, checking the back view was good also. I look like I'm on holidays, without a care in the world, she thought, before taking a deep breath. After this weekend she could be on an endless holiday, or maybe she should just refer to herself as 'unemployed'.

When Simon knocked at the door of her unit she felt like a teenager, her stomach did little flips and she stood still, nervous about opening the door.

'Come in, it's unlocked,' she called out, grabbing a chilled bottle of wine and waiting for him to enter.

His body filled the doorway as he walked into the room. Casual shorts showed off his tanned legs and a dark blue collared shirt matched the colour of his eyes. His hair was neatly brushed, with no hat to hide it, and he was cleanly shaven, his wide smile making her heart pound.

'You look gorgeous,' he said, his words tumbling out fast. 'Wow!'

Frankie smiled back. 'Thank you. It feels good to get dressed up and to be taken out.'

She walked towards the door. 'You've left your phone on the table,' he said.

She didn't look back, just kept walking towards his car. 'I know,' she replied.

10

Simon took the main road before turning off onto a dirt track that ran through the fields. A large moon shone down on the tops of the cane, its golden glow casting a dreamy haze over the stalks standing still in the night air.

'This is the track we travelled over on the tractor, that day you arrived,' Simon swerved to avoid some potholes and Frankie bounced up and down, laughing as she hung onto the side of the car. 'My farm runs from the main road, nearly through to the town. I only bought it about seven years ago and it's small by farm standards around here. It's misleading which way you're headed once you're in amongst the cane.

'I have no idea which way we're going,' Frankie peered out of her window, the red eyes of small animals caught in the headlights, flickering as they jumped out of the way of the tyres.

'We're heading east now. We've looped behind the town and these tracks will take us to the homestead, which is on the other side of Dingo Beach. About ten miles as the crow flies.'

The cane fields soon changed into paddocks, the cattle grazing near the barb wire fences, lifting their heads to watch them go past. 'I run a few head of cattle but the cane's my main income. Steven bought another farm on the western side of Dingo Beach around the same time I bought mine. Actually, he called around to see me this afternoon. He's not that happy with you.'

'Word travels fast.' Frankie looked out the window, annoyed that she had been a topic for conversation once again.

'You did the right thing. All he wanted is to get rid of that block, he doesn't care who buys it. That was just a perfect opportunity. It's a five-acre block that's been split off but once these new laws come in, he won't be able to develop it.'

'That's a shame, but it's not my problem.'

'It won't be anyone's problem because I've told him to do up a contract for me. I've bought it for a good price. It's a nice block on the beach and maybe one day Eli will want it. Steven's always made out he's a big shot businessman, but I'm not sure what he does with his money, because he always seems to be out of it. This way, I get a good buy and he has some cash to get him out of other trouble he's got himself into at the moment.'

Typical, Frankie thought. All this for nothing. A broken car, a situation where she had vomited everywhere, weeks spent driving up the coast and now no job. And all with no outcome or sense of achievement for her. No one else cared. Steven had sold his block, Larry and Bob would move onto the next project and Gary would find a new employee to suck in with his promises. Her car wasn't the only thing that had been shat on!

'You're not saying much but I can see you're thinking hard.' Simon flashed her one of his smiles and she couldn't help but smile back.

'I'm glad everyone is happy.' She shook her head and looked out the car window, a winding track taking them up through the hills and down the other side until they were on flat land again.

'So cynical for one so young,' Simon said as he swung the car through an open gate and onto a gravel driveway.

Soon the lights of the house were visible and she looked up at an old Queenslander style homestead with a verandah wrapped around it. Wide stairs led up to the front of the house, its exterior walls made up of large windows and doors that during the day would allow the cool breezes to flow through. Hibiscus bushes grew in a small garden near the stairs and Frankie stopped to look at the orange flowers covering its branches. A sweet aroma from a magnolia tree nearby wafted through the evening air and she inhaled the scent as she looked across the yard, a familiar ute, she recognised as Rose's, parked near the side of the house.

Simon stopped beside her; his eyes also drawn to the hibiscus flowers. 'The garden has been neglected, it was beautiful when we bought here, but I just don't have the time.' He turned his eyes to Rose's ute, a frown on his face. 'Eli and Rose were here all day today. In his bedroom listening to music and laughing, and who knows what else.'

Frankie followed him up the stairs. 'They're only young, maybe they were studying.'

'That's exactly what they said,' Simon replied, his eyes following her as she walked along the wide verandah.

'It's just like my grandparents' old house in the Gold Coast hinterland. They had a dairy farm, and the house was remarkably similar to this one.' She turned around and looked back the way they had come. 'I'm completely disorientated though. Usually I can tell which direction I'm facing, but not this time.'

Simon pointed over her shoulder. 'Dingo Beach is that way on the other side of those hills and Airlie over there in the other direction.' He led her along the old timber floorboards, towards the back of the house. 'And around the back here …' He kept walking, down the back stairs and onto the grassy area behind the house. 'You will see …'

Frankie followed him, looking upwards as they walked under sprawling fig trees, their branches silhouetted like huge arms in the sky. Bats chatted excitedly from above and she jumped as an owl launched from a bush nearby, the flapping of its wings and eerie calls loud in the quiet of the night.

'Look ahead,' Simon said as they passed under the last tree. In front of them a white sandy beach was lit up by the glow of the moon high above them, its light creating a golden path across the ocean.

'The jewel sea,' Frankie gasped, turning around and checking the way they had walked. 'When we drove here it seemed like we were heading in the opposite direction and not at all towards the ocean. This is so beautiful. Your house is right on the water.'

'It's deceiving, especially at night. This area is full of headlands and bays and it's hard to pick the direction unless you're familiar with it. Here, sit down.'

Heavy wooden chairs were positioned next to a round table, an ice bucket, complete with champagne and glasses arranged in the middle of it. 'I thought you might like a drink before dinner.'

Simon poured her a drink, both of them laughing as the fizzy bubbles frothed and spilled over the top of her glass. They sat together gazing at the ocean. Simon spoke slowly, his voice deep and soothing. 'It has put on a display for you tonight. A full moon and rising early.'

'I'm lost for words.' The ocean held her gaze, the shore lined with tall swaying palms, laden with coconuts, casting dark silhouettes along the beach. Curlews called from the bush beside them and she shuddered when a dingo howled from the range of mountains that stretched across the horizon to the south.

'Those hills are full of dingoes. You get used to them. They mostly stay away from us.'

'I don't think I've ever heard one. Do you have dogs?'

'I do, two of them. I locked them in before I left, otherwise they follow the car. They're bitsas. You know, a bit of this and bit of that.'

The moonlight shone on Simon's face and his eyes lit up when he talked about the farm and what it meant to him. Where they were sitting was his favourite spot and he often came here to think or watch the moon come up.

Voices sounded behind them and they turned to see Eli and Rose walking under the trees towards them. They held hands and Simon's smile turned to a frown as they approached.

Frankie noticed they no longer held hands once they neared Simon, both sitting in the sand closest to her.

'I think you already know Rose,' Eli introduced the young girl who sat quietly next to him. 'She said she washed your car when you first arrived.'

'Oh, was that you. I thought Bert must have cleaned it. Thanks so much, that was kind of you.'

Rose's voice was barely audible, her eyes downcast when she

spoke. 'My brother said it's nearly ready. They'll have the parts in late Friday and they'll have it fixed by Wednesday.'

'I hear you're both about to finish year twelve.' Frankie turned to them, interested in what they were studying and intended to do after they finished. Soon she had Rose opening up and chatting about her subjects at school. The young girl's voice became more confident and she told Frankie that she found it hard sometimes because she had to have time off to work, but she was managing to keep up and her marks were good.

Simon had gone quiet, taking long sips from his drink as he stared out across the ocean. Eli and Rose sat cross-legged in the sand, like two kids, excited but also anxious about the year to come.

Eli's voice was not as deep as his father's, and where Simon's legs and arms were strong and muscly, Eli's were wiry and thin, his blonde hair long and his face tanned and youthful. Their mannerisms and the way they spoke was similar and she noted the fond way that Eli looked at Rose when they were speaking. The young girl was beautiful in the moonlight and Frankie looked with envy at her long eyelashes and full lips.

Eli gave his girlfriend a gentle shove. 'Rose has been selected for a scholarship in Medicine at Qld University next year. She's already been accepted and it's a full scholarship for the entire course.

'As long as I pass my final exams and hold my marks.' Rose giggled and nudged Eli back. 'It sounds real when you say it out loud.'

Simon turned towards Eli. 'You never told me that. That's a big call. Well done, how many years of study will it take to complete that?'

Rose sat up straight and looked at Frankie when she spoke, not Simon. 'It's six years all up, but I can do it. I'll be the first one in my family to go to University. It's a wonder you haven't heard, Mum's been telling anyone who will listen.'

Frankie plied them both with questions. Eli had also received early acceptance into a Science course at Griffith Uni on the Gold Coast. 'That's not far from me', Frankie said. 'Perhaps I can help out with accommodation until you get on your feet.'

Eli's eyes lit up as he spoke, and he looked towards his father who nodded in agreement. 'That would be great. We don't know anyone down there and Rose's accommodation comes with her scholarship, but I'll have to find somewhere to live.'

Simon waded into the conversation and Frankie smiled to herself when he asked Rose more questions about her course and then complimented her, telling her she should be proud of herself; she was used to working hard and being so independent already, she might not find it so hard to study.

~

AFTER ELI AND ROSE LEFT, SIMON AND FRANKIE SAT IN SILENCE, BOTH wrapped up in their thoughts.

The moon rose higher, the foreshore bathed in light that filtered across the bay. Gentle waves lapped the beach, and the calm surface of the ocean was broken when something jumped and splashed back down.

'Probably a ray or a turtle. The bay is full of them. You'll have to come back during the day to see it properly.'

'It's pretty spectacular tonight.' Frankie leaned back in her chair, her eyes focussed on the track of the moonlight on the ocean, a pathway to the sky. 'As of Monday, I don't have a job. They've stood me down, using the excuse they had to make cuts to their budget.'

'Mongrels,' Simon growled, shaking his head. 'But then again, maybe it was better to find out early in the game, rather than get tied up in their corrupt deals.'

'Strangely, I'm not upset at all. In fact, it's a relief.' She turned to him. 'I feel like a different person up here. I don't think I'm going to go back to the same type of job. It's time for something new. I'm not sure what but I'm done with deadlines and deals and always trying to please someone. It's time to move on.'

'Time for dinner also.' Simon jumped up and helped her to her feet, his hand holding hers until she stood. 'Come and help me bring out the food. Mud crabs for entrée and freshly caught Coral Trout for main. Let's see if I can outdo the pub meals you've been having.'

~

THEY WALKED BACK UP TO THE HOUSE AND SIMON OPENED THE BACK door, ushering her into a spacious room lined with shelves, a large pine table surrounded by a number of brightly coloured wooden chairs positioned in the middle. It was an old-style kitchen, reminding her of times when families sat together for dinner enjoying good food and talking about the events of the day. If she looked out through the open casement windows that lined the wall she could see across the back yard and to the ocean beyond.

The walls were timber, the high ceilings adorned with ornate edges and a large rose- patterned plaster setting encircled a light that hung down on a long cord. She ran her feet over the floorboards, their wide golden colour cool and smooth, remnants of another era, she reminded herself, when life was simple and the internet and mobile phones didn't exist.

Earlier in the night they had discussed the simplicity of life in previous eras. Were they better off today with technology and constantly being in contact with everyone, or was life better, when time went slowly and people appreciated the simple things in life?

He'd laughed when she said that she didn't care what happened anymore, as long as she could get to eat fresh fish and mud crab, which was now the best food she'd ever tasted.

'Plenty of it around here,' Simon replied as he carried the platters and drinks back to the table near the beach. Frankie leant back in her chair, impressed at how the food was displayed, the meat of the crab already separated and resting loosely in its shell, grapes and slices of watermelon cut and ready to eat in bowls placed in front of her. The aroma of the food wafted across the table; her plate soon piled high with delicious seafood. A candle in the middle of the table and a string of fairy lights twinkling in the bushes imbued a romantic atmosphere, the scented oil of bamboo flares scattered nearby keeping the insects at bay.

The white flesh of the fish melted in her mouth, a mixture of lemon and lime squeezed onto it, a zingy combination of seafood and citrus.

Simon placed another piece of fish and chunks of crab on her plate. 'You eat a lot. For someone with such a trim figure I'm surprised at what you can put away.'

She sniffed the steam rising from the fish. 'I've never tasted anything as good. The pub meals have been amazing, in fact I didn't think I'd ever eaten better.' She popped a piece of crab into her mouth. 'This, however, is another level up.'

'Don't tell the chef at the pub that. He prides himself on his menu. People come from miles around for his food and you know it's good when the locals eat there.'

They chatted continually over dinner and when the meal was finished, she sat up straight, her stomach full, her skirt tight around her waist. 'I'm so full I could burst,' she remarked, breathing in as they walked back down to the water. They sat together on the sand, the granules running through her fingers as she picked up handfuls, letting them drop back down again.

'When do you leave?' Simon asked, stretching his legs out in front of him, his arms behind him as he leaned back on the sand.

'I guess I'll go this week. The motel unit is paid up until Friday, so if my car is ready, I'll leave Saturday morning.'

Neither spoke. A cloud passed in front of the moon and darkness cloaked the beach, the only sound, the waves lapping at the water's edge.

11

It was nearly two o'clock in the morning when Simon drove her back to Dingo Beach. She was so full she was sure she wouldn't need to eat for a week. At least she wouldn't be hungover tomorrow, the wine and beer turning into tea and coffee early in the night.

It had been a quiet and slow trip back in the car, neither of them speaking until they reached the unit. Simon turned the engine off and stared at her. 'It's a shame you're leaving. I enjoy being with you.'

She looked back at him, hoping that he would reach across and kiss her. But he didn't and a knot formed in her stomach as he hopped out, coming around to open her door.

'Goodnight Frankie,' he said.

'Goodnight Simon.'

AN EMAIL ON MONDAY FROM GARY CONFIRMED THAT SHE WAS NOW without a job. They would pay her up until Friday but that was it. No thanks, no questions just, c'est la vie!

The week passed slowly and she continued to walk, do her exercise and eat meals at the pub. One day she picked up a beer in the afternoon from the bar and walked across to where Pickles sat with the other locals. There were eight of them crowded around the high bar, a few standing barefoot in the sand, the others perched on stools, drinks in hand.

The conversation had gone quiet as she approached and she put on her most friendly smile, asking Pickles if she could join them for a drink before she left at the end of the week. 'Of course, you can my love. Here you lot, move over. This here is Frankie and she's from the Goldie.' Pickles did the round of introductions and soon they were all asking her questions, where she came from, where was she going to and what did she think of Dingo Beach. They had laughed when she had repeated the cow shit and then the vomit story, each one of them sharing similar disastrous tales of their own.

The lady she sat next to was very thin, with dark eyes and olive skin, her dark hair tied up in a loose messy bun on top of her head. Her name was Sylvia and she'd just turned forty-three as well as recently recovering from cancer. She was attractive for her age and it was obvious her husband, who sat the other side of her, doted on her, his hand caressing her arm as she spoke. The two of them soon had Frankie laughing with their stories of hospitals and life in Brisbane when Sylvia had gone for treatment.

'Don't ask questions of these others,' Pickles gave her a wink. 'You don't want to know their stories.' Some of the men nodded quietly, a few of them not joining the conversation, just sipping their drinks slowly and smiling or nodding at her occasionally. She wished now she had joined them when she first arrived. They were friendly and genuinely interested in what she was going to do now she didn't have a job. Their take on life was relaxed and they clearly enjoyed the simple things in life. A quiet beer with mates, catching fish from a small boat or just sitting and watching the world go past. She listened to their words of advice, particularly Sylvia's remarks about what stress in your life brought with it. 'Take it from me,' she told Frankie. 'Grab opportunities for a peaceful life when you can.'

They hugged and shook hands with her when she got up to leave and Pickles walked back through the pub with her, his skinny arms wrapping around her for a big hug when she finally said goodbye. His eyes were bright in amongst the wrinkles and lines of his wizened face. 'You know Simon has not had a partner, not even dated anyone, not even danced or shared a meal with anyone since those kids were really little tykes.'

'Thanks Pickles,' Frankie gave him another big hug in return. 'I've just got my car back so I'm having a farewell dinner with him tonight at his place. Hopefully I'll see you again one day.'

'Everyone returns to Dingo,' Pickles called out as he waved his hand high in the air. 'It's like a boomerang, you'll always come back.'

SIMON HAD CALLED TO CHECK SHE WAS STILL PLANNING TO COME FOR dinner. He was still out in the paddocks and needed to clean up and asked if it was okay if he sent Eli in to pick her up late in the afternoon. He didn't want Frankie driving her car through the cane, not when she'd just had it fixed.

Eli had only had his license a few months, but he was a good driver and took the track slower than Simon had. His father had given him a lecture about how to drive and not bounce Frankie all over the place.

'He's a good dad, your dad,' Frankie said, enjoying looking out the window at the cane which towered high above the car. She wound her window down, letting the cool air wash over her. She had worn her favourite floral dress that ended just above her knees, its neckline low and cool in the September heat. The humidity was starting to increase and at night she now had to put some natural smelly stuff on her legs to keep the midges away. A variety of different larger bugs now also clustered underneath the outside light of her hotel room and she had learnt to keep the door shut to keep them from joining her inside. Heavy clouds with dark bruised bottoms hovered over the ocean in the afternoons and the mood of the sea was changing, awaiting the rainy season that would arrive in a couple of months.

Eli hadn't answered her.

'It can't have been easy bringing you up by himself,' she added.

'He is a good dad,' Eli finally replied, 'We've always got on, but he doesn't like Rose. The other night was the first time he's actually talked to her properly. He just judges her on her family. Something he's always taught me not to do, to judge other people, and now he's doing it himself.'

'Parents go through different things in their lives. When you're a kid you don't realise the impact that other events have had on them.' She sighed. 'I guess you just think of yourself and what you want. I was the same at your age. Not really realising what my parents had gone through.'

Eli slowed as an echidna plodded across the road in front of them, its spiky back moving from side to side as it manoeuvred through the potholes in its path. 'Sometimes he treats me like a kid still. He doesn't realise that Rose and I have plans of our own.'

'It would be hard for him letting go. If it's just been the two of you for so long, he naturally worries and wants the best for you. You might find he comes around after the other night. Rose is a lovely girl and it will be helpful for you both to experience life in Brisbane for a while. It's always good to put yourself out of your comfort zone.'

'Did you mean what you said the other night, about your unit,' Eli turned to her, a hopeful look on his face.

'Definitely! I need to work out what I'm doing, but at this stage I'm not going to go back. When I leave here I'll probably head north.' She looked out the window and pulled her sunglasses over her eyes. She didn't want Eli to see she was upset. That she had no idea what she was going to do or where she was going to end up. What she did know though, was that there was nothing for her in her old life. It was good timing because she'd need someone in the unit to look after it. He could move down there in a couple of months or whenever he wanted and pay her minimal rent when he could afford it.

There was excitement in Eli's voice as he gripped the steering wheel and turned slowly into the gate and onto the gravel driveway. 'I'll get a job down there easily. I've done bar work and labouring and I'll pick up something that will pay the rent and keep me in food. I don't want much and I own my car. Rose will be down there as well so we can help each other out with money.'

They had pulled up in front of the house and the two dogs that had been locked up last time came bounding out to greet them. 'Watch out,'

Eli called out, 'Dad usually locks them up, they're not used to visitors.' The big spotted one was called Macee and the smaller one, Demi. They jumped all over Frankie, their tails wagging, their loud barks alerting Simon who came around the side of the house.

Frankie's heart thumped and she felt her face redden as Eli turned to talk to her. 'You've gone red,' he said, pushing the dogs away.

'It's just the heat,' she replied, averting her eyes and staring at Simon as he came towards them. She could tell he had been rushing to get ready and for once he seemed flustered and lost for words as his eyes met hers.

12

―――――

The three of them sat together as they worked out the details of her flat. Simon had raised his eyebrows and sat up straighter, his shoulders tensed and a quizzical look on his face when she explained that she wasn't going back south. She was going to head north.

She was more than happy with receiving minimal rent because it saved her having to find someone else to take care of it. When Eli arrived down south, he could work out the space and just move her stuff out of the way and put it all in the main bedroom. In fact, she said, 'Just claim the main bedroom and store my stuff in the spare bedroom. I really don't care.'

Eli had left to visit Rose, shaking Frankie's hand at first and then hugging her. He was grateful for the offer and the accommodation would help him settle in and alleviate the worry of where to live.

Simon to show her around the property and along the beach. The bay he lived on reminded her of the one they had swum at on Gloucester Island and she dipped her toes in the water, remembering the salty feel of the water on her skin that day. When she looked up towards the house she was met with a colourful view, the huge clumps of bougainvillea that grew either side of the fig trees were in full bloom, the crimson and orange flowers vivid amongst the backdrop of dark green. The dogs bounded alongside them and she threw sticks for them to fetch, calling out when they swam further and further out to retrieve them. When they arrived back at her feet she squealed as they shook the water from their coats, both lying at her feet as she rested on the sand.

Simon was quiet and after a while she stopped talking and asking him questions. He sat next to her, an old pair of boardshorts and a faded t-shirt looking as good on him as when he dressed up. She had an urge to run her hand over the fair hairs on his legs, to wiggle her toes on top of his bare feet that were pushed into the sand, but she sat still, pulling her hat down lower, her sunglasses hiding her eyes.

As the glowing ball of the sun eased down under the trees behind them, the heat of the day lifted. Shades of pink and orange filtered across the eastern clouds beyond the ocean. A reverse sunset, Simon told her. They sat together on the warm sand while the light dimmed, the first stars appearing in the sky.

'You're quiet, she finally said.

He jumped up and grabbed her hands. 'Sorry, I just have a lot on my mind at the moment. Let's have dinner.'

This time he made her stay seated on the chairs on the beach and brought the food to her on a large platter. There was a combination of fresh prawns, crayfish and mud crab and her mouth watered as he placed it in front of her, squeezing a lemon and then a lime over it for extra taste. A bottle of champagne complemented the dinner and they laughed together when the bottle popped, the cork flying up into the trees and scattering a couple of owls that had bunkered down for the night.

The conversation picked up and Simon seemed more upbeat. They veered around the topic of her leaving and she wondered if he would offer to keep in touch with her or perhaps mention they might catch up again one day.

She closed her eyes and lay back in the chair, the champagne and delicious food leaving a fuzzy warm feeling, the balmy night air relaxing her entire body.

Simon stood up and leaned over to fill her glass again.

'Who's driving? 'she asked as she sat up. 'Will Eli be coming back?'

He stopped pouring and only filled her glass. 'I'll stop now. That way I can drive you back.' He hesitated. 'Or you could stay the night. I mean not in that way, but you could just sleep in the spare bedroom.'

She stared hard at him and frowned. 'Are you going to remain single forever?'

The words came out before she could stop them and she stood up, watching him as he turned away. His back was to her and his words barely audible. 'I don't know.'

He turned back towards her and stood close, placing his glass down on the table. Both hands came up and he gently cradled her face, the heat from his fingers sending shivers through her as he looked straight into her eyes. Every nerve in her body clenched as he pulled her towards him, strong arms wrapping around her as their bodies pressed together. His lips were warm and soft and she kissed him back, the touch of his hands soft on her skin. Her back arched as he caressed her and she held him tightly, as he kissed her again and again.

WHEN SHE WOKE UP BESIDE HIM LATER IN THE NIGHT SHE STARED AT THE ceiling, remembering where she was and who she was lying next to. Moving onto her side she pulled the sheet over her nakedness, staring straight into his open eyes. 'You're awake,' she whispered.

Simon's warm hands stroked her back and strong arms held her as his naked body pressed up next to hers. He kissed up and down her neck and she giggled as his hands roamed over her body, her eyes closed, her body on fire, tingling from the aftermath of their lovemaking.

His voice was husky. 'Stay with me Frankie. Don't move on. I want you to stay. It doesn't have to be in this house with me if that's moving a bit too fast. We could take it slow. There will be a little place to rent in town or on the other hand if you wanted to, I'd love you here with me. The decision is yours but please tell me you'll stay.'

'I had planned to travel on further to Cairns.' She paused and leant up to kiss him, their eyes meeting. 'But that plan just went out the window.' She threw her leg over his body, pressing in close to him, her head snuggling into his chest, her words muffled when she spoke. 'I've also had a job offer.'

Simon leant up on one elbow, his face worried as he looked down at her. 'In Cairns?

'Actually no, at Airlie Beach. A lady from the council rang me yesterday.

She said that she had been keeping an eye on the project I was supposed to sign off on and they were impressed that I didn't give in. They thought it was a done deal and wouldn't be able to stop it. I was surprised that she knew what I'd been sent here for.'

Simon shook his head. 'Everyone knows everything that goes on around here. Don't forget we're a country town. Did they offer you something?'

'They did. Rose's cousin works with this lady and she'd told them that I had a background in business.'

'How would Rose's cousin know that?'

She lay back, enjoying the sensations as Simon's hands caressed her. 'I'd talked to Rose about what I'd studied at Uni and what I did before I started this latest job. Someone has just left a position without much notice, so they need someone with experience to start immediately. It would just be casual until they advertise it later in the year and then I'd have to actually apply for it to see if I win the permanent position.'

'That sounds alright.'

'The lady asked me about my previous jobs and then wanted to know if I'd consider working with them on a project that involves monitoring and preserving the breeding grounds for the marine life in the bays to the north and south of here.'

'Do you have to work from a boat?'

She laughed. 'That was also my first question and thankfully she said I would be land based. I'd be her personal assistant as well as taking care of the general office work and looking after their data collection.'

'Sounds great. What did you tell her?'

'I told her I'd let her know by Monday.'

'That's a big decision to make. You're a long way from home.'

'It's actually not a big decision. I don't think I've ever been surer about something. Both the job and also staying here with you.'

Simon stroked her face. 'I know it's only early days but …' He paused for a long while. 'I've fallen in love with you and I'm hoping like crazy you feel something similar for me.'

Frankie closed her eyes, her heart full. 'I knew the last time I was here with you. The night you drove me back to the pub. I haven't stopped wanting to be with you since then. All I can think about is seeing you and hoping you wanted me in the same way.'

'I haven't had feelings like this since, well…' he hesitated.

'It's okay to say it,' she interrupted, 'since you were first married?'

'Yes.'

She looked up at him and smiled. 'Sometimes things happen when you're least expecting it. This was certainly not what I planned when I drove up here a month ago.'

He kissed the top of her head, drawing her in closer. 'So, will you stay?'

Without hesitation, she replied, 'I will. I want to be with you and now, nothing else matters. I've found you and love, at a little place called Dingo Beach.'

A wide smile covered Simon's face, and he pulled her closer, his words sweet in her ears. 'You've also found yourself.'

'You're right. I have, and all because of you and this beautiful area.'

Simon wrapped his leg around her, his kisses sweet and long. 'I want to share it all with you, Frankie. To go to sleep with you at night and wake with you in the morning.' He smothered her neck in kisses, making her wriggle in his arms. 'I found love with a city girl in a muddy ditch in the cane fields.'

She smiled and snuggled in close, his body warm against hers. 'I found love, by the jewel sea.'

THE END

core
of my
Heart

He's hungry for more than her baking,
but she's on a no-man diet

Louise Forster

Love in a Sunburnt Land anthology

CORE OF MY HEART

LOUISE FORSTER

For my soulmate, you're always there for me.

Louise Forster

1

———

Madeline Crowe shot upright out of a deep sleep, and in a croaky morning voice, cried, *'Shit!'*

Feeling hot and bothered, she shoved the mountain of feather-down doona off her body and slowly took a few deep, calming breaths. 'Wherever he is, he's safe.' She repeated her mantra as a shiver ran through her. 'Get over it already.'

Heart pounding, she waited for her eyes to adjust to the grey dawn light. 'Okay, I'm good,' she mumbled into the room and rolled out of bed. Toes hitting the cold hardwood floor, she tiptoed into the bathroom to shower and get ready for the day.

She loved her new home in Liana Valley, named so because an early surveyor believed that's what he saw; when in fact it was a Happy Wanderer vine. Which would've been a bit of a mouthful anyway.

Mornings were a mixed bag of, Oh God, it's so freaking early, and freaking cold, but quickly forgotten as excitement kicked in of what she could bake today? Would the locals flock in and try a Bedouin sweet recipe of dumplings coated in date syrup and sesame seeds? More importantly, will the vet drive past? Just hoping he might, made her pulse quicken.

She turned the shower off in her quaint, pastel pink country bathroom. A month into her new life, she still wasn't sure she could stick with her aunt's carefully chosen muted pastel tones, of flowers and frills, décor. It wasn't Madeline's style, though it complimented the stone-built colonial home and its adjacent bakery.

Now her bakery.

She towel-dried her hair and finger-combed the wet auburn strands off her face before slapping on moisturiser. She pulled on a pair of well worn, many times washed, comfy jeans and a long-sleeved white T-shirt emblazoned with bright red, shiny letters, *Just A Blip*. Stroking the words, she hurried off.

Madeline made herself a coffee, shoved her feet into sneakers, shrugged on a puffer jacket, and headed out to the veranda. Gazing out into the dawning light had quickly become a morning ritual, a precious moment for herself. The crisp autumn air refreshing. She wrapped her hands around her mug, leant against a post, sipped her coffee and listened to the early morning bird calls.

A heavy fog blanketed the town this morning. A short distance across the road, large eucalypts stood in the ghostly grey light. The sound of clanging and thumping had Madeline turn towards the bakery. She caught her reflection in the windowpane and hardly recognised the woman looking back. Yes, she was still pale, but her life had turned around. And mornings like this were her favourite. She looked past the mist-shrouded gum trees enjoying the tranquil scene of fields and cattle grazing. She was reminded of Dorothea Mackellar's awe-inspiring poem, *I love a sunburnt country*. But the first line in verses four and five captured her emotions, *Core of my heart, my country!* She'd travelled the world, including remote countries and villages, but this delightful country town was where Madeline felt truly at home. She loved the valley, loved how after years of appalling drought, dried pastures, dusty creeks and dams — were once again lush green, interspersed with cops of magnificent eucalypts. The lake was full, and the water birds had returned. She wouldn't miss these mornings for anything.

Stretching the sleepy kinks out of her supple body, she suddenly stood perfectly still, listening to the familiar engine. Then slumped against the verandah railing trying to look casual, just as the vet's refurbished old ambulance came into view. He slowed the old truck, looked straight at her and called out, 'Morning, Maddie.' Smiling, he gave her a hasty salute before driving on.

Heart thumping, Madeline straightened and mumbled, 'Oh-my-God. The hot country dream? And me behaving like a delirious rock fan, and at my age.' She thought about that for a second and decided she didn't care. At least she knew he was the hunky local vet and wasn't a stranger. Since becoming a teenager, she'd been aware of him when allowed to stay with her aunt and uncle during school holidays. For which she would be eternally grateful. She'd much rather spend time with them, have fun cooking, and enjoying their company, than being *made* to join her parents at the club. Which would've been okay except they'd leave her sitting in the wild, raucous children's crèche while they played Cribbage.

Over a succession of yearly holidays, she'd heard more about Ash Cooper. He was labelled a wild child, but even from a distance, she hadn't believed it. Just because he was a handsome kid, did well at school and sport, there had to be something wrong. Whenever she stayed at the bakery, and he saw her, he'd smile and wave with the same snappy salute as he sailed past on his bike. And he was still interested enough to give her a friendly wave decades later, which made her day.

Humming a tune, she turned back to her cottage, and like every morning, lights were on in the bakery. Her baker, Doug, was already pulling freshly baked bread out of his oven. At least she could sleep in for a couple of hours. One day she hoped her body clock would catch on that this was it, six am starts. She could handle that.

Sure, her life fell apart when at forty-two, the man she was about to marry after ten years of living together found someone else better suited — the narcissistic sleaze. She'd fought long and hard for her rightful share of the house they'd bought together — with *her* deposit. The bastard and his new squeeze could have the furniture. The last thing Madeline needed was a reminder of the man she once loved bonking his new-beloved on the couch and other places. She informed her well-meaning friends, she wasn't going to call the bimbo out for man-hunting. A man can only be hunted and found if he wants to. In other words, 'bitch stole my husband, she's a home-wrecker, etc. is just so much bullshit. It makes men sound like they could be led astray by a perky nipple, with not another thought in their heads. There's not a real man who would say, 'The bitch stole me,' she mused, quietly giggling at herself, 'How pathetic would that be?'

In Madeline's mind, he was the guilty one.

There was one thing Madeline was grateful for, the bastard and his shit hit the fan pre-wedding vows.

Six months later, still feeling raw over the breakup, her Aunt Bea and Uncle Peter offered to sell their bakery to her at a price she couldn't refuse. Which was their plan, of course. After searching their faces for regret, or, oh shit, did we really say that — offer that? But all she got was a shrug and big innocent eyes. A few seconds later, Aunt Bea said, 'For goodness sake, Maddie, help us out here; we need to retire. We have plans to visit England and Europe.'

Having that cleared up, Madeline felt blessed and smiled at her good fortune. All three had a good laugh and a long, meaningful hug.

Before moving to Liana Valley, Madeline had an established career writing about baking. It meant lots of research and travelling world-wide seeking out recipes handed down from generation to generation. And a few new ones that, over time, would become old favourites. There was always more to explore. Her next trip was going back deep into the heart of the country. Thankfully much of her travel research could be done online. When the time came to make another trip, Doug Taylor, her new friend and baker, told her not to worry, he'd take care of everything. They signed and sealed his generous offer on a hand-shake. Which to Doug was more binding than a contract.

After turning the lights off in her quaint cottage, Madeline made fresh coffees. Shoving open the kitchen door with her hip, she walked through her laundry along the glassed walled hallway filled with a beautiful display of ferns and orchids, then through another door to the bakery's kitchen. Hit by warm air and mouth-watering aromas of freshly baked bread, pastries and pies never got old.

She placed one of the coffees on a bench, slapped a hand on, all-round-good-bloke, Doug's muscled shoulder, giving it a friendly squeeze. He had a few years on her, but he was all wiry lean muscle and, as her aunt and uncle said, 'Doug's as fit as a Mallee bull.'

'We all set?' Madeline asked, flicking her wet hair back as she sipped her coffee.

'Sure, go ahead, open up.'

She gave him an okay nod and headed to the business end, the shop.

Doug's strong hands pummelled a mound of dough, and he didn't stop as he peeked across his shoulder, a big grin on his well-worn face. 'You do know your hair is dripping?' And then he winked.

Madeline smiled back. 'By the time customers start arriving, the ovens will have dried my hair to a crisp.' She kept walking through to the shopfront, wondering what was so amusing. Reaching the glass-fronted door, Madeline swung the sign around to *Open* and called out, 'You're such a flirt, Doug!'

'There's no denyin' it,' he chuckled. 'Told you that when you took me on.'

'True … my aunt and uncle did insist you were a terrific bloke, to ignore your flirtatious ways, and give you plenty of cheek!' Unwanted images flashed in Madeline's mind when she mumbled, 'I'd better rephrase that.' She yelled toward the kitchen, 'They told me to give you plenty of sass.'

Doug chuckled, 'You could try.'

She took a deep breath and gazed out the plate glass window towards the lake. A light breeze swept and swirled a heavy mist across the water. She called out, 'You're going to make every woman in town cry into their tea or coffee, not to mention diluting the G&T's.'

'Why's that?' he called back.

'Don't play coy with me. I can hear the chuckle in your voice. But I'll humour you. It's because you're a good looking bloke for a man your age —'

'Hey,' Doug cut in, taking exception, he hollered, 'I turned grey in my twenties, and I'm just as vir—'

'Doug!' Madeline chastised. 'You're a free agent and, you're not really chasing anyone. But you are single and flirting a hell of a lot.' And while working to unlock the bolted door, she mumbled, 'The town's women looking for a bit of love or companionship in their lives think you're a —'

'Think I'm a what?' Doug cut in right next to her.

Madeline jumped. 'Crikey, Doug! That's it, I'm buying you a pair of shoes that play a tune every time you take a step. And I know exactly where to find them, the shoes that is.'

Doug went very quiet as he took a couple of deep breaths to control his emotions flitting across his face. His happy-go-lucky expression disappeared, becoming drawn.

'Doug?'

Head bent, he stared at his flour-covered work boots. Straightening, he leant against the counter and slowly crossed his ankles and arms. For the most part, his emotions were back under control. His mouth fighting a wry grin, yet his eyes were sad.

Yep, he was hiding something, and it would appear it was something quite distressing. Shit. And damn it, she didn't know what set him off. And knowing him a little now, she wondered if she ever would.

His stance softened. 'What are they thinking?'

'Never mind that. I believe I've hurt your feelings over …' she gave a little shrug, 'something.'

'Don't worry, my problem, not yours. It's all good. Now, what am I supposed to be doing to the single women in town?'

'You're playing them all along and that you're not interested in any of them.'

'*Hmm.*' A grumble was all she got as Doug strode back to his bench and his dough.

Madeline grabbed an empty basket to fill with warm, crusty bread and hurried after him.

'Doug? I'm sorry if I spoke out of turn.'

'Nothin' to be sorry about. To be honest, I'm the fool.

'I can't see that in you, Doug,' she told him earnestly.

'Well, you'd be wrong. I put my heart and soul into my Finnie, but it wasn't enough.' Doug waved a dismissive hand, effectively putting an end to any further discussion. He fixed his blue eyes, glinting with a hint of sadness, on Madeline. 'Flirtin', and I hope it's fun flirtin', ye know, not creepy?'

'God, no.' Madeline shook her head. 'If I was creeped out, you'd be outa' here so fast your arse'd be on fire.'

'Crikey! Good to hear you're no push-over. As for flirtin' with you and banterin' about all kinds of stuff, it breaks the day. And it's fun cos you always bite. Can't help yourself.' Doug shook his head and chuckled; lines fanned out from the corners of his eyes and deeper lines down his craggy cheeks

'I can so, you big walrus.' Madeline filled her display basked with a collection of bread straight out of the oven.

'And I was just about to say that you have a great mind.' Doug shoved a fist into a mound of proved dough. 'Are we into playground name-callin' now?'

'Nope,' Chin up, Madeline struck a snooty pose,' Great mind, hey.'

'Knew I should've kept me mouth shut. You'll bring it out any time you think your argument is goin' down the toilet.'

'I heard that,' she called out just as the doorbell tinkled. Grinning, she mumbled, 'Oh, yes, I'll bring it out a lot.'

She strode into the shop and greeted her first customer of the day. 'Hi, Mrs Risso. You look gorgeous, but then you always do. Red suits your complexion.'

'Thank you,' she said, smiling and adjusting her jacket. She slanted her head, pursed her lips and sighed. 'Please, it's not Risso, people will think I'm a meatball.'

'What? How?'

'You just add the L, Rissol,' she gave Madeline big brown eyes. 'You pronounce it Ritzzo, like it had a soft *T* in front of the *zz* and cut the O off quickly, so it doesn't become an *Oh*.'

Madeline gave Anna's surname another shot. Mrs Rizzo slapped a hand over her heart, shook her head, looked up at the ceiling and moaned. She let out a huff. 'There is no hope for you, call me Giovanna.' She frantically waved a hand. 'No-no, wait, you do terrible things, just call me Anna.'

'Mrs Rizzo!' Doug called out as he strode into the shop.

Anna beamed. 'See, Doug has no trouble.'

'Well, you know you're my favourite,' Doug told her, wearing his buttery-smooth smile.

'Oh, favourite what?'

'Customer, of course.'

'Every single woman in town thinks they are your favourite. Yes, Mr Taylor,' Giovanna reached over and cupped his cheek, patting it a few times, while saying, 'I am on to you, Dougie.' Then Anna dropped her hand and gave him a seductive slow wink.

Madeline, couldn't believe her eyes, the way those two were looking at each other, they should get a room…probably-maybe. After all, Madeline's track record was crap. Anna turned aside, cutting Doug off, but then perhaps not, because Doug left with the last word.

'*Tiamo*, Anna.' His deep chuckle receded around to the kitchen.

Anna shook her head, leaned across the counter and whispered, 'That man,' she gave a sideways nod, 'is giving women of all ages, all over town, hot dreams.'

'Oh,' Yes, that was familiar territory. Madeline leaned closer, 'You too?'

'No-no.' Anna waved a dismissive hand. 'Doug is just a flirt.' But her give away were flushed pink cheeks.

'I don't think Doug was the only one flirting.' Madeline suggested.

Giovanna smiled coyly. 'Hmm, maybe I was. I can give just as good.'

'I just bore witness to a master at,' Madeline leaned closer, 'flirting. You could teach me a thing or two.'

'Something tells me you'll do fine.' Giovanna looked at her watch. 'Oh, *Cavalo!* I must hurry. I'll have two sourdough loaves and eight custard and apple Danish's.'

'You expecting visitors?' Madeline asked, wrapping the bread and placing the pastries in a box.

'No, not yet, Mondays I give the farm hands a treat. Fridays we supply food and beer for a barbie, but they have to do the frying.'

'What a lovely idea.'

'You keep the workers happy, do right by them, they stay loyal. Makes my heart glad.'

Anna paid with her card, and off she went with the usual verbal poke at Doug, 'You come out of that cave you're hiding in yet, Doug?' she never waited for an answer. The doorbell tinkled and, Anna was gone.

Head down and giggling, Madeline wiped the glass-topped counter. She arranged the loaves of bread neatly in their baskets and made sure the pastries and cakes in the display case looked tidy.

A distant rumbling caught her attention. She swung around and waited as it came ever closer down the main road. Moments later, a massive black motorbike appeared and stopped right in front of her bakery.

2

———

She'd seen and heard the bike quite a few times since arriving. Knew it was Ash Cooper, the vet who rode it, sitting comfortably, as one with the machine. Once when Madeline had to stop at a give way sign, he'd come through, hit the open road, switched gears, accelerated, and that, she had to admit sounded hot. Still, if Madeline, by some miracle, was invited on the back for a ride, she would definitely decline.

Head turned slightly to look at the shop, she assumed he was making sure *Butternut Bakery* was open.

The leather-clad, booted, helmeted with dark face shield vet was not a risk-taker the locals had made him out to be while growing up. To Madeline's way of thinking, his relaxed movements were born of repetition. He sat astride his rumbling Harley, feet comfortably splayed to keep his bike steady. Carrying his masculinity well with his, I'm cool with everything, stance. Super virile, like a panther waiting to pounce. And maybe she should get a life and cut back on her reading genre. Was Madeline impressed? Not really, just curious.

Hah!

Stepping back, she took a deep breath, crossed her arms and casually rested against the shelves behind her. She silently thanked Doug, who knew a thing or two about looking casual while oozing country-style charm.

In her short time here, she'd only ever managed to catch a glimpse of him as he drove past, like earlier this morning. She wondered what he looked like close up. And she may just find out now. Watching him yank his thick bikie gloves off to reveal strong, masculine hands quickened her pulse. He casually looked around, acknowledging farmers and locals who were going about their early morning business. He shoved his gloves into the pocket of his jacket, unzipped it, shrugged it off and dropped it across the seat behind him.

'Wow…' Madeline breathed, butterflies swirling in her stomach while she enjoyed the scene. Ash had a perfect physique. The dips, valleys and rounded musculature, beautiful. She'd happily spend an afternoon exploring every inch of him. Take a few pics and send them to Bastard and Bimbo. She covered her mouth, stifling a giggle. Of course, he had tattoos; what man in his right mind, dressed like that, riding a beast like that, wouldn't have at least one. His tribal tattoo was definitely an owl. The claws peeked out from under the sleeve, the owl's feathered ears and big round eyes peeked over the neck of his shirt. If this was by design, then Ash Cooper had a sense of humour.

He unbuckled his helmet and, reaching up, pulled it off.

Mesmerised, Madeline drank in his every move. Beautiful, big hands lifted his helmet. He twisted around, almost facing the road now, flexing powerful, broad shoulders and back as he placed it on top of his jacket.

Madeline's heart thumped; she licked her lips and sighed, 'The Vet is …'

'What are you doing, Maddie,' Doug said, quietly right next to her ear.

She clutched her heart and squealed. 'Jesus, Doug!'

Movement outside caught their attention. The vet, who must've heard her squeal, swung around, and with a questioning look, caught her eyes.

'Oh Mother Mary,' Madeline sighed.

'You know Cooper, the vet?'

'No…Yes. Maybe.' She wasn't going to mention that she knew him from when she'd visited during school holidays. They never spoke, so she doubted he would remember the gawky, shy teenage girl. And she certainly wasn't going to give Doug any ammo by letting him know her past and where she took her coffee most mornings. 'I know of him since visiting Aunt Bea and Uncle Pete, but we never met. If he's not at the clinic, he's tearing off somewhere or tearing back.'

'Apparently, he's been away for a while. Come home for good. Bit like you, seeing the world. He's already got a reputation.' Doug chuckled.

'Travelling is mind-expanding,' she told him pointedly.

'I'll ignore that. Anyways, I reckon Cooper'd eat you alive.'

'Oh, I can only dream.'

Doug threw his head back and laughed. 'Rubbish, just say the word, he'd have you on the back of his Harley riding off into the sunset, just like those books women like to read.'

'Is that what it is, a Harley.' Madeline pasted I'm-an-oh-so-innocent-slightly-bored face on. 'I would never have guessed.' She glanced at the fabulous chrome and black leather monster. 'And I certainly would never get on one. I don't want anyone scraping me off the road with a spatula.'

Doug pulled a face. 'Crikey, you paint a gruesome picture. You have to take risks now and then. Live a little. You're worth lookin' at any time of the day, even at six in the mornin'.'

'Aw … thank you, Doug, you're so poetic.'

Brow furrowed, looking ready to slay a fiery dragon, the vet strode towards them.

'Quickly give me something believable for squealing like a banshee. I have a strong feeling he's going to ask why.'

'Um … you saw a cockroach?' Doug grinned, ever on the wrong side of helpful, whilst enjoying the process of reeling her in, of course. Sometimes his statements, and ideas were so outrageous she had no choice but to bite.

Eyes big, mouth pressed together, she rounded on him and thumped his arm. 'This is a bakery, Doug! A place where food is prepared.'

'I'm jealous and, I tried to kiss you?'

'Are you out of your fucking mind?' Madeline thumped him again.

'What, I'm not your type?' Hand on his heart, Doug hammed it up looking utterly crestfallen, even added and lip-quiver.

The door opened *and,* usually, the tinkling bell would be just that, a sweet tinkle. But this morning it echoed inside Madeline's head as if heralding a person of celebrity status. And in this small town of Liana Valley, they'd call a town meeting ASAP and set a day aside for an annual celebration of said celebrity.

For goodness sake woman, get a grip!

'Hope I'm not interrupting?'

Oh, there is a Goddess. His deep, rumbling voice rivalled the sound of his heavy-duty bike. She tried to look beyond the ruggedly handsome, strong jaw, a face that smiled a lot and his grey-green eyes with laugh lines fanning out from the corners. It didn't take long for her to realise that pretending he didn't have an effect was futile. Madeline straightened her spine, swallowed, and turned away from Doug to face the man with the voice that made her body throb. The vet's t-shirt stretched and clung across his muscled chest, shoulders and biceps. Perfect.

I need to get laid. That's just so wrong. No, he's *wrong. He's trouble, with a capital T, and married* … probably.

'G'day, Coop. How're things?'

'Busy, I need an extra pair of hands.'

Madeline fidgetted with her damp, wavy hair that she'd only run her fingers through earlier to get it off her face. *Shit!* Oh, what the hell, she wasn't interested anyway. Who was she trying to kid? She took hold of a thick strand and flung it back over her shoulder. And at that very moment, she caught sight of two wet patches over her breasts. Her lacy bra and perky nipples now clearly visible through her see-through T-shirt.

He hadn't missed it, Madeline saw his eyes slowly trail down to her boobs, and a barely perceptible smile played his mouth. She quickly folded her arms across her chest and glared at him. His smile grew, and God help her, he had the sexiest, most wicked grin. Madeline was struck when, without saying a word, he smiled and shrugged an honest and sincere apology, then almost shyly dipped his head.

Doug elbowed Madeline while dangling his flour-covered apron in front of her. 'I scared Maddie with a rubber spider,' He slung the loop over her head.

She quickly adjusted the bibbed front, grabbed the ties and made a bow around the back.

'Thank you, Doug.' Madeline meant every word. Then told herself to behave like an adult. Oh crap … had she blown it already? It happened, it's over, move on. 'The spider sitting on my shoulder was hairy and very realistic. I squealed and smacked it off. God only knows where it is now,' she rambled, peering at the floor. Popping up again when she heard the vet chuckle.

'Hairy huh. I'm with you, Madeline. I would've squealed as well.' He said, kindly. 'Spiders give me the shivers.'

He knew her name, it just rolled off his tongue like he owned it.

'Aha,' Doug asked, 'what if I'd done it to you?'

'I'd have pulled out my dart gun with enough tranquillizer to down an elephant. And you wouldn't be standing right now.' His eyebrows did a little comical dance. 'I'm kidding.'

'Well, that's a relief — I think.' Doug hammed it up with an exaggerated slump of his shoulders.

An oven timer went off. 'Maddie'll look after you.' Doug grinned and winked. 'Babe, sorry about the spider.' Disappearing around the corner, he called out, 'I'm right here if needed, *Babe!*'

This was beyond bantering and calling each other shit names. *So* not caring what the vet at the counter thought, after all, he'd seen so much already. She strode to the doorway leading to the kitchen and yelled, 'Babe!?'

'Yeah, payback for callin' me a walrus.'

'There's a difference, Doug. You are a walrus, but I'm not *your* Babe.' Well, someone had to make that clear.

'You okay out here, Coop?' Doug asked, head stuck around the doorway. 'Maddie's a bit tetchy this mornin'.'

'Really? I hadn't noticed,' Ash drawled slowly, on a playful grin.

His voice, calm and warm, sounded like a deep purr. Madeline refused to be affected by his charm — mentally perhaps that might work — physically, her knees took a hit. She had to grasp the counter for support and hoped he hadn't noticed. *Stop!* was a cry in her head, *Enough of this crazy shit.* She took a deep breath and gathered her composure.

'How can I help you?' She sounded normal, or so she thought.

Cooper dipped his chin and, those grey-green, penetrating eyes captured Madeline's. *'Hmmm,'* his tone a thoughtful sigh.

She cleared her throat and aimed for a calm façade. Reminding herself of what happened last time she got involved *and* lost, after giving the relationship her everything for years.

Wait a minute, could she have guilt-free fun? Guilt-free sex?

Only if he wasn't married.

Her girly bits hadn't shrivelled — yeah — but wake up smarty pants, this guy looked like he'd left broken hearts every place he'd been. *So,* not reacting to whatever that is he's trying on.

He chuckled. 'Sorry, I believe I made you feel uncomfortable. It's just that you … never mind,' he shook his head as if to clear his thoughts.

'Are you here for a quick breakfast? A snack to tide you over? The cheese and bacon croissants are delicious.'

'They look great, but I've eaten. I'm just here to find out if you're available for a little catering. About the Rizzo's Saturday week?'

Madeline cut in, 'But Anna was…'

Hands up facing her, in a stop right there gesture, Ash added. 'I'm not family, but in their misplaced wisdom, they invited me. Probably because I spend a lot of time at their place.' Looking baffled, he shrugged, saying, 'Honestly, I have no idea why I'm doing this, but hey, I'm happy to be here doing it.'

'They asked me to drop in and order a shit-load of …' he peered down at the display case, 'cakes, and erm, shit.' He nodded for emphasis.

'You seem unfamiliar with cakes?'

'Yep, you could say that.'

'Okay, er, Ash, or do you prefer Coop? Do you want us to make a selection?'

Extending his hand and smiling, he said, 'Ash.'

'Bullshit!' Doug sang from out the back. 'Coop to all his friends.

And something tells me, *Babe…*' he chuckled wickedly, 'you are going to be friends.'

'Pay no attention to him,' Madeline waved a dismissive hand in Doug's direction.

'We're not going to be friends?'

Ignoring his question, she automatically took his hand, and immediately thought, *shit*. Her stomach contracted with the most wondrous feeling. Strong fingers wrapped her hand as he pressed the firm cushions of his palm into hers. His strength and sinewy toughness came through without overstepping and crushing her bones. He felt incredible, this brief connection held Madeline transfixed. Euphoria bubbled inside her, much like coming home after a long trip away. She'd look out the plane's window to see the first dawn split the horizon with a sliver of the brightest yellow quickly changing to the deep reds to beautiful shades of purple. A magnificent sunrise slowly sending its rays across the vast country.

A breathless all-encompassing exhilaration.

She blinked a few times and took a couple of deep breaths to bring herself back from tripping into la-la land, or was it too late for that as well. And though he seemed reluctant to let go, she managed to ease her hand out of his, determined to plough on.

'Well, Ash,' Madeline said graciously, 'as you are a guest, what would we bake for you? There has to be something?'

His steady, sensuous gaze fixed on hers when, he rumbled, 'I know nothing about cakes. I think your cakes look great, the best.' He obviously thought he'd taken it far enough, paused and looked up at the ceiling, presumably searching. 'Okay,' he grinned with a telling twinkle in his eyes. 'Got one, Mongolian Sweet Dumplings.'

Where did he know that from? Madeline narrowed her eyes at him. 'Interesting choice, made from goats and or yak milk, fermented on the roof of a Ger. Then shaped into little patties and occasionally served with dried fruit such as dates, or if they're lucky, honey.'

He chuckled, 'I'm impressed.' His phone buzzed in the back pocket of his leather pants. He pulled it out, thumbed the screen and muttered, 'Okay, got to go in five.'

'Right, what's the occasion? Is it a celebration, an event of some sort? Someone getting engaged, married, anniversary perhaps?' She asked brazenly fishing.

'It's for the Rizzo family get-together and —'

'Oh...' She cut in enthusiastically pointing at the door. 'You just missed Giovanna, um Anna. Why didn't she ... Um wouldn't she be preparing her own Italian sweets and pastries?'

Looking comically confused, Ash asked. 'Yeah, why isn't she?' A knowing grin eased into his handsome face, he was thinking something up, she just knew it. Then he threw his head back and laughed, making his mischievous eyes crinkle.

'What's so funny?' Madeline was feeling a giggle starting in her stomach.

'The Rizzo family, or specifically, Giovanna,' Ash replied, humour obvious in his voice. Shaking his head, he rested his big hands just below his hips, casual-like.

'And?'

'It's nothing, don't worry,' he waved it off.

Disappointed she wasn't getting an answer, Madeline put her feelings aside, he was a customer, so be nice. 'I haven't known the Rizzo...' Madeline, forgetting herself, stopped short. 'Oh my God, I just said her name perfectly. I nailed it.' She laughed, and Ash grinned; those happy lines spreading out from the corners of his eyes. He was so easy to be around, no wonder he had a reputation.

'From where I stand — absolutely did nail it.'

What *was* he saying? Had she nailed something else? The man spoke in riddles, and his smile, his eyes were saying something, but what?

Madeline hadn't come down in the last shower, she knew want and desire when she saw it. Get on the back of my bike and we'll ride off into the sunset. *Hah.* Didn't matter, she believed brain and heart were disconnected — other parts not so much. But nothing was going to happen between them. She was in lust, an unemotional reaction to wanting something. The sweet tingles between her legs should've been proof enough that body and mind *were* in sync. Denying it wasn't going anywhere. But un-inhibited, lusty-sex was not something she'd ever succumbed to, and she wasn't about to start.

Instead, she used correct phrasing as a ploy to derail his *subtle* innuendos. 'I'll have to try Anna's surname again, make sure it's not a fluke.' Rolling the R and softening the T, the way Anna had described, she gave it her best shot. *'Rrrritzo.'*

'Yep, sounds good to me,' Ash said, chuckling. 'Anna will be impressed. 'Watched you grow up all through high school, until I went to Uni, and life took over. How long have you been back?'

'Not long about …'

'Four weeks, and counting,' Doug called out. 'Not that I'm listenin', mind.'

'Trust me, he isn't counting. I'm the one that's counting!' Madeline called out toward the kitchen. Facing Ash's bemused expression, she felt the need to explain. 'He gets far too much enjoyment out of teasing me. And I fall into his trap every time. There's possibly no end in sight.' She ran her fingers through her drying hair and sighed. 'Anyway, get Anna to email me a list of what she'd like, we'll make sure it's fresh and ready Saturday afternoon.' She slid a business card across the counter.

He took a moment to read her card, then shoved it in the back pocket of his leather pants. Ash started to leave and hand on the door, slowly turned his broad shoulders and beautiful head her way. *Sigh.* Eyes capturing hers, he added, 'If you need help with anything, let me know.'

He strode back to her, hand reaching out. Head to one side, he asked, 'Phone?'

'You want my phone?' The butterflies just became a stampede.

'Yeah, I'm adding my number to your contacts; otherwise, how're you going to ask for help?'

'Call, Anna?'

'Uh, no. She'll send someone who won't remember why they came and get lost. I say that with the utmost respect. I'm looking after their safety – and the town's time and energy because the cops will ask everyone to drop what they're doing and go look for them. See, calling Anna will just make it harder.'

'She was here earlier, so she'll probably come herself. If not, how about children, nieces and nephews?'

'Sure, but they live closer to Sydney, and Anna won't leave the farm for a while. I just came back from there, and four of her prize ewes are heavily pregnant and, she's keeping a close eye.' Adding quietly, 'At least that's what she told me … The rest of Anna's family aren't arriving until late Saturday week.'

'Oh?' She narrowed her eyes at him. 'I don't know about you, but I think there's some sort of bullshit going on.' Goodness, that was bold. 'But okay—' After opening her contact page, Madeline handed Ash her phone.

He keyed in his details and handed it back. 'Be seeing you, Maddie.' He gave her a quirky, lopsided grin.

She bloody hoped so, just to chat, mind you. And who was she kidding? Anyway, she hadn't found out yet if Ash was either married or had a girlfriend. Decades had passed since crossing paths occasionally in town or seeing him across the sports oval. Back then, she was painfully shy, and his boyish yet confident hello waves and crooked grins always sent her into a tailspin. Still, during those early teenage years, she looked forward to school holidays, which they all did. But for Madeline, it meant visiting with her aunt and uncle, which meant she might get a glimpse of Ash, might even pluck up the courage to talk to him.

3

____

Days went by, and Madeline was both relieved and pissed. Waiting for her phone to ring all the bloody time, in case *he* might call, had finally made her grumpy — damn it. She bristled with every clang, thump, clatter and ding Doug made. Normally, not the sort of noises that concerned her at all. Doug was an exceptional baker, and bakers used utensils and machinery; all of them made a racket. She learned very quickly that despite all the noise he made, Doug had excellent peripheral hearing.

'If I hear one more grumble or heavy sigh out of you,' Doug began, 'one more look at your phone, I'm gonna ring the bastard me-self.'

She should be happy seeing him most mornings. Quietly cursing, she knew Doug was right and turned her phone off for both their sakes, only checking in at night. Ash never called. She was so annoyed with herself for being gullible, taken in by a scruffy, tattooed, leather-clad vet on a bike that she decided to delete his number. But, she had to be honest with herself, he wasn't a bit scruffy. Ash just looked as if he'd washed his hair, towelled dried it and stuck his helmet on.

After a restless night, Madeline dragged herself out of bed, showered, dressed, even added a little makeup, determined to enjoy Saturday. She looked forward to spending the day with four high school students who helped out, on rotation, swapping jobs every weekend. Two at the counter, while another two helped in the kitchen. Getting a life lesson from Doug, who had many great stories to tell, was a bonus. He made them laugh, and for a little while, worry less about upcoming exams. He was brilliant with them, and she loved him for it.

Towns in the shire took turns with having Saturday market day. Those days were put to good use with fundraising stalls, sausage sizzles, homemade jams and pickles. The *Butternut Bakery* stall, where her helpers were today, donated bread and pastries towards upkeep on the sports fields, gardens in town and whatever else needed doing. The sunny but crisp early winter morning brought people out from all over to enjoy the day. The market was a big drawcard with extra foot traffic past the bakery windows. And who could possibly pass by without buying a delicious fresh hot pastry or pie?

Madeline waved their last customer out the door. She paid her staff of teenagers who worked hard for a good course selling *Butternut Bakery* pastry snacks and bread at the market.

Having started at three am, Doug was long gone. Though dead on her feet, she locked the door, put earbuds in and listening to her favourite tunes, she mopped the floor.

Exhausted, when her phone lit up, she flinched. Grabbing it off the counter, she read Ash's message. Of course, she hadn't deleted his number for real. With nervous fingers, she keyed in her password and listened to what he had to say. Difficult when your heart is beating so hard you can feel it.

'G'day beautiful —' Her hand flew to her throat, her pulse racing. Bizarrely, she thought that it must be genetic. Her mother reacted in the same way when shocked by bad news on the stock market and their investments. Her hand would fly to her throat as if she might stop her heart from leaping out of her chest.

Madeline hadn't had to deal with a trigger like that in a while.

'Okay, I'm okay.' She told herself sharply.

Unshed tears blurred her vision, she blinked them away, and taking a deep breath, continued to listen to Ash's message.

'If you get this, the Rizzo's are a force — I need rescuing from too much huggin' and, kissin' and mountains of food, and arguin', Jeez …

the big gathering isn't until next weekend.' Ash paused. 'Listen, I'm kidding, love them all. And I enjoy a good debate. But after a few wines, common sense is lost. Listening to each other's point of view is lost. It becomes an argy-bargy farce, with a whole lota love thrown in. But, I digress, it's a warm balmy evening and, if you feel the need to wind down, I'll be at the lake just past the swing rope … about six this afternoon. I'd enjoy talking with my fascinating, old but new friend, a childhood friend I've wanted to know for decades. But hey, with all that's been going on in town today, you're probably dead on your feet, so *please* understand, if you'd rather not, I'm totally good with that.'

Madeline swallowed, wiped her eyes, and decided she'd take her 'fascinating' self to the lake. Straight after she freshened up and changed her clothes.

An hour later, Madeline wondered what the hell she was doing but parked her bright red Suzuki Swift at the lake anyway. She took a steadying breath, hauled herself out, and straightened her black hoodie, which was long enough to cover her jean-clad arse. She had a thing about her arse, a legacy of high school taunts. And now she wished she'd had more confidence in herself and worn the scooped-neck, snug-fitting, long-sleeved T-shirt and slung her hoodie casually over her shoulders. A brain flick told her, that was pandering to the wants of men.

She rolled her eyes heavenward and asked the early evening stars, 'So why am I here then?'

Because she wasn't running away anymore?

Running to a new life? *Yes.* Determined to put the past behind her, *Yes.* Her mother leaving her father for her new Lawn Bowls partner, Sally? *Yes.* No wonder their focus on making a good impression was such a thing; one of them, her mother, the worst exponent, was hiding her sexuality. How positively awful. And what a turn around that was, their 'clubby' community would've been aghast, or maybe not. And her non-supporting father's good riddance attitude? *Yes.* Her aunt, Bea, bless her cotton socks, offering the bakery. *Absolutely, Yes.* And the real biggie, kicking Bastard's arse, *yes.* Her recent dramas made leaving the bustling city to country, an emotional, but welcome trip. And —

could she write cookbooks here? 'Hell, yes!' She punched the air with her fists.

Madeline took the path along the water's edge and saw the swing rope ahead.

There he is. *Oh God no — Oh God, yes!*

Under the tree sat Ash on a park bench, his familiar, large, yet, athletic physique appeared relaxed, in jeans and black leather jacket. She slowly stopped walking and watched him pull his arms off the backrest and folded them across his broad chest. Leaning back, he crossed his ankles as well and, with a contented smile, gazed out across the water.

Getting to know someone was taking a chance, and taking a chance was scary. But for fuck's sake, she was forty-two. He asked to see her, so plough ahead and grab life with both hands.

A big fat — *Yes.*

Walking on, she heard the ducks making a racket, which made the galahs try to compete. Ash, shook his head and chuckled, muttering, 'Crazy ducks.'

Doug had told her, 'Ash is a good bloke, born and raised here. Came back after seeing something of the world; helping out when needed volunteering his veterinary skills. He joined World Vets, International Aid for Animals. Came back where his heart is, in this country, in this town,' he'd emphasised with a nod. Adding, 'And I'm not just saying that to hear meself talk.'

4

———————

Feet crunching on gravel caught Ash's attention. The vision coming towards him caused a physical reaction. His heart boomed, sending blood all the way down to his abs and further. 'Jesus,' came out on a whispered breath. He needed blood directed to his brain, not elsewhere, potentially causing embarrassment. He'd had a feeling the moment he walked into the bakery that the stunning girl he knew back in high school had become an incredible woman. And here she was, walking towards him. Madeline was out of the ordinary, uniquely funny, beautiful. But he wasn't expecting a physical reaction so soon. He felt utterly euphoric, which made his face crease into a wide grin. Her step faltered. Fuck, did he look like a maniac? Quick, speak.

'Madeline,' Ash surged to his feet, 'my rescuer, I'm glad you're here.' He strode the few meters towards her.

'You don't look like you need rescuing.' A tentative smile kinda made its way across her beautiful face. 'I might be the one who needs rescuing?'

'From me,' he shook his head, 'never.'

Should he embrace her? Shaking hands seems too impersonal. Shit, just relax and do what comes naturally — sure, but don't fuck it up.

Arms out, he tucked her into his chest, and thankfully she responded by wrapping her arms around his back. He took a deep breath, savouring her scent of fresh citrus sweetened with something exotic.

She loosened her hold and, he stepped back,

'You smell amazing,' he murmured.

She searched his face. He didn't know what she found but hoped it was his honesty. Sadly, what he saw took him by surprise; fresh pain clouded her eyes.

And then, Madeline went right to the crux of the matter.

'We've both been around the tracks a few times. We know what's going on here, yeah? So you'll have to convince me of a lot of things, but especially that we're not wasting each other's time.'

'I know I'm not wasting mine.'

'Right,' Madeline's smile wavered. 'You smell great too, I might add.'

'Good to know. And you're welcome to have a good sniff anytime.' Her brows pinched, concerned? *Shit, what're you trying to do?* Ash quickly ploughed on, 'Uh…best you ignore what comes out of my mouth, for the moment anyway. Seems I've lost my brain to the teenager in me…still lurking, obviously.'

'No, that's not it, Motorcycle man,' she honoured him with a tentative smile, and his heart boomed some more. 'You're … different. Don't worry, it's *my* long story.'

'I hope it's one you'll share … once you're ready. And I feel the same. I've never met anyone like you.' He rubbed the stubble on his jaw and immediately wondered if he got to kiss Madeline, how much damage he'd do to her lovely skin.

He offered Madeline his hand, and thankfully she took it. His strong fingers wrapped around hers and gave her hand a little tug to start them walking along the path skirting the lake. Feeling encouraged to take it further, he brought her hand up and tucked it into his side, utterly relieved that she didn't object.

'I only just managed to escape Wattle Tree farm. The moment I grabbed my jacket to go out, Giovanna's face changed. I've never seen that spritely little woman move so fast to question me before I left.

Actually, it was more of an interrogation. Anna *is* relentless. So the truth came out that I was hoping to meet with you. And all hell broke loose.' He felt a wry grin tweak the muscles on his face, and looking at Madeline, her hazel eyes expectant, he had to come clean with the rest. 'They've been trying to match me up for years, it's been one disaster after another.

'But why would they do that?'

'Though I'm not related, I'm considered the odd one out. They're all married or remarrying. From the very start, the family wanted to include me, wanted me to be miserable or deliriously happy, one way or the other, they don't care.' He gave her hand a little squeeze. 'We both know that Anna was matchmaking sending me into your bakery about the Saturday family shindig. And now I'm thinking, I've gotta kiss Anna's feet, nothing less will do.'

Madeline laughed. 'You must've had girlfriends … lots of girlfriends? How many times have you done that — kissed Anna's feet?'

'I haven't been celibate. I mean, that would be worrying, wouldn't it, a man my age never having had sex. But to answer your question, I've had a few girlfriends none were worthy of kissing anyone's feet.' He tried not to grin at her not so subtle research about his past.

'Where are we going?'

'Right here on the park bench. Okay?'

'Yes, sure.' She sat and started to rub at her thighs.'

'Fuck, you've been on your feet all day. I should've picked you up.'

'No, it's fine. I'm still getting used to early starts, and because of the market, I was up really early. I didn't realise that my high school part-timers needed to help their school raise money for final year camp, so I was short-staffed as well. And I'm more than okay with that, shows their priorities are in the right place. They're a great help and, I wouldn't like to be without them every Saturday.'

'I can massage your feet if you like?' Ash studied her face. 'But I see your silent questions.' He waggled his eyebrows. 'I'm guessing, but I'm rarely wrong. You think I've lived a carefree life with no responsibility, know nothing about true love or empathy.'

'Yep, that's exactly right.' Madeline laughed. 'You're so innocent. The last couple of years in high school, you had your own fan club.'

'Yeah, well,' Ash gave a one-shoulder shrug. 'Not my doing, and think about it. The constant crap I got because of the fan club from so-called friends made a *carefree* life impossible. I was itching to leave town.'

'I'm sorry, Ash. Thinking back, I can see how hard it must have been.'

'I'm the kid who waved every time I saw you. I'm also the kid who needed to leave the passive-aggressive bullying behind.' Ash studied her face. 'What I really see ...' he said, index finger circling her face from a respectable distance, 'is wariness. You want to believe, but someone broke your trust.'

'It's a long, ugly story that I won't go into right now.'

'Fair enough.'

Madeline toed her shoes off, raised her legs, swung her pretty arse around and rested her calves on his lap.

'All-righty', he grinned, and using his thumbs, started massaging the balls of her feet, the arch, heel and calf.

'Oh ... you *are* good.' Madeline sighed, letting herself relax against the armrest and closed her eyes. 'You have great hands.' She bolted upright. 'I'm very verbal with you, shit just pops out.'

'It's not shit, Maddie, I can't vouch for you, but from where I'm sitting, it looked to me like an honest response.' He waggled his brows. 'Keep it coming, you make me feel like a hero.' And then he chuckled. 'Am I talking shit? Nope. Right now that's how you make me feel.' His strong fingers dug into her calves. 'Don't give me that look, you don't want to know what I'm thinking right now.'

'Oh sure —' she stopped mid reply and, head back, moaned, 'What you're doing there for my legs is amazing.'

'Good to know, for future rub-downs.' He chuckled, adding, 'I'll tell you what else, I'm going to teach Doug how to for Anna's sake.'

'You've seen that too?' Madeline asked, lazily. 'they should stop dancing around each other and just date or something ... Oh my God,' she purred through a pleasured hum, 'That, what you're doing behind my knees ... gosh,' she sighed.

And right then, her stomach grumbled.

'Maddie, wow, that was some complaint,' he chuckled. 'Have you eaten at all today?

'There was a mini-break and, I scoffed an apricot Danish with coffee.'

'That's it?'

'Yep.'

'You want to share a sandwich? I made extra.'

Madeline sat up. 'Sure, I'll eat anything right now.' A flush crept up her neck and into her face. She covered her mouth to stifle her snort-laugh.

'Yeah, I wouldn't say that at the local pub,' Ash warned, a big grin on his face. He bent down and pulled a picnic cooler bag out from under the bench, unzipping it to reveal two packets of generously filled sandwiches, two glasses and a bottle of Rosé.

'You didn't really know I was coming yet you came prepared.'

'Yep, I live in hope,' he felt self-conscious, not knowing what was okay and what wasn't, but smiled at her anyway.

Their eyes locked, something profound passed between them, and Ash felt his pulse accelerate. He dared to lean in closer. Madeline's gaze dropped to his mouth, then slowly drifted up to meet his.

He murmured, 'I really want to kiss you right now.' Madeline looked away. *Fuck. Too soon?* Pressure in Ash's throat thickened like a big ball of dread, but heart thumping, he waited, hoping for a positive sign.

Madeline's gaze roamed everywhere except at him. He didn't rush but was thankful when her hazel eyes found his. She leaned in closer, her chest rising and falling; he wasn't the only one nervous. And then she whispered, 'I'd like that.'

As her lids slowly fell, Ash closed in. With her warm mouth soft, and playful, she swung around onto his lap and sat astride his thighs. He ran his tongue along her lips to the silken underside. She sucked on the tip and kissed him with breathtaking passion, her breasts soft against his chest. He cupped her face and ran his fingers into her hair. She moaned her pleasure and, he responded with a deep rumble, letting her know that he felt it too, the passion, the fire.

He pulled back to catch a breath, needing to see her beautiful face. Deep in thought, she studied him, their connection all-encompassing.

Madeline Crowe opened his heart and stepped right in. Overwhelmed, he whispered, 'Fuck!'

'Holy Fuck!' Madeline whispered back, looking a little alarmed now.

Madeline swung her legs off of him, and he immediately felt the loss. With a nervous laugh, she stood and started pacing back and forth at the water's edge. The ducks took off, chasing each other across the water with loud splashing and complaining. Watching Madeline closely, he thought her adorable when she tried to stifle a nervous giggle. He loved every moment of her spontaneity but was Madeline embarrassed that she'd taken the initiative?

Edgy with worry, Ash waited for a reaction, something, anything. Their kiss had been intense, and he wanted more, a lifetime more. He knew instinctively that Madeline would fulfil his dreams. Make his world.

She stopped pacing and, arms wrapped around herself, gazed out across the water.

'Maddie?' Ash called softly.

She swung around, and focused on Ash, made her way back to the bench.

'You know back when I straddled you, and we kissed?' she asked softly.

'Yeah, ingrained on my soul, fucking magnificent,' he grinned.

'Um, yes … well … what I'm trying to say is … I've never been so bold.'

'What?' Ash asked, a little stunned. Then to his alarm, Madeline started shaking. *Fuck!* What should he do? Instinct took over. He grabbed his jacket, swung it over her shoulders, wrapped his arms around her and held on, whispering, 'It's all right, Maddie. It really is.'

Slowly, her rapid breathing returned to normal. Straightening, she grabbed the lapels of his jacket and pulled them together, literally creating a shield. She took a deep breath and slowly let it go. To Ash's astonishment, Madeline leaned into him, resting her head on his shoulder. He kissed the top of her head, lingering to savour the delicate perfume of her shampoo.

After a stretch of quiet reflection, Ash whispered, 'Maddie, you okay?'

'Yes, I'm very comfortable. I should apologise for throwing myself at you.'

He leaned back to get a better look at her face. 'Are you kidding me? I just lived every man's dream.' He gave her big eyes and, a few very affirmative nods, and felt her quietly laugh against his chest. He smiled, 'There you go. As Anna would say, a pair of strong arms can fix anything. I hope your giggling meant I could do that for you.'

Madeline twisted around to see him and said, 'You do a pretty good job.' She cupped his face. Ash leaned into her palm, then turned a little to bury his face in her open hand, kissed her there, and then placed her hand on his chest. 'Want to talk about it?'

'My mouth is parched. I wouldn't mind a drink of water first.'

Ash grabbed a bottle out of his pack, screwed the cap off and handed it to Madeline. She took a few long swigs and set the bottle on the bench next to her.

Ash waited while she pulled herself together. 'I'm a vegetarian,' he blurted out, hoping it would break the awkward silence.

Head to one side, Madeline studied his face then burst out laughing.'You really needed to share that. How long has that been bubbling just below the surface?'

'To be honest, since we met at your bakery and I saw the array of meat pies.'

'Gosh, it doesn't bother me in the *slightest* that you are. Each to their own,' Madeline replied softly.

He smiled and stroked her cheek with the back of his fingers. 'Maddie, I really want to know what happened. Is it something I did or didn't do that I should've?'

'No, relax, Ash. I discovered, at the most inappropriate time that I buried something deep. But why did I dig it up now?' She shrugged. 'Are you sure you want to hear the sordid details?'

Ash poured them both a glass of Rosé. 'While you're sipping, I'll go first. I need to clear something up. Having said that, you wouldn't be here if you were in any way disturbed by it. And even though I'm scared shitless that it might change the way you think of me, here goes.'

5

———————

Madeline turned to face him and propped one knee on the bench. 'As long as you haven't committed a terrible crime, I'm all ears.'

'No crimes, too busy studying. You know how I catch you some mornings as I drive past your place. Occasionally, I take a detour to see if you're there, to give you a wave.' He took her hand and held it to his chest. 'I'm not stalking you. I just hope to see you there all rugged up, warming your hands around a mug of coffee. I smile all the way to work. You make my day.' He shrugged as if to say, that's just how it is. 'Don't care that half an hour later I'll have my arm up a cows arse feeling for a foetus.' His quirky grin made her smile, even laugh a little.

'It's okay, Ash. To be honest, after my first day here, I asked myself, what the hell have I done — I haven't thought this through at all. I know everything about baking, but no idea how to run a bakery. The romantic-idea-bubble had burst, and now I was stuck. *Soo* out of my depth, I had a shitty first day with Doug nattering about stuff I had to do, and his, 'ovens are waiting,' cry to get me moving. I hid under the bed, metaphorically speaking, for a few days. Woke up one morning, thought I'd better change my attitude and focus on a plan. And maybe reading Aunt Bea's notes would be a good start,' she said. 'After reading them, I had a huge grin on my face and praised my Aunt Bea as I stood out on the front verandah with my coffee and let all that information percolate. Then one morning, you drove past and gave me a sideways nod and blokey salute, which made *my* day even better. So now I stand out there hoping you'll come by.'

A long, eye searching pause, and she knew it, it wasn't her imagination, she felt that same deep and profound connection between them again. It scared the pants off her. And it hurt to realise she wasn't yet ready to take another chance. She told herself, it was better this way, far less painful...surely.

'You're not ready.' Ash kissed her palm and placed her hand back in her lap.

'Yeah, I think we're rushing things … I need to go home.' Madeline mumbled while getting to her feet. 'Thanks for the picnic.' She gave him a sad smile and started walking.

'Maddie,' Ash called out and hurried to her side. 'The deal was honesty. I feel like a gawky teenager, not knowing what to say or do, so I say what I feel needs to be said and to hell with the consequences. Because not airing shit gets me —' he pointed back and forth between them, 'us, nowhere. And if you're looking out for me in the early mornings, then aren't we both feeling the same thing. If I'm reading you correctly then, yeah, fucked up shit happens to all of us.'

She took a deep breath. 'It's not a secret, I just don't want my fucked up shit invading my life all the time. The fear of it happening again …' Madeline shook her head, took a deep breath, and decided he deserved to know. 'About six weeks ago, after two years of court cases and unnecessary ugly fighting, I finally got my separation, and awarded what was due to me and fair.' Her voice trembled recalling how close she came to losing everything.

Brow furrowed, Ash nodded. 'I can see you're finding it distressing, but if you can keep going, I need to hear the rest.' He took a moment to study his feet, then looking up, his gentle eyes greener than usual, searched hers. 'Sorry, that came out — wrong.' He rubbed his jaw and let out a long sigh. 'I hope you feel comfortable enough to tell me more?'

'I'm okay. I was told not to let my past drain any more of my energy and, that I'm entitled to be happy.' Madeline folded her arms. Defensive? Probably, she still felt something was lacking within her. 'My ex tried to cheat, plot, scheme, swindle my house and my hard work away from me. After living together for over ten years, he believed he was entitled to the house, the contents, and half my earnings. Considering my hard work paid for everything, I wasn't about to let that happen. His endless excuses for not contributing were wearing thin. And then there was photographic proof of his infidelity and his forging my signature on documents.' She paused, thinking infidelity was too nice a word, and forgery…well, she stopped putting tiny little hearts over the *i* in her name years ago. And she didn't need psychoanalysis to figure out why.

Ash's expression hardened. Madeline could see that he tried to control his anger. And she thought, there you go, like a ripple in a pond, what hurts one continues on to touch others.

Madeline's anger started to rise, she didn't want that happening, not now, and took a deep breath determined to shake it off. 'I would love something wonderful to happen between us,' she continued. 'But I just realised he's done a lot more damage than trying to send me broke and have me couch surfing at forty-two.'

'Some …' Ash paused.

Seeing frustration and empathy wash over his handsome face, Madeline's anger softened further.

Ash ran his masculine hands through his hair, then dropped them down to rest on his hips. He ducked his head and let out a breath.'Okay, first off … I'm sincerely and genuinely sorry that you had to go through that. Also, I'm here, not going anywhere —'

'I have this terrible doomed to fail shit happening in my head —' Madeline cut in. 'It's horrible. I know while living with Bastard, I did nothing wrong. Yet the whole time I was with him …' she had to stop before she became a blubbering mess. She cleared her throat and mouth quivering, Madeline put an end to their evening. 'Coming out here to the beautiful, serene lake today, I thought I could beat it.'

'I understand, Maddie, I really do.'

I'm not sure you do, Ash. I'm sorry. I have to go.'

'Wait … please. Can I take you home? I'll bring my bike around.'

'Bike!' Madeline yelped. 'No thanks, my car's not far.'

'Okay, but first …you asked about girlfriends. I know in this day and age, this will sound weird. Sure, I didn't lead a celibate life; there were girlfriends. But never anyone I thought seriously about — Until you?'

Yes, she had to admit she was a little shocked but could she trust that he was honest? Her legs and feet felt like they were stuck in quicksand.

Gathering her inner strength, she asked, 'So you're about the same age as me and, and you're saying there wasn't a girl who was truly special for you?'

Ash's face became suspiciously blank until he couldn't hold it any longer, and a guilty look crept into his features. 'It's been you from the first day I saw you, back when we were teenagers, but I never had the courage to ask you out.'

Madeline's mouth went dry. 'Please go on.'

Tension tightened his body, making his muscles flex and veins pop. He moved closer. 'I'm at a loss as to where I should go from here without causing more upset. But hey, you asked, so here goes.' He took a deep breath and shoved his hands deep into the pockets of his jeans. 'Coming to terms with the past is like ripping off a bikini wax, hurts like a mother, but worth the pain. And I know from experience.' He tilted his handsome head as if weighing up whether he might offend. But his grin told Madeline that he was going to say it anyway. 'Cos you women seem to like going through it, it has to be worthwhile…yeah.'

She shrugged, 'Oh come on, don't tell me you watched while a girl-friend had her bits waxed?'

'Hell no! But if she'd let me, I'd hold her hand. The truth is a bunch of us were on a bucks night and, since the bride was having hers waxed, we told Fritzy he should get his junk tidied. In our drunken state, it really wasn't as bad as it should've been. Nevertheless, with the first strip-rip, Fritzy passed out. The rest of us lasted through the ordeal.'

Madeline covered her mouth, laughed — *and* cried. Extraordinary, she didn't think that was possible in real life; movies, yes.

He stepped closer, his worried face within kissing distance. 'One more question, please, Maddie.' His compassionate tone melted her resolve.

'As you've driven me to hysteria, why not?'

'Hysteria? Nuh, your emotions are justified. You invested your life with someone you loved and trusted. I can see that what you went through is still raw. And I bet family and friends have urged you to move on. But it's not that easy, far from it. Hence ripping off the past and going naked into the future.'

Madeline's laughter echoed across the lake.

Even through tears of mixed emotions, it was pretty clear that Ash empathised. His honesty clearly written on his face, but especially his warm, caring eyes.

Madeline pulled herself together and asked, 'Ash, what was your question?'

'The T-shirt you wore the first time I walked into the baker, on the front in bright red it said, *Just A Blip*. I can make a wild guess if you like?'

'Sure, give it a go.' Madeline said bravely and held onto her heart.

'Was that a blip from an ultrasound? Were you pregnant?'

There was no stopping it, emotions got the better of her, and now her nose and eyes pricked with tears; they welled and rolled down her face. A sob choked in her throat, she quickly covered her trembling mouth.

'Maddie — I'm so sorry, I didn't mean to hurt you. It was careless of me. I am truly sorry.'

Unable to stop a sob from escaping, Madeline made a dash for her car.

If anyone asked, she had a ready-made answer for the words on her T-shirt that she wore on the twenty-fifth of June every year, and that was, life is a blip, a moment in time. In reality, it was the date her baby boy was born, and without her consent, taken from her. Days later at home, grieving and utterly distraught, Madeline discovered what her mother had done. Regardless of how much Madeline loved and wanted her baby, she was still a minor, and they were *not* going to allow her to keep him. Her mother found a hospital where they would accommodate her every wish without question. Therefore, the nurses or midwives arranged to have her baby adopted. After a difficult birth, a nurse gave her medication intravenously. Before it knocked her out, she heard a couple of nurses discuss that at seventeen and living alone, how could she possibly look after a helpless baby? She was just a child herself. To Madeline's horror, one said, *True, and besides, to this young girl, the boy was just a blip, and much better that she doesn't see him at all.*

Fear had gripped her young heart. Boy, she'd had a baby boy — hers to love and nurture. Madeline struggled to make a noise, to cry out *No!* But sadly the strain, the heartbreak, the injection only sent her deeper into blackness. And when she finally woke and screamed her outrage, the unbearable loss for both her and her baby, who she used to sing to, their cold reply was, he's gone. And that she should thank God and be grateful that he's with good people. Madeline wasted no time at all seeking help to find him, all to no avail. In the end, a legal aid lawyer strongly suggested she get on with her life. Madeline raged at her parents, running away several times, only to be brought back and be told she was an embarrassment.

Were you with that boy again? Are you pregnant again?

How could you behave this way after everything we've done for you.

All of their anger, accusations and disappointment enraged Madeline. After that, any questions they had, she answered simply with a yes or a no, never giving more than that. Her Aunt Bea and Uncle Pete did all they could to persuade her parents to be more forgiving. Keep the baby they'd said; he's your grandson, all of it landed on deaf ears. Forced to stay in her parental home, she spent most of the days and months to come in her bedroom. When she turned eighteen, there was no birthday party, no friends around, nothing. The moment she knew her parents were asleep, Madeline grabbed the bag she'd packed for this very moment, left the house and ran. She caught several trains and a bus all the way to her Aunt Bea and Uncle Pete's home in Liana Valley. They helped Madeline pursue her passion, Food Science. She promised to pay back every cent, which she did. She never let her parents know where she was and never saw or spoke to them again. Determined to make the most of what her aunt and uncle had done for her, their happiness, their love of baking, became hers as well. Madeline carried on with her life and made a successful career for herself. She never forgave her parents and never came to terms with losing her baby boy. So every year on his birthday, she wore a T-shirt emblazoned with the words *Just A Blip*. But in reality, so much more than a blip. Those three words held meaning far beyond anyone's understanding.

And then Ash nailed it.

She liked him more than a lot, and that in itself was scary.

6

Madeline swung her hand over to thump the button and stop the dreadful noise coming out of her alarm clock radio. A flush of adrenaline made her gasp. She sat up, and feeling tense stared at the wall opposite as memories of the previous evening played in her mind. What should she do, go out on the porch with her coffee or stay indoors and hide like a frightened rabbit? Neither was easy, but the latter seemed unnecessarily childish. She jumped in the shower, dressed warmly, quickly made herself a coffee and headed out to the porch. Trying for nonchalance, despite butterflies partying in her stomach, she casually leant against the porch post. Oh yeah, very casual.

Meanwhile, as she fidgeted for that casual pose, the familiar sound of the rumbling vet ambulance came ever closer. Madeline's hesitant smile caught his attention, and poor guy, he looked worried, which made her feel bad for running off the night before. Ash turned the van to park up against the kerb opposite. His phone rang, but it wasn't the default bubbly tune, the vet had a rooster crowing most urgently. After listening to the caller, he gave instructions, satisfied he ended the call, shoving the phone on the dashboard mount. The driver's door creaked open, and Ash surged out of his van. A quick glance left and right, all clear, he jogged across the street towards her, his handsome face a mixture of apprehension and sheer joy.

Endearing soft eyes studying her, he stopped at the porch steps.

'I thought I was past it,' Madeline began, 'but you just made me giggle.'

His loud and infectious chuckle resounded in the quiet early morning as he strode up the short rise of steps. He took her coffee mug and placed it on the handrail before wrapping Madeline in his arms. Taking a moment to make sure this is what she wanted, he saw something in her hazel eyes that he liked and returned her smile. Barely seconds went by, slowly, his lids lowered. Body tingling with expectation, Madeline sighed. The warm cushions of his supple lips covered hers. He was a *fantastic* kisser. She clung onto the sides of his winter puffer jacket and pressed her body against his. Without the slightest pause, he kept his sensuous kiss going while moving back slightly. Unzipping his jacket, he opened the front panels and wrapped them around her, pulling her into him, where it was warm. His unique woodsy, citrus scent enveloped her … heaven.

Lost in his kiss, her hands trailed up his back and pushed up past his collar, her fingertips finding the back of his neck. Madeline took pleasure in caressing his warm skin.

She'd never felt so at one with herself. So comfortable, sensual.

His beautiful mouth slipped away, leaving Madeline in a daze.

'I have to go — a cat's waiting — got kicked by a cow this morning while trying to help himself to milk — from her teat.'

Madeline gasped, 'The cheeky bugger, I hope he's alright.'

'Being smacked in the face with a hoof, I dunno, he may be missing a couple of teeth, but then farm cats are agile creatures.' He cupped her face and caught her gaze. 'I'd like to see you again. Sadly my schedule is pretty full at the moment. But I need fuel; otherwise, I'll fall flat on my face. So when I get a window of opportunity, can I bring us a quick meal?'

'Sure, sounds good to me.'

A happy smile eased into his features. 'Later then.' His deep, sexy as hell voice coupled with a kiss made her body tingle with anticipation for *later then*.

To have a life, she had to shake off the vulnerable feeling constantly taking hold of her. The past is just that — past — history — gone. Besides, she told herself firmly, there really is no comparison. She was an adult and, she must accept that she's in a far better place than she'd ever been in her entire life. Even when growing up. Anything would've been better than that.

'I've lost you,' Ash murmured against her mouth.

'Sorry, I was thinking how lucky I am to have landed here in Liana Valley. And one thing led to another.'

He chuckled softly. 'I'll have to try harder next time and keep all other thoughts from invading your head.'

'I'm sorry, Ash,' Madeline smiled, 'I have … never mind, you'd better get going, or your patients will get cranky.'

He nodded and kissed her briefly before murmuring, 'We wouldn't be human if we hadn't fucked up now and then. Whenever you're ready, I'll share my fucked up shit, and trust me, I've got some beauties. Feel free to ask me anything about my life so far and, I'll answer honestly. I hope you'll be comfortable enough to share what else is troubling you? Right now, I'm looking at a beautiful woman with a gentle heart.'

Madeline opened her mouth to speak.

'Don't worry, it'll keep, Maddie.'

'I know. It's all a bit overwhelming and, I'm second-guessing everything.'

'Yeah, I get that, but I very much like being with you. Let me know if I'm moving too fast.' He kissed her again, brief and sweet. 'Later then,' his rumbling tone, intoxicating. He let her go and, with an over the shoulder grin that seemed to convey, stop worrying, it's all good, he took off across the street to his van.

Madeline shook her head and wandered inside to refresh her coffee and take one in for Doug. Walking into the warm hub of the bakery, the usual flour haze hanging in the air, she placed Doug's mug on his bench.

'Thanks, boss,' he mumbled, pulling a tray of croissants out of the oven.

Madeline moved to the shop's door to swap the closed sign to open. Staring across the road to the tall eucalypts and lake and foothills beyond, her spirits rose. Her body tingled with anticipation; what would the day bring. More to the point, what was Ash going to bring into her life?

Doug broke into her thoughts. 'Hey, daydreamer!'

As Madeline turned, she pasted a dreamy, lost look on her face.

'Yes, Doug?'

'Oh crikey, what've they done to me boss?' he asked, feigning panic. 'Someone give Maddy her brain back.' Hands resting on hips, Doug slanted his head as if sussing out what was going on. 'I'm assumin' you've ordered all the ingredients necessary for Anna's do, or is there no brain space left?'

'Ha-ha, very funny. Of course, I ordered. The warehouse promised delivery sometime tomorrow.'

'Okay, good. You doin' the baking?'

'We've already discussed that. Why are you all toey about Anna's do?'

Doug waved her off. 'No reason … making sure you don't forget anything, is all.'

'Oh, hang on, I know why. You and Anna have a thing, but neither is willing to say so out loud, but you want to make an impression just the same.'

Doug harrumphed without further denial, but his guarded, clear blues peering at her over the rim of his mug said a hell of a lot more than words ever could. Doug was in emotional pain; perhaps he desperately *needed* the one that felt out of reach. She'd heard from Aunt Bea that when Finnie left with the local librarian, he lost all confidence, so best to flirt with someone he felt was out of reach.

Should she play matchmaker when she can't even give herself permission to find love again? *'Hmm,'* Madeline studied him, ascertaining how far she could go and gave him an, I know more than you think, arched eyebrow. 'Well Doug, you're going to have to help me out at Anna's. I suspect she'll be directing her family on working the ovens and side dishes and all the other incidentals that go with a friends' and family get-together.'

'Sure, but I won't be stayin',' he answered tersely. Wandering back to the bakery kitchen, he muttered, 'I read the list. I'll make all the *focaccia*, the crusty bread, and pastries. Just the way Anna likes it. And you can read into that whatever you like. You can make the *cannoli*, *zeppole*, and the *bombolone* and make sure they're bite-sized for twenty plus guests. Don't be surprised if Anna decides to spring more requests on you … cos she will. My advice is, be strong, but gentle.'

'Of course, Doug … er, boss,' she said, a wry smile curling her mouth.

'Uh-huh,' Doug pulled a face and nodded. 'And just a heads-up, don't allow yourself to get dragged into rumours and gossip. People like to bring stupid shit up every so often, don't listen to them.' He stopped and stared at her.

A shiver ran through Madeline as goosebumps rose across her neck into her hair and down her arms. 'What are you *not* telling me, Doug? Stop fobbing me off. It's insulting in a way. You think you can't trust me, is that it?' Madeline was getting a little irritated over him saying stuff, but not giving what really needed to be said.

He rubbed his face. 'All right — Finnie and her pal left a trail of destruction just sayin' gossipin' is not my thing. I've had enough. And I know, Anna doesn't like it — not one bit. If guests or locals want *you* to join their natterin', don't. My advice, that's all.'

'Okay, Doug, I'll be very polite and tell whoever, I'm too busy to notice anything.' Madeline shrugged, happy to leave well enough alone. She'd endured hurtful, malicious, gossip while getting rid of Bastard, and really didn't want to deal with any more.

Doug wasn't grumpy often, but like now when she really looked at him, he couldn't hide how he felt. She'd seen right through his, jokey guard, and what she'd found was grief, despair, and a look that said, leave it the fuck alone. Yes, Madeline understood only too well. She straightened her spine and gave him an understanding nod. He gave her a nod back, and that was it — done. A silent agreement that Madeline had seen men give each other all over the world. A man-code of silence.

Perhaps Doug was coming around a little. A couple of weeks after moving in, Madeline told Doug that she was a good listener, anytime he wanted to talk for whatever reason. The look he gave her then would've dropped a lesser person to their knees. But thanks to her tough upbringing and a recent breakup, Madeline had armour-plated her emotions. Or so she believed, and belief was just as good as anything, wasn't it? In her most desperate moments, she'd hoped that a time would come when someone cracked her façade wide open, and make it disappear with a look, followed by a bone-melting kiss. Perhaps she needed to acknowledge that Ash had already broken through.

Accept? Ooh, scary.

EARLY SATURDAY MORNING, MADELINE THUMPED THE SNOOZE BUTTON ON her alarm and snuggled deeper under her bedding. *Just a few more minutes.* She'd had a rough night, wild dreams keeping her awake. Finally, she'd fallen into a deep sleep and, that's where she wanted to stay.

Thumping on her door woke her after what felt like only minutes had passed.

'Maddie — Maddie! Get up!' Doug yelled.

'Oh, shit! I'm up — I'm up!' she croaked back.

'I made coffee, it's on the kitchen bench, tastes like shit, but who cares, right?'

Hands covering her face, Madeline quietly groaned. 'I'll make us a fresh one.'

'Good, but not moving until I hear the shower,' Doug called through the door. 'By the way, Ash dropped by with a bottle of Anna's Amaretto.'

'Ash?' Madeline scrambled out off the bed and flung open the door.

Just as Doug yelled, 'No, the tooth fairy!' His fist clenched ready for another go at her door. He stared at her. 'Fuck woman, you look like shit, rough night?'

'A bit …' Madeline nodded.

A familiar voice sang out, 'Doug, where the hell are you!' And his footsteps came closer. And then there he was standing right beside Doug.'Morning beautiful.' he grinned.

'Get *her* sorted,' Doug chuckled, moving away and disappearing down the hall.

'Ash!' came out as a squeak. She cleared her throat. 'Well, there's no point in making a hasty retreat. You've seen me at my worst. You still want to date?' she waved her hands up and down her body clad in a large T-shirt that barely covered her thighs.

He stepped across the threshold and shut the door with his foot. His seductive grin, the sexiest she'd ever seen, turned her insides warm and fluttery, her fingers tingled, her toes too. Heat rose from her chest, up her neck and into her face; burning desire rushed in the opposite direction. Her girlie parts were singing with joy. Captivated by his sensual masculinity, Madeline fantasised that he'd make passionate love to her all day and into the night.

What an excellent idea. Do it, Ash, her heart pleaded.

He moved into her space and murmured, 'Fuck, you're the woman I'm desperate to explore. Just beautiful! You blow my mind.' He cupped her face and kissed her tenderly.

Eyes brimming, Madeline whispered, 'Um … Ash?'

'Right here for you, Maddie.' He pushed her mass of bed hair back and planted soft kisses all over her face. 'How about we make a day where we both have time to comfortably talk without worrying about promises that need to be kept?'

'Yes, thank you. I'd like that, very much.'

'Go, take your shower, I'll make coffee.'

'Do I have to worry how this coffee turns out, or has Anna trained you as I'm sure she's trained everyone in her family?' She pulled him in, kissed him with passion and felt his body mass increase with plea-sure. Taking a breath, she murmured, 'Leaving you standing here, looking at me like I'm the best cupcake you've ever tasted is um … difficult.'

'Cupcake? Nah,' Ash shook his head ever so slightly, Brandy plum tort with lots'a cream running over it,' he said softly but wickedly.

'Oh, that hit my gir …' Madeline quickly covered her mouth, mumbling. 'Shit, I said that out loud.'

His relaxed, happy laugh was so infectious that Madeline forgot all about her embarrassment.

Grinning, he kissed both her cheeks, rubbed her arms, growled with pleasure and left her room, calling out, 'Get your arse into gear.'

Twenty minutes later, Madeline hurried to the kitchen. 'Where's Ash?'

'Had an emergency, a stray dog had pups under someone's house. I think she's in pretty bad shape. He said he'd get to Anna's as soon as he could.'

'Thanks, Doug,' She started on the pastries Anna had ordered, and adding some of her own to the mix. With two hours to spare, Doug helped place Anna's delicacies into boxes. Madeline told him to stop fussing and shooed him off to shower and change while she finished off and did the same.

7

———

Arriving at Wattle Creek Farm, just outside Liana Valley, was like walking into high-octane mayhem, a good description and one Madeline took in her stride. She'd seen families cook together all over the world. Most were like this, they appeared rowdy and chaotic, but look closely, and it was organised chaos.

Doug led her straight to the kitchen and enormous walk-in pantry beyond where non-perishables were stored. Also, standing side by side were two massive fridges. 'I'll get the boxes, you make sure no one tries shoving anythin' in this fridge,' he ordered with a slap on the door.

A little bewildering, but okay, she could do that.

Doug eyed her and patted her on the shouldered, mumbling, 'That a girl.'

What was wrong with him? Did he expect that she'd have to fight for a fridge?

She barely registered he was gone when two burly guys rocked up.

'S'cuse us, love.' The bigger one sidled closer, getting flirty? '*Hmm,* you're that cook from outa town, takin' over the bakery. Heard you're makin' some really good stuff.' He looked around to see what the crowd was doing — eating, chatting, oblivious.

'Stuff?' The idiot made her lip curl. He was using the gathering, thinking she wouldn't protest and cause a scene. And he was right. He pressed in closer, Madeline backed up and hit the fridge door. He raised an arm and slapped his hand on the door near her face. The way he was leering at her, she really wanted to bop him one in the nuts. If they were somewhere else, she certainly would've enjoyed making a scene.

Unfortunately, he went on, 'Yeah, ye know pies, sausage rolls, snot-blocks.' He edged closer. He took a deep breath through his nose. 'Hmm, you smell good.' And then his hand came up reaching for her hair that hung in soft curls over her shoulders.

She slapped his hand away, and through clenched teeth, growled, 'Listen, Romeo, you're at a family gathering maybe you should just go find something to eat.' Madeline leaned in, instantly inflating his misplaced ego. But hey, having travelled extensively, she knew a thing or two about self-defence. 'Fuck off, before I hurt you.'

Face set in a questioning frown, it looked as if he could go either way. And for a split second, Madeline thought he might get nasty. But he laughed it off and, raising his voice to be heard above the raucous clamour, he yelled, 'You? Hurt me?' He threw his head back and roared.

Before she *could* knee him, familiar hands came around her waist, his voice softly murmured in her ear, 'My tigress.' Madeline instantly relaxed into Ash, smiling, she turned her head, and holding onto his grin, he kissed her nose.

'Very unprofessional,' Doug quipped in passing, armed with boxes of their pastries.

'Hey!' the big guy protested.

Short in stature, Anna was a powerful force to be reckoned with. She took them all in and yelled, 'Stu!'

Doug grinned, and so did Ash.

Stu shot straight up, and hands diving into his pockets, stepped back and headed for Anna.

'What did I say before my party even started?' Neck craned, finger jabbing near his nose, she gave him a dressing down with one word, '*Vaffanculo!*'

Stu shrugged as if to say, 'Eh, you can't blame a bloke for trying.'

'Yes-I-can!' Anna stated emphatically. Followed by a string of colourful Italian.

Madeline was dying to know what Anna said to Stu.

Doug had the answer. 'She pretty much told him to fuck off. For the rest, she spoke too fast, but it wouldn't have been pretty. Aside from that, it's all in her tone and the fire in her eyes.' His wide unabashed grin said it all — admiration.

'You're quite intimate with Anna's temper.'

Doug looked mighty pleased, even if his smile was edged with heartache. Should she get involved?

Anna frequently visited the bakery, mostly to ruffle Doug's feathers. Madeleine knew Anna quite well by now and admired everything about her. Especially family love, how she managed her farm, how she treated her employees and supported local businesses. Her stylish dress sense, even her casual work clothes were to be admired. It all contributed to Anna's aura of trusted boss, estate owner, but especially mother and grandmother. A role model.

Anna, Giovanna, was a true matriarch in the best sense of the word.

Ash closed in and whispered, 'No, you shouldn't.'

'What the — I never said anything.'

'You don't have to.'

Madeline passed her hand down her face and changed her expression to blank. 'How's that.'

'Scary…' Ash chuckled and kissed her sweetly on the mouth.

In her peripheral vision, Madeline spotted Anna watching and smiling. She beckoned Madeline over to join her table where women of all ages were making gnocchi. Ash escorted her all the way, his excuse? Apparently, he didn't need one.

It had been a very long day. Although Madeline felt drained, she stayed longer to be polite. Leaving them with enough gnocchi to feed the town plus neighbouring communities, she thanked Anna for including her and headed for her car.

Ash jogged to her side. 'Wait up.' Taking her hand, he brought her fingers to his mouth and kissed her knuckles softly, sensuously. 'It's been a long hard day, and you haven't eaten. There's so much good food here. Let me come by with some?'

'Don't you have to go check on the stray and her puppies?'

'It's all been taken care of.'

ASH WANTED TO WRAP HIS ARMS AROUND MADELINE AND HOLD ON. SHE'D just given him a nod and a barely visible one-shoulder shrug. Which he read as; make up your own mind. So true to his word, by early evening, he'd phoned asking Madeline were there any requests for dinner. She'd told him that nothing came to mind. And yes she was hungry and lazing on the couch with her feet up, and she wasn't moving. So he could find his own way through the house.

Carrying Anna's basket heavy with hot food containers, Ash walked in through the back, down the hall to the living room. He stopped short at the doorway, unable to move, a deep breath lodged in his throat. His heart just didn't give him a break. He needed Madeline in his life and, with everything he had, he hoped that she needed him. He caught a whiff of her exotic fragrance wafting through the room and closed his eyes, capturing Madeline's signature scent. She'd showered, her damp, auburn hair fanned out on a cushion. Dressed in comfortable leggings, fluffy socks and a warm, long-sleeved fleecy top, she lay back across her aunt's couch in a sea of colourful printed flowers.

She smiled and tucked a cushion further under her head. 'Hi, Ash. Hmm, I smell delicious food.'

'Christ, I nearly dropped the lot.' He sat the basket on the coffee table. 'Don't move a muscle, not even if you feel my hand.'

'Oh, hang on a minute, you're not trying for anything kinky are you?'

'What? — No. But hey, I'm up for games, within reason.' He dared to give her a slow wink. 'We'll talk about it. Right now, don't move.'

'Talk about it?' she started to sit up. Ash gently pushed her back down. 'Is there something I need to know?'

'Relax, We'll work something out.'

'Ash!' Madeline cried out and paused as she studied his face, and yeah, she connected the dots. 'Okay…' Hands fidgeting, she went all coy. 'It'll allow me to explain why I have kneehigh, black patent leather boots, a leather bustier and a whip.' She snuggled deeper into the cushions. 'I love a little whip cracking.'

'Great, I can't wait,' he wisecracked, and knees popping, Ash hunkered down.

'Crikey!' Madeline cried out, opening one eye.

'Shush, just an old football injury.' Imagining Madeline as a Donna Matrix made him uncharacteristically hot. He cleared his throat, but couldn't stop the grin.

Madeline brought her hand up to rest on the cushion.

'Stop moving,' he murmured, 'I wanted to do this the moment I walked in.' Bending closer, and with the softest touch he could manage, he lightly pressed his lips to one eyelid then kissed his way across to the other. Studying her face, he saw straight through Madeline's emotional smile; though her eyes were still closed, her lashes were wet.

'Open your eyes, Maddie,' Ash murmured, and when she did, more tears welled. He watched as one then another slowly slip across the bridge of her nose and into her hair. A couple more fell, and he kissed them away. 'What's up?'

'I'm okay.'

'Then why the tears?' It worried him when Madeline paused. 'Say something, Maddie. I'd prefer it if you were brutally honest. You know, like the bandaid, rip that sucker off.'

'Okay here goes.' She turned on her back, looked at the ceiling and, slowly, painstakingly her feelings tumbled out. 'Part of me is sad because I've never experienced anything as heartbreakingly sweet as what you just gave me. But, elated that you did.'

''Scuse me, why the fuck not?' Ash cupped her face and using the pads of his thumbs, stroked the wetness away.

Madeline gave a halfhearted shrug, moved his hands away and softly said, 'I really like what you do to me. But I can't talk if you keep being so affectionate.'

'Ah … sorry … I see you and, I'm pulled in. You're a magnet.' Ash ran both hands through his hair, then tucked them across his chest. 'Your experiences?'

'Experiences? No, more like totally wrong — bad choices. Seeing qualities in someone that, in hindsight, were never there.' She sat up, raised one finger as if she'd suddenly discovered something important. 'Trying to keep friends happy with my choices was a big mistake. Listening to those friends who heaped accolades on my ex, telling me I'd be stupid to let him slip out of my grasp. For them, it was all about prestige and money. Sure he had connections that proved he supported charities, and during the divorce proceedings, the truth came out. He couldn't hide what he'd been up to. The help he told everyone he gave charities free of charge — was not. If he did donate, he'd cook the books so that they were eligible for tax deductions. And of course, he was using me all along. The young woman who'd done well with her books, her recipes. The young woman who went into ghettos teaching families how to cook healthy food and wisely, without breaking the budget.' Madeline took a deep breath and sighed long and hard.

Ash hoped she was letting go of her disappointment, her anger.

'My self-esteem, which was sadly lacking anyway, hit rock bottom.' She rubbed her arms, gathered a blanket from the back of the couch and slung it around her shoulders. 'Because I'm not a total fool, I did learn a few things. Hence when someone is as honest as you are, when you're so loving, so affectionate, I come apart at the seams.' She shrugged again. 'Is that a good emotion for me? I don't know. Am I falling into my own needy trap? At my age, you'd think I'd have my shit together.

Ash's heart rate kicked up as Madeline cupped his face, fearful of what might be coming he braced himself for the *but*.

Smiling tenderly, she told him, 'I'm okay with all of that now … not going to give what happened any more energy. I'm throwing caution to the wind and trust my emotions without others putting their two cents worth in to muddle my brain.'

Ash let go a breath he hadn't realised he was holding. 'I'm relieved. I can't see myself changing, nor do I want to. I like how you make me feel.' Well, that was an understatement. His grin widened. 'So it's all good.' Madeline took his offered hand. He loved her hands, soft yet strong. And just as he was about to break out the food, his phone rang. 'Damn.' He pulled it out of his jean's back pocket, hoping it wasn't an animal needing his immediate attention. Reading who the sender was, he laughed and read out the message in a strong Italian accent. *'Don't forget to give Madeline a serviette and a nice plate from Bea's display cabinet, and a glass of wine, use the crystal ones.* Anna's enthusiastic instructions, love her to bits. I also have to make a creative spread. All you need to do is point, and I'll dish it up.' Smiling warmly, he eyed his phone, shook his head and answered Anna with a thumbs up icon.

'Okay, but not huge amounts, bite-size would be good.'

Ash sat cross-legged on the floor, back resting on the couch with a plate in his lap. While eating, he answered Madeline's questions mostly about his life spent in countries where he was often called upon for his Veterinary skills. Occasionally giving care to animals that, anatomically, Ash knew very little about. When in doubt, he'd call, or where possible FaceTimed colleagues who looked after exotic zoo animals. They were always happy to help.

Madeline tasted Anna's gnocchi made with her homemade creamy sauce and asked for seconds. 'Oh, that was delicious.' she said, easing the waistband of her leggings as she reclined back on the couch. 'I wonder would she share her recipe?'

'Anna doesn't have a problem sharing her recipes. It's a compliment to her cooking. Her sentiment is, why shouldn't everyone taste good food. For Anna to buy Aunt Bea's, now yours and Doug's bread and pastries is a huge compliment.'

'Yes, I feel that?' Madeline beamed.

'Look at you, all lit up,' Ash chuckled.

'I have a plan for Anna's superb cooking. I hope she'll agree to a collaboration.'

'She'll jump at the chance.'

'Do you realise we've been eating and talking since about nine-thirty? It's after one. Oh my God, it's Sunday already.' She yawned, stretched her arms above her head, brought them down and flopped sideways lying back on the cushions. She giggled, 'You've got a beautiful, deep voice ... want to tell me a story?'

Ash laughed, picked up his glass and took a swig.'Ask any vet, we've all got great stories. It's a given that pets will get sick, have an accident or get up to something on weekends. Fretting owners come in asking, why on the weekend, why couldn't Miss Peabody be an idiot during the week? No, it had to be Sunday when every vet within a hundred k's is closed.'

'Of course, that's their mission in life …' Madeline mumbled, drowsily. 'Fuckup the weekend of their food source…'

Ash chuckled. 'I should introduce you to a few.'

'Hmm-hmm, look forward to it.' Madeline was losing the fight to stay awake.

'Just last week, I helped deliver six pups, each one a little dynamo with its own personality. You'd love them.' Ash smiled as Madeline's eyelids slowly dropped. Mouth relaxed, she murmured, 'So good, keep talking …'

'The Liana Valley wildlife rescue centre has a variety of local fauna. My favourite would be the wombat. Especially Pav, short for Pavlova.' He spoke about Pav for a bit until Madeline's soft breath told him she was fast asleep. He couldn't leave her like that, so scooped her up, and carried her to the main bedroom; laying her carefully on the bed.

'Wait.' Madeline wriggled out of her clothes except for her T-shirt and undies.

It took all of Ash's willpower not to let his hands stray. Thankfully, Madeline hopped into bed and pulled the covers up her lovely legs all the way to her shoulders.

Ash turned to leave, when Madeline whispered, 'Please stay.' At least, he hoped that's what she said. He needed confirmation.

'What was that, Maddie?'

'Stay …' She pulled at his hand and, that was all he needed. He kicked his shoes off, and everything else, except his jocks and T-shirt, then carefully slipped into the opposite side. Not moving he lay on his back, murmuring, 'You know the poem, I love a sunburnt country?'

'Hmm, beautiful.'

He began reciting Dorothea Mackellar's poem. 'I love a sunburnt country. A land of sweeping plains…' Her soft breathing lulled him, so much so, he became relaxed and whispered, 'You are the *Core of my heart.'* That came out of nowhere, and now, he was bloody wide awake. 'Shit.' He whispered into the night.

8

'Damn that screaming rooster,' Ash whispered, reaching for his phone, quickly muting it. The noise was such that it made sure he never missed a call, but on days he'd hired a stand-in vet, he usually muted the ringtone. Perhaps he had more interesting things on his mind. With Madeline's sudden, sweet request to stay, everything else left his brain. He looked across at her sleeping form and noticed the enormous kingsized bed looked even larger in the daylight.

Next to him, she suddenly bolted upright. Back straight, looking as sexy as hell with amazing bed-hair all over the place, she squinted in the dawn light. Rubbing her eyes, she mumbled, 'I'm going to kill that rooster — better still, I know someone who can castrate him.'

'Ouch,' Ash cringed.

Madeline squealed, 'Holy crap, Ash! What the…?'

'Yeah, who else,' his tone incredulous. 'I'm only here because you pulled me into your bed.' Hearing that come out of his very own mouth sounded horrible, he imagined Madeline would verbally beat him to a pulp.

'You mean to say, had I not coerced you, you wouldn't have bothered!'

Yep, there it is. *Shit, like to see you get out of this one pal.* 'Madeline,' he pleaded, 'Aside from not wanting …' She gasped, and mouth agape she stared at him. '… to leave you, I asked you to repeat what you said to make absolutely sure I heard right *when,* holding my hand you said, please stay.'

A lightbulb moment? 'Oh yeah, I did, sorry.' She flopped back onto her pillow and sighed. *'Yay…'* was a feeble cry. 'It's Sunday, I can sleep in.'

Laying on his side, elbow jammed in the pillow, chin in hand, Ash took pleasure watching this amazing woman. Her eyelids slowly fell, her breath softened as Maddie nodded off. This was the woman he intended to wake up with every morning for the rest of his life. He was smiling so hard his jaw ached.

MADELINE TURNED TO FACE ASH AND IMMEDIATELY WANTED TO KNOW what he was grinning at. 'Good morning Ash. Why do you look like, a …' she was going to say handsome prince but decided he didn't need any more encouragement, 'a version of the Joker? Without make-up, of course.'

'Morning Maddie. You okay?'

'I'm excellent, thank you,' her voice muffled behind the doona because morning breath was definitely a turn off at this stage. *And what stage was that, Madeleine? Wanting to jump his bones?* 'What are you grinning at?'

'Happy to be here. Happy to see you. Happy to have platonically spent the night with you.' He gave her arched brows and a wide-eyed look. 'And don't go reading anything into that other than, it's you … I enjoy being with you.'

Her heart just somersaulted, at least that's how it felt. 'Um … I'm going to use the bathroom,' she said, daring to lift an arm out of the warm cosy place under the doona to wave towards the en-suite. Grabbing the bedding off her body, she rolled out of bed and hurried to the bathroom to do her thing, most importantly, brush her teeth. She heard movement through the door and hurried; Ash was not leaving, not now when she'd made her mind up to take things past hot and heavy kissing.

She opened the door a smidge and called out through the crack. 'Ash! Are you leaving?'

'No … you want me to?'

She paused, weighing up the pros and cons. 'Um … No!' came out a pitch too eager.

'Okay,' he called out. 'Was on my way to the other bathroom, back in a sec.'

Madeline took the opportunity to grab a quick shower and stay naked. With her hair falling in waves over one shoulder, she covered herself and lounged provocatively in bed, waiting. She needn't have rushed; Ash's *sec* felt like half an hour. Moments later, he walked in, carrying a tray still wearing his T-shirt and jocks, making her feel awkward and — even more naked.

Ash had made coffee and something else that smelled deliciously familiar.

'Wow! I'm impressed,' Madeline announced. She tucked the doona further under her arms and shuffled back to sit straight and accommodate the tray Ash placed on her lap. He sauntered around to his side of the bed and made himself comfortable.

'*Hmm*…Madeline stirred her coffee. 'Ash, does this feel peculiar to you? Here we are sitting in this massive bed like it happens all the time, yet we haven't … you know, done anything.'

'By anything you mean had crazy-monkey-sex?' Ash asked, deadpan.

Madeline was at that very moment, sipping her coffee. She didn't swallow quickly enough and nearly choked as spontaneous raucous laughter competed with the coffee going down. She coughed until red in the face but kept her mug steady, not spilling a drop.

Chuckling, Ash gently slapped her naked back, which soon became stroking her naked back. She was already red in the face, so blushing made little difference.

Madeline held up her hand for him to stop. Clearing her throat, she squeaked, 'Don't think you're helping.' And dared to take another sip of coffee. She grabbed a tissue from her bedside table, dabbed her eyes, cleared her throat and sighed. 'Oh, I'm glad that's over.'

'Yeah, me too. You turned a very becoming but scary shade of red.'

He lifted a serviette off a plate to reveal four steaming scones. He cut one in half, spooned strawberry jam and a dollop of cream on either side and handed it to Madeline.

'Crikey, how on earth did you manage this?'

'Part of Anna's basket of goodies, with handwritten instruction of how to warm them up.'

'So she expected you to stay?' Madeline took a bite. 'Hmm, delicious.'

'Don't know, don't care. Anna can get too involved when she should look after her own affairs.'

'You mean Doug?'

'Yeah, they should be together.' He gave an impatient shrug.

Ash curled his finger around a lock of her hair.

They talked in early morning hushed tones as if they might wake someone when there wasn't anyone to wake.

'You've got cream on your nose.' He reached out, swiped it off and sucked the cream off his finger, then shook his head and moved away.

'Where are you going?' Madeline asked, swinging out of bed to sit on the edge.

'I was headed for the kitchen, is there something you want?'

'Oh, bloody hell,' Madeline whispered, diving under the bed covers. She peeked over the top and watched Ash put the tray down on the dresser. Her body trembling with desire as he turned to face her with his soft smile, both serious and amused.

'Maddie, I'm not sure what you mean by *Oh, bloody hell?*'

'I don't want you to leave,' the nervous tremble in her voice made her wince.

'You don't sound sure, Maddie.'

She badly wanted this. Needed to feel, needed to connect with her emotions. 'Ash, I'm nervous. It's been a very long time since I — let's be blunt since I had sex with anyone. And I so want to …'

Ash cut in, 'If I stay …' he began and paused to study her reaction. 'Then, I need to know that you're serious and that there'll be no regrets. Because once I make this commitment with you, we don't keep it hidden and play silly games like the two old fools we know about because, for *me,* there'll be no turning back. I know this is early for a relationship, but Maddie, I love you. I have since high school.'

'Oh …I …' Madeline murmured on a breath.

'Maddie, you don't need to reciprocate.' And with a sweet smile, he added, 'Though naturally, at some point, I hope you will.'

She pushed herself up, knelt on the bed and let the covers slowly slide down her body. 'I very much want to feel again, and the only one I want to share that with, is you.'

Within seconds, Ash hauled his jocks and t-shirt off. Long, lean muscles covered his impressive, athletic physique. He looked powerful as he moved to the edge of the bed. Raising one knee then the other, he headed for her on all fours.

'You are spectacular,' he rumbled low, a wicked grin playing his features. 'Am I reading you correctly, Maddie? Do you want us to have crazy monkey sex?'

Madeline let all her negative crap go, fell to one side, laughing loud and free. Calming down, she nodded, 'Yes, please.'

She already knew Ash was an incredible kisser making every part of her tingle until her knees threatened to give way. But his giving of himself for her pleasure was on another level of sensuality. His big, strong hands caressed her skin and gently massaged muscles underneath. She felt the warm cushions of his lips between her breasts. Then trailing soft kisses, he reached her nipples, adding a swirl of his tongue to each one, making them peak and pebble. Softly, he blew a whispered breath over them. Anticipating what might come next, Madeline's breath quickened. Ash's mouth leisurely nipped, kissed all the way to her jaw, the corners of her mouth, her cheeks, to her temples. He nibbled her neck and shoulder, sending tingles through her body. But as she reached for his mouth, he only allowed a whisper-touch, a hint of his lips, a tease before continuing with his slow, sexy seduction. Ash was unravelling her. All care evaporated, and Madeline let herself go. She felt light, yet grounded, floating, yet absorbed, totally caught up in Ash's arousing lovemaking.

And when he kissed her mouth, all Madeline's doubts and fears evaporated.

9

Ash woke to find Madeline face down, half-buried in her pillow next to him, breathing softly, her thigh across his, forearm and hand resting on his abs. He desperately needed the bathroom, and trying not to wake her, he slowly eased out from under her relaxed, heavy limbs.

'Where're you going?' came her muffled voice.

'On my way to the bathroom.'

'Wait.' She reached for the neck of his T-shirt, tugged it down, and traced his owl tattoo with her index finger. 'What's with the owl?'

Ash peered down at his shoulder. 'A couple of years ago, while staying in a small Bavarian village, I helped out the local vet. A teenager came in with an injured Long-Eared Owl, hoping I could help. The owl made it, and after a couple of weeks, the young bloke let him free where he'd found him. His father was a tattooist and offered me a tattoo. With the kid's help, I chose this one.'

'Got to go!' Ash hastily kissed her fingers, hurried around the bed, and caught a glimpse of Madeline struggling to raise herself.

'Aw… that young fella will never forget you,' she called out sleepily.

'*Aaah,*' his relief echoed through the tiled room. Hearing Madeline laugh made him smile. Satisfaction on several levels was a wonderful thing.

He took the opportunity to take a shower, and towel-drying his hair, wandered back into the bedroom, his senses immediately hit with mouthwatering breakfast aromas. 'You made coffee and …' he breathed in through his nose. Smiling at Madeline, the most beautiful woman inside and out, he tossed the towel over a chair. His only hope for a happy life was that, not too far in the future, Madeline would be ready for something bigger…long-lasting.

'Fluffy scones won't last the distance. I made us brunch, my take on toad in a hole, a little tomato, basil, cheese, and of course, eggs. Done in five minutes tops.' Madeline handed him a plate. 'Thank you,' Ash took a bite. 'Hmm…very good.' Swallowing the tasty morsel, he asked, 'Hey, since we both have the day off,' he began, silently hoping, 'you want to come see my menagerie?'

Madeline put the tray down between them; she tried to control her growing amusement, but a sniggle-snort escaped, 'Sure, I'd love to.'

'Okay, you've made my day! But you've gotta let me in on the joke?'

'It's not funny. In fact, it's not at funny all,' Madeline shook her head. 'When you said, come see my menagerie, it reminded me of what my Pop used when I first started dating. *Don't follow anyone who says, come see my etchings…*or whatever was popular at the time like, come see my Pokemon, my x-box. It's a metaphor for…'

Ash burst out laughing. 'Who would say something that stupid? And who would believe it?'

'I did — I was naïve, though I did ask Pop what are etchings and why would a guy say that? Pop would just roll his eyes and tell me to ask my parents to explain. And because they'd rather call Granddad all sorts of names, I never asked them. I didn't find out until it was too late. Though in my defence, the predator was a lot more sophisticated.'

Ah…here we go, perhaps with a bit of luck, Madeline trusted him enough to open up about what he'd touched on when they first met at the lake, and he asked about the words on her T-shirt. *Just A Blip.*

'Too late for what, Maddie?' Ash asked softly and with care.

She ducked her head, but before dark wavy hair fell like a curtain hiding her emotions, he caught a glimpse of her grief-stricken face, and his heart ached for her. He needed to do or say something, but what? How could he help Madeline get through this? She sniffed a couple of times and took a deep, shaky breath.

Scenarios of what may have happened bounced around in his thoughts, none of them good. But with little to go on, his gut feeling was that he should wait. Whatever demons Madeline fought, she needed to trust him and find the strength to verbalise them. Say it out loud, air the dirty laundry and accept that an unspeakable, traumatic event actually did happen.

After what seemed like an age, he asked, 'Can I get you a glass of water?'

Madeline nodded, 'Thanks, Ash.'

The way she whispered his name, Ash felt a sudden, but by now, familiar ache in his chest. He rubbed at the spot with the heel of his hand. She gave him a sense of belonging that he could only describe as home; he was home, Madeline was home. A relationship, a team of two, whatever, he'd make it work. He handed her a tumbler of water from the bathroom and waited while Madeline drank down a few longs sips before placing the tumbler on her nightstand. She drew her hair back off her sweet face and somehow tied it in a knot.

'Wow,' she dabbed her face with the cuffs of her long-sleeved T-shirt. 'It's staggering how the mind works; you hear a word and, it takes you right back to a moment.' Madeline looked to the ceiling and heaved a sigh.

'You can trust me, Maddie.' He dare not move or touch her in case she closed off again. 'Please trust me.'

'I do trust you.' She touched his knee, then withdrew her hand to clasp them in her lap, taking a deep, steadying breath before diving in the deep. 'I fell pregnant at seventeen.'

'Whoa — sorry, please go on.' Ash grabbed a box of tissues from the nightstand, pulled several out and handed them to Madeline.

'Thanks,' she wiped her face and blew her nose. 'My parents were ready to disown me. They were even colder towards me than before, which I didn't think was possible. I was a mistake, an embarrassment. I cramped their style, a nuisance to have around. Can you imagine them taking on another child – mine? How would they explain that? To absolutely put an end to it all, to make sure that finding him would be impossible, I was never informed about the thirty-day revocation. And for that matter, was my son ever noted down anywhere? Too much time has passed. I'll never know what happened to him. And that's the worst pain,' she finished, voice breaking.

'I'm so sorry, Maddie.' He cupped her face, and using the pads of his thumbs, Ash gently wiped fresh tears off her cheeks.

'Despite them, I managed to pass my high school certificate with honours. Before I really started to show, my parents took me away to their holiday house. I could not leave, so I spent the last few months hidden away from prying busybodies. They did their best to make me feel I'd done something so despicable that I would need to be punished. So when my time came, I was hurried off to an accomodating hospital where my mother's wishes were followed to the letter. I gave birth to a healthy baby boy.' Madeline let go an anguished sob.

His gut tied in knots, Ash desperately wanted to hold her, make it all go away, but he couldn't, not yet. Madeline needed to finish what she'd started. The whole ugly, devastating time of her young life needed to come out. A few more deep breaths and she pulled herself together. And he got the entire heartbreaking story. Strangely, he felt honoured that she trusted him enough to unload this heavy burden.

'They took him from me.' Seething, she angrily added, 'They said he was just a blip.'

She gave him an intense look, a mix of grief, hopelessness, even determination, but most of all, love. Madeline Crowe loved her son wherever he might be. All of this fucked up shit broke his resolve to keep a steady head and heart. Hands clenched, knuckles turning white, Ash searched for control of his own anger, for the injustices, and for the massive hole in Madeline's life that may never be fulfilled. Emotionally drained, Madeline sagged. Ash gathered her up and wrapped his arms firmly around her. He gently pulled her to his side.

Holding and being held was how they stayed until he felt her relax, and her breathing calm. Utterly spent, she'd fallen asleep. Now was a good time to close his eyes and think things through.

MADELINE WOKE TO A HAPPY FACE. ASH LAY ON HIS SIDE, GAZING AT HER. The depth of feeling he conveyed was something she'd never before experienced. His emotions laid bare took her breath away.

She pulled herself together; after all these years, it was second nature. 'How long was I asleep.'

'Half an hour, not long. I was hoping you'd wake up.' He reached forward and kissed her lightly on the mouth. 'I didn't want to have to leave a note that I have to check on my patients at home. You're welcome to come along?' Ash said, wandering into the bathroom.

Madeline had looked forward to this moment. But now that it was here, it scared the pants off her. In her mind, this meant another move forward in their relationship. It meant taking on the responsibilities of having a partner. Suppose she tossed aside the possibility of a life filled with joy and true love. Would she, years later, see herself as a cranky, dried up lonely old lady whose life had been devoid of emotional colour? Devoid of love. Sure it was scary to try again. To change from making decisions about life and career with only herself to consider. To have a partner would mean consulting with each other. Well, bugger scary — what was wrong with consulting and going ahead with what needed doing anyway. There had to be a reason for the old saying, *two heads were better than one.* Madeline decided on taking the bold step forward and let Ash take her to his place. And whatever happened — happened.

Ash wandered back in from the bathroom, freshly showered and smelling divine.

'Would love to.'

He looked a little confused, arms leaving his sides, palms facing her, he asked, 'Would love to, what?'

She gave him an impatient look. 'But I'll follow in my car.'

Ash chuckled, crawled across the bed on all fours and kissed her with passion.

❧

ASH'S HOUSE WAS SITUATED ON THE OUTSKIRTS OF TOWN WHERE THE terrain sloped up to join rolling hills that overlooked the village below. Madeline followed him, turning into his driveway lined with tall eucalypts that led to his sprawling sandstone homestead with deep verandas all the way around. The timber-framed sash windows and panelled doors were painted white offsetting them beautifully against the sandstone walls. She loved the pretty cottage garden, flush with colourful flowers, a haven for birds and bees.

As soon as she parked, Ash threw the van door open and jogged towards her.

From the top of his driveway, the vista was breathtaking — an eagle's eye view of the deep valley below. Untouched national park meant forests were left to flourish as they rose up from the foothills covered in vineyards. Lush green fields butted up against the tree lines and Madeline could just make out the brown and white dots of grazing cattle, sheep and a few wallabies. The sun shone in an azure sky, indicative of Australia. And it was so quiet — just birdsong and the slightest rustle of leaves.

'First, come and see my patients.'

A row of cages and runs designed for all species, big and small, were lined up on a grassy lawn a few metres from the back of his house. Not a dog or cat to be seen.

'Meet Clive, our Wedge Tail eagle.' Ash fitted a gauntlet to his right hand and arm, entered the large cage and held out his arm for the bird. Clive flew down, settled on his arm and devoured his meat treat. Ash looked him over before lifting his arm again. The largest most magnificent bird she'd ever seen flew back to his perch.

'What happened to him?' Madeline asked.

'A good Samaritan found him on the side of the road and brought him in. Clive had a broken leg. I managed to align the bones, he's convalescing well, and if all goes to plan, he should be released some-time next week.'

'He's powerful. A magnificent bird.'

Ash walked her past all his patients, leaving the wombat for last. She followed him to the edge of the vast lawn towards an embankment where she could see a large burrow had been dug.

'When I call out his name, he'll come out to see what I've got.' He pulled a couple of carrots out of his jacket pocket and called out, 'Dozer, hey Dozer … *Do-z-er!*'

'Oh, very original.'

'Yeah well, with so many animals coming through, I run out of ideas.' Dozer came lumbering out and headed straight for Ash, letting him scratch his head while he happily munched on a carrot.

'I can see why you called him Dozer, I reckon he could dig his way out of anything. He's big, and also very cute.'

'Here you go,' Ash handed her a carrot. 'He won't bite unless he's annoyed, irritated, frustrated or hungry.'

'I should be fine then, seeing as I'm so calm.' Madeline gave him a hoity-toity face. Bending down, she fed Dozer his carrot and felt the power of this small, cute animal as he bit down and munched.

They left the animals and headed back to the house.

Ash took her hand and escorted her through the sprawling home-stead to the updated conservatory with picture windows facing the panoramic view. A spacious flagstone patio had a set of outdoor seating just waiting for them to relax and gaze out over the most beautiful vista.

'Are you warm enough to sit outside for a bit?

'Sure, lead the way.'

Leading her out through the conservatory doors, he took her to the outdoor setting. 'Take a seat,

'I — ' She stopped herself

'Yes.' Head bent, he moved closer. 'Whatever it is, you know you can tell me.'

'Okay,' she answered, giving him an honest, apologetic smile. 'Sorry, I … we need to talk some more.'

'Should I be worried?'

'No, I just need to drop a shit load of crap that I've been hanging onto long enough. And seeing as you have …' Madeline paused to take in his physique, 'broad shoulders, I'm hoping you can handle it?'

'I don't know what it is, but you're still standing, so it can't be deadly.'

Madeline laughed. 'No, but perhaps a little heavy.'

'Okay, not a problem, at all.'

'Coming here was a big step for me. I know I'm no different to many women out there. But I can only speak for me. My life has had its dramas, the first one devastating. The last one traumatic, like the stuffing, had been kicked out of me. I almost lost everything. My confidence regarding business returned when I managed all the legal matters during the separation. I don't have to worry about my investment, the bakery, or worry about the money from book sales that he tried to get the rights to. But diving into a relationship is something else again. You said I'm like a magnet. Well, you're no different, you're *my* magnet. It's like I need to see you drive by in the morning; otherwise, my day is crappy.'

A lopsided grin played his mouth. 'How crappy?'

Madeline rolled her eyes. 'Really? Are you that needy? Okay, I wonder why you didn't drive past, or if you were fed up with driving past and found another interest. You know, that sort of horrible merry go round.'

'Maddie.' He wrapped his arms around her.

'Yes, Ash.'

The days I don't drive past is because I have an emergency or something is going on the other side of town.' He shrugged. 'That's all.'

Madeline slid her hands up into his hair, fingers spread she pulled him down to her waiting mouth.

His powerful arms around her, his warm mouth, soft and supple, all-consuming. Madeline could've been in the middle of a bustling street, nothing mattered, nothing penetrated her focus. There was just Ash. His wide shoulders curving around her, and broad hands slowly caressing her back. His beautiful, relentless mouth sending her to a dreamy place where her knees grew weak. Ash's kiss wavered and became a smile. Hanging onto his shoulders, Madeline felt a giggled start in her chest and pulled back far enough to see his face.

'I don't know what I did,' he whispered in her ear as he nipped and gently sucked on her earlobe, 'but you have no idea how good you just made me feel.'

'Oh, do tell?'

'Your response to my mouth on yours. We've kissed on your verandah, at the park, and earlier in your cottage. You being here is different for some unknown reason. And something else, I might be in my forties, but I was the most nervous I've ever been. And I think the more we kiss, the less nervous I'll become, which could mean one thing, I've jumped that hurdle and my kisses could only get better.' He ended with waggling his brows and a wild, roguish grin. His comical expressions had Madeline laughing, which echoed across the valley. Wide-eyed, she covered her mouth.

'I like your confidence,' she informed him.

'Good, because of you, I've now got a shitload.'

'Good because you'll need it around me.' She slapped him on the shoulder.

'I look forward to the challenge.' He took her hand, kissed it and left her to enjoy the view.

The setting sun cast its orange glow across this vast panorama. Madeline gazed across the valley and mountain range, the changing early evening light, spectacular, taking her back to Mackellar's most well-known, beloved poem, *My Country*. Especially the line where she wrote: *Core of my heart, my country! Land of the rainbow gold*. Perfect for this very moment.

Carrying a bottle of wine, two glasses with a packet of chips dangling from between his teeth, Ash returned to join her on the patio.

They sat watching the sunset in peaceful silence. And then out of the blue, 'Damn! I'm up early tomorrow.' Madeline frowned, 'Shit, I said that out loud.'

Ash snort-chuckled. He turned to face her, and said, 'That statement is up for *all kinds* of interpretation.

He cupped her face and kissed her softly, his passion igniting her core.

He was perfect.

Was true love like that? She had never experienced this feeling before. Her sweet Aunt Bea and Uncle Pete gave her unconditional love. Though she was never given a chance to hold her son, she felt unconditional love for him.

But this was so very different.

True love?

10

Wiping down countertops and shelves was her least enjoyable chore, so when her phone beeped, alerting her there was a message, she dropped everything. Peering at the screen, she smiled, emotions getting the better of her as happy tears welled. She murmured affectionately, 'Aunt Bea. Thank goodness.' She had to admit her aged aunt and uncle taking a trip overseas was a bit worrying. Madeline read the message where her aunt explained why she texted instead of calling. They were running late for their scheduled flight home, and she hoped she wouldn't get car sick texting from a moving London Cab. 'Well, that doesn't make sense, just call me Aunt Bea.'

'What doesn't make sense?'

Madeline jumped with fright, nearly dropping her phone. So engrossed reading Bea's message she hadn't heard, Doug sidle up.

Hand to her heart, Madeline chastised him. 'Bloody hell, Doug.'

'Crikey, a bit tetchy?' He leaned back for a better look at her, then quirked an eyebrow.

'And what is that supposed to mean?' she asked, waggling her finger in his face.

'Who me — Nothin' at all. What gives, what's new?'

Wary about Doug's motive, she decided to ignore him and peered back at her phone. 'They're on their way to Heathrow in a London Cab, Aunt Bea sent a text because she's worried that she might get car sick.'

'You're right, that doesn't make sense.'

'Hmm, anyway, there's no need to pick them up at the airport because they've organised a car. And they'll be in to visit as soon as they've caught up on sleep.'

'Okay, it'll be great to have them home,' Doug enthused as he wandered off.

Madeline knew all about jetlag. She sent them another message saying she understood and was thrilled to hear they'd be home soon and more than happy to wait for all the exciting travel news.

A few days passed, but Madeline kept her word and waited. Bea rang, and they had a long chat on Saturday afternoon, mostly about how well the bakery was going. When Madeline redirected the conversation to their fantastic trip, Aunt Bea mentioned how wonderful the Kensington gardens were and asked Madeline to come for dinner. Better to share their photos and experiences over a glass of wine and good food. And since hearing through, who else but Anna, that she and Ash were dating, he was invited as well.

Madeline started walking up the garden path. Ash took her hand, which she thought was odd since it made walking along the narrow pathway awkward. *And* he had a strange look on his face. She couldn't work out what was on his mind.

The door opened, and Aunt Bea, arms wide, called out, 'Madeline, you look beautiful as always!' Bea hugged her tightly then turned to Ash. 'Who's this scruff you've got with you.' Aunt Bea joked, her arms wide, ready to engulf Ash. 'Come here, Coop, give your favourite old lady a hug.'

He mumbled in Bea's ear, Madeline couldn't hear what he'd said, but he looked deadly serious.

Aunt Bea stood back and said, overly bright, 'Yes, everything is as it should be.' She hooked her arms through theirs and led them into their sparkling new home. 'Come, Pete's waiting inside.'

Madeline heard softly spoken voices filter down the short hallway. Pete wasn't alone.

11

———————

A tall, athletic young man stood next to him.

Did her sweet, kind aunt and uncle pick up a lonely backpacker? The young man gave her a warm, tentative smile. And that is all Madeline could see; everything, everyone around him disappeared in an emotional haze.

God — that look — that smile. It can't be...

Trembling from head to foot, desperately wanting to believe but not daring to. He looked to be the right age. But really, he could be anyone. And anyway, how was this possible after all the years of searching? It felt like a trick — too good to be true.

'Maddie?' Bea prompted. Madeline blinked to clear her head and glanced at her aunt, who gave her an endearing smile and one short nod.

Disbelief warred with the truth. Aunt Bea would not lead her astray, so surely this was confirmation that this strapping young man was her son?

Overcome and light-headed, her mouth felt dry, and the blood drained to God knows where; her fingers tingled, and her feet seemed rooted to the floor.

'Mum.' The young man's deep, softly spoken voice penetrated her crazy thoughts.

'Mum?'

He called me Mum. Oh my God, he did, he called me Mum.

One hand flew to cover her mouth while the other went to grip her stomach and hold on. Madeline let out an anguished sob, a heartbreaking cry. Over the years, she'd kept a vice-like grip on her devastating loss. She'd study young men of his age and wonder what her son looked like. Though she never gave up hope that one day her son would find his way home. Her baby grew up without her. Did this mean she had the chance to learn about her son's life? Dare she hope to even be part of it?

Ash caught her up, his arms encircling, holding her tightly. Another pair of strong arms, she knew belonged to the young man, wrapped around her. Tissues fluttered under her nose; Madeline grabbed them, slowly straightening, she dabbed her face. Ash momentarily released his hold before his hands went to her waist and turned her to face the young man — her son.

Mentally unravelling, she took a steadying breath and studied this tall, broad-shouldered, muscular young man. His angular features still held a softness, no doubt that would change as he aged. His intelligent dark brown eyes were gentle, caring, but most importantly, they glistened with compassion.

Heart pounding, Madeline embraced recognition, acceptance and love. Her son's eyes glistened, and his mouth trembled. The deep emotional connection between them, palpable.

He gently held Madeline's shoulders. 'Hi…' And his smile was just like her own, kinda quirky. 'I'm Madison Swift, your son.'

'Yes,' came out in a whisper. She tried to smile and made an effort to form a coherent reply. 'I can see – bits of me in you. I hope – you're okay with that?'

'Very okay.' Madison pulled her in for a tight hug. 'Mum,' he said with meaning.

'Yes,' Madeline murmured, voice shaking, 'I've missed so much. All those growing years. I'm so sorry I wasn't there for you. I would've given anything — *anything*.'

'It's okay. I know what happened,' Madison quietly said, with care and understanding.

Still holding her, Madeline felt him ease back. He studied her; a soft, sympathetic smile eased into his face. 'There are several people who need to be sorry. But you most definitely are *not* one of them.'

'Thank you. I did try everything in my power to find you,' Madeline told him, dabbing her face again.

'I know, Bea and Pete explained,' he leaned in and quietly added, 'in great detail. Your Aunt Bea is a wonderful, caring woman, but boy can she talk.' Madeline agreed, nodding with an apologetic shrug. 'It was quite a conversation, but they needn't have worried about me not wanting to fly here and meet you.' His hands dropped away, but Madeline took his offered arm. 'Bea and Pete thought of everything; they set up drinks for us out the back.'

Turning, Madeline noticed Ash, Bea, and Pete were gone; they'd silently slipped away. She followed Madison out to the patio surrounded by Bea's flower-filled garden. A bottle of wine and two glasses sat in the centre of a small table surrounded by four cushioned wicker chairs.

He pulled a chair out for her, his one-sided smile endearing. 'They're giving us a moment. Actually, their exact words were, take as long as you both want.'

'They're adorable, and it's typical of them both.' Madeline sat, nervous about what was to come next. Was Madison leaving soon? After all, he must have a life, a girlfriend, or perhaps a wife to go back to … another thought blind-sided her … did she have grandchildren?

'Madison?'

He stopped pouring her wine and looked up. 'Yes. You okay?'

'Do you have a girlfriend, maybe a wife …' Madeline drew in a steadying breath. 'Do I have grandchildren?'

'Good Lord — no to all the above. I would've brought them along if I had.'

'Yes, of course.' She took his offered glass of wine.

Madison sat and raised his glass for a toast. 'To the future.' He made a face and frowned. 'Sorry that's *so* lame. It's a long trip from London to Sydney; my brain feels like a dried prune.' He rubbed his face and, mumbling behind his hands, said, 'throw in relentless jetlag and crazy back to front seasons.'

Madeline's heart sank. She wondered whether Madison would be here long enough to experience one of Australia's hot summers. How would he cope when it was difficult enough for the locals. 'I know what you mean. I dreamt of this moment, never thinking I'd ever see you in the flesh. That I could hug you and chat with you ...' Madeline started reaching for his face, but something told her she might be rushing things and let her hand drop.

Madison took her hand, clasping hers with both of his and voice just above a whisper, he told her, 'Yeah ... I had no idea.' He released her hand and took a deep swig of his wine. 'Faced with the truth, my parents regretted keeping you a secret. In their defence, they loved me and didn't want to see me leave the country. But, here I am anyway. There's something else, and it's kinda weird. As soon as I could read a map, I was drawn to Australia, this massive island in the pacific. Since you've travelled a hell of a lot, you might think that's nothing new. But my fascination continued throughout my adult life. I never knew why, until now.'

'Madison, how do your parents feel?' Though it wasn't the least bit cold, Madeline rubbed her arms. 'I hope they're coping, but I imagine they'd be worried ... you know?'

'I reassured them as best I could. Growing up, I overheard snippets, missteps in conversations that led to subtle hints that I didn't know what to do with. They'd had the perfect opportunity to set things right anytime, but they didn't. Not happy about that.' He shook his head.

It was wrong for sure, but Madeline was not going to undermine what he had with them. 'They must miss you.'

'Unfortunately, yes, but it can't be helped. Having said that, I have been away studying, and we often face-timed to catch up. But...' Madison hung his head, fighting to control his emotions. 'They were naïve and not terribly honest, and part of me understands that. Still, another part of me wishes they'd trusted me.' Madison pulled at a loose thread on his shirt. 'Once Bea and Pete knocked on our door, there was no hiding the truth anymore. My parents often worried that one day someone would come looking for me. I'm sure this feeling was exacerbated when the 2000 New South Wales Adoption Act allowed Bea and Pete to acquire information regarding my adoption. According to the paperwork at the hospital where I was born, the file said that my birth mother was a teenager who couldn't cope and gave me up for adoption. My parents were horrified to learn that your signature had been forged. They couldn't believe they'd been lied to in such a despicable, cold-hearted way. But they also lied to me and kept it up for twenty-five years.' Madison ran a hand into his dark wavy hair. 'I have to come to terms with that.' He searched her face. A slow, understanding smile played across his features. 'One thing my parents caught by accident during an interview was your Christian name, Madeline. Asking for more information on *Madeline's* background, they were told there was no record of anyone ever saying that. I believe choosing Madison for me was in recognition of my birth mother.'

'That's very sweet of them. When did your parents take you home to the UK?'

'They left Australia soon after the adoption papers were signed.'

Leaning across, Madison's jaw set, determined to control his emotions. 'Thank you for trying so hard to find me.'

'I couldn't do anything else.' Madeline decided then and there that anytime she felt like it, she would hug her son. She put her glass down, stood and did just that; Madeline hugged him. Sniffling, she sat down again. 'You're going to have to put up with a lot of this.' She heard him chuckle, and what a blessing to be able to feel his happiness. 'Shall we go and find where *our* family have got to?'

Madison dug his phone out. 'I'll text Pete.'

WHILE WAITING, MADELINE ENJOYED SHARING STORIES WITH HER SON. THE journey of getting to know each other was something she only ever dared dream of. Uncle Pete cleared his throat, and deep in conversation, Madeline let out a startled cry.

'I'm not that scary,' Pete grinned. 'We've got reservations at *The Eagles Nest*,' he announced at the open door. 'If we don't hurry to claim our table, they're real quick to offer it to a bunch of others. Probably the highest bidder,' he chortled at his own wisecracking. '*But*, you take your time — and we mean that. Follow us when you're ready — and we mean that as well. We'll be the ones beating people off with a French breadstick — no one's gonna pinch your chairs.' And with another guffaw, he wandered off.

Aunt Bea strolled past and gave them a *melodramatic* eye-roll.

Madeline swung around at the exact moment Madison did. 'Yeah, let's all go,' they said in unison.

Her beautiful son tucked her hand in the crook of his arm and murmured, 'Great to have you in my life.'

'Oh, yes, same here with bells on.'

'Bells on? That sounds exciting.'

'Oh, it is!'

Madison threw his head back and laughed. That simple, everyday happy sound was so very precious.

ASH WAS WAITING BY HIS CAR, HIS HANDSOME FACE LINED WITH A MIX OF concern and curiosity. Madison released his grip on her arm, kissed her cheek, and jogged straight for Ash. She couldn't make out what they said, but chuckling, they shook hands, then gave each other a man hug with a couple of blokey slaps on the back.

Madison, *her son*, waved and headed for Bea and Pete. 'See you up there!' he called out.

Madeline hurried to join Ash. Alarmed, she gripped his shirt, 'Help me, I have this overwhelming anxiety welling up inside that, if I let him out of my sight, he'll vanish.'

'He'd better not, I've got plans.' Ash quickly added, 'He's with Bea and Pete. After travelling seventeen thousand kilometres to find your son, they're hardly going to lose him now, here on home turf.

'Yes, of course ... but why do I feel like someone threw me in the deep end without my water wings.'

'I get that, I really do, but hey, I won't let you drown.'

'And I'm very confident that you won't. But please bear with me; I'm a mess — a very grateful, happy mess. I'm living a dream, every nerve ending frayed. I'm exhausted,' Madeline giggled as tears welled.

'Hop in,' Ash opened the passenger door of his vet ambulance and helped her climb in. 'Bea, Pete and I were chatting. Madison is a terrific guy. Very well mannered, well-spoken of — a good bloke.'

'Yes … I-I gathered as much.'

'Okay — buckle-up, let's go get to know your son. And by the way, you'll have to design a new T-shirt.' He grinned, sliding behind the wheel with another suggestion. 'Perhaps just ad a word, *Never Just A blip.'* Or, *The Blip Came Home.*

'I like them both, so getting a couple of each.' Madeline craned her neck to see what it was like in the back of his van and, shaking her head, mumbled, 'Organised chaos.'

'Don't know Madison well enough to stick him with that. He could be a very tidy guy.'

'No, that's *your* T-shirt. Unless someone gets in here too —'

Horrified, Ash jumped in, 'No one is allowed to touch, organise or tidy up my stuff. I know where everything is, and that's all that matters.'

'Good to know. By the way, I've heard of *The Eagles Nest* but never been there. Where is it?'

'It's not far from my place; they've got an even better view of the valley.'

Suddenly awash with uncontrollable emotions, Madeline grabbed Ash on the thigh and choked out, 'Pull over, please — pull over!' She couldn't hold back any longer. Something, she didn't know what, had to work its way out.

But Ash kept going.

'Ash, please stop!' Madeline pleaded, and then she saw the park gates. Ash drove in, swung around, and parked under a big stand of trees. He dived out from behind the wheel, jogged to the passenger side, unbuckled her seatbelt, hands around her waist, he hauled her out and wrapped her tightly in his arms. Murmuring sweet words of love and understanding until the trembling stopped.

'Bloody hell, I hope that's it,' she hiccoughed, 'I don't have the energy for more.'

'Maddie!' He moved her back far enough to see her face. 'You're dwelling on the past — stop it, right now.'

Feebly, she nodded. 'I am, aren't I?'

'Yeah, honey.' His serious face softened. 'I understand your sudden renewed anger and grief of all the times you wanted to be there for him. You *can't* go back. Don't waste a moment now feeling sad for a life that should've been. You need to embrace what your aunt and uncle, *and* Madison have given you. Think of the possibilities. He's in your life now; you can expect amazing times and celebrations. One day he'll find the love of his life, and you'll get to have that. Birthdays, Christmas, New Year and, for just because-get-togethers.'

'His life is in London, and you're talking as if he might stay.' She argued and shoved her index finger into his chest. 'A moment ago, Madison was with you saying goodbye or see you later, but it was more than that, wasn't it?' Madeline focused on his face and, he looked as guilty as sin. 'You're so bad at this, Ash. You can't hide anything.' His desperate attempt at concealing something was so absurd, he made her laugh through her tears. 'Come on, stop keeping secrets; we're not starting that bullshit.'

'Okay, Madison mentioned that he wanted to stay for a while and hoped you had enough room for a guest. Also ...' Madeline thought he looked cagey. 'if I had time, he'd love to see where I worked.'

'Right, where *you* work? Interesting.' Eyebrows arched, Madeline hoped she conveyed a goodly amount of scepticism.

'Yeah, and stop looking at me like that.' Ash gave a nervous chuckle. 'Look,' he began, 'like most people from overseas, the first thing they want to see is our wildlife.'

'*Uh-huh*,' Ash tried to give her the runaround, but she knew something was going on. 'There's nothing else?'

'Nope, not yet anyway, but give it time, something always crops up. I told Madison I'd ring him when I had a moment, not saying anything else.' Ash rubbed his jaw, 'Give this a thought. For the foreseeable future, *your son* will be staying with you. And thank Christ you've got an ensuite.'

'Nice try, Ash.' Madeline was onto him. 'You'd have to be the worst ... not liar exactly, but worst omitting the juicy bits.'

'Who me? Nah, it's all good, couldn't be better. Stop giving me that dramatic, confused, lost-babe look. I just want to wrap you up and kiss you until your body melts...' He looked past his brow at her and pursed his lips against another full-blown chuckle. 'You may not have noticed because you were busy kissing me back — but your mouth on mine,' he snapped his fingers, 'I melt. I stagger to my car and have to adjust my jeans before I can sit down.' He pulled a funny, I'm-so-screwed-face.

Madeline laughed, and it felt so good, the best feeling she'd had in a very long time. The release she needed.

'You have to tell me what turned your mood around; I might need to file that away for future reference.'

'Oh, nothing, just the expression on your face right now. The gobs-macking, awesome moment I met my son. My amazing aunt and uncle …and, your turn of phrase.'

'Good to know – got lots more phrases.'

Of course, Ash was right about a lot of things, but then so was *she*. Her old *and* renewed grief had blown right open, and what a mess that was. Deprived of happy memories: tooth fairies, scraped knees, sport, long pants, big shoes, excursions, amazing achievements, first loves, lost loves, tears and joy.

'You ready?' Hand extended, Ash waited.

Madeline slipped her hand in his. He pulled her in for a kiss then helped her climb in the van. She smiled as he made his way around the bonnet, hamming it up like he was weak in the knees.

'You poor old thing,' Madeline crooned as he curled himself in the driver's seat.

'What, no adjusting your jeans? I'll have to try harder.'

'Oh please, tease me all you want,' he nodded, grinning to himself, 'blokes hang out for that shit.'

12

───────

Madeline saw them first and pulled Ash behind a water feature. 'They're here, together.'

'Who are?'

Madeline pointed across the room at Doug, with who else but Anna.

'Are they dining or waiting for us?' Madeline asked.

'I don't know.'

'But I think you do. In fact, I think you had a big hand in the whole search and find my lost son.'

'Really, you have a wild imagination.' But Madeline could see straight through Ash and his oh so innocent look.

'I will find out soon enough, so you may as well fess up.'

'Look, they're moving,' Ash pointed at the two lovebirds.

Madeline peered past his shoulder and gasped. 'They're kissing. Doug has his hand on Anna's cheek. They're sitting so close she's almost in his lap — canoodling. Ash,' she elbowed him, 'you could learn a thing or two.'

'I don't think so since Doug came to me for help.'

Another open mouth gasp. Madeline could tell he wasn't kidding.

'Anyway, who cares, they're together.'

'Did Doug say anything about Finnie?'

'Look,' Ash took her by the hands, 'I'm not going there. It's up to Doug.'

'Of course,' Madeline agreed. 'It's private. Doesn't mean I'm not dying to know.'

Their attention was drawn back to the two lovebirds, nattering and laughing. And far too focused on each other to notice anyone standing nearby a water feature watching them. Seeing them together like this was icing on a cake.

Doug must have felt eyes on him; he turned suddenly and quickly scanned the restaurant, spotting them, his face lit up.

'We're sprung.' Madeline laughed.

Ash clasped her hand and urged her out of their hiding spot.

Alerting Anna, Doug scooted across the padded booth. Standing, he held his hand out for her. She looked gorgeous as always. On this occasion, she wore a black fitted pantsuit with an indigenous printed scarf showcasing colours of Australia's red centre.

'Wow, look at you two. I would never have guessed, 'Madeline quipped. 'Gosh, you make a beautiful couple. You look gorgeous by the way.' Madeline kissed Anna European style on both her cheeks. 'And Doug, it's fair to say you outshine us all.' And weirdly out of character, no jokes flying back, Doug dropped his chin and wrestled with a grin.

'*Grazie mille.*' Anna said, smiling big and looking incredibly happy.

'Thank you,' Doug beamed, arm firmly around Anna's waist. 'In case you're wondering, I listened to Anna's advice, and she listened to mine — then we threw all the unnecessary dross out the window.

'Thank God. You two were so frustrating. We all knew you needed to be together,' Madeline chastised.

Familiar voices trailed through the restaurant. Bea and Pete arrived, chorusing their approval.

Madison stood back smiling. Not wanting him to feel on the outer, Madeline sidled up next to him. 'What do you see?'

'A crazy, chaotic bunch of caring people.' He laughed as Anna went off, spreading her happiness with Doug.

'Sorry lovies,' Bea bustled past, 'but I need to sit.' Adding dismissively, 'Anna, Doug, Madeline has news. And don't look so worried, as far as I know, she's not leaving town.'

'That's right, not leaving. But I've just had…' Madeline worked hard at keeping herself together. 'My life has been turned on its head in the best possible way,' she began, 'Doug, Anna, twenty-five years ago I had a son who was … *Who*, without my consent, was taken from me. Thanks to Aunt Bea and Uncle Pete, and I'd say recently Ash had a hand in it too, my son Madison Swift,' she wrapped an arm around his waist, 'will be joining us for dinner.'

He raised his hand in greeting. 'Hi everyone.'

Chaos ensued, something Anna did well. The Italian came out in a melodious string of colourful language and so much love.

Anna firing off questions no one understood. Her passion undeniable; she stood on tiptoe and, cupping Madison's face, kissed his cheeks several times.

Arms wide, eyes glistening, Doug mumbled, sincerely, 'I'm guessing the, *Just A Blip*, T-shirt you wore the other day, is going to be shoved in a drawer somewhere.

You'll have to design a new one with, *Found the Blip*. You sure know how to liven up a party. It can't get much better than this…can it, kiddo?'

'No.' Madeline sucked on her bottom lip and shook her head.

Doug's eyes lit up. 'I've got a great idea. We'll hold a competition, impartial judges will pick a winner for your new T-shirt. Money raised will go to charity. Whadaya think?'

'Super idea, have fun organising that.'

'Noo-noo, I had the idea now someone else can do the organising.'

Anna sidled up. 'Doug, I overheard about the T-shirt. What a great project. I'll help you. I know businesses in town who will love to help out too. This is *the* most wonderful moment. What a great, uplifting story to share.'

'*Ooh*, me and my big mouth,' Doug grumbled good-naturedly.

Madeline left them to their ideas, seeing Ash and Madison standing aside deep in conversation as her son flicked through photos on Ash's phone. Both smiling and full of enthusiasm. Intrigued, she was about to join them when Aunt Bea called her.

Uncle Pete had made sure they had one of the best tables in the house. One where they all had the most stunning valley and mountain views of misty clouds drifting across the mountain range with their first dusting of snow. Perfect.

'Thank you both for this amazing gift. I have no words. And I can't think of anything that would suffice where I could demonstrate how much this means to me.'

Aunt Bea clasped her hand, 'Seeing you both, so happy, is our gift.'

Pete clasped the other. 'We love you kiddo …' mouth trembling, he trailed off as the rest of them could be heard coming to join the table.

Once seated, a waiter patiently circled the table taking their orders. Their drinks waiter arrived and, Uncle Pete motioned for him to come closer. The waiter nodded, clocked eyes with Madison, smiled, and strode off, coming back with an ice bucket and one of the best Australian sparkling wines. With glasses filled, it was time for a toast.

Uncle Pete stood and raised his glass. 'I'll be real short.' After a few snorts and giggles, he repeated, 'No, it's so short you have to listen carefully. Here goes: The bureaucrats never stood a chance against my beautiful Beatrice. To you my love.' And then, God love him, he drained half his glass while Aunt Bea did her utmost to control her emotions.

Madeline noticed through a delicious dinner, then desserts and coffee that Ash answered Madison's many questions. The usual hubbub through the restaurant prevented her from overhearing what their discussion was about. But Ash and Madison were animated, happy, nodding agreement, and getting on really well.

Sipping her coffee, she suddenly saw Madison move his chair back and stand.

'Excuse me, everyone. First, thank you all for your wonderful welcome.'

Madeline's heart sank, sure that her son was about to tell them all that he was needed back home, and he must leave soon.

Doug called out, 'Hey Mad, Sonny, Sonno, Maddo. Hang on, I've got it, Swifty. Is your speech going to be as long as Pete's?'

Madeline thought that was awful, but the whole table erupted in laughter.

'Maybe The Blip Returns,' Madison suggested.

Madeline had just taken a good sip of wine and covered her mouth; before she sprayed it across the table. In desperation, she tried to swallow before it came out through her nose. Grabbing her serviette, she gulped her mouthful, wiped her face and dabbed her eyes.

Through noisy chuckles around the table, aunt Bea called out, 'Maddie sweetie, breathe through your nose.'

Madeline nodded and slowly gave her aunt's suggestion a try… and it seemed to work. Or was it because Ash was gently rubbing her back?

'You okay, Mum?' Madison asked, leaning forward to see her face.

'Yes, I'm good,' Madeline squeaked and cleared her throat. It was going to take a little while before she got used to being called mum. She loved it and would definitely never, ever take her new title for granted.

Madison rested his hand on her shoulder and continued. 'Because it took me a long time getting here, twenty-five years doesn't mean I feel like a stranger, far from it. You've all made me feel very welcome. Thank you for your friendship.'

'Quit that; you'll have everyone blubbering into their wine,' Doug announced, swiping at his eyes.

'Okay, but you all know what I mean. As I was going to say, I have some amazing news.' He took a good sip of wine, paused, took a deep breath and smiled at Madeline. When her son's gaze moved to Ash, she didn't miss but also didn't understand when Ash gave Madison raised brows, a quick shrug coupled with a nod. 'Um …' her son hesitated.

'Hey Blip,' Pete called out, and everyone laughed. 'Stop leaving us in suspense.'

Doug, with a wicked twinkle in his eyes, was the loudest. 'Come on, it's not hard.'

'Okay, maybe not for you, and although you've taken me into your fold, I'm a newbie at this.' He rubbed his hands together. 'Right, here goes … I've been offered a job. I'll be staying for the foreseeable future.'

Madeline covered her gaping mouth as silent tears slid down her face.

Anna leaned forward and asked, 'Where is this job? What will you be doing because I have lots of jobs if you'd like where you can make good money.'

'Thank you for your kind offer, Giovanna,' Madison gave her a slight nod of respect. 'I'm a vet and, I'll be working with Ash.'

And the room erupted!

MADELINE'S ALARM WENT OFF, AND SHE DIDN'T CARE. AFTER A NIGHT OF so much joy, she could not stop smiling. Her early morning, *Oh God is it that time already*, hadn't entered her mind. Yesterday, her son came home. They'd had an unforgettable time together, talking well into the night, and Madeline soaked up every moment. The way Madison used his hands, the way he described his happy childhood, the look in his eyes when he talked about his school days; she'd missed so much. But she was smiling hard this morning. Madison stayed the night making himself at home in the spare room.

She threw the feather doona aside and hurried to use the bathroom, still grinning and so emotional at the same time. Dressing quickly, and thanks to Doug, who'd left a sticky note, 'Mornin' Princess, yours', with a red arrow pointing to her ready-made coffee. Giggling at how wonderful her life had turned around, Madeline went out to the front veranda. Ash waited in his *Pet Ambulance* across the street, sipping coffee from his travel mug. He looked across the road, gave her a wicked grin, put his coffee down, curled out of his van, jogged across the street, and enveloped Madeline in a warm, loving hug.

He whispered in her ear, 'Hey …' which sounded very much like a question, then he leaned back to study her face. Madeline assumed it was to get her attention, so she gave him her undivided.

'Your calm quietness is making me nervous,' she murmured, stroking his neck.

'Don't want to do that, not while I'm taking in how much I love you.'

Madeline's lips parted. Heart thumping, she wrapped her arms around his neck and kissed him passionately — until his knees did buckle.

~

SIX MONTHS LATER THE WEDDING:
Low-key and relaxed.

THE BIG DAY HAD ARRIVED. THE AFTERNOON WEATHER WAS COOL BUT sunny for early spring in the highlands.

Madeline slipped her feet into a pair of ivory satin heels. Her satin wedding dress with three-quarter sleeves reached mid-calf. And to set it off, the boat neck bodice was overlaid with delicate lace. Elegant and understated. Perfect for an outdoor wedding.

Her hair was styled in a mass of soft curls at her crown with just the right amount of escaping tendrils, pinned in place with a small spray of fresh flowers.

She checked herself in the cheval mirror to make sure her makeup, hair, dress and shoes were as she'd hoped.

A knock on her door caused another flutter of excitement.

Aunt Bea sang out, 'Maddie, are you decent?' Not waiting for an answer, she opened the door and walked in wearing an indigo chiffon frock that suited her perfectly.

'Thank God you're here, Aunt Bea. I'm so ready, I don't know what I'll do with myself for the next half hour — probably pace the floor.'

'Thought as much,' Bea smiled affectionately, 'You were always ahead of time. Never late for anything.'

'I don't think you could say that anymore. It's taken months to get used to early mornings. I can't wait for daylight saving,' Madeline quipped facetiously as she nervously fiddled with her hair.

'Stop fussing. You're stunning. You could easily model for Vogue.'

'Thank you, Aunt Bea, but I think you might be a little biased.' Madeline kissed her cheek. She peered at her reflection, turning to the side and back again, 'I don't wear much makeup at any time. So I made sure I had plenty of time to get dolled up. Have I gone too far? Is it too much? I didn't use a professional makeup artist for that very reason. They do a great job, but I didn't want to end up looking … different. And now maybe I've done that to myself.'

'Maddie, relax! Gosh, you'll wear yourself out.' Bea took hold of her hand. 'Keep going like this, and you'll fall headfirst into your wedding cake.'

'Jokes aside, you look like an angel.' Uncle Pete grinned as he came through the door misty-eyed, looking distinguished in his dinner suit.

'Yes, you do,' Aunt Bea chorused, mouth trembling as she quickly grabbed a hanky from somewhere within her clothes and dabbed her eyes. 'You look beautiful.'

'Thank you both for always being there for me.' Madeline kissed them and slipped her arms through theirs, one on either side of her to give her away.

'You ready?' Uncle Pete asked.

'Absolutely!'

Fairylights festooned the patio and surrounding trees. The wedding guests were seated in rows on either side of a red carpet running down a centre aisle. The celebrant, wearing a turquoise suit and with her fair hair pulled back in a tight chignon, waited in front of the timber arbour, festooned with ribbons and native flowers.

The music Madeline and Ash chose for her walk down the aisle was not what flowed out of the speakers.

Keith Urban's cover of the Bee Gees song, *To Love Somebody*, caught Madeline by surprise. Heart and breath quickening, she sniffed back tears.

Ash and best man Madison, both looking handsome in their dinner suits, turned and smiled affectionately.

'Maddie honey,' Bea prompted, jiggling a folded handkerchief. 'You might want to try smiling.'

God, did she look scared out of her wits? Madeline took a breath, then slowly let it out.

Aunt Bea whispered through the side of her mouth, 'That's it, Maddie, another one of those, and you'll be fine.'

Uncle Pete squeezed her hand. And whispered, 'Ready – set – go.' He took a step forward, tugging Madeline along.

Laughing at her uncle's crazy humour, it took a couple of steps before Madeline got a grip on her emotions. Bea was laughing too, so no help there. Madeline playfully slapped him on the arm; nevertheless, she silently thanked him for breaking her train of worrying thoughts; has Madison remembered the rings. Will her ring still fit. And shit, I need a drink of water — no, maybe a brandy.

Ash blew her a kiss. Madeline clutched her aunt and uncle's arms and breathed, 'Oh my…sex in a tux.'

Beside her, aunt Bea gave a little gasp and reflexive squeeze of Madelin's arm. Out the side of her aunt's mouth came, 'Ooh, you are naughty,' giggle-snort.

'Aunt Bea?' When Maddie had her attention. 'I love you both. You're awesome,' and they both giggled nervously.

On Madeline's other side Pete ordered, 'Will you two stop playing about? This is serious business.' His over the top pompous, po-face ready to crack as he chuckled under his breath.

All the way down the aisle, Ash's loving eyes were on her and never wavered for a moment.

Reaching the arbour, the celebrant smiled and said, 'Who presents this woman to be married to this man?

'We do,' Bea and Pete announced before kissing Madeline's cheeks. They placed her in Ash's tender care and turned to take their seats.

For Madeline, it felt like the ceremony was over in a blink when she heard,

'I now pronounce you husband and wife.'

Madeline wasn't surprised when Ash didn't wait for the *okay* you may kiss the bride. He wrapped his arms around and went for a passionate smooch.

Ignoring wolf whistles erupting all around, Ash whispered against her mouth, 'Bloody hell, you're gorgeous.'

The celebrant smiled, waiting patiently until they came up for air.

Then someone called out, 'Save it for your honeymoon!'

Then another bright spark yelled, 'Get a room.'

Ash whispered in her ear, 'Do you want to make a run for the car and leave this crowd to their party?'

'Are you kidding? Anna made a croquembouche,' Madeline said, tongue in cheek.

'Oh, in that case…' But when he gave her that sexy half-smile, she almost took him up on his offer.

'I love you, Mr Cooper.

'Love you too, Mrs Cooper.'

Arm in arm, they slowly walked back down the red carpet, savouring every moment.

'You know what's going to happen, don't you?' Madeline asked.

'Yeah …' he drawled and topped his seductive ways with a sexy-as-sin wink. And for his efforts, she playfully slapped his arm.

'What … no foreplay?'

And in her ear, he whispered, 'I foreplay all day.'

'I'm blushing, Mr Cooper.'

He studied her face.

'You won't find it, but trust me, it's there under my makeup.'

'Hey, love birds!' Doug's deep voice boomed, 'It's time to cut the cake!'

THE END

ABOUT THE AUTHORS

Leanne Lovegrove is a lawyer, wife and mother and a lover of romance and reading.

Her law career created an addiction to coffee but provides countless story ideas. The author of four romance novels, this is her first anthology. Leanne likes writing sweeping love stories with happily-ever-afters with strong female heroines and set in the beautiful landscape of Australia. She lives in Brisbane, Australia with her husband and three children.

www.leannelovegroveauthor.com

https://www.facebook.com/leanne.lovegrove.545/

https://www.instagram.com/leannelovegroveauthor/

Susan Mackie is the author of Amazon best-selling novel *Charlie's Will*, the first in the Barrington Series. Book Two – *A Place to Start Over* is ready for release now. Susan writes romance novels filled with vibrant, authentic characters and a touch of mystery, set in Australian country towns. Oh, and there's often a horse or two, and maybe a dog, in her stories. This is her first novella and anthology participation. Susan also edits and publishes for other authors, under her *Small Town Publishing* imprint. Susan has two grown daughters and lives in Warwick, Queensland, with Bloke.

www.susanmackie.com

https://www.instagram.com/susanmackieauthor/

https://www.facebook.com/susanmackieauthor

Emma Powell, author of all things romance and funny and female lives in Melbourne, Australia with her human kid and fur babies. Her hobbies include, chicken chips, reading, true crime docos, politics and sleeping. Her other career is as a theatre actor which she has done for the last three decades. So as an actor and a writer she is able to do what she loves best - tell stories.

Emma has three romance books available:

https://www.emmapowell.com.au/

https://www.facebook.com/Emma-Powell-588701104921778

Rhonda Forrest is an Australian author who writes captivating contemporary and historical fiction about relationships, family life and social issues. Over the last five years she has published five novels, all set amidst beautiful and uniquely Australian landscapes.

Rhonda teaches English and History to high-school students and along with her husband, divides her time between Tamborine Mountain and a 100-year-old cottage, overlooking the waters of the Whitsundays.

She continues to write and document stories that bring to life the remarkable characters and settings that make up our wonderful Australian heritage.

https://-/www.rhondaforrest.com/

https://www.facebook.com/valeenapress

https://www.instagram.com/rhondaforrestauthor/

Louise Forster is the author of bestselling novels in the Tumble Creek series, with the 5th book well on its way, titled, Tumbling Back. She lives on the far north coast of New South Wales, Australia, five minutes from the Pacific Ocean with her childhood sweetheart, extended family and a menagerie of pets. She loves writing edgy romance with a touch of humour, mystery, and loving, sensual passion.

She enjoys writing from a hero's point of view, resilient, straightforward men who love their women unconditionally. They can also fix anything, including a broken heart.

Her sassy heroines are strong and stand up for their beliefs, even when they feel vulnerable.

www.louiseforster.com

https://www.facebook.com/Louise-Forster-Romance-Writer-146905226005690/

www.instagram.com/louise_forster_author/

Support for Independent Authors

The authors hope you enjoyed reading Love in a Sunburnt Land as much as we enjoyed writing each story within. As independent authors, we rely on readers rating and reviewing our books, and we would love you to leave a rating and/or review on Amazon or Goodreads.

Thank you.